The Illusion of Desire

A Second Sons Inquiry Agency Mystery

Featuring:
Kathryn Whitethorn-Litton and Captain
Nicholas Ainsley

By
Amy Corwin

Copyright

The Illusion of Desire

Contact information: contact@amycorwin.com

Cover Art by Amy G. Padgett
Publisher: Fireside Mysteries
Editorial Services provided by: Vince Dickinson

Publishing History
First Edition, 2014

Synopsis

Partially disabled during the Napoleonic wars, Nicholas Ainsley is desperate to prove that he is not useless, so he accepts a position at the Second Sons Inquiry Agency. Unfortunately his first case, an inquiry into the death of Lord Taunton, proves more challenging than he anticipated. The murder weapon, a knife owned by his mistress, is missing. Even the victim seems determined to obstruct the investigation through a series of illusions created to hide the details of his private life.

Then, Taunton's close friend, Harry Silsbury, accuses Taunton's mistress, Kathryn Whitethorn-Litton of the murder. But, Harry disliked the woman and may have had his own reason for murdering Taunton. To complicate matters, Nicholas is attracted to Kathryn, despite the evidence that she may have murdered her lover.

Nicholas soon has reason to question if Taunton and Kathryn were, in fact, lovers. Their relationship seems to be nothing more than another illusion created by Taunton to hide his sexual preferences.

As the inquiry continues, Nicholas uncovers evidence of an even older tragedy. Was Taunton's death related to a murder that happened seven years ago? Whatever the truth, Nicholas is determined to expose the murderer and bring him, or her, to justice.

Facebook and Newsletter Connection

Connect with Amy Corwin and "like" her page on Facebook at http://www.facebook.com/AuthorAmyCorwin for fun news and book teasers.

Sign up for her newsletter for information about new releases, book sales, and freebies on her webpage at http://www.amycorwin.com or through her Facebook page.

Chapter One

9:30 PM July 10, 1821 – Wrexley Hall, Somerset

Kathryn Whitethorn-Litton paused at the doorway to the drawing room and rubbed her damp hands against the sides of her dress. She hated supper parties, they always brought out the worst in everyone. Malicious remarks seemed to be the order of the day, and she was heartily sick of it all.

A small cluster of guests caught her attention and with relief she recognized Rose Mardling. The young woman was about the same age as Kathryn, and she decided to join her, only to stop a few feet away. Rose seemed to be engaged in a tense conversation with her parents, and Kathryn was loathe to intrude.

"Please, Christian, I beg of you—reconsider." Mrs. Mardling leaned toward her husband and gripped his sleeve.

Rose, standing next to her mother, fixed her gaze on her father. A small V of worried concentration wrinkled her brow as she glanced from one parent to the other. Despite Kathryn's nearness, the young woman did not notice her.

Mr. Mardling ignored his wife's quiet plea and watched their host, smiling. When Lord Taunton glanced at him, Mr. Mardling

1

raised his glass of brandy in a brief salute.

"Christian!" Mrs. Mardling's hand tightened on his sleeve, her knuckles whitening. "Please."

Her husband shook her off. "If Rose marries Lord Taunton, she will have all the dresses and jewels any girl could desire. I would think it would please you to know that she would never want for anything." He glanced at his daughter, his gaze brushing over her face and pale, blue silk gown with the air of a horse trader assessing a likely colt. "You will much prefer being rich, Rose, I assure you. Taunton can provide you with a future while my secretary can not even afford the dress you are wearing this evening. I suggest you consider that before you throw everything away."

"But I love Frank!" Rose stamped her foot and then looked over her shoulder in the direction of Lord Taunton. She shifted uneasily and turned her back on their host. "He has asked me to marry him."

"Frank, is it?" Mr. Mardling frowned at her. "A bit forward for a mere secretary, is he not? Well, I am warning you now, I will not allow you to throw away this opportunity for a foolish infatuation—a school girl fancy. If you persist, you will force me to let Mr. Westbrook go. Then you shall both find out how unpleasant life can be without position or funds."

Mrs. Mardling slipped an arm around her daughter's waist. "You cannot do such a thing,

Christian. You would not—"

"Would I not?" Mr. Mardling chuckled low in his throat and took a sip of his brandy. The sound made Kathryn take another step backward though she kept her gaze on Miss Mardling, wishing there was something she could do to help her. "I know what is best for my daughter. Rose, you must see that regardless of this nonsense about love, you will be far happier married to the earl. Put your faith in me. I know what is best for you."

Rose stared at him, her face set in tense, unhappy lines.

"You mean you will be happier with an earl for a son-in-law," Mrs. Mardling shot at him when her daughter did not respond.

"Of course," her husband agreed complacently. "I will not deny that such a connection would be a useful thing. A very useful thing. So you will both stop this foolishness about Westbrook. And Rose, it would not be amiss if you were to cultivate a friendship with Miss Whitethorn-Litton. The earl would surely notice such kindness on your part, and it can only be to your credit."

"She cannot. It is most improper. That woman is clearly his—" Mrs. Mardling stopped abruptly, pressing her lips together and avoiding her daughter's curious stare.

Kathryn cringed inside and edged in the opposite direction. She should be hardened to such slights, but she could not help wishing for something other than disdain from the women in the house party. The fact that her presence in Taunton's household was intended to create precisely the impression that Mrs. Mardling hesitated to mention did not make Kathryn any happier.

Drowning in grief after her father's unexpected—and suspicious—death seven years ago at Taunton's country estate, she had foolishly agreed to trade her respectability for a place to live. She had hoped to discover what had truly happened to her father. The earl assured her that he had died peacefully in bed, but she could not accept his comforting answer. Her father had been young—he was not yet forty—when he passed away. Several times, she had tried to obtain Lord Taunton's journal to discover what he had written in private about the incident, but she had never been able to locate it.

And over time, she had realized that Lord Taunton had gotten the best of their arrangement. By creating the illusion that she was his mistress, he had put an end to unsavory rumors about his personal life. Unfortunately, his success was at the cost of her future.

She had learned nothing about her father's untimely passing and had only a small room and a few dresses to her name. Now, even that status appeared fragile. Why had Lord Taunton suddenly decided to marry?

"His mistress?" Mr. Mardling shrugged.

"What of it? An intelligent man makes use of any tools at his disposal. Rose, it would not be amiss for you to use the woman's position to attract Lord Taunton's attention. Of course, once you wed the earl, you can insist he get rid of the chit, though you must expect a man in his position to have an occasional dalliance. Even you are not that naïve, my dear. It means nothing, and you should take no notice of it."

"He may prefer Mary Dudley or Elizabeth Reeve. They are both here." Rose's eyes flashed. Defiance straightened her spine. "Have you thought of that?"

Her father laughed. "Those dowds? You little minx—you know better than that. You are fishing for a compliment, are you not? Well, you are prettier by far. You have no competition from those girls."

"Well, I won't do it." When Rose moved, she caught Kathryn's gaze. Rose flushed, but she was too caught up in the discussion with her parents to acknowledge her.

"You will." Mr. Mardling studied his daughter with hard eyes.

"I will not. And I warn you, if he offers, I will not be responsible for my actions. You can not force me to marry him, and you will both rue the day if you do not listen to me."

"Nonsense. We both know that if you will not be responsible, it is because nothing shall happen except for your marriage—"

"Marriage!" George Inglewood, one of

the bachelors Lord Taunton had invited to even the numbers of single men and women, approached the Mardling family. His brown eyes widened in surprise as he glanced from Mr. Mardling to Rose. A smile slowly grew on his face. "If you are expecting news of a betrothal from our host, I fear you are doomed to disappointment. Lord Taunton is a confirmed bachelor."

The slim, young man trailing him chuckled. "Or so you hope, Georgie." Bartholomew Palmer gazed at the ceiling, pressed his palm to his breast, and released a melodramatic sigh. The gesture annoyed Kathryn, and she suspected that irritation was precisely the emotion what he hoped to provoke. "Methinks you wear your heart upon your sleeve, following Taunton around the way you do."

Despite his amusing tone, Kathryn had noted that Inglewood's hero-worship of Lord Taunton angered Palmer. He had spent the last few days dogging Inglewood's heels and attempting to monopolize his attention while Inglewood seemed equally determined to monopolize Taunton. Neither man had been particularly successful.

Inglewood flushed. "He is an earl and worthy of my respect, while you are but a fool."

"Then we are two fools, dear Georgie," Palmer replied in a light voice. "Blinded by the illusion of desire."

Noticing the growing cluster of guests, Harry Silsbury joined them. Harry always seemed impelled to thrust himself into the center of any crowd. He could not tolerate being ignored. Or remaining silent. Kathryn hid a smile by gazing at the floor.

"Illusion of desire?" Harry repeated the phrase, a faraway look glazing his hazel eyes. "What a felicitous phrase. I shall write a poem—an ode—with the title, 'The Illusion of Desire' and dedicate it to...who, I wonder?" He glanced from Palmer to Inglewood and chuckled. "Methinks the Earl of Taunton. As my patron, he deserves nothing less. And my ode shall be a marvel of subtlety. What the world observes as desire—or love—is so rarely what the heart truly feels." He gazed at the gold-adorned crown molding in the corner of the room and pressed a slender hand to his forehead, brushing back a thick, brown curl. Then he sighed and shook his head. "What the heart feels... It is often such a mystery to us all, is it not?"

"Your *patron* has a great deal of patience if he willingly listens to that sort of nonsense." Mr. Mardling snorted. He hurriedly drained his glass and turned to his wife and daughter. "You both appear in need of refreshment. Please excuse us, gentlemen." Without waiting for a response, he steered his wife and daughter away from Kathryn and the loose semi-circle of men.

Harry lifted his glass in mocking salute to the family, a smile lifting one corner of his mouth. "Will you follow their lead, Kathryn, and abandon us?"

"I have not decided. I suppose if you wish to be alone to discuss your desires...?" Kathryn let the question drift off and raised her brows. For once, a sharp retort had come to her before Harry Silsbury walked away in smug superiority. She hoped she had caused him at least a small twinge of embarrassment. He had certainly brought many blushes to her cheeks in the past.

Palmer and Inglewood chuckled as Harry's eyes narrowed. "Watch those claws, my little kitten, or you may find yourself scratching the wrong hand."

She smiled but before she could answer, Palmer glanced past Harry's shoulder. "Ah, Mr. and Mrs. Croftson," Palmer greeted the quiet couple as they walked by. "Did you enjoy your supper? I thought the lobster was particularly well done. Delightful sauce."

"Yes." Mr. Croftson nodded and his gaze slid past Kathryn without acknowledging her. The earl's brother did not approve of her, and he and his wife generally behaved as if she simply did not exist. "We have always had excellent fare at Wrexley." The note of satisfaction in his voice conveyed the impression that Edward Croftson felt the credit for the menu belonged to him instead of his elder brother.

Kathryn stifled a laugh behind her hand. If only Taunton could hear him. For once,

Croftson was almost complimenting the earl.

However, her brief good humor turned to anxiety when Palmer greeted Croftson's young wife. "You're looking remarkably lovely and well-rested, Mrs. Croftson."

Please don't tease her. Kathryn stiffened, hoping Mr. Palmer would not say anything to embarrass the young woman. Mrs. Croftson was at least ten years younger than her husband and seemed confused and easily hurt by those around her. In fact, she seemed far too soft-hearted, and Kathryn frequently went to the lady's aid to protect her from the supposed witticisms of Taunton's other guests when Mrs. Croftson appeared overwhelmed.

"Th-thank you." Mrs. Croftson blushed and glanced up at her husband for approval.

Mr. Croftson frowned at Palmer.

Palmer's smile broadened. "Has he set a date, yet?"

"A date?" Mrs. Croftson stared at Palmer in confusion.

"For his wedding. I understood that Lord Taunton is planning to wed, and I suppose you are assisting him with all the details. It must be quite an undertaking for one so young, but I'm sure you will handle it with all the grace and aplomb for which you are so well known."

This was precisely what she feared. Kathryn's stomach fell. She stepped forward to distract the young men from teasing Mrs. Croftson further, but before she could say

Amy Corwin

anything, Mr. Croftson said, "You have been drinking, Palmer. It has clearly addled your wits. My brother is a confirmed bachelor and has no plans to wed."

"*Au contraire, mon ami.*" Palmer lifted his brandy and saluted Mr. Croftson. "Quite the contrary. I have heard that our host invited all these delectable ladies and their parents in order to make a selection."

"Don't be absurd."

"Absurd?" Palmer shook his head. "Not so. And I'm afraid you are not the only one destined to be disappointed." He cast a pointed glance at Inglewood, who flushed and drained his glass of sherry so quickly that he broke into a choking cough. "It appears unlikely that either you, or your offspring, will inherit the earldom. Taunton intends to marry and produce his own heir."

Croftson shrugged, although the pinched look on his face betrayed his anger. "I hope he does marry, then. He deserves some happiness. But we shall see what the future brings, shall we not?"

Kathryn studied Croftson with dismay. Why did all of Taunton's guests seem so bitter? This wasn't the first time she had noticed that the earl seemed to churn up a great deal of resentment in his wake. Perhaps all powerful men created conflicts among their friends with everyone vying for attention. She shook off a feeling of trepidation and looked over her shoulder at the doorway. Would anyone notice if she escaped to her room?

She could not imagine anything worse than spending the rest of the evening fending off barbed comments. Or deliberately losing at cards in order to placate the other guests as she had two nights ago.

Even Mr. and Mrs. Reeve and their pretty, dark-eyed daughter, Alice, seemed distracted and ill-tempered. They strolled around the room as if unable to find a comfortable place to sit despite an abundance of unoccupied chairs and cozy sitting areas.

Perhaps they had noticed that the earl did seem to prefer Rose, just as Mr. Mardling had anticipated. Taunton's attentions had been marked last night. He had courted Rose, making sure her glass of ratafia was always filled and that she lacked for nothing during a long evening playing game after game of speculation. He had even replenished her supply of farthings when she persisted in losing.

The two other single ladies, Alice Reeve and Mary Dudley, had been virtually ignored until Kathryn took mercy on them. Despite the unhappy looks of their parents, the three women had settled at the pianoforte and amused themselves playing favorite tunes including "The Joys of the Country" and "O Waly Waly" while the gentlemen gossiped or played cards with the earl, Rose, and her parents.

Even Mr. Reeve, an accomplished master of the violin, had deigned to join them. Smiling, Kathryn was about to ask the Reeves if they wished to join her at the pianoforte again when Lord Taunton nodded to her.

"So there you are, Miss Whitethorn-Litton." Lord Taunton's eyes glittered as he smiled at her. The purring note of satisfaction in his voice warned Kathryn to be on her guard. "I feared you might be suffering another of your headaches and had already retired to your room."

"No, my lord. I am quite well." Uneasy, she glanced around. The room had grown quiet, and she was now the unhappy center of attention.

Taunton stepped closer and threw a heavy arm around her shoulders, preventing her escape. "Excellent." He squeezed her shoulder and before she could slip away, he brushed his free hand down her neck and plunged his fingers briefly down her bodice. Before she could twist away, he pulled out the slender dagger that rested between her breasts.

Several women gasped in shock. Kathryn's face burned with humiliation. He had ordered her to wear the knife that evening, and though she had been reluctant to do so, she had complied. She never dreamed he would behave in such a cruelly callous manner to her in front of all his friends.

"None of you suspected that the jewel

Miss Whitethorn-Litton wore was not a brooch but a stiletto, did you?" Laughing, Lord Taunton held up the blade and tilted it to watch the ruby inset in the handle gleam in the candlelight. "I designed it myself. What do you think?" He pointed the sharp tip toward Miss Rose Mardling, who blushed and stared modestly at the floor. Lord Taunton's smile widened. "Every young maiden needs a protector, does she not? And Miss Whitethorn-Litton has always seemed to be in great need of protection."

When Kathryn tried to edge away, Taunton caught her wrist and placed the blade in her palm.

"Take care not to lose your protection," Taunton warned her, a strange look in his blue eyes.

"You are very kind, my lord." Kathryn reluctantly took the blade, holding it awkwardly at her side. She refused to slip it down her *décolleté* with all the men in the room eyeing her. "However, with so many kind gentlemen present, I cannot believe I would ever need such a cruel device."

"Cruel it may be, but also very effective in hands as adept as yours." Taunton gave her a slight bow.

"You flatter me." Glancing around at the cold, almost hostile faces, she decided she had had more than enough. "And I hope you enjoy your evening. I believe I shall retire after all, my lord." She curtsied and walked quickly through the door before he could stop her.

As she passed into the hallway, a babble of voices erupted behind her. Most were shrill with outrage at the small scene Taunton had arranged. But above them all, she heard the earl's boisterous laughter.

He might not be so amused if one of his guests decided he had finally had enough.

She shook her head and tried to forget the tension chilling the air of the drawing room. Unfortunately, the sound of Taunton's laughter followed her all the way up the staircase.

Chapter Two

Three months later...
2:00 PM October 13, 1821 - London

Nicholas Ainsley hesitated before he stepped into the main hallway at Second Sons Inquiry Agency, just off Clerkenwell Road. His shoulders tightened uncomfortably.

This is a mistake. Why would they hire a man with only one good arm? Thrusting his doubts aside, he forced himself to relax and enter the office.

The agency's founder, Knighton Gaunt, walked forward to greet him. "Good afternoon, Captain Ainsley."

"Mr. Gaunt, thank you for this opportunity." Nicholas offered his hand. Noting Gaunt's funereal garb, a sense of hollowness settled into his chest.

His luck had not changed for the better. Someone overcome with grief was hardly likely to exhibit much enthusiasm for hiring an unknown man. This was all yet another waste of time.

As they shook hands, the movement drew his attention to Gaunt's arm. His sleeve lacked the traditional black armband of mourning. Apparently, the man simply preferred somber black to more fashionable colors. Nicholas smiled as a *soupçon* of tension slipped away, making his own tailored jacket seem less restricting than it had been.

Gaunt nodded and sat down, waving to the chair in front of his desk. "Please be seated, Captain Ainsley. I was intrigued by your application. There aren't many gentlemen of your standing who wish for a career as an inquiry agent."

"No, I suppose not." Nicholas eased himself into the indicated chair, careful to clasp his useless left hand and place it in what he hoped was a natural position in his lap.

"What persuaded you to apply?"

For a moment, he couldn't seem to think of an answer.

Pointing out that any position would do since England in general, and London in particular, contained a superfluity of wounded, and therefore unemployable, war veterans didn't appear to be an appropriate answer.

Nicholas shifted in his chair. The wooden legs screeched against the wooden floor. He frowned and straightened, determined to give the impression of thoughtfulness instead of discomfort.

"The work sounded interesting," he said at last.

Gaunt nodded. "Some find it so, despite the social disadvantages. What qualifies you to perform inquiries?"

"The fact that the social disadvantages don't bother me in the least," he replied dryly before he could censor his cynical words.

He was well aware that men from the

lower orders generally performed inquires and caught thieves and other miscreants. Some considered them as bad, or worse, than those they hauled off to gaol. However, being shunned by the *bon ton* did not bother Nicholas. In fact, he viewed the possibility as eminently satisfactory as he wanted nothing more to do with his previous associates.

He had suffered enough petty humiliations and slights after his return a dozen years ago from the war in Corunna. The worst had been his discovery that his betrothed had deserted him in favor of a man with two good arms. The thought still had the power to make his gut twist with disappointment and anger. She'd been married for seven years now and had three children, but the bitter memory still burned like sour wine in his stomach.

To his surprise, Gaunt's mouth quirked in a half-smile before Nicholas continued, "I studied Philosophy at Cambridge, as well. The tenants might prove useful in unraveling some of the knottier mysteries humankind inflicts upon itself."

"Yes, I often find philosophy to be very useful, particularly moral philosophy. Anything else?"

"I'd like the chance to do something of benefit." Nicholas halted, fumbling for the words to explain. He scarcely understood himself what drove him. Something in him longed to right the wrongs the war inflicted, to do something to bring into his life a sense of justice, no matter how ephemeral.

Gaunt leaned back, hands steepled in front of his mouth. He studied Nicholas for a full minute in silence.

Some men might have found the prolonged quiet so untenable that they would say anything to break it.

Nicholas was not one of those men.

With his tension abating, he grew aware of his exhaustion. He'd been living on his nerves the last few days, eating little and sleeping less, waiting for this interview. He fought the urge to fall asleep as his thoughts drifted.

In a well-meaning effort to offer guidance, his mother had opposed his notion and suggested the church. Perhaps a nice vicarage in the country would do. Nicholas had shrugged off that idea. He couldn't imagine anything more deadly dull. When she persisted, he had found lodgings elsewhere.

As he sat in the rigid, wooden chair, his left arm tingled and ached. He tightened his right hand around the wrist of the left. He refused to rub the wasted appendage even if it felt like an entire colony of ants marched up and down his bare skin under his sleeve.

The doctors may have saved the limb, but his forearm and hand hung stiffly at his side as if carved from a block of wood. Useless, worm-eaten wood.

"I see," Gaunt said. "Well, as you might

expect, I've spoken to several of your associates to obtain references and determine your character."

"Associates?"

"The men who served under you in the 50th Foot. They spoke very highly of you, Captain Ainsley. Your men indicated that even in the heat of battle, you kept your wits about you. Self-possession is an excellent trait for our line of work. Corporal Myles, in particular, declared that you thought more of your men than yourself and in fact, led far too often from the front for good sense or safety."

Forgetting his useless hand, Nicholas released it. His wrist hit the armrest, calling attention to his disfigurement.

He grabbed his cold hand and clasped it, staring at the edge of Gaunt's desk as a deep flush heated his face. He could imagine what Gaunt was thinking. To forestall any discussion of what he had experienced during the war, he said, "Indeed. In the heat of battle, it's easy to mistake idiocy for valor."

"Very likely. However, Myles also mentioned that you saved his life. That action seems to prove his point that you did, indeed, consider the lives of others first."

Nicholas shifted on the hard, wooden seat and regretted doing so when the chair legs squealed against the floor. Again. "I've always found little point in thinking about anything in the heat of battle except staying alive. When one panics and stands to run, one merely makes a larger target. The Corporal may have mistaken my actions as more courageous than they were."

"Perhaps, though your fellow captains disagreed with your assessment. They had nothing but praise for you, as well. I understand you were awarded several commendations upon your return. You acquitted yourself with honor when you led your men in that charge on a French cannon entrenchment at Elvina. That took courage, Captain Ainsley."

No. It took nothing but terror. Anger, and a refusal to see any more of his men die, had driven Nicholas that day, not courage.

His head throbbed with the pounding sound of the French cannons that day. The frogs had merrily lobbed cannon balls at the English, turning the earth into billowing clouds of dust. A deep, soul-shattering sickness had grown in Nicholas as he watched the blood and pain they inflicted. The carnage and his bitter fear had eaten away at him until he could no longer bear it. In the end, he could only think with relief of standing up in the middle of the battle and screaming until some thoughtful Frenchman put a bullet through his head.

But no one had seen fit to do him that small favor.

And now his nights were haunted by the soft, whimpering cries of those who had not died immediately, the men who stared out of grimy, bloodstained faces with anguished eyes. As the rout in the battlefield around Corunna continued, they watched the port with increasing desperation, praying that the British ships would arrive before it was too late. Most knew they would never see England again, and their hopeless realization of approaching death tore at him.

He shrugged and stared past Gaunt to the window behind him. That battle was the last time he had been whole. He couldn't remember the last time he had slept the night through without dreaming of the blood.

"I was trying to sleep at the time." Nicholas met Gaunt's steady gaze and added in a light tone, "They shot the bloody cannons all night. The noise annoyed me so much I decided to do something about it."

"Were you wounded in Corunna?" Gaunt asked.

"Yes." There it was. A bitter taste filled his mouth as he replied, "You may as well know, my left arm is useless."

"Corporal Myles explained your situation."

"That is it, then, is it?" The muscles in Nicholas jaw tightened. The anticipation of another dismissal hung in the air between them like the sulfurous smell of gunpowder.

"I beg your pardon?" One of Gaunt's dark brows rose.

"Is the interview over?"

"Not unless you want it to be. Do you?"

Nicholas shook his head.

"Myles sent his regards, as well. And I was about to ask if you wished to know how he was faring."

"Good God, no," he said without thinking. Nicholas didn't want to know how any of his men fared these days.

The losses at Corunna had to have been worth something. He had to believe that his remaining men were happy now and growing fat sitting in front of a crackling fire. In the quiet periods between battles, Corporal Myles had talked incessantly about a brown-eyed girl named Violet waiting for him at home. Surely, he had married his Violet, and they had five or six noisy children stumbling over their feet in their parlor by now.

If Myles' fate were otherwise, Nicholas preferred to maintain his fantasy.

As the silence stretched, Nicholas swallowed, his mouth dry. Finally, he felt forced to continue. "Sorry, yes. How is he?"

"Doing well. He owns a tavern near Brighton." Gaunt paused and clasped his hands on his desk, studying Nicholas. "He said to tell you his wife, Violet, sends her regards."

Thank God. At least one of them made it. Nicholas let out a long breath. "Thank you. I am relieved to hear it."

"He also explained how you received your injury. Apparently, you pushed him out of the path of a bullet." Like the physician who had saved Nicholas's arm, Gaunt's dark eyes held a kind of detached assessment. "Well done. And that said, do you believe your injury will prevent you from performing inquiries?"

Rage momentarily tightened Nicholas mouth, choking off his voice. Here it was. Gaunt was going to dismiss him, saying that the work was too difficult or dangerous for a cripple. He met his stare. He didn't see curiosity, or worse, the pity that he'd seen so many times before, but he didn't know how to evaluate Gaunt's expression.

Tension cramped his lungs eased. He coughed before he could speak. "The bullet severed ligaments in the elbow when I pushed the corporal out of the line of fire." He'd been fast, but not fast enough. Nicholas clasped his left hand more tightly in his lap. Suddenly, he wanted to explain what had happened. He wanted to talk about the injury, honestly and openly. "I lost the use of my left hand for most purposes. I have retained some sensation, though. I know when I stand too close to the fire, for example. However, I cannot lift my forearm, and my grip is gone."

"And what is your assessment of your condition?"

"I can ask questions well enough." Nicholas smiled. "I would not have applied otherwise."

"And you are right-handed, so in fact it is not much of an impediment, is it?" Before

Nicholas could answer, Gaunt nodded and stood. "Very well. I believe you might be suitable and find the work interesting enough. At least, I hope so." He held out his hand.

Nicholas got to his feet, feeling as if he'd suddenly lost his bearings. They shook hands. "I'm not sure I understand. The interview is over? You are hiring me?"

"Yes. I see no reason to prolong matters. I am privileged to offer you employment with Second Sons, Captain Ainsley. I am assuming that suits you?"

"Yes, and I'm grateful for the opportunity." He wavered, wanting to confirm that Gaunt realized the extent of Nicholas' injury. "My arm—it is a disadvantage."

"Perhaps to you. I find your arm does not bother me in the least. And as you said, it will not prevent you from pursuing inquires." Gaunt's dark eyes glittered with what looked to Nicholas like amusement.

"Thank you," he mumbled, light-headed with relief. While he had wanted the position, he hadn't realized precisely how much until that moment. "But I prefer *Mr.* Ainsley, now. If you don't mind."

"Certainly. Well, come around tomorrow morning by nine sharp. We will have something set aside for you to review." When Gaunt opened the office door, Nicholas hurried out, almost afraid to converse any further lest his sudden good fortune vanish like a drop of dew in the sunlight.

Chest tight, Nicholas blinked in the brilliant London sunshine and made his way back to his apartments. He might be searching for a lord's lost dog tomorrow, but at least for today he had a renewed sense of purpose.

He only hoped fate would not find a way to make him regret his good fortune.

Chapter Three

12:00 AM—Midnight October 23, 1821

Kathryn Whitethorn-Litton watched Mary Dudley hesitate with one foot on the bottom step of the carriage. "Pray make haste, Miss Dudley. We don't want your parents to see us and wonder why you are getting into the carriage of a notorious harlot, do we?"

"Harlot?" Mary's large brown eyes grew even larger and her face paler if that were possible. "You shouldn't say such things. Rose said—"

"Never mind what Miss Mardling said. Do you want to be seen dawdling on the street at this hour?"

Night already shadowed London, and flickering streetlamps made the damp pavement glisten. The misty air chilled Kathryn's cheeks, and her thin gloves were insufficient to keep her hands warm. Her icy fingers felt numb as she gave Mary a gentle nudge.

To confuse prying eyes, Kathryn had arranged to meet Mary three blocks from her home. But that maneuver couldn't preclude the curious from noting the young woman who lacked the wits to hide her hair and face beneath the hood of her fur-lined cloak. Kathryn glanced around uneasily. She pushed Mary a bit harder.

Finally, Mary climbed into the carriage with unseemly haste, tripping over the hem of her gown. She fell to the floor and gave a whimper of pain before scrambling up to one of the seats.

Kathryn followed more slowly and then leaned out of the window to call to the driver, "Move on!"

When their conveyance jerked forward, Kathryn settled back in her seat and studied the woman in front of her. She would never have expected Miss Mary Dudley to be in such a predicament. Mary was certainly pretty enough in a plump, brown dove way, but she was not a distinctive beauty and right now the tip of her sharp nose was bright red with agitation and worry.

Mary rubbed it nervously with a fluttering handkerchief.

Well, no wonder she was on edge. They were both well on their way to committing what Society dubbed an appalling crime. Their Christian souls were in peril, although that thought didn't scare Kathryn. Her soul could take care of itself.

What bothered her was being abroad so late at night without anyone to defend them against footpads.

"No one will know, will they?" Mary asked, her voice high and faintly lisping like a young child just learning to speak.

"Not unless you tell someone," Kathryn answered harshly, trying to sound nonchalant and experienced. She chewed a snag on her index fingernail, thinking about the irony of her situation. "You did not tell anyone, did you?"

"Oh, no!" Mary shook her head vigorously. "Who would I tell?"

"Who, indeed?"

After an uncomfortable minute listening to the horses' hooves go clippety-clop down the street, Mary pressed one hand to her belly and asked, "Will it hurt?"

Knowing nothing about the procedure, Kathryn shrugged. "I expect it will be uncomfortable, but I am confident you will face it bravely." In fact, she was no more certain of Mary's courage than she was about how abortions were done. However, Kathryn was supposedly Lord Taunton's mistress and therefore the worldly one who knew about such things.

Clearly, Mar y had far more carnal experience than Kathryn. The highly regarded and morally upright Miss Mary Dudley had unwisely given in to the blandishments of a persuasive, young gentleman. As is so often the case, after she had accepted his attentions, he had fallen desperately in love with a different young lady. The second lady had the advantages of a title and a plump dowry, so he had married her forthwith. He expressed no interest in the fact that he had left Mary quick with his child.

It struck Kathryn as unjust and bitterly ironic that Society should accept Mary as a chaste maiden, not knowing her condition, and yet shun Kathryn merely because she lived with a man to whom she was unrelated.

Nothing in life was fair.

As the carriage passed through pools of light cast by the streetlamps lining the narrow street, a golden glow lighted the interior of the coach. Kathryn studied Mary's pallid face during a brief moment of illumination. Was she as terrified as she appeared? Kathryn's frown deepened, pinching the skin between her brows.

Mary's eyes blinked rapidly and her gaze flitted from one window to the other as if she feared to catch sight of an acquaintance peering into the carriage.

"You must try not to worry." Kathryn patted Mary's arm. What could she say to reassure her? She had no idea what lay ahead of them and her ignorance increased her anxiety.

Mary moaned and rubbed her stomach before pressing her fingers into the softness cradled within her hip bones.

"What is wrong? Are you ill?" Kathryn asked sharply. "Surely you are not far enough along to suffer birthing pains?" Some women gave birth prematurely. She prayed that would not happen.

"No. I am only a few weeks as far as I can tell," Mary whispered, her hand pressing harder.

Perhaps she hoped to squeeze the unborn child out of her without the need of a midwife. Kathryn immediately regretted the churlish thought and blamed her anxiety for her meanness.

"No one can hear us. There is no need to whisper." Kathryn took Mary's hand in hers and rubbed it. She could feel the chill in Mary's fingers through her gloves. "Are you in pain?"

The girl snatched her hand away with a grimace. "I am quite well," she said in a cold voice, clearly trying to regain control of herself. Her inability to stop casting frightened glances at the increasingly shabby streets ruined the effect.

Fewer and fewer streetlamps lit the narrow lanes of Whitechapel and in the distance, they could hear raucous laughter and singing from a tavern. Darkness clung to the alleys and walkways, giving them a sinister gloom. Men in heavy shoes and worn jackets staggered by, shouting to companions. One man with a filthy cap pulled low over his heavy brown kicked a starving dog out of the way when the animal did not move fast enough to avoid him. The man glanced up at the carriage, his red-rimmed eyes watching them, glazed with hopeless rage. Kathryn closed her eyes and looked away, feeling ill and trapped. The buildings appeared to lean over their fragile carriage as if about to fall over and crush them under a pile of bricks and rubbish.

Kathryn's chest tightened when she dared to open her eyes again. She had never been to this area of London, and she prayed they were not lost. She wanted to complete their errand and return home as quickly as possible.

Finally, the conveyance jerked to a halt. The two women stiffened. Mary grabbed Kathryn's hand as they listened to the thumps and grunts of the driver descending from his perch. He jerked the door open and lowered the steps. A heavy draft of cold, damp air rushed into the carriage and swirled around their ankles.

"Is this it?" Mary's eyes were wide with terror. Her white hands flew to her belly, covering it protectively.

Kathryn swallowed and forced a smile, all the while hating herself for accompanying this woman on this appalling mission. Why had she agreed?

The poor baby...

What did she know about Mary, after all? She had seemed sweet enough, but Kathryn had only known her for a few months. She drew a long breath. No matter. Even if they had been strangers, she would have assisted her, given her abandonment by the man who had seduced her.

Kathryn could not help but sympathize with Mary's situation. No matter how silly the girl had been, she didn't deserve the ostracism she would suffer if she bore the babe out of wedlock. She didn't deserve to face the consequences of her actions, alone.

Kathryn nodded to Mary. "We're only a few minutes away from the townhouse. We couldn't ask the driver to take us to her very door, now could we?"

"No." Mary looked as if she were ready to faint.

"Never fear, Mary—Miss Dudley. It will soon be over," Kathryn said reassuringly. She gripped Mary's elbow and guided her through the carriage door.

The two women descended, their breaths turning to misty clouds in the cold night air. They stood for a moment on the walkway, staring around in confusion. Neither had ever set foot on this particular street. The wretchedness and filth seemed threatening even though black shadows obscured the worst details. The street smelled of bile and excrement, forcing Kathryn to breathe through her mouth to avoid being sick.

Remembering the directions she had obtained from a "friend of a friend," Kathryn finally moved to the left. She hoped she had judged their course correctly.

"Is it far?" Mary asked.

"No." Kathryn didn't actually know where the midwife lived. However, from the address she had been given, she thought they were walking in the appropriate direction. She slipped an arm around Mary's waist, drawing courage from their shared warmth.

Before long, they came upon a nondescript brick building wedged between a taller building on its left and a dark, narrow alley on its right. The roof sagged above dark, shuttered windows. To Kathryn, the narrow house seemed to cower against its taller neighbor as if the slightest breeze would topple it. A crumbled pile of bricks lay in the alley. A few feet above the rubble, a black hole pierced the brick wall.

She had heard of buildings collapsing without warning in the poorer sections of London. Surely, that wouldn't happen, now. She shivered. What happened to the poor families living in them when it did? To the children? The thought of living in a building that threatened to fall on her at any moment seemed unbearable, but perhaps the inhabitants felt that any shelter was better than none. She glanced at Mary, hoping she had not noticed. Worrying about the walls crumbling around them would only deepen Mary's fears.

"Is this it?" Mary stopped.

Kathryn gripped her elbow and pulled her up the four shallow steps to the black, peeling door. "Yes." She tried to sound confident, but her taut nerves and the knot in her stomach made her voice quaver. She was just as nervous as Mary as she knocked on the door, her fingers glazed with ice despite her gloves.

Not quite as frightened, she reminded herself. She was not pregnant and seeking to be rid of her unborn baby. Her parents would claim I am just as bad, or worse, for assisting their daughter in the commission of the crime of abortion.

The thought didn't bear scrutiny.

She pulled her shawl more tightly around her shoulders and smoothed the concern away from her face. Mary might believe Kathryn routinely visited midwives willing to "take care of awkward matters" for a fee, but Kathryn had never been to such a place in her life. She had no idea what went on behind the black door. She could only hope the authorities were not waiting for them. Uneasy, she did her best to appear unconcerned for Mary's sake. The procedure would be over soon, and they both would return to their homes before anyone missed either of them.

Kathryn raised her hand to knock again when she heard a noise. Hinges screeched and the black door opened partway.

A woman peered at them through the gap. "Who are you?"

"Miss Dudley and Miss Whitethorn-Litton. I believe we're expected."

The woman's dark brown eyes looked them up and down, her glance resting longer on Mary's pale face. "Expected?"

"By Mrs. Cushway. Are you Mrs. Cushway? We are, um, friends of Miss Singleton. She indicated Mrs. Cushway would be expecting us. We have an appointment." Kathryn bit her lip to stop from rattling on from sheer nerves.

Rose Mardling had told Kathryn that Miss Singleton had visited Mrs. Cushway on numerous occasions in the past. Mentioning her ought to reassure Mrs. Cushway, if this was indeed the woman they sought. Kathryn smiled though her lips trembled.

"Miss Singleton?" The woman didn't budge. She stared at Kathryn, her eyes shadowed by her heavy, frowning brows.

"Miss Singleton made the appointment for Miss Dudley. Please take us to Mrs. Cushway immediately." Kathryn could understand the woman's nervousness, but they couldn't stand here chatting.

Someone would notice the two well-dressed women standing in front of this unprepossessing door and make note of it. If anyone discovered their purpose, all of them would be arrested. Their fates would rest in the hangman's calloused hands.

"Please let us inside." Kathryn stepped forward and placed a hand against the door.

The woman stood aside and let them enter the dank hallway. She glanced outside, studying the street, before shutting the door.

In the faint light from a small lamp sitting on a nearby table, Kathryn eyed the woman's plain face. Deep grooves ran from her stub of a nose to her thin mouth, and the skin of her strong jaw sagged slightly above a thick, wrinkled neck. The woman was perhaps in her late forties, Kathryn judged, although her heavy, worn features made her seem far older. A crude, bullish air hung around her, and Kathryn almost expected her to snort and trample over them like fragile blades of grass obstructing her path.

The hallway around them was barren of furniture except for the rickety table and lamp. The wooden floor was worn and dusty, and a narrow stairway led upwards into the darkness of the first floor. No pictures hung on the soot-stained walls, and Kathryn had the distinct impression that if she stumbled against the wall or fell to the floor, splinters from the rough wood would pierce her palms. The sound of pattering feet and scratching alerted Kathryn to the presence of rats. As if to confirm her fears, a black rodent the size of a small cat jumped off one of the stairs and skittered away down the hallway, disappearing into the gloom.

Mary gripped Kathryn's hand harder, squeezing the bones together.

Shaking her hand loose, Kathryn put her arm around her waist. She had the wild urge to drag Mary outside and run away, fleeing this wretched house filled with vermin and shadows. But where would they go? What would they do?

Over the years, Kathryn had pawned some of the gifts Lord Taunton had seen fit to give her, replacing the items with cheaper versions. She knew that one day Taunton would get rid of her, and she placed no reliance on his sporadic generosity. She needed the funds to support herself when he asked her to leave.

However, despite her best efforts, her nest egg remained small. She lacked the resources to support two women and a baby. And unprepared for Mary's situation, Kathryn had only a few shillings in her reticule.

So what could she do? Taking Mary to one of the houses for unwed mothers didn't bear consideration. A friend had once dragged Kathryn to see one, and she never wanted to see another. It was a grim place, filled with empty-eyed women who paid for their sins with a restricted life of unbending rules, poor food, and unceasing toil.

That such places existed made her ill, doubly so because she knew the institutions were needed. Dozens of desperate women with no means to support themselves lacked a better alternative. Given a choice between Hell and the unknown, many preferred Hell.

"This way, then," the woman said, gesturing for them to move in front of her.

She herded them down the hallway briskly, past the staircase, and into the blackness beyond. At the end on the passageway, Kathryn saw the wavering, smoky glow of a lantern streaming through a door on their right.

"I'm Mrs. Cushway." The brusque woman all but pushed them through the door.

Two battered lamps hung from hooks in the ceiling. Their wavering light pooled over a wide table that nearly filled the cramped room.

To the left of the door, a cheap wooden chest of drawers with one broken leg leaned against the wall. A pile of dingy white towels, a bowl, and a large pitcher of water stood on top of the chest. As Kathryn glanced around, appalled by the barren, utilitarian room, Mrs. Cushway brushed past her to open the top drawer.

Her clothing exuded the rank odors of sweat, mustiness, and gin. Kathryn turned away and held her breath, blinking her stinging eyes.

Mrs. Cushway pulled out a bundle that she unrolled next to the towels on top of the chest. Several evil-looking, instruments clanked loudly in the silence. Kathryn flinched. Mary gave a sharp, audible gasp and gripped Kathryn's right arm with both hands.

"Well?" Mrs. Cushway turned to them, holding a long, thin metal tool that looked like a knitting needle with a hooked tip in her hand. Her plain face hardened. The lines surrounding her thin mouth etched more deeply into her weathered cheeks. Instead of understanding Mary's fear, her mouth tightened with impatience. "Lift your skirts and climb up on the table, girl. No point in dawdling. None of us wants to be here. But you came to me, not otherwise, so come along with you."

Biting her lower lip, Mary retreated until her back pressed against the edge of the table. She placed her hands on the filthy surface and stared at Mrs. Cushway with wide-eyed terror. Her body shook, rattling the table.

Kathryn put an arm around Mary's shoulders, feeling an absurd desire to protect the young woman. "Here, let me help you. It will be over soon." She could feel Mary's trembling increase. "Have courage."

"I cannot do it," Mary whispered. "I simply cannot."

Kathryn caught Mrs. Cushway's unsympathetic gaze. The older woman shook her head. "It makes no difference to me, but I will have my five pounds no matter what you decide. I risked my own life to help you in your time of need." Her lips twisted over the last words as if she'd swallowed a spoonful of vinegar.

Kathryn leaned closer to Mary and squeezed her shoulder. "It is your decision, but what will you do if you remain pregnant? What will you say to your parents?"

"I don't know!" Mary turned and buried her face into Kathryn's shoulder. A muffled sob broke from deep within her throat.

"Tell them you wish to go to France, then. Surely, you must have an elderly relative, some lady who could chaperone you. Then leave the baby on the doorstep of a church when it is born. Others have done it, why should you not?" Kathryn rubbed her shoulder. They should leave this dreadful place, no matter what the consequences were. She could not let Mrs. Cushway touch Mary, not with that dreadful, hooked thing in her hand. She thought about her small nest egg. Perhaps she could give it to Mary. Somehow, she could find a way to replenish her funds.

"I cannot. My parents would never understand. They will send me to one of those places—one of those *terrible* places for unwed mothers. Oh Kathryn, what am I to do?"

Mrs. Cushway shifted her feet impatiently. The soles of her shoes scraped the grit on the battered floor. "Make up your mind, girl. Leave, or stay and be done with it."

"I—oh—" Mary doubled over.

Kathryn felt the muscles in the girl's body tighten. "What is it?" She tried to raise Mary's head, but her tightening muscles resisted Kathryn's gentle touch.

Sweat beaded Mary's pale forehead. Droplets rolled off her and soaked through the bodice of Kathryn's dress. "Nothing—" Mary gasped. "Oh, it hurts!"

Placing a broad hand on the girl's belly, Mrs. Cushman pressed for a moment and then stepped back. "Lucky girl, God has blessed you despite your sins. He has sent an angel to take care of you tonight."

"What do you mean?" Kathryn struggled to keep Mary on her feet, swaying under her weight. The girl leaned over and clutched the side of the table.

"He is purging her of her shame without any assistance." Mrs. Cushman grabbed Mary's damp hair and raised her face. "Unless you have taken something. Poison? Is that it, girl? You took poison thinking to die here and place the blame at my door?"

Whatever was wrong, Mary couldn't answer. Sweating and gray-faced, she moaned before she crumpled onto the filthy floor.

Chapter Four

12:00 AM—Midnight October 23, 1821

"Well Mr. Bottom, what do you think, then?" Richard Toddy asked his portly companion as they stood in the shadows across the street from Croftson House. "A sweet house, to be sure."

The grand townhouse sparkled like a golden jewel. The glow of brilliant lights poured from the windows. Toddy's heart expanded with joy at the thought of all the small, highly portable objects that surely lay within those thick walls. Those objects, so often meaningless to the wealthy men who owned them, would buy dozens of warm, hearty meals. Toddy could almost taste roast beef, swimming in thick, rich gravy, or perhaps a steaming slice of steak-and-kidney pie. His stomach grumbled hollowly. It had been days since his last meal. The shriveled apple and stale bit of bread were distant memories.

Albert Bottom and Richard Toddy had been watching the residence for the last hour, disappointed that the earl had apparently decided to host a party on this of all nights. Why had he selected this particular evening? The same night the two men hoped to obtain a small bauble or two in order to meet their most pressing needs. A bit of sustenance and a pint of ale weren't too much to ask, were they?

Nonetheless, the earl seemed determined

to be most unaccommodating.

No guests had arrived or departed while Bottom and Toddy waited, however. After another hour, the two relaxed.

"I believe we may have misjudged his lordship, Mr. Toddy," Bottom said. "Perhaps our host is merely having a quiet evening in his own abode, no doubt sitting in front of his fire roasting his toes and enjoying a pint or two."

"No doubt." Toddy rubbed his thin hands together. The night breeze chilled him to the bone and made his joints ache. His portly companion seemed oblivious to the freezing temperature and looked as content as ever with the icy wind blowing past his double chin. "Upstairs or downstairs?" Toddy asked, referring to the earl in residence.

"Library, no doubt, on the ground floor," Bottom said in his rich, solemn voice. Then with a tone of regret he continued, "Brandy, I should think, on a night like this. His lordship would have brandy instead of ale, wouldn't he? I wouldn't mind a glass of brandy, myself."

"No doubt. If we have guessed a-right, then the second floor corner is quite available, Mr. Bottom, for our, um, exploration. The master's bedroom to be precise." Toddy smiled and rubbed his itchy nose that someone in a monumental fit of drunken temper had once likened to the twitching, pink nose of a rat.

The insult had bothered Toddy initially. Then he found the charity within himself to forgive the rudeness a good ten minutes before the executioner had dropped the floor out from under the miscreant's kicking feet a week later. Remembering the incident fondly, Toddy adjusted the heavy coil of rope that hung awkwardly over his left arm, hampering free-and-easy movement. He yanked the irritating coils again as he glanced around.

In the dimness, he spotted something that brought a grin to his narrow face. For once, luck was with them. They might be able to forgo the use of their rope, after all. The painters who had spent the last two days refreshing the shutters of Croftson House had obligingly left a ladder behind. The handy contrivance nestled against the wall in the narrow alley running front-to-back along the length of the townhouse.

When the workmen's activity first came to the attention of Toddy and Bottom, Bottom had tsked over their slow and not particularly well-done work. The peeling, deep green shutters on the top floor remained untouched despite the sloppy progress on the lower floors that left tracks of paint running down the brick walls. The painters were apparently not only slow, but careless enough to leave their tools lying around where anyone could borrow them.

Poor, slovenly craftsmanship, truth be told. Toddy shifted from one cold, aching foot to the other as they studied the house. The lazy workmen had not even finished half the job, although by rights they should have done so the previous day.

"Shall we, Mr. Bottom?" Toddy bowed to his companion and gestured toward the shining beacon of Croftson House, Lord Taunton's magnificent town residence.

"Indeed we shall, Mr. Toddy." Bottom smiled and nodded.

The pair retrieved the ladder from its "hiding place" behind a messy stack of canvas and buckets. The two removed it so delicately that even the tabby cat hunting a mouse a yard away in the alley never twitched at their efforts. Toddy and Bottom maneuvered the ladder around to the rear of the townhouse and propped it up against the brick wall.

Bottom had one foot on the first rung when the cat shot around the corner of the house. The animal brushed Toddy's legs as he braced the ladder and leapt through the kitchen garden as if a pack of wolves were snapping at its heels. Both men immediately stiffened. Movement attracted attention and that was the last thing they wanted.

The kitchen door creaked. A light step and the brush of a heavy cloak against the wooden door broke the silence. Toddy was so startled that he turned his head in the direction of the noise although every instinct warned him to remain still. A slight figure stood for a moment in the open doorway. Toddy could just make out the gleam of pale, silken skirts beneath the heavy cloak.

The woman turned her head as if listening. A flickering light from the kitchen illuminated her face and hair for a moment. Then she pulled up her hood and ran towards the alley, never realizing that the two men stood not ten feet away, gaping at her.

When the sound of hurried footsteps faded into the night, Toddy glanced at Bottom. "Housemaid out for a lark, I suppose." He frowned, thinking about the gleam of her skirts. Far too rich for a mere servant. A cast-off dress, no doubt, from her mistress.

Nice bit of finery, that. One that would fetch a pretty penny at a second-hand shop. Assuming he ever happened to find a garment like that in his hands.

"I sincerely hope she doesn't suffer for it. 'Tis certainly a shame she is so careless as to go out on a night like this." Bottom shook his head as he eased off the ladder and motioned for Toddy to ascend, instead. "Bound to end badly."

"Indeed, yes," Toddy agreed. The woman had been pretty, at least what he had seen of her. It would be a shame if she were to be blamed for their misappropriation of her master's goods.

However, that eventuality couldn't be avoided if he wanted a decent supper anytime this week. He could not be sure that the workmen would continue to be as unconsciously generous with their ladder as they had been this evening. Any use of the contrivance had to occur now. He dropped the rope, relieved to be rid of it. Using the rope had always been a risky second choice in his opinion.

Toddy glanced around. There was no other movement and since Bottom seemed too nervous to go first, he climbed up the ladder, keeping his gaze fixed on the windowsill above him. When he reached the window, he paused to listen before pushing it open. His shoulders rose as if to cover his ears at the shriek of wood rubbing against wood.

A few feet below him, Bottom waited. He had picked up the rope Toddy had discarded and stood with one hand holding the rope now looped over his shoulder as a precaution. He had once told Toddy that he didn't trust ladders. The unwieldy devices had a mind of their own and in the past, had often abandoned him right when he needed them the most.

In truth, Bottom had lost his position as a schoolteacher to one such incident when he had simply been trying to supplement his meager income. Toddy considered him lucky to have only lost a position he had secretly despised and not to have lost his life in the process.

Thievery was not a sport for amateurs and frequently led to an untimely demise.

Toddy swung a leg into the richly furnished room, easing noiselessly to the floor. With a satisfied smile, he thrust his arm out of the window to assist Bottom, who begrudgingly ascended the ladder.

Both men stayed near their potential escape route for a minute while they assessed the glittering potential of the cozy room.

A fire crackled and blazed merrily on the hearth. Three brass lamps cast a warm, golden glow over the furnishings. One lamp sat on a delicate, curved-leg desk in the corner a few feet from the window, the second sat on a round table next to the bed, and the last lamp lit the room from atop the fireplace mantle. Despite the lights and the cheerful fire, the room appeared to be empty of life and the door safely closed.

Raising his brows, Toddy glanced at Bottom. "Wasteful bloke. All these lights burning for naught."

*

Bottom frowned and pulled his lower lip. "I have the distinct feeling that our dear earl wandered away from his bed chamber a mere minute ago." He ran his hand over the smooth coverlet gracing the bed, smiling at the feel of the soft, deep blue velvet nap of the rich fabric.

What it would be like to sleep on clean, linen sheets again, with a thick, plush coverlet pulled up to his chin to keep him toasty against the winter's damp chill?

Bottom felt fortunate on those few nights when he and Toddy managed to find a place to sleep sheltered enough to avoid waking up with icicles hanging from the tips of their noses. Once before he died, he would like to sleep in a warm, comfortable bed again.

Not for the first time he regretted the loss of his position as a school teacher. The pay may have been insufficient for his needs, and he had developed an utter distaste for porridge, but at least he had slept quite peacefully in a real bed.

"Mr. Bottom," Toddy gripped Bottom's arm. "I believe we are not alone."

Bottom ceased all movement and waited, his heart pounding deep within his chest. He'd been expecting this, however he had hoped tonight would not be the night when the authorities finally caught up with them. It all seemed so unfair. All he wanted was a warm bed and something to eat.

Was that really so awful?

As Bottom watched, Toddy crept forward. He moved toward the cheerful fire in the fireplace, walking softly on the balls of his feet.

"What are you on about?" Bottom whispered, edging close enough to grab his companion's sleeve.

Shaking him off, Toddy tiptoed around a wing chair. He stopped and stood staring at the floor. "It appears our dear earl has suffered a terrible misfortune." He nudged something with the toe of his worn, leather shoe. "And is, regretfully, now our dearly *departed* earl."

Nerves shaking like a wagon wheel over cobblestones, Bottom eased around the chair.

A man lay on partially on his side, long

49

legs sprawled over the carpet, his wavy hair bright gold in the firelight.

When Toddy nudged the man's shoulder again with his toe, Bottom gripped his friend's shoulder. "Don't be a nodcock. He is only drunk—do you want to awaken him?"

Toddy ignored Bottom and knelt to push the man over onto his stomach. "He was past awakening these last ten minutes or more, Mr. Bottom." He gestured toward a jeweled knife sticking out of the man's back. It jutted out from a spot just under the man's left shoulder blade.

With a quick glance around, Toddy pulled the knife free and wiped it clean on the shoulder of the earl's brocade jacket. He grimaced and scooted back a few inches when a small rivulet of dark blood oozed out of the wound. With a nervous twitch, Toddy turned the body over onto its back as if to hide the small, reddish-black stain on the carpet.

Bottom felt a jolt of shock as he watched his companion's actions. How could he touch a corpse? He frowned and brushed his fingers over his coat with distaste. Although he tried not to stare, he noticed that only a few sluggish drops of blood fell when Toddy removed the dagger. The stain on the carpet was small, almost non-existent. And smoothed of all human worry, the earl's face appeared as lovely and cherubic as a plump-cheeked girl. For a moment, Bottom wondered if they really were too late to save him.

"Should we send for a physician?"

"Don't be daft," Toddy replied in a harsh voice.

Bending closer, Bottom noted the earl's eyes were half-open beneath their heavy lids, and death had already glazed them over.

It was most assuredly too late. He propped his hands on his knees and straightened, trying to ignore the crackles and snaps of pain in his back. The cold sank sharp and brutal claws into his aging bones. How much longer would he be able to maintain his admittedly thin stream of income through these nightly jaunts with Toddy?

Not much longer. He shivered. Their future didn't bear consideration. He had yet to learn the main lesson poverty taught all her students: think only of today, this hour, this minute. He still worried and fretted over what *might* be instead of what was.

"Nice little trinket." Toddy held the knife up in the firelight to admire the large ruby at the tip of the handle. "Gold and a fine ruby. Should fetch a nice price."

Bottom hummed a bit, trying to clear his mind. Murder had been done and Toddy proposed to abscond with the weapon used in the commission thereof.

Bottom's joints ached with cold at the thought. "Leave it. We should depart before his servants come. 'Tis not safe here, not with him lying there."

"What and leave with nothing to show for our pains?" Toddy eyed him, his thin face twisting with distaste. "Neither of us has had a morsel to eat for two days. I don't propose to suffer a third night with nothing but frost on my tongue." He slipped the knife into a capacious pocket and glanced around. "Our dear earl here no longer has any need of his earthly wealth, and we have need aplenty." He stood and patted his tattered coat. "Have a look, then, at our lovely gent's desk."

Ill-at-ease, Bottom complied. In the narrow, top drawer of the desk, he found a leather purse. He hefted it in his hand and heard the welcomed clink of heavy coins. Toddy glanced his way at the sound and stopped his own search to watch his partner.

Bottom hooked a finger into the purse's opening and widened it before dumping the contents on the desk's blotter.

Gold! Several new sovereigns rolled an inch or so and then fell on their sides. A bloody fortune in gold. While there were several other coins of smaller denominations, it was the gold that caught his attention and made his heart throb in his chest. He licked his lips. His mouth watered at the thought of what he could do with so many guineas. A real dinner, piping hot from the oven, and a bed. A roof over their heads that didn't leak and windows that didn't rattle and let in every errant, freezing draft.

A squeak from somewhere in the house

interrupted Bottom's dreams. He looked at Toddy. Toddy lifted his head. His nose twitched as if scenting the air like a dog.

He jerked his chin at Bottom. In utter silence, the two collected most of the coins as quickly as possible.

Showing remarkable restraint, Toddy pressed a finger to the side of his nose and caught Bottom's eye before he elaborately returned a few coins to the purse. "No need to make them think his lordship has been robbed. No need to send the authorities looking for us."

Of course! Why hadn't he thought of that? Bottom winked his agreement. He eased the purse back where it belonged and shut the desk drawer before slipping over to the window.

While he refused to admit the weakness out loud, he held the superstitious belief that if he looked over his shoulder, he would see something he didn't want to see. So despite the creeping sensation that they were observed and about to be caught, Bottom did not glance behind him. He grimly held the top of the ladder steady while Toddy clambered down, all the while feeling the hairs on the back of his neck stiffening.

As Toddy stepped off the last rung, Bottom heard the sound of a leather sole on wood. Another floorboard creaked behind him, this time closer. His heartbeat doubled and then trebled, but he remained silent. He didn't move until Toddy waved.

Climbing out of the window, Bottom slipped down three rungs before easing the window shut behind him. No point in leaving it open as a calling card. Moving as quickly as he dared, he descended the ladder rung by painful, slow rung until he felt the lovely ground beneath the worn sole of his shoe.

He grinned at Toddy and nodded. They gripped the ladder, and then as quiet as mice, they lowered it and slid it back under the pile of tarps at the side of the house. By the time they finished, it had started to rain again, a cold rain on the biting edge of freezing into snow.

Cold droplets trickled under Bottom's chin, around his neck, and down his tattered collar. The precipitation started out as a spitting, icy dribble, but soon turned into a regular torrent. He hunched his shoulders, trying to protect his neck, but the persistent rain beat through the thin defenses of his woolen jacket. The fabric had more moth holes than cloth and the freezing torrent easily breached its thin defense.

A block away, despite the increasingly inclement weather, Toddy began whistling in his odd, out of tune way. A street further on, Bottom spotted the watch on the opposite side of the avenue. The heavy-set man turned to look at them, tapping a cudgel against his thigh. Bottom touched the brim of his hat in acknowledgement as they passed, hoping they appeared as innocent as angels.

The watchman did not follow. Bottom's thoughts soon turned to the roast beef dinner he was going to enjoy tonight—that is, tomorrow—since it was already well past midnight.

The evening was already too far gone to do more than escape from Mayfair and find an inn that wasn't too full to accommodate them. They would be lucky to obtain a leftover crust of cheese or a moldy bit of bread to fill their bellies at this late hour. However, a bit of food and shelter didn't seem like too much to ask on such a miserable night.

Bottom's warm thoughts turned icy, though, when he remembered the watch.

He meant trouble for them. Toddy and Bottom didn't belong in Mayfair, and the watch knew it. Bottom could feel the man's suspicious gaze following them through the damp streets.

That meeting and the dead man's knife in Toddy's pocket were bad omens. Those were the kinds of things that tripped a man up when he least expected it and paved the way to the trapdoor under the hangman's noose.

Amy Corwin

Chapter Five

3:00 AM October 23, 1821

"You cannot leave us!" Kathryn said as Mrs. Cushway picked up her shawl and wrapped it around her shoulders.

"She don't have no need of me now, does she?"

"She is bleeding—we must help her!" Kathryn knelt next to Mary. After a moment's examination of the unconscious woman and filthy floor on which she lay, Kathryn turned her over so that her head rested in her lap. She brushed a streak of dirt off of Mary's damp cheek.

Mrs. Cushway dragged open a drawer, ignoring the horrendous squeaks the wood made. Harsh clinking noises erupted as she fumbled through the contents before she finally dragged out a small glass bottle. She uncorked it and bent over, waving it under Mary's nose.

The sharp, ammonia odor of *sal volatile* caught in Kathryn's throat. She coughed and turned away. After a second, Mary twisted and hunched over, pressing her face into Kathryn's belly as she choked and gasped for air.

"There." Mrs. Cushway struggled to her feet, stepping on her hem and stumbling against the wooden chest of drawers behind her. "The bleeding will stop soon enough since she's rid herself of the babe. Now you two must leave while I clean up her mess. This were a bad notion as I told that Singleton girl, and I don't do this no more."

"Then why did you agree?" Kathryn asked curtly.

Shrugging, Mrs. Cushway laughed and ran a filthy rag over the pool of blood on the floor. "A few coins is always welcome. Now I am going out the back way. You leave when you're ready. Don't wait too long. There be too many eyes with nothing better to do than watch these streets at night." She eyed Mary who clung to Kathryn sniffing and shaking with tears. An emotion that looked suspiciously like sympathy passed through Mrs. Cushway's cloudy eyes as she looked at them from the doorway. "She will be right as rain once you get her home, never fear. She may wish herself to the devil now, but she'll forget all of this soon enough. You'll see. She were lucky the good Lord took care of the matter for her."

Before Kathryn could respond, Mrs. Cushway disappeared into the shadows. Less than a minute later, she heard the slam of a door echoing down the empty hallway.

Except for the sound of Mary's soft, heart-wrenching sobs, the house seemed oppressively silent, almost menacing. The peeling, mildewed walls loomed over them to disappear into the shadows obscuring the ceiling. Suddenly, Kathryn could not breathe. The odors of damp wood and the metallic scent of blood filled her throat and choked her.

She put an arm around Mary and pulled her to her feet. "We must go. Please, Mary, we cannot remain here any longer. It is over, and you must return home to rest."

"It hurts so," Mary gasped, hunched and holding her belly. Perspiration dampened her gray face and her eyes appeared sunken into dark hollows. Her blue lips trembled.

Kathryn adjusted her grip to hold Mary's arm with her free hand. "Can you walk?"

"I cannot." Mary's mouth compressed into a harsh line, and she trembled with weakness. "I'm in pain—" She panted and gasped for breath. "It is beyond bearing!" A deep breath whistled in her throat. "I cannot walk. Have...mercy..."

The house whispered and creaked around them as a gust of wind kicked the doors and shutters. The windows trembled and clacked in their frames. A tendril of frigid air squeezed through the cracks to twine around Kathryn's ankles. Shivering, she glanced around, desperately wanting to leave and forget this terrible place. The floors and walls seemed to have absorbed all the fear and blood that had soaked into the fabric of the wretched room.

She squeezed her eyes shut, trying to shut out the notion. She had never hated a place before and the violence of her revulsion for this townhouse frightened her.

"You must master yourself. I am sorry, but we must leave. It is only a few blocks to the carriage." She brushed a few damp curls away from Mary's forehead and tucked them under the edge of her bonnet. Kathryn carefully straightened the confection, retying the blue silk ribbons under Mary's trembling chin. "The cramps will ease now that—" She halted, feeling ill. *Now that your baby is gone.* She couldn't say the words. "Come, Mary, please. You were strong enough to come here. Now you must find your strength again and return home."

Tightening her grip, she drew Mary toward the door, trying not to wobble under the weight of the woman leaning against her. Somehow, she managed to maneuver her out the front door and down the four steps to the walkway.

Outside, Kathryn took a deep breath, relieved to flush the scent of misery from her lungs. Her second breath hitched as she looked around. Why had she expected the street to be deserted? Several men staggered past, leering at the two women. Kathryn felt exposed to the gazes of the inhabitants. Two drunken men called out, making lewd comments and laughing coarsely.

She had no way to protect Mary against the louts. Three men lounged against a wall at the mouth of a nearby alley, watching them. She drew Mary closer. Even Mary seemed aware that they were vulnerable. She straightened slightly, although she slipped an arm around Kathryn's waist for support as they walked. When they passed the alley, they walked more quickly and ignored the men. Kathryn heard a stumbling step behind them, and dragged Mary forward, nearly running. The footsteps faded, though Kathryn's heart continued to pound in her chest as they hurried through the misty streets. The three blocks to the carriage seemed endless.

Kathryn's breath was ragged when they finally located the conveyance and climbed inside, weary beyond bearing.

"You cannot tell anyone." Mary gripped Kathryn's hand and squeezed, her shadowed eyes shiny with fear within the airless confines of the carriage. The air reeked of worn leather, dust, and the metallic scent of Mary's stained skirts. "I cannot bear the disgrace. How could this have happened?"

Kathryn choked back a tart reply that Mary could not be that foolish. She most certainly did understand how she came to be in this sorry state. Kathryn shook her head and patted Mary's hand, striving to reassure her.

Their conveyance jolted the two women as the horses plodded into the street, their iron horseshoes ringing loudly against the cobblestones. Kathryn lifted one of the leather curtains covering the window and peered outside. Everyone on the street must have heard the rattle of the carriage wheels and clattering trot of the horses. Thank goodness they had used a hired carriage instead of one that could be identified as belonging to Mary's family.

"I will not gossip," Kathryn promised, letting the curtain fall back into place. She rubbed Mary's cold fingers. The icy flesh seemed to absorb all of Kathryn's heat without warming. "I promised you I would tell no one, and I will honor that vow. You have nothing to fear from me."

"Father would consign me to a Magdalen home, if he found out. I—I could not bear it. I would die if I went to such a place."

"He shall not find out from me." Kathryn could not imagine any father doing such a thing though she knew it was a sadly common occurrence. He might as well take a pistol to his daughter's head and pull the trigger.

No, she would not tell Mary's sad story to anyone, and not simply because of Mary's fear of her parents. From a purely pragmatic standpoint, Kathryn knew if she mentioned this incident to anyone, she would be subject to arrest just as surely as Mary Dudley. Both women would be disgraced and accused of conspiring in the death of the unborn baby, even if their plans proved unnecessary. Seeking such a procedure was considered immoral and was most definitely illegal. Neither of them would escape punishment if the authorities learned of this night's activities.

Their only safety lay in silence.

Weeping quietly, Mary sagged in the shadowed corner while Kathryn tried to relax against the hard squabs of the seat back.

Although the entire trip took no more than twenty minutes, it felt like hours before the carriage jerked to a stop at Mary's residence. Their coachman clambered down, shaking the conveyance before yanking open the door to let down the narrow steps.

When Mary did not move, Kathryn gripped her wrist and pulled her to the door. "Remember—if your maid notices—the blood on your skirts is normal. You started your monthly courses without realizing."

"I don't know if I can." Mary stared at Kathryn, her face as white as fresh linen. "I don't know if I can tell such a lie."

"You told lies about where you were when you took a peer into your bed." Kathryn's grip on Mary's wrist tightened. "So you can most certainly lie about such a paltry thing as your time of the month."

"I feel ill. Can you not come in with me?"

"No—I cannot. How would you explain my presence at this time of night? It must be nearly four in the morning." She shook her head and transferred her grip to Mary's shoulder to encourage her to step down the two steps to the walkway. "Despite our recent friendship, you are not supposed to be such close friends with women like me. If anyone saw me, all this would be for naught. You would most surely be disgraced. So go to your room and go to bed. Complain of a headache, or your monthly courses if you must, but whatever you do, forget what truly happened this night. Forget you saw me this evening."

"But—"

"It is for the best. Now goodnight, Mary—Miss Dudley. Rest. And good luck."

Kathryn would have shut the carriage door in Mary's frightened, pallid face except for the small matter of the steps.

The coachman made the awkward situation even worse by gripping both sides of the door and sticking his head inside. "I am sorry, Miss, but the horses is knackered, and I don't go no further tonight. You must walk if you wish to go further than this house tonight."

Flushing, Kathryn stepped out of the carriage, pulling her shawl around her shoulders as she brushed past him. The air felt cold against her cheeks and small puffs of mist followed each breath.

I should be used to such slights. No matter how she tried to ignore the coachman, his words made her feel ashamed.

"Go on, Miss Dudley." She gave Mary a small, encouraging push toward the narrow alley leading to the back of the house. "Go through the servant's door and go straight to bed. There is nothing to fear."

Mary opened her mouth as if to protest, but Kathryn turned on her heel and strode away. She had a long walk ahead of her, and she was exhausted. There was nothing more she could do for Mary except wish her well. As long as the girl remained silent and behaved with propriety, her unfortunate affair would be forgotten. The peer who had ruined her had surely already forgotten her.

And unlike Kathryn, Mary would have the opportunity to marry. She would never have cause to speak to a member of the demi-monde like Kathryn, again.

As always, when she remembered her position, or lack thereof, in Polite Society, Kathryn experienced dismay and a vague sense of envy. She felt trapped and helpless to change the opinions of the women who despised her as soon as they discovered who she was.

Mary was the lucky one, although she probably didn't feel that way at the moment. Despite her current difficulties, Mary's placid life would continue quite happily. She could dance on her merry way without another thought for this awful night.

Kathryn could not envision such a bright future for herself. Her only consolation as she trudged through the nearly empty streets was the knowledge that her protector, Lord Taunton, never seemed to care where she went, what she did, or when she came home. In that respect, she had complete independence. She would not be scolded for being out all night, even if Taunton discovered her absence, which she sincerely doubted.

Taunton encouraged her to roam London at will and do precisely as she wished. She used to fret about his lack of concern. Now, she suspected that it might be due to the fact that other mistresses appeared to share a bed, at least at times, with the men who claimed their attention. Her protector preferred the company of his young gentlemen.

She knew that well, but it still bothered her that Taunton expressed no interest in her. While he publically paraded her around as if she were truly his mistress, once they were home he waved her off, uninterested in her company. She had freedom, a few bits of jewelry, and nothing more. But she longed for much more. She wanted Taunton's eyes to hold something other than mild interest when he looked at her.

Still, she had to be grateful to him. When her father had died under mysterious circumstances during a visit to Wrexley Hall, leaving her alone and motherless at sixteen in a houseful of men, Lord Taunton had offered her a home in exchange for her appearance as his mistress.

And true to his promise, she had been safe. In a houseful of men, no one had touched her. No one even seemed interested in her. Why? Was she so repulsive that they could not stomach the sight of her?

She sighed. To be fair, Taunton had done the best he could, given her circumstances. He was an honorable man and hardly had any choice but to claim her as his mistress when she was orphaned and left in his charge. Her reputation had already been ruined by her presence in his household without even a maid as duenna. Her feckless father had seemed unconcerned about her future. He had dragged her along with him and left no will or instructions about who would act as guardian to his daughter if he passed away.

But then, he would have hardly thought he would die before he even reached his fortieth birthday.

Thankfully, Taunton had enough respect for her father to come to her aid in her time of mourning. He'd offered her a room when she had no place else to go.

It should have been enough, and she should have been grateful. She should have been happy. Many other women would have been giddy with joy to have such independence despite the loss of respectability.

Instead, she felt as if Mary were the lucky one despite everything that had befallen her. Mary's parents cared enough to want their daughter to remain safely under their protection until she married well and left for a home of her own. She might resent their strict regulation of her life, but she had to acknowledge that it was the best course for a secure future. She had not gotten into difficulties until she had slipped out of their control and mistaken the illusion of desire for love.

Kathryn pulled her shawl ever tighter, watchful for footpads and other inhabitants of

London's night-world who might believe a woman without protection was fair game. The walkway glittered with early morning dew under the glow of the streetlamps. She hurried, feeling the moisture seep into the thin soles of her shoes. Her toes were numb with cold when she finally rounded the corner and saw the unwelcoming façade of Lord Taunton's townhouse.

There were no glowing lights, no signs of life, as she set one foot on the bottom step of the short flight leading to the front door. Even the empty windows stared down at her with cold disdain. After a moment's hesitation, she backed away and slipped around the side of the building, heading for the kitchen entrance. No sense in waking up the Kirby to let her in the front door. The butler obtained little enough sleep as it was and would soon be up with chores of his own to attend to.

Her hem caught on something in the alley, and she flung a hand against a brick wall to prevent a fall. Wood clattered against the walkway. The painters had left behind their ladder, and one of the supports had caught her hem, nearly ripping it out. She freed her skirt and chiding herself for her clumsiness, entered the house just as the clock in the grand entryway chimed four AM. The mellow, low bell of the clock echoed through the empty hallway, audible even from the back of the house.

Thinking of nothing but sleep, she quietly

climbed the servants' stair. When she got to her room and began to disrobe, she found the hem of her gown stiff with dirt. No wonder the ladder had caught it when she passed. The material must have brushed through Mary's blood and hardened into crusty, dark red stains as it dried. Then the round imprint of her knee, about twelve inches above the sullied hem, caught her attention. She stared at it with distaste, remembering the sticky feel as she had knelt in the small puddle of blood on the filthy floor of the townhouse.

Balling up the dress, she thrust it into the bottom of her wardrobe. She was too tired to wash it out before retiring for the night. The gown could wait until morning.

In fact, as she climbed into bed, she realized it was unlikely she would ever want to wear that particular dress again, anyway. Too much suffering clung to the pale blue dress. She could not wear it without seeing Mary's pale face and desperate eyes or hearing the rats scrabbling in the darkness. In the morning, she would rinse it out and give it to one of the maids. Someone else could get some use from it.

Then perhaps she could forget Mary Dudley and her unfortunate affair.

Chapter Six

9:00 AM October 23, 1821

Unable to sleep, Nicholas threw the covers off and sat on the edge of his bed. Despite the October chill, the room felt stuffy. The air was thick with dust although the woman he hired to keep his flat in order had been there yesterday. Even the wooden floor felt gritty beneath his bare feet.

If the offices at Second Sons hadn't been closed at this hour, he would have been happy to go there. Anything was better than sitting here in the dark, his mind restlessly chewing over every weakness, every fault that Gaunt might discover in his newest employee.

Ridiculous. The fact that Gaunt had hired him should have been sufficient to prove it, but Nicholas could not quite lay to rest the notion that he would be let go without warning. Just the way his betrothed had walked away from him when he returned from the war.

When would he forget?

He ran a hand through his sweat-dampened hair, shivering as a draft from the window curled around his neck. A fluffy ball of gray dust skittered across the floorboards, pushed along by a random eddy of air. He couldn't help a small smile at the sight. Maybe Mrs. Hurley had better things to do than clean. He strongly suspected she merely shifted the dirt around without actually removing any of it.

However, since she always arrived on time, left him alone, and did a masterful job on his cravats, he was willing to accept her little foibles.

There were worse things than a bit of dust.

With a sigh, he lit the lamp on the small chest by his bed and opened the top drawer. After scrabbling through the tangle of handkerchiefs, old newspapers, and other odds-and-ends, he found the contrivance his brother's interfering and overly concerned doctor had designed for him. As far as Nicholas could determine, the two wooden grips connected to a metal coil were little more than a diabolical torture device. The physician's recommended exercise regime had done him little good since his injury at Corunna in 1809.

Despite his frustration, he could not quite erase the hope that one day his muscles and nerves might miraculously heal. So he continued to use the damn thing, cursing all the while and wishing the doctor to the hottest pit of Hell.

He put the V-shaped device in the palm of his unresponsive left hand and concentrated, trying to make his recalcitrant muscles grip the wooden handles. A prickling sensation ran down his arm, giving him a brief flare of hope. The moment passed, however, when his fingers refused to tighten. A bead of sweat trickled down his temple.

"Come on, damn you." He struggled to

make his wasted muscles obey him. His arm twitched, but his fingers never moved. Finally, he let out a long breath and clamped his good hand around his left, forcing the dead hand to compress the two handles. Despite the resistance of the metal coil, he managed to increase his grip until the pieces of wood clacked together.

"One, two, three ..." he chanted, counting off the clicks. Sweat stung his eyes, but he kept on, pressing the handles together twenty-five times before his hands cramped. Five more than yesterday. Was he improving or just deluding himself? He had to believe the prickling sensation and the cramping meant something, even if his good hand did the work.

At least there was a slight feeling, something to bolster his flagging hopes for a miracle. He wiped the tail of his shirt over his damp forehead before massaging his left arm, trying to knead life back into the limb as he watched the first red streaks of dawn touch the chimney pots and roofs of the slumbering city. A faint, bluish fog curled around the corners of the buildings, leaving damp patches that glittered dully as the pale sunlight gradually burned away the mist.

When Nicholas grew restless in the early morning silence, he left his apartment and walked swiftly through a freshly awakened London. He arrived at the walkway leading up to Second Sons' front door at eight-thirty AM, a good half hour before he was expected. For nearly two weeks, he had been working on writing the final reports for cases that other agents had investigated. The opportunity to see how others worked and the logic they used to complete their tasks intrigued him at first, but the novelty had long since worn off.

However, he didn't complain. He sensed that Gaunt was using the mindless work to evaluate him. The thought irritated him when he thought about it, and Nicholas was already chafing under Gaunt's discreet scrutiny. He wanted to get out and do something, not sit behind a desk and review the trivial cases and dry conclusions of others.

He stared at the front door. If he went into his office now, his impatience would be imprinted clearly upon his face. He absently rubbed his left wrist before stepping away from Second Sons. As he continued around the block at a slow pace, he tried to enjoy the crisp, autumn air. A freezing draft wriggled under his waistcoat, and he awkwardly buttoned his heavy outer coat more tightly around his throat with one hand. Truthfully, the temperature was more chilly than crisp, and the city sparkled with an icy clarity leant to it by the cold weather.

When would Gaunt trust him with a case of his own? Nicholas thought about the stack of folders on his desk with distaste. Perhaps Gaunt had already concluded that a man with only one good arm could only handle deskwork.

Preoccupied by the irritating thought, Nicholas tripped over a bundle of rags. He barely stayed upright by looping his good arm around a nearby lamppost.

"Wot'cher, mate," a low voice exclaimed.

"What the devil?" Nicholas glanced down.

A man, or at least a pile of dirty fabric and matted hair, huddled on the walkway with one leg stretched out toward the road. The creature swore at him, and Nicholas swore back with equal creativity. He almost strode on when something familiar about the man sprawled across the curb caught his attention. He stared into the glinting blue eyes and remembered another man—a soldier—with similar, brilliant blue-green eyes.

"Sergeant Dalton?" Nicholas asked, shocked at his condition.

Dalton wore so many layers of stained, tattered coats that he appeared to be a pile of refuse thrown onto the curb for the rag man to collect. Each jacket was a different hue, showing rainbow-like glimpses of color through the numerous holes of the tattered outermost one. Dalton's brown hair and beard were matted and oily-looking. His skin was so filthy and burned by the sun that it was nearly indistinguishable from his hair. Only his blue eyes shone clear and bright under his bristling eyebrows.

"Aye, Captain is it?" he asked, blinking in the early morning sun.

"What are you doing here?"

Sergeant Dalton laughed, spittle dampening his ragged beard. "Resting a minute or two, as you can see, while I wait for my carriage to come for me."

Nicholas flushed at the bitter sarcasm in Dalton's words. "I thought you went home to Richmond, your wife—"

"Ran off with a man with two legs, didn't she?" He leaned over and spit into the street then wiped his mouth with the back of his hand. "But you would know how the words to that song go as well as I, now wouldn't you?"

The muscles in Nicholas' jaw tightened. He knew those lyrics and didn't need to be reminded of it. "What are you doing here?"

"What do you think?" he shrugged. "Not much call for a one-legged man these days." He glanced at Nicholas' left arm. "Just like I doubt but what there's not much use for a one-armed man, neither. But then, the rich never have to worry about being useful, do they, Captain?"

"I haven't the slightest idea," Nicholas replied more sharply than he intended. "I am hardly wealthy enough to test that theory."

The sergeant shrugged and drew a pair of crutches into his lap. His muddy fingers played over the rough wood.

Nicholas hesitated. The condition of Sergeant Dalton was precisely why Nicholas had told Gaunt that he had no wish to hear about the fate of his men. He feared their lives were not what he wanted for them, and he choked back a futile sense of bitterness, faced with the miserable results of the war. The smoke and bloodshed of battle had been sickening enough without coming home to the realization that the very country they had fought for so desperately had no need of them now that they were maimed.

Time and society had moved on without them, happy to ignore their suffering.

Nicholas dug into his pocket and withdrew a few coins. He tossed the silver to Dalton, hardly able to look at him. "Get something to eat."

"Kind of you, Captain." Despite his words, Dalton's voice grated with bitter sarcasm.

Nicholas reached down and helped Dalton to stand, holding his breath at the foul stench of the sergeant's greasy clothing. Before Dalton could respond, Nicholas pulled out a slim card case, a remnant from better days, and extracted a card. He shoved the small square into Dalton's muddy hand. "And after you clean yourself up, call on me. Understand?"

"I'm no charity case."

"Did I say you were?"

Dalton stared at him for a minute before glancing down at the curb. "That's as may be—"

"Do as you please," Nicholas interrupted him. "It is your decision, after all."

"Aye, Captain. So it is, so it is." Sergeant

Dalton shook his head. Then he swung away and thumped down the street, heading in the direction from which Nicholas had come.

Nicholas watched him for a few minutes before continuing around the block to arrive at the front door to Second Sons once more at precisely five minutes to nine. The black door opened just as Nicholas raised his hand to knock.

"Ah, there you are, Captain Ainsley." Stepping aside to permit Nicholas to enter, Gaunt's servant, Mr. Sotheby, waved to the open door of the first office on the right. "Mr. Gaunt is expecting you."

Nicholas nodded, surprised at Gaunt's summons. A trickle of excitement tickled him. Perhaps Gaunt would finally assign him something more challenging than cleaning up old files.

When he entered Gaunt's office, his employer stood. "Good morning. Have a seat, if you please. I have something a bit more interesting for you this morning." He was again dressed in black, and he waited for Nicholas to cross the room to the chair in front of the desk before he reseated himself. "We just received a message from Lord Taunton's townhouse in Mayfair."

"The Earl of Taunton?" Nicholas frowned, trying to recall what he knew about the earl. Other than the name and the fact that he had his seat, Wrexley Hall, in Somerset,

Nicholas knew nothing else. He had never met him, as far as he knew.

"Yes, in a sense. A friend of his, Mr. Silsbury, sent his card requesting our assistance."

Nicholas shifted in his chair. "What sort of assistance?" He had unpleasant visions of following Gaunt around the earl's hallowed townhouse halls like an ill-trained puppy while his employer took care of whatever annoyed the earl. He had no desire to be anyone's assistant.

"Mr. Silsbury was unclear concerning that aspect." Gaunt's mouth twisted into a wry smile. "However, I gather he felt it was urgent enough to request our presence as soon as humanly possible. He also sent a retainer of nearly two hundred pounds which I find remarkably interesting, not to mention compelling. If you are not too busy with the files, perhaps you would be willing to visit the earl's home? Determine what has upset him and merits such a hefty sum." Gaunt studied him with curiosity and a hint of challenge in his direct gaze.

"I haven't quite finished the work you assigned me." The thought of escaping from the pile of folders on his desk filled him with relief. He felt like a school boy who has managed to escape his tutor for the day.

"It can wait. Unless you are not interested in this case?" Gaunt shrugged. "After all, it may be nothing."

"No—I am interested. Very interested. Am I to go alone?"

"Of course. I do not hire men who are incapable of working independently. I hope that doesn't inconvenience you."

"No. Not at all." His first case. This was why he had applied at Second Sons. He had a chance, now, to prove what he was still capable of. A spark of excitement sizzled inside him before dying abruptly. He had never done anything even remotely similar. What made him think he could succeed? He shook the thought off. He could manage this deftly enough. He stood, holding his limp left wrist with his right hand. "Is there anything else, sir?"

"No. I'm sorry I have no additional information regarding this request. Whatever it is, I feel sure you will acquit yourself well. Send word if you need assistance." Mr. Gaunt smiled before picking up a small pile of letters from a low wooden box at the edge of his desk. "I don't expect you will, however. Good luck, Captain Ainsley."

"Thank you." Nicholas strode out, hardly noticing Sotheby as he opened the door for him. His mind was too busy churning over what Gaunt had said. Precious little, to be sure. In fact, nothing more than a summons and the promise of a hefty reward.

Back on the street, Nicholas glanced down the walkway, aware of a return of his previous feeling of uncertainty. He was walking into the unknown—he didn't even know what this mission involved. He didn't like the feeling, and for a brief moment, he almost regretted leaving the military. At least there he knew what he had to do. The tasks were simple and repetitive: arm himself, run towards the enemy, and hope for the best. Dying for his country was easy enough although he managed to fail at that and return crippled.

Life is really no different than war. The thought jolted him. All he had to do was run forward, oblivious to bullets and shrapnel, and pretend that neither fear nor doubt ever crossed his mind. It was simple enough, even for a cripple. He was almost smiling when he finally turned the corner and headed toward Mayfair. A small portion of his confidence returned, buoyed up by the simple fact of having a task to perform.

When he arrived at the earl's townhouse, his good humor faded. He stared at his first obstacle. Front door or servants' door? It wouldn't do to antagonize the inhabitants on his initial approach. He eyed the rich green paint covering the front door and the elegant swan's head brass knocker.

Most butlers would agree that an inquiry agent had no business calling at the front door. He should use the tradesmen's and servants' entrance. An innate streak of stubbornness made him take another step forward. Although Nicholas didn't place much importance on his captaincy, it might suffice to allow him through the door used by visitors and socially acceptable guests.

In for a penny, in for a pound.

He straightened, walked up to the front door, and knocked. The door was literally thrown open before he lowered his fist. A man, presumably the butler, stood there staring at Nicholas as if he were a Christian facing a lion. His pudgy face was flushed and his clothing gave the impression of utter disarray.

Nicholas stepped back, startled. All the buttons of the butler's formal coat were buttoned, and there was nothing out of order if one overlooked a few wrinkles here and there, and yet he seemed disheveled. Perhaps it was the man's breathlessness and red face that created such a sense of panicked disorder.

"Wha—yes?" the butler asked, his thick fingers fumbling over his collar, clearly trying to bring himself under control.

"Captain Ainsley to see Mr. Silsbury. He is expecting me." Nicholas handed the butler his card. Only three more cards remained in the card holder. He frowned, flicking the edges with his fingernail. He hadn't used, or needed, them for years. The loneliness of the remaining cards chided him for his recent lack of sociability.

Well, he needed them now, and he'd have to order more if he managed to remain employed by Second Sons.

"Wait here, if you please, sir." The butler

started to leave and then turned back in a flurry, waving at one of the brocade-upholstered benches in the hallway. "If you please?" He gestured again and then hurried past the grand staircase toward the back of the house.

Looking at the bench with distaste, Nicholas remained standing. He wasn't tired by his brief walk and wasn't so crippled that he felt the need to sit. He looked around, reluctantly impressed by the earl's subdued good taste. Nothing was too garishly new. In fact, the brocade on the bench appeared rather threadbare in patches as if dozens of posteriors had worn away the golden threads over the years. A few good portraits, dim with age, stared at him. Most of the stiff-necked men and women had sour expressions and pale blue eyes. Their cold gazes seemed to follow him as he paced from one wall to the other.

"This way, sir." Sweating and red-cheeked, the butler gestured to him before he padded up the grand staircase, muttering under his breath.

"I beg your pardon, did you say something?" Nicholas asked when he thought he heard the man say something in a particularly vehement voice.

The butler halted abruptly and looked over his shoulder, his eyes wide. "No. I did not. Why would I have anything to say, sir?" Without waiting for a response, he continued past the first landing to the second floor. "What could one in my position possibly have to say?"

Nicholas followed in silence, his curiosity increasing when the butler led the way to a door at the end of the hallway. In most townhouses, they would be standing in front of the door leading to the master bedchamber suite.

The butler tapped the door once and then opened it with a flourish. He bowed as he intoned, "Captain Ainsley, sir."

The minute Nicholas stepped into the room, the butler closed the door behind him. He did it with such unseemly haste that the edge of the door brushed Nicholas' back.

He didn't have time to worry about the abrupt gesture. A man stood in the center of the room, staring at him. An apology leapt to Nicholas' mouth, but he managed to remain silent.

The slender, brown-haired man wore a soft, blue velvet jacket and a rumpled linen shirt open at the neck. He seemed abnormally pale and he blinked several times, his large, hazel eyes suspiciously wet and ringed with red. Nicholas had the sense that something calamitous had occurred, and he waited for the other man to explain.

"Captain Ainsley?"

"Yes."

"I am Silsbury, Mr. Harold Silsbury." He held out a slim, white hand that shook ever so slightly.

Nicholas shook hands, trying not to crush

the limp, damp fingers. "You sent a message to Second Sons Inquiry Agency?"

Silsbury let out a long breath and blinked more rapidly, dabbing his eyes with a lace-edged, white handkerchief. "Yes. Thank God, thank God you have come!"

Taken aback by the overly dramatic statement, Nicholas nodded and waited. He knew many such personages, both men and women. They were so emotional that they could never tolerate the occasional quiet moment in any conversation. They felt compelled to rattle on, even if they spoke insipid nonsense, and fill any silence with the sound of their own voice. Nicholas only had to show patience and allow Silsbury the opportunity to speak.

"I did not know what else to do." Silsbury's fingers tightened around his handkerchief for a moment before he waved it toward the fireplace. "I have been distraught since I found him."

Glancing past Silsbury's narrow shoulder, Nicholas noticed a pair of black leather shoes lying on their sides near the fireplace. A closer look revealed that feet still wore the shoes and that legs clad in gray trousers were attached to the feet. He moved forward to get a better look.

A man lay on the floor facing them, his half-opened eyes staring vacantly at their feet, clearly deceased. Nicholas had seen enough death at Corunna to know a dead man when he saw one.

"What happened?" He studied Silsbury, filled with suspicion. A man susceptible to strong emotions might kill in the heat of the moment. And a murderer might wish to be present when the body was examined in order to manipulate any evidence discovered by the investigators.

Silsbury stiffened and frowned. "I found him like this." He gripped the back of a nearby wing chair. "He has been stabbed—he is dead!"

"Who is he?"

"Why the earl, man! The Earl of Taunton. How can you not recognize him?"

"Forgive me. I have never met the earl. Have you sent for the coroner and constabulary?" Nicholas knelt down on one knee and gently moved the corpse onto its belly to view the wound in his back. There was not much blood on the floor beneath him, and the tiny rent in the back of his jacket was barely noticeable.

A thin blade, then. A stiletto, perhaps, that did its damage internally. He glanced at Silsbury again, noting the clean white cuffs peeping out from the sleeves of his elegant, velvet jacket. Nicholas frowned. The lack of stains in this case meant very little. There was virtually no blood on the victim's clothing or on the carpet beneath him. There was little likelihood that whoever had killed him would have any telltale "Lady Macbeth" stains, either.

As he eased the body back into its original position, something flashed, a small pinpoint of light glittered at the edge of the tear in Taunton's jacket. Frowning, Nicholas took a closer look at the wound. A very small diamond was caught in the thick strands of wool near the area where the knife had entered. The tiny stone was the sort often used to encircle the larger center stone in a piece of jewelry such as a ring. Dried blood had glued the diamond into the fabric.

So whoever had murdered Taunton must have been wearing a ring. And that ring was now missing this small stone.

He shook out his handkerchief, picked the diamond out of the tear and gently folded it, along with a few bloody strands of the jacket, into a square. He tucked the packet into his pocket and studied Taunton's wound and the floor beneath him one more time. No other clues of importance appeared.

When he glanced up at Silsbury, the man stood in front of the mirror, staring at his reflection. He artfully adjusted a strand of his black hair to curl over his forehead, tilting his head first one way and then the other to view the effect. The movement of his hands made his rings glitter in the sunlight, their flashing lights reflected by the silvered glass.

Were any of the rings he wore missing a stone? If only Nicholas could resolve this case so easily. He crooked his mouth at the cynical thought and concentrated on the task at hand.

"Did you notify the authorities?" Nicholas prodded him again, irritated by Silsbury's artificial air of vanity and nonchalance.

"No, I have not." Silsbury turned. His eyes flashed with mockery that did nothing to conceal the hard gleam of underlying anger. "You cannot expect me to deal with such persons at a time like this. It is beyond bearing."

"Did you notify anyone, then?"

He waved his handkerchief in front of his aquiline nose. The ring on his right, index finger bore a large, oval emerald surrounded by brilliants, but none appeared to be missing. "I sent my card to your inquiry agency. Surely, that is sufficient? Can you not see that I am overcome with grief at the loss of my closest and dearest friend?"

"May I offer my condolences?"

Silsbury nodded, pressing the handkerchief to his mouth as if so overcome with emotion that he was unable to speak.

The gesture irritated Nicholas with its false drama. "What about the servants?"

"What about them?" Silsbury asked sharply, his finely arched brows snapping down over his nose. It seemed to Nicholas that the emotion that had so overwhelmed Silsbury earlier was more anger than grief.

"Do you know if anyone in the household sent word to the constable?"

"How should I know? Ask them if you wish. That is what you are here for, after all. I don't know how much more I can manage under these tragic circumstances. I'm nearly prostrate with the pain of this tragedy. I am a poet, as you surely must know. You can see how sensitive I am." He blinked and focused on Nicholas. "We have lost a great man, today. The earl supported many artists and was my patron. He made my existence possible. Perhaps you have heard of me?"

"Perhaps." Nicholas had never heard of Harold Silsbury. And from his first impressions of the man, he wished he had never been privileged to make his acquaintance. He had no patience with dramatics or lies.

"My sensibilities are far too acute, I fear. This is all more than I can bear." He stared at Nicholas, brows raised, mouth half-open, clearly expecting some sort of sympathetic response. "I cannot remain here with this— this—" He waved at the corpse before glancing away in an overly theatrical way.

Nicholas got to his feet and brushed off his knee. When he looked up, he noticed Silsbury staring at his flaccid arm, a malicious little smile curving his mouth. A spurt of hot anger erupted inside him, but Nicholas tamped down the emotion. It was useless and would only increase Silsbury's joy at his discomfiture.

He returned his attention to the investigation, ignoring Silsbury's exaggerated pronouncements. "That is an interesting ring, Mr. Silsbury. May I see it?"

Silsbury eyed him as if he suspected trickery.

Nicholas stared back, maintaining a bland expression. After a moment, Silsbury shrugged. He held out his limp hand, gave a long-suffering sigh, and gazed at the ceiling. Gripping the cool fingers, Nicholas bent over the emerald ring.

None of the brilliants surrounding the emerald appeared to be missing, and the other rings on Silsbury's right hand were single stones. Nicholas was not interested in the rings on his left hand and didn't bother to look at them. He'd already noted that Silsbury was right-handed.

"Very elegant. Thank you." He released Silsbury's hand and stepped away. It would have been encouraging if he could have proved that Silsbury murdered his patron and closed the case within an hour of arriving. "I'll ask your butler if the authorities have been notified. What is his name?"

"Kirby."

Rather than chasing after servants through the corridors of an unfamiliar house, Nicholas glanced around the room. He found the bell pull hanging in the corner nearest the grand mahogany bed. With a nod to Silsbury, he strode to the corner and yanked. Lowering his hand, he studied the bed. The thick covers had been folded back, exposing crisp, white linen sheets, and the bed curtains were still tied back to the four tall posts. A long nightshirt, padded silk robe, and tasseled nightcap lay draped over the pillows. The maid would hardly have laid out Taunton's nightclothes this morning with Taunton lying dead on the floor.

"The earl does not appear to have gone to bed," Nicholas observed.

Silsbury shrugged.

"Who was the last one to speak to him last night?"

"I don't know. I retired early, myself. I was quite exhausted." Spite brightened Silsbury's hazel eyes as he glanced at the door. "Perhaps you should ask his bit o'muslin."

"He has a mistress?"

"Indeed, yes. He installed her here several years ago after her father had the poor manners to be strangled in the garden. I suppose he felt pity for the orphaned creature and kept her. She has a room down the hall. On the right."

A remarkably long and lucid statement for one supposedly too prostrate with grief to speak. A statement overripe with bitterness and anger. In a flash of understanding, Nicholas realized Silsbury was jealous of the earl's mistress. The notion cast an interesting light on the situation in Taunton's townhouse.

"What is her name?"

"Kathryn   Whitethorn-Litton.   Miss

Whitethorn-Litton." Silsbury quickly suppressed a malicious grin as he flicked a sidelong glance at Nicholas. "If you wish to know Taunton's last words, you should ask her. I am sure *I* can not tell you."

"Would he have invited her to his bedchamber?"

Again, Silsbury shrugged. He glanced down at his left slipper and studied it as he rubbed his toe against the edge of the carpet.

"Do you have any reason to believe she was here last night?"

"I thought I heard voices—his and a woman's. Who else would it have been?"

"You *thought*? Did you not recognize her voice?"

For a fraction of a second, Nicholas thought he saw uncertainty cross Silsbury's face. He glanced at Nicholas and then raised both hands, palms up. The handkerchief fluttered between the fingers of his right hand. "Upon my honor, I heard a woman's voice. They were arguing. That is all I can say."

"Was it Miss Whitethorn-Litton, or did you merely presume it was?"

Silsbury shrugged.

"He could just as easily have been arguing with a maid, could he not?" Nicholas waved toward the bed. "Perhaps he was dissatisfied with how she prepared the bed. Or something else in his room." He strode to the mantle and ran his good hand over the surface.

There was no dust, no grit, but he remained distrustful of Silsbury. The inclination to pick a fight with him was difficult to withstand.

"Disbelieve me if you must, but I would interview her. Ask *her* if she argued with my dear friend last night and murdered him in a fit of rage. Ask her if you wish to find the truth."

Grim determination settled within him at Silsbury's subtle challenge. Nicholas watched him for a moment before nodding. "Never fear, I shall speak to Miss Whitethorn-Litton. And I shall discover not only who argued with Lord Taunton before his death, but who took his life, as well."

"You may certainly *try* my pretty captain. We shall see if you succeed."

Chapter Seven

10:00 AM October 23, 1821

Something warm and sticky covered my hands. My first thought was that honey covered my fingers, but where had it come from? I didn't remember eating anything with honey on it. Then, a stark sense of terror made my heart race. The substance wasn't anything so benign. It was horrible, just horrible!

I moaned and shook my hands. The harder I shook, the more I smelled the thick, metallic odor that made my stomach churn. I swallowed, trying not to get sick. I couldn't stand the filth covering my fingers, drying into red, crumbling patches. I wiped my hands over my skirts again and again, desperate to be rid of the stains and trying to ignore the dark, flaky streaks left behind.

I will never be clean again. That terrible smell—I can't stand it! I brushed my skirts faster and faster, but the odor intensified, and the dreadful, crimson stains on my hands deepened no matter how hard I rubbed them. I can't remove it...

A rapping noise rattled the door. The key clacked within the brass lock, jiggling and adding to the noise as it almost bounced out of its slot under the assault.

Kathryn sat up in bed, confused and staring at the familiar bed-curtains surrounding her, shutting her in. Her heart pounded. Her nightgown clung to her in constricting twists, drenched in sweat. A nightmare, that's all. There was nothing to fear. She was at home and in bed. Safe.

The door shook again as someone pounded on it.

"Miss Whitethorn-Litton!" Harry Silsbury called, his voice muffled by the thick, wooden door.

Pulling back the bed curtain, Kathryn blinked, striving to collect her wits. Her heart raced from the nightmare. She couldn't seem to catch her breath, and her eyes ached as if someone had thrown sand into them while she slept. Weary beyond bearing, she swung her legs out of bed. She shoved her cold feet into her slippers and collected the robe she'd left hanging over a chair near the bed. Why was Harry thumping on her door at this time in the morning?

Most of the time, he preferred to pretend she didn't exist. Why did he choose this wretched morning after her first restless night in ages to annoy her?

A strong beam of sunshine squeezed through the draperies covering the windows. She yanked one curtain aside and took a step back, jerking her hand up to shield her eyes from the harsh light. The strength of the sunlight burned her vulnerable skin. Based upon the bright sunshine streaming over her shoulder, she assumed it was late morning. When her vision adjusted, she glanced at the ornate ormolu clock sitting on the narrow mantle over the fireplace. It was a few minutes to ten.

She felt as if she had climbed into bed only minutes before. She frowned at the door, feeling unsettled and irritated. All she wanted was a few hours of sleep. Was that really too much to expect?

"What is it?" Hand on the brass doorknob, she rested her forehead against the cool wood of the door.

"May we speak to you?" Harry responded quickly.

Swallowing a sharp retort, she unlocked the door and opened it. "What is it, Harry?" She stopped abruptly at the sight of a tall, dark-haired man standing at Harry's shoulder. Her stomach clenched. His rigid stance and ramrod straight back brought back all the terrors of her nightmare.

Had Mary confessed to her parents? Was this man here to arrest her?

So soon? Please don't let it all fall apart so soon.

A tremor shook Kathryn and she involuntarily tightened her grip on the doorknob until her fingers ached. Could he smell the blood on her?

How could he? She had washed, scrubbed her hands until her skin was raw. Surely, no betraying scent remained, nothing that would reveal what she had done last night.

But this man—what was he doing here if not to arrest her? The serious expression on his face would have convinced her of it if she hadn't already felt with absolute certainty that it was so. When her knees threatened to fold, she leaned against the door, feeling vulnerable and conscious of her undressed state.

Harry eyed her with the hint of a spiteful smile curving his mouth. He always enjoyed discomforting her and his expression served to further confirm her fears.

Mary *must* have confessed. Her parents must have subsequently informed the constabulary to arrest her for having corrupted their daughter and taking her to an abortionist. It was the only explanation for Harry's appearance at her door with this stranger at his heels.

Her chin lifted. "Well, Harry, what is it?"

"This is Captain Ainsley, Miss Whitethorn-Litton," Harry replied, emphasizing her surname as if he barely knew her.

Kathryn flicked a glance at the taller man. The captain appeared grimly decisive, an impression strengthened by a very strong chin. She did not offer her hand, nor did he move except to meet her stare with an assessing look. She would not be intimidated by him. No matter what he said or what happened to her, she knew she had done the right thing. She had tried to help Mary, which was more than anyone else

95

had done.

Her gaze lingered on the captain, searching for any hint of sympathy. His straight back and wide shoulders exuded an air of command and authority, but his face remained unreadable in the slanted sunshine from the window behind her. He was not as beautiful as Harry, but something drew her to him and suggested that he was a man she could trust.

Nerves taut, she took a deep breath to master her emotions. Her glance drifted to his left arm. She couldn't help but note that he held the limb awkwardly. Had he been injured? Wounded in the war with Napoleon? When she looked once more at his face, his dark brows were drawn together as if he had seen the direction of her glance and it displeased him.

"Perhaps there is a sitting room where we may speak?" Captain Ainsley broke the silence.

They both looked at Harry, who shrugged. "Of course. The Chinese room should do."

"I will join you there in fifteen minutes." Kathryn gripped the edge of the door, determined to delay matters until she could dress.

Could she escape while they waited? Climb out of the window and run...to where? She had no sanctuary in London and no funds. And even if she had a purse full of coins, there was no handy trellis below her window to climb down. There was only a sheer drop to the brick walkway below.

"That is acceptable," Captain Ainsley said in a curt voice. "We will be expecting you, Miss Whitethorn-Litton. Fifteen minutes."

As if she needed the reminder that she only had a quarter of an hour.

She shut the door in their faces and held her hand to her chest, forcing her thoughts to stop churning and her heartbeat to return to normal. After a long, deep breath, she moved quickly to dress. She pulled out a sprigged muslin with rich green embroidery around the neck and hem and lovely, hunter green ribbons fluttering from the sleeves. She splashed her face with cold water in hopes of soothing her eyes and twisted her heavy hair, holding it with one hand to pin it up as best she could.

Scrutinizing her reflection, she hastily covered the lackluster coils with a lacy cap. She was not at her best this morning. The harsh light from the window did not bring out the rich, chestnut highlights of her brown hair as it seemed to do when she was happy. The sunlight drained the color from her, leaving her hair mousy and making the dark, puffy skin under her eyes seem as black as soot.

The clock chimed the half hour. She was five minutes late. Her stomach twisted, and as she picked up a light green shawl, her nervous fingers fumbled and dropped it to the floor. She picked it up and ran lightly to the stairway, descending as quickly as she could to the second floor.

The door to the Chinese drawing room stood open. She entered quickly, pausing briefly on the threshold to adjust her shawl around her shoulders. The rich, red walls with their gold trim framed and enhanced several small, white pedestals graced with delicate blue-and-white Chinese porcelain vases. Fans with oriental scenes and paintings of birds from China glowed on the walls with evocative power. The room had always delighted her, but today the deep, bright colors seemed garish and overpowering. Her eyes ached and she blinked self-consciously.

Captain Ainsley stood in front of one of the Oriental fans, and he turned when she entered. "Please be seated, Miss Whitethorn-Litton."

"Thank you." She hurried to a settee that formed the backbone of a group of chairs near the windows overlooking the street. At the last moment she stopped, not wanting to risk having Harry or the captain sitting so close to her. She knew it was ridiculous, however she couldn't help the notion that they would smell Mary's blood on her.

Finally, in a flurry of skirts, she sat on an elegant white-and-gold wooden chair across from the settee. The window would be at her back and merciful shadows would hide her face.

"Would you request a maid to join us?" the captain asked Harry.

Both Kathryn and Harry stared at him in surprise.

"Of course." Harry moved reluctantly to the bell pull. He frowned at the captain while they waited in silence.

When the girl, a young upstairs maid named Nancy, opened the door, she peered cautiously around the edge. Captain Ainsley strode forward, cutting off Harry. Irritation flickered over Harry's alabaster features but the expression was gone so quickly that only someone who knew him as well as Kathryn would even have noted it.

"Please come in." Captain Ainsley looked around and then gestured to one of the chairs at the far end of the room. "We require your presence for a half hour or so."

Twisting the hem of her apron in her reddened hands, Nancy stepped cautiously into the room. When she caught Kathryn's gaze, her blue eyes grew round, and she raised the apron's hem to cover her mouth.

"Well, go on! Sit over there," Harry said when the maid did not immediately comply.

When Harry took a few steps toward the seating area where Kathryn waited, Captain Ainsley touched his sleeve, bringing him to a halt. "I would appreciate it if I could speak to Miss Whitethorn-Litton privately." He nodded briefly toward the maid. "She is properly chaperoned, now. There is no need for you to remain."

The maid glanced at Harry and smothered a giggle with her apron hem. Harry's head snapped around to frown at her. She caught his glance, paled, and hurried toward the far corner, her shoulders hunched and head down.

"Perhaps Miss Whitethorn-Litton would prefer it if I remained. A friend, you know," Harry said. "Someone who can show her some sympathy..."

Kathryn stared down at her hands so he would not see her smile. Harry was the least sympathetic person she knew. In point of fact, he simply wanted to see her humiliated if possible and satisfy his curiosity if nothing else. "I am content to speak to Captain Ainsley in private, Harry. There is no need to detain you any longer. I know how busy you are."

The captain had moved to stand by the door, his hand on the doorknob. He moved the door ever so slightly and watched Harry, as if silently encouraging him to leave as expeditiously as possible.

"Very well. You may send for me if you require my assistance." Harry sniffed and brushed past the captain, ignoring Kathryn entirely.

"Thank you for granting me this interview, Miss Whitethorn-Litton." Captain Ainsley joined her and sat in the middle of the blue, watered silk settee, directly across from her.

She nodded and waited.

"There are some questions I must ask about last night."

Her muscles stiffened. Ice filled her veins, numbing her limbs. She remained silent, watching him, waiting to hear the words she dreaded, that Mary Dudley had confessed.

"I apologize." He looked at her steadily. She could have sworn that his brown eyes were filled with embarrassment. "However, I must ask if you remember what time you last saw Lord Taunton yesterday evening?"

"I beg your pardon, but I don't understand the question." Her thoughts whirled crazily like autumn leaves stirred by a gale. "Whatever can you possibly mean?" She almost stuttered, unable to properly focus on his question. What did Taunton have to do with Mary Dudley?

Unease settled into her bones.

Had Taunton discovered she was gone last night? Had her absence angered him? Her evening forays had never bothered him before, what had changed? Sitting here, she sensed something different, something almost evil in the house, like the walls were drawing closer and closer too slowly for her to notice.

"Did you note what time you said goodnight to Lord Taunton?" he asked, slightly rephrasing his question. He leaned forward as if to place a hand on top of her damp, knotted fingers. At the last moment, he restrained himself and gripped his knee.

"Last night? Why at supper, sir! What business is it of yours?"

"At supper?" He glanced over his shoulder at the maid. Nancy was busily chewing on her nails and kicking her heels against the edge of the carpeting, obviously bored. "You did not see him after dinner?"

"No." Again, her stomach contracted. She felt hollow and dizzy, wishing she had taken the time to eat. Waves of ice and the clenching sensation of acid eating away at her disturbed her concentration. As her confusion grew, so did her fear. In a burst of panic, she added, "I went out after supper. I did not see him last night. Surely he told you that—did you ask him?"

Her question appeared to startle him. He sat back, his skin paling enough to emphasize a dark shadow covering his chin and lower cheeks. A few, very short bristles showed on his left cheek. He had missed a spot shaving, and for some odd reason, she found the slight imperfection rather endearing.

He cleared his throat. "When did you go out?"

"I went to my room immediately after supper, around nine or so. I rarely join Harry and Taunton in the evening unless we go to the theatre or opera. I remained in my room until quite late and then went out. Does that satisfy you?"

"Where did you go? How late did you

leave?"

She shrugged. "Lord Taunton encourages me to attend a variety of entertainments. I met some friends—women." She waved vaguely, trying not to flush. She could not understand where the interview was leading. The thought squeezed her stomach with cold fingers.

"Women?" His brows rose as if he mistrusted her statement.

"Yes. Demi-monde, if you must know. Surely you guessed."

He looked past her shoulder toward the window, but not before she saw the ghost of disappointment in his eyes. What did he think? She was an unmarried woman living with a man unrelated to her. Despite the sad fact that she was more virtuous than the socially acceptable Mary Dudley was irrelevant. Kathryn's circumstances dictated her position in society. She had accepted that with as much good grace as she could.

"Will any of them be willing to confirm that?"

She laughed. "Why should they? No. They will not, and I will not give you their names. Why are you questioning me?"

"Please, I beg your indulgence. Let me confirm, then, that the last time you claim to have seen Lord Taunton was last night at nine p.m.?"

"Yes, of course. Ask Harry if you don't wish to bother Lord Taunton. He can confirm that I have told you the truth. He and Taunton spend a great deal of time together. If you wish to know who spent the evening with Taunton, you must ask Harry."

"I have spoken with Mr. Silsbury. He indicated he heard a woman speaking with Lord Taunton late—sometime after midnight, I believe."

"He could have been requesting water for a bath." She shrugged. "Did Harry say he heard me?"

"Yes. He indicated it was your voice."

"How could he? I was not here at midnight." She sighed and felt the stirrings of impatience. "If you are concerned about this matter, then you must ask Lord Taunton. He can surely tell you what you want to know and identify the woman he spoke to last night. Although I am quite sure he was simply asking a maid for some everyday item like a towel or fresh soap. It is not unheard of, you know."

A few moments of silence followed this, and once again her confusion stirred. Why did he persist in asking her about Lord Taunton?

"You must realize, surely..." His words trailed off. He studied her, a speculative gleam in his brown eyes.

More and more, she had the feeling that she was unaware of something terrible. There was some fact she ought to be aware of and yet she was not. What had happened while she accompanied Mary Dudley? The sensation of missing a critical point grew almost unbearable. Her fingers twisted together in her lap, stiff and damp.

"Lord Taunton is no longer in a position to answer my questions." Captain Ainsley leaned forward, his right hand gripping his knee. "He died last night."

"Died? I don't understand you. How could he die?" Her voice rose shrilly as terror gripped her. "He was young—too young to die— I refuse to credit it. You must be lying!"

He shook his head. "I am sorry, but I am not lying. He passed away last night. I am attempting to ascertain his last movements and who might have seen him before, well, before tragedy struck him down."

"I don't believe you." She fought a maelstrom of emotions ranging from disbelief to bone-freezing terror.

"It is quite true, I assure you. Now would you be so good as to tell me the truth?"

"I already told you, I did not see him after supper. He was perfectly healthy at that time. You must be mistaken. He simply cannot be dead. He was barely thirty-five. The idea is ridiculous, and this is a cruel joke, a terribly cruel joke." She tried to stand, to walk out of the room, but when she tried to rise, her legs crumpled beneath her. She sat and clasped her hands, twisting her cold fingers together until the knuckles whitened. After a deep breath, she forced her hands to relax in her lap. She refused to cry.

"I am not mistaken."

"Then how—"

"He was murdered."

She couldn't draw in a single breath. Air rasped in her throat but did not find a way to her lungs. Her corset felt too tight and her ribs ached with the need for release and a sweet breath of air. As she stared at Captain Ainsley, sparks flashed and glowed in a darkening veil. Through the dimness she watched his mouth move, but his words were a faint buzzing sound like a hive of anxious bees.

Her cheek stung. The sound of a sharp slap focused her attention. She rubbed the left side of her face and eyed Captain Ainsley, her mouth open with shock.

"Are you well?" He shook her shoulder brusquely. "Do you feel faint?"

"Yes—no—don't!" She raised her left arm to block him when he appeared ready to slap her again. "I am not going to faint."

"Are you sure?"

"Of course I am sure. How dare you presume such a thing?" She rubbed her cheek.

He studied her. "Have you eaten this morning?"

The unexpected question caught her by surprise. She lowered her hand and studied him in silence. Did he believe she had something to do with Taunton's death? The idea was incredible. She shook her head. The room spun around her. A tiny pinpoint of pain ignited just above her right eyebrow. Striving to maintain control, she stared down at the red-and-gold carpet and rubbed her brow.

She couldn't believe what he had told her. How could Lord Taunton be dead? She had had supper with him just last night.

Murdered.

No. It was inconceivable. It had to be a mistake.

"Nancy?" Captain Ainsley stood and spoke to the maid. "Fetch tea and whatever you have to eat. And brandy. Miss Whitethorn-Litton has had a terrible shock. And ask some other maid to attend us while you are gone."

Nancy got up. Smoothing her apron, she looked at him, her mouth gaping.

"Go. Now, if you please," Captain Ainsley ordered.

As he watched, Nancy reclaimed a bit of wit and scurried away without argument.

"You did not know?" He turned back to Kathryn.

She shook her head and then pressed her icy fingers against her throbbing temple. "No. How could I? I did not return here until late this morning, and I went directly to my room. Lord Taunton does not—did not—like to be disturbed after he retires—retired—to his room. How did he ... how did it happen?"

"As I indicated, he was killed—"

"How can you be sure?"

"He died a violent death, Miss Whitethorn-Litton. It was obvious someone decided to end his life."

"He did not kill himself?"

"No. He couldn't have done so." His head tilted to the side. "Did you have a reason to suggest Lord Taunton would take his own life?"

"No. It's just that—it's just less horrid to believe he took his own life than that someone—a stranger—came here and murdered him." She stumbled over her words, her mind rushing in panicked, restless waves.

What would she do? The funds she had managed to save would be insufficient to support her for more than a few weeks. What would happen to her after that? Selfish questions tumbled through her thoughts despite her efforts to focus on the tragedy of Lord Taunton's death.

In truth, she could not help worrying about her future. Death had come again to force yet another major upheaval into her life. The last time it had visited her, her father had died, leaving her alone at a house party consisting solely of young men. She had not asked for the subsequent changes in her young life, and nothing had been right since then. Now the specter had arisen again to rip the fabric of her life asunder. Everything would change and not for the better. She struggled to understand the implications and make plans, but all she could think about was her lack of funds and how small her nest egg truly was. Even a small cottage in a remote village was out of the question, and she could not find a respectable position without a reference. She had no family, no resources to rely upon.

She was alone.

"How? When did it happen?" she asked at last, breaking the uncomfortable silence.

"Last night," he answered, though she barely heard him. "Sometime around midnight."

A single image haunted her, arising like the specter of an unbearable future: Whitechapel. She had passed through the area in the safety of a carriage and could not forget the heart-wrenching despair she had witnessed. The dirty streets had smelled of alcohol, vomit and the despair of the destitute. Red-rimmed eyes had watched them, glazed with hopelessness.

She couldn't go there. Where, then? None of Taunton's associates desired her as their mistress. No one cared if she starved in the street with the mongrel dogs. She had no illusions that Lord Taunton had been concerned enough about her wellbeing to make arrangements for her in the event of his death.

Why should he? She knew her status in his household and had agreed to their bargain. She was part of the illusion he created to convince Society that he had no secret life with private, illicit desires. He had offered her a home after her father had unexpectedly died during a house party at Taunton's country estate, and that was the extent of Lord Taunton's generosity. He felt nothing for her that would impel him to make provisions for her in his will.

She had nothing, was nothing, but a discarded bit of muslin. A desperate, agonizing sob of grief, mixed with fear, caught in her throat. Her eyes filled with tears. She could flee, go to the country and live for a few weeks, but then what?

What was she going to do?

Chapter Eight

10:22 AM October 23, 1821

Albert Bottom eyed their pile of riches. They had spread out their takings on a handkerchief on the wooden floor of a disreputable boardinghouse run by a woman claiming the title of Mrs. Smith. Bottom rather thought it more likely that she was Miss Something-quite-other, but as she charged only a few shillings a week for a room that was more than sufficient for both Bottom and Toddy, he was happy to use whatever title she desired.

Staring at the dagger and gold coins, a cold knot formed in his belly. They were not the sort to have such riches and would be hard pressed to explain possessing them. In fact, he wished the earl's purse had held only a bob or two. That was a reasonable sum for the two of them to possess. Where could they spend gold coins without being questioned as to their provenance?

And yet...he could hardly have left the gold behind. That much honesty would have been beyond his meager capabilities. He looked from the coins to the thin-bladed dagger and eyed it with increasing anxiety. He wished Toddy hadn't felt it necessary to take it. Like the coins, it would be difficult to pawn and even more difficult to explain. Staring at it gave him an unsettled feeling, especially since the weapon's last sheath had been the earl's back.

Toddy picked up the blade and turned it in his thin hands. He smiled. "Fine little dagger. I am almost inclined to keep it. Such a toy may prove to be useful, eh Mr. Bottom? Particularly in our line of work."

"I don't care for it, Mr. Toddy. Not at all. Too flashy by half and not the thing our sort should be carrying around. If you understand my meaning."

Laughing, Toddy flipped the dagger into the air. He caught it expertly by the handle before it could fall to the floor. "You worry overmuch, Mr. Bottom."

"Mark my words, the thing is unlucky. It was unlucky for the earl, and it will be doubly so for us."

"Next you will be saying as how we should never have taken those guineas, neither. Would you have us hand them back? Where is the profit in that, I ask you?" Toddy stared at him, a cold light hardening his eyes.

Toddy had a temper. He frightened Bottom when he looked at him like that, but Toddy's moods didn't last long. And he did ensure that both of them ate on a fairly regular basis. Bottom couldn't fault him for that.

However, he couldn't change his feelings about either the knife or the gold. They would both be lucky to avoid the hangman's noose after last night. He shivered and drew his coat more tightly around him.

When Bottom didn't answer, Toddy

shook his head and delicately replaced the knife on the handkerchief. His long fingers stroked the pile of coins as if they were a lovely woman's warm cheek. "I always said you didn't have the heart for the adventuring business."

"One of us needs to keep a level-head. And how do you propose to use those coins? The moment you offer one to a merchant, he will know you for a thief and have you arrested." Bottom pulled at his plump lower lip. "The gold is nothing but a liability."

"Then we exchange them for shillings and such. I know a fellow who might be willing to make a trade."

"You will never get what they are worth."

Shrugging, Toddy picked up five of the golden guineas and dropped them in his pocket. "'Tis the cost of adventuring, Mr. Bottom. We'll get enough for our needs."

When Toddy picked up the dagger again, Bottom's heart fell to his worn boots. "What are you planning, then? Why do you need that cursed dagger?"

"It is a decent weapon—"

"You already have a knife in your boot. I should think you would find that sufficient." He worked to put the proper note of disdain into his voice. "You can hardly call that flashy thing useful."

"It was useful enough to do in his lordship, wasn't it?"

"Leave it here, Mr. Toddy," Bottom

pleaded, leaning forward to place his hand on Toddy's thin sleeve. "I tell you the thing is cursed. Nothing good can come of it—nothing."

Toddy shook him off and stood. "That is where you are wrong, my friend. I intend that much good shall come of it." He patted his pocket, causing the coins to give a mellow clink. "We are not without resources, now. I shall turn this trinket and these coins into a purse full of quite spendable coin, never fear. After that, I think a tankard of ale and fine platter piled high with roast beef are in order. What say you?"

"I say again, nothing good will come of this." Bottom struggled to his feet, his bones snapping and creaking like brittle ice as he straightened. "But I cannot let you go alone. I only hope that I am wrong."

"You shall see, Mr. Bottom." Toddy slapped him on the back. "We are destined for nothing worse than indigestion. Place your trust in good old Toddy. No harm shall ever come to you—not while Dick Toddy has a say in it. You shall see, right enough."

"That is precisely the problem," Bottom murmured as he followed his friend through the door. "I am afraid I shall see and will not like the results in the least."

Chapter Nine

11:00 AM October 23, 1821

"Are you honestly unaware of the manner of his death?" Nicholas asked Miss Whitethorn-Litton again, searching her face for a glimpse of the truth.

"No. I am not."

If pressed, Nicholas would have sworn that the news of Lord Taunton's death had surprised her. Her face was pale, her blue eyes staring. Every few seconds, something akin to a convulsion rippled up her neck and over her features. In its wake, she would blink repeatedly and swallow until the wave passed. Her lashes were dark with tears and she kept blinking as she looked at him. It took him a minute before he realized she was straining to hold back tears.

This mute evidence of her grief made him pause. He was pushing her, perhaps past her endurance. She seemed to have difficulties understanding the situation, and her evident confusion almost convinced him of her innocence.

When she caught him staring, she held his gaze, catching her lower lip between her teeth. One trembling hand rose to touch a curl covering her ear before she lowered her eyes.

Her movements made him intensely aware of her. The spark of intelligence and even humor had flared in her eyes when they first met, but now the dark depths held despair and near-panic. She attracted him, and he feared his unwanted emotions might affect his judgment. He had not expected her to be so lovely, though he should have, considering her position in Lord Taunton's household.

Her chestnut hair glowed against her creamy skin in the light from the window, drawing his gaze. He glanced away, unwilling to be caught staring at her again.

Despite his sympathy, he sensed a reckless, impulsive nature that whispered she might be capable of stabbing Lord Taunton. If they had argued last night, she might have thrust a knife into her lover's back before she realized what she was doing. He could not forget that Harry Silsbury thought he'd heard a woman speaking to Lord Taunton in his room. Harry had identified the woman as Miss Whitethorn-Litton.

Nicholas could not ignore the information.

Had Taunton been trying to rid himself of an unwanted mistress? The possibility provided her with an excellent motive. As he considered the matter, he realized there were several ways to interpret Silsbury's statement. The poet might have lied about hearing a woman in Taunton's room to deflect attention away from himself.

Nicholas ran a hand over the back of his neck as he picked apart his reactions and searched for a fair balance between intuition and logic. He was reluctant to brand him a complete liar, if for no other reason than that Silsbury irritated him. Nicholas was not a man who made friends easily. Perhaps he might be judging Silsbury too harshly simply because he did not like him.

And he might be searching for a way to prove Miss Whitethorn-Litton's innocence because she attracted him.

When he eliminated his emotional response to the two most important people in the Taunton household, he realized he believed both of them. Unfortunately, their stories seemed to conflict.

The arrival of a maid distracted him. She slipped in and sidled over to stand against the wall near the door.

"Well?" Miss Whitethorn-Litton tugged at a lock of her hair. "Can you tell me what happened, or must I go to his room to find out for myself?"

"Lord Taunton was stabbed."

She pressed her fingers to her mouth, trying in vain to suppress her startled gasp. "Stabbed? How could he have been stabbed? Who would do such a thing? Are you sure?" Her questions flew at him, each one shriller and more urgent.

"That is what I am trying to determine," he replied in a dry voice.

She was either one of the most accomplished actresses he had ever seen, or she truly did not know.

"I did not do it—how could I?" Her mouth compressed into a thin, bitter line. "Why would I? He was my protector. Without him, I don't know what I will do, what will become of me." She glanced away, but not before he saw a look of anguished panic darkening her eyes.

"I can think of many reasons why a woman in your position might undertake such a desperate measure."

"You think he wanted to rid himself of me?" She laughed, the sound sharp and bitter. She shook her head. "Why should he? He scarcely knew I existed. I was little more than a ghost in his household."

Her words only seemed to confirm his doubts. If Lord Taunton was no longer fascinated by her, then the possibility that he had tried to rid himself of her increased in likelihood. "Can anyone confirm where you were last night?"

"No. No one will help me. You must either believe me when I tell you I was not here, or not. I have no proof either way."

"Surely your friends—"

Her blue eyes hardened. "My *friends* will say naught. And I shall not betray their confidences by giving you their names."

Before Nicholas could swing the direction of his questions to another tack, the butler knocked on the door. "Your pardon, sir, but I took the liberty of sending for the coroner.

He is here with his men. Do you wish to join them?"

Nicholas glanced from the butler to Miss Whitethorn-Litton.

She caught his gaze, small wrinkles of anxiety creasing her forehead. "Will you—are you going now?"

"Yes. I think it is best if I attend. May I ask that you remain available? I don't expect to be occupied longer than a half hour or so." He glanced around ruefully. He wasn't going to get a cup of tea, after all, as the maid who went for refreshments had not returned.

She made a small, dismissive gesture and stood. "Where would I go, Captain Ainsley? I need hardly say I will remain at your disposal. Assuming I am allowed to remain at all and am not arrested simply because Harry believes he heard Lord Taunton speaking to a woman at some point last night. An *unknown* woman, I might add."

"I assure you that will not happen." Unfortunately, he was by no means certain that the constable would not be escorting her away when he left. Either Miss Whitethorn-Litton or Mr. Silsbury were the most likely murderers, and Nicholas did not know which way the coroner's jury would lean after viewing the scene in Taunton's bedchamber.

It would have been satisfactory for all of them if he could have blamed the servants, but as they would have known that they would be likely to lose their positions when Lord Taunton died, it was highly unlikely that any of them would have murdered him.

Miss Whitethorn-Litton nodded and brushed past him, the green ribbons on her sleeves fluttering as she passed him. The clean scent of soap and lavender surrounded her, leaving in her wake a freshness that reminded Nicholas of the sea. He collected his thoughts and then followed, striding into the hallway intent on collecting as many facts as he could.

Information first, action second. That process, simplistic though it was, had served him well in the military, and he expected it to serve him equally well now.

The butler had waited for him. When Nicholas caught his attention, he nodded and led the way to Taunton's room.

The spacious bedchamber seemed positively crowded when he entered. A group of men, hastily gathered to serve as jurists, were bending over Taunton's body, oblivious to Nicholas' entrance. They whispered to each other, some with their hands covering their mouths, as if afraid the dead man might hear and be offended by their comments. A small, tidy man gently rolled the body over. He lifted the hems of the shirt and jacket to expose the small but deadly wound in Taunton's back.

When Nicholas moved closer, the little man straightened. He was short and lithe and moved with sharp gestures as if his small body contained too much energy to control. His hair had receded from his high forehead and a fringe of graying brown hair fluttered around his rather prominent ears. He had a thin, intelligent face and sharp, hazel eyes that moved in an assessing manner from one object in the room to the next. Catching his gaze, Nicholas felt an immediate sense of trust, almost bordering on relief.

He'd known one or two men like this one in the past. They were good, honest souls one could rely on when difficulties tossed stones into the path. One man, remarkably like him, had dragged Nicholas, wounded and half-conscious, onto the British Naval vessel that saved his life.

"And you are?" the man asked.

"Captain Ainsley. Mr. Silsbury requested assistance from the Second Sons Inquiry Agency." He felt reluctant to identify himself as an inquiry agent when his employment was still at the probationary stage.

"I am the coroner, Mr. Flatman." His curt reply and a flicker of disapproval in his eyes as he gazed away in a dismissive gesture made Nicholas rethink his optimistic first impression. The coroner's face gave nothing away now as he resumed his study of the corpse. Perhaps he anticipated difficulties working with a private agent. If that was the case, his anxiety was unnecessary. "I gather you arrived earlier this morning, Captain Ainsley. Is that true?"

"Yes." Nicholas clasped the wrist of his

useless arm, striving to give the appearance of a competent, uninjured man at ease with the situation.

Unfortunately, Mr. Flatman had already noted the awkward position of Nicholas' arm. He gazed his left side with indifferent eyes, making Nicholas realize the futility of his effort. He straightened his shoulders.

"Did you remove the knife?"

Nicholas' grip on his useless hand tightened. "No, I did not. It was not present when I arrived to view the deceased."

"Did you move or disturb anything in this room?"

"I shifted the body slightly to inspect the back. I did not remove the clothing, however. Mr. Silsbury was present during my examination and can confirm."

"We have already spoken to Mr. Silsbury." Flatman's mouth thinned slightly.

"Then he must have stated that I took no actions other than those I mentioned." His heart pounded, almost as if he were the one suspected of murder instead of an investigator.

"Very good."

Then Nicholas remembered the tiny diamond in his pocket. He had removed it from the corpse, but he was reluctant to offer the evidence to Flatman or the constable when the coroner confirmed that murder and not natural death had taken the life of the earl. The more people who knew about the gem, the more likely it was that the information might reach the ears of the murderer. If he, or she, discovered they had the diamond, he might get rid of the damaged ring and destroy any chance of identifying the culprit.

If Nicholas wanted the diamond to remain secret until they obtained more information, it had to remain safely in his possession. The fact that the coroner's jury only had to determine the manner of death, not the identity of any presumed murderer, offered his conscience a bit of salve.

Eyeing Flatman, he shifted his feet to relax his stance a fraction. He had a right to be present, and Flatman could not exclude him from the investigation. With a deep breath, he strode further into the room and then stilled, surprised by an errant breeze. His head lifted and he sniffed the air, the hair on the back of his neck prickling.

While war had nearly destroyed him, it had bestowed one gift, or curse, depending upon how he viewed it. Where once he had been almost oblivious to his surroundings, now he was aware and therefore wary. He had learned to sense when something was not right, when the enemy had him in their sights or had laid a trap. His life had depended upon the skill. Now, he sensed something wrong in the room, something he had not noticed earlier due to his surprise at discovering the earl deceased.

"Did you open the window?" he asked

Amy Corwin

abruptly.

Flatman's brows rose in surprise. He glanced over his shoulder at the windows and then looked at his men. They stared back at him, mouths agape, like seven confused children staring at a teacher who had just finished a lecture on an utterly indecipherable math theorem.

"Did anyone open a window?" Flatman aimed the question at his men.

They shook their heads and glanced at each other, appearing ill-at-ease as they shifted from foot to foot.

"Then, no, Captain. We have not opened a window." Flatman turned and studied the windows again. "I do not see any left open. Why do you ask? Was one open earlier?"

Nicholas strode to the furthest window and bent down. Sure enough, whoever had shut it had not done so properly. The right side was jammed down to the sill, but the left side slanted upward, leaving a gap of about a half of an inch. Cold air streamed through the narrow opening, curling over the floor to pool around their ankles. The draft had alerted him.

Of course anyone, even Lord Taunton, could have left the window like that. And yet... He felt that prickling sensation again, the intuition that something was not quite right.

A suspicion of danger, whether that danger was past or present, took root.

He gently lifted the window, carefully

124

examining the white paint of the sill. Scratches marred the smooth, satiny paint, along with a smear of mud. A faint footprint soiled the floor below the window. Oddly enough, the heel was an inch from the wall and the toe pointed into the room. Whoever had left the footprint had been standing against the window, facing into the room. A strange position unless one had just climbed through the window.

He pushed up the window and glanced out, examining the outer edge of the window. The white paint had been recently scraped off in several places, leaving behind freshly exposed wood. Leaning further out, he examined the rear of the townhouse, looking for a reason for the marks. Some of the shutters below glimmered with fresh glossiness, showing that they had been newly painted. However, the ones on either side of the window where he stood had not been painted recently. The old, green paint was cracked and flaking.

"Mr. Flatman, you may wish to question the staff and Mr. Silsbury. Ask if this window was open and if any of them shut it. I see marks here that need investigation."

When Flatman joined him, Nicholas pointed to the footprint and the scratches on the windowsill, both inside and out.

Flatman nodded. "Then perhaps this was an attempt at burglary."

"Has anyone ascertained if anything was stolen?" Nicholas asked.

The coroner's jurymen glanced at one another before they each shrugged. Nicholas took a fresh look around the room, noting all the expensive and very portable contents. Nothing appeared to be missing. In fact, the room was uncomfortably cluttered. Every surface supported one or more expensive objects. Porcelain figurines jostled each other and a pair of Venetian glass paperweights stood on either side of an extravagant, gilded clock on the fireplace mantle. Piles of expensively bound books teetered on the edge of a table near the bed and on the floor next to a nearby chair. Nicholas couldn't help but think a burglar would have taken some of the articles, leaving behind a bare spot.

Mr. Flatman strolled over to the desk and opened the top drawer. He shoved the contents around with his fingertips, crumpling some papers before pulling out a leather purse. He loosened the drawstrings and dumped out the contents. A few golden guineas, shillings, and a handful of pence tumbled out. The coins rolled over the felt blotter and almost tumbled off the desk before Flatman slapped his hand over them.

"If it was an attempted burglary, Lord Taunton must have interrupted them before they could take anything." A thoughtful expression creased Flatman's forehead and deepened the brackets around his mouth. "His death must have frightened them away."

Nicholas nodded. "That would also explain the missing knife. The thief stabbed him and then escaped, taking his knife with him." He walked over and bent down on one knee beside the body. "May I?" He glanced at Flatman.

"Of course." Flatman turned to watch him.

Gently smoothing Taunton's linen shirt and jacket down over the cold flesh, he examined the shirt and hem. A faint, brown smear showed on the part of the jacket covering Taunton's hip. "There is a stain here that appears to have been made by wiping the knife clean. I wish to check one more thing. Will you excuse me for a moment?"

Without waiting for a response, Nicholas left the bedchamber and went downstairs. He was surprised by a sense of relief when he breathed in the fresh, cooler air outside of the over-heated townhouse. Perhaps it was only the tension of the investigation, but he felt as if the house had been suffocating him. He walked around the corner and through the alley to the rear of the building until he was directly under the windows of Taunton's bedchamber. Initially, he feared that the hard surface of the walkway would not reveal what he wanted to find, but there was a narrow strip of soft grass between the walkway and the foundation of the house.

He had almost given up the search when he noticed a lighter, gray streak on one of the bricks of the walkway. Upon closer inspection, he saw two rectangular depressions in the grass. They abutted the walkway, as if a ladder's supports had rested on the ground, braced against the firm bricks of the walkway.

The positioning made sense. If the end of the ladder had rested on the walkway, it would have slipped. Placing it on the dirt adjacent to the path's edge ensured the ladder would remain firm and the marks left were obscured by the transition of grass to the brick of the walkway.

He walked back toward the alleyway. In the narrow space, he ran into three workmen bending over a pile of painting supplies.

"Excuse me, may I ask if you left your supplies and ladder in this alley last night?"

An older, gray-haired man dressed in a paint-spattered smock glanced up. Thick brows hung over his sunken eyes, giving him a belligerent appearance that seemed all too appropriate when he responded, "And who do you be to ask such things, sir?"

"I am with the Second Sons Inquiry Agency. We are investigating a suspicious death on the premises. May I ask who you are?"

"George Horner of Horner and Sons Painters." Horner straightened, still frowning with suspicion. After studying Nicholas a moment, he gestured to one of his companions. "This is my assistant, Mr. Glover."

"Sir." Glover pulled his cap off his head,

his gaze locked on his dusty, worn-out shoes.

"I am pleased to make your acquaintance. I am Captain Ainsley. Now, if you have a moment, could you tell me if you left your supplies and ladder here last night?"

"Yes, we did," Horner said. "Though what that has to do with any death, suspicious or otherwise, is beyond me. We left before sunset and have not returned until this very minute. Whatever has happened is no concern of ours."

"No one is accusing you. I hoped you could tell me if your ladder was where you placed it last night?"

Horner flicked a quick look at Glover who stood next to him, twisting his cap between his hands. Glover glanced from Horner to Nicholas before once more staring at his feet. Despite his smooth, unlined skin, he had already begun to lose his sandy hair, making his freckled face and balding head appear curiously vulnerable and baby-like.

"Well, Glover?" Mr. Horner elbowed him. "What of it? Was the ladder where we left it last night?"

"Ye—yes, sir," the young man stammered. "It was here, right where we left it, sir."

"You were not afraid it would be stolen?" Nicholas walked over to the ladder to examine the ends of the supports. A few blades of grass, still green but beginning to dry in the sunshine, clung to the ends of the ladder. Running his hand along the length of it, he found some flakes of white paint near the top.

The paint was not proof, of course. The men were busy painting the townhouse and could have scraped the paint from any sill as they worked. However, it was an interesting coincidence when considered with the relatively fresh grass and dirt clinging to the foot of the ladder.

"It were only overnight." Glover's voice shook. He tilted his head up enough to glance at Horner. "We meant no harm, sir."

"I understand perfectly." Nicholas took one last glance around. "Thank you for your assistance."

"Who do you claim passed away?" Horner took a belligerent stance in the middle of the alleyway, meaty hands on hips. He stared up into Nicholas' face as if convinced he had lied.

"Lord Taunton."

The simple statement brought Horner up short. Hands falling to his sides, he paled. "We had naught to do with that. You cannot blame us. We were gone by dark."

"I understand."

"You cannot claim otherwise," Horner insisted. "We left the ladder there as we needed it today. No sense in dragging it through the streets of London. You cannot claim we were negligent or planned to do ought else. We knew nothing about his lordship until you came here, accusing us—"

"As I mentioned earlier, no one is accusing you. I merely wanted to know if you had noticed anything unusual. That is all."

"Will we be paid?" Horner moved closer, the lines bracketing his mouth tightening. "We have the work half done. There is no sense in continuing if we are not to be paid."

"I am afraid I don't know what arrangements will be made. You must ask Lord Taunton's solicitor, or his man of business." Without waiting for a response, Nicholas pushed past the burly painter. The nape of his neck itched, and he knew Horner continued to stare at him until he existed the alley.

At the curb, he glanced up and down the street. A phaeton with gaudy red wheels flashed by. A heavily laden wagon caught his gaze, coming from the opposite direction. His shoulders tensed. The phaeton barely missed the wagon, swerving at the last moment. Contemplating the busy avenue, Nicholas considered what he knew.

It was precious little.

A young boy of about twelve strolled into view. The urchin walked in a jerky fashion with one foot in the gutter and one on the walkway as he searched the ground for any coins or refuse he could trade for a few pence.

"Hey, boy!" Nicholas called.

The boy's head jerked up. He stared at Nicholas with wary brown eyes. His thin body tensed as he prepared to run, looking for all the world like a squirrel about to dash up a tree.

"Do you want to earn a shilling?"

The boy licked his lower lip, although he didn't come any closer. He nodded once.

"What is your name?"

"Jack, sir. Jack Jones." He kept his distance and even clasped his hands behind his back as if he feared Nicholas would try to catch him.

"Where are your parents?" Nicholas searched the jostling passersby for a likely adult, but found no likely candidate to speak to about an errand for the boy.

"Parents?" Jack scoffed. "What parents?"

"You're an orphan, then?"

Jack shrugged. "As well as. If I've got parents, I've never met 'em."

"Very well, Mr. Jones. Then I have a job for you. I need a good lad to run an errand. If you are willing, there is a sixpence for you now and another when you return after discharging your mission. Are you game?" Nicholas smiled and took a step forward.

Eyeing him, Jack backed up, maintaining a good five feet between them. "What were this mission, then?"

"I need to send a request to a friend, Sergeant Dalton. He should be easy enough to find—he only has one leg and often strolls along the streets near the Second Sons Inquiry Agency. Do you know where that is?"

Jack nodded.

"Do you think you can find him?"

"Yes, sir."

"Excellent." He fished yet another card out of his card case and the stub of a pencil from his pocket. "Can you hold this so I can write on it?"

Jack nodded and darted forward to twitch the card from between his fingers. He held it in the palm of his outstretched hand and watched Nicholas warily.

He scrawled the address of his flat on the back. "Tell the sergeant that Captain Ainsley would like him to nose around and discover if the night watch saw anyone lurking near Lord Taunton's townhouse in Mayfair last night. Ask him to find out if there were any thieves or other notorious persons seen. Do you think you can remember that?"

Apparently not given to extensive conversation, the boy's head bobbed once in the affirmative.

"Give him my card." Nicholas tapped the calling card. "Tell him I will pay him for his time and any expenditures he might incur in the commission of his investigation."

The card disappeared into the boy's pocket. His head tilted to the right. A considering look passed through his large eyes. "I could find out what you want to know, sir. No need to annoy the sergeant."

"I have no doubt you could." Nicholas

chuckled. "How is this, then? I will pay both you and the sergeant if you will act as Sergeant Dalton's assistant and discover if anyone saw anything. It is possible someone committed burglary." He gestured at the townhouse. "If you find evidence of that, I will gladly repay your efforts."

"It'll cost you more than a shilling, sir, if I were to do all that."

"Agreed."

A crafty look narrowed Jack's eyes. "How much would it be worth to you?"

"I will pay you the full shilling after you locate the sergeant and give him my message. If you then discover any information about thieves seen in this area last night, and news if any of Lord Taunton's property has been pawned, then there will be an additional payment." Nicholas smiled.

Jack licked his lower lip again, his brown eyes alight.

"But I shall need to confirm the information," Nicholas continued. "I will not pay for speculation. How much you receive will depend upon the success of your venture. Are these terms agreeable to you?"

"Yes, sir." The lad stepped closer and held out his hand.

Nicholas dropped a sixpence onto Jack's grubby palm. "I shall want a report from both of you. And don't forget—no lies. If I cannot confirm the information, I shall not pay for it."

"I don't lie, sir." Jack's bony chest puffed out with pride.

"Indeed." When Jack flipped the card over and stared at it with a puzzled look on his face, Nicholas added, "The sergeant can read. He will be able to guide you to my flat when you have information for me." By not giving Jack his address, he could ensure that the boy would do his best to find Sergeant Dalton so that he could receive at least one sixpence.

"You will not be here?" Jack stared at the façade of Lord Taunton's townhouse.

"No. You must come to my flat this evening if you wish to be paid."

"Your flat?" A hard look flickered in the boy's eyes. He frowned and glanced again at the townhouse behind Nicholas, apparently considering what it meant that Nicholas did not live in Mayfair.

"You need not come inside. I will come out, if you wish. Never fear, I shall not cheat you. If you believe I am not to be trusted, ask Sergeant Dalton about Captain Ainsley."

"Yes, sir." The shuttered look on Jack's face made Nicholas think the boy might simply pocket the first sixpence and go on his way, forgetting about the rest of the shilling. Even at his young age, he obviously had had enough bad experiences with adults to be distrustful and suspicious of their intentions.

The thought saddened Nicholas. "If you don't trust me, ask the sergeant. He and I served together in Corunna."

Jack nodded and spotting a gap in the carriage traffic, dashed away.

As the boy ran around the corner at a cross street, Nicholas turned to face the placid exterior of the townhouse. At least the boy had headed in the correct direction to find Second Sons. Perhaps he truly would find the sergeant and enlist his aid instead of running off to enjoy whatever comforts he could purchase with a sixpence. With luck, the sergeant and Jack might even locate the man who had broken into Taunton's townhouse the night before, if he existed.

With a sigh, Nicholas set his foot on the bottom step only to halt when the front door opened. Flatman and his jurymen filed out and formed a motley cluster on the walkway. They slowly filled the stoop and steps, forcing Nicholas to the edge of the walkway. Droplets of water, carried on a cool breeze, sprinkled over Nicholas' hand. He glanced over in annoyance. A small fountain sprayed water through the air, decorating the narrow space between the townhouse and the walkway on their right. He moved further away to avoid the chilly spray, irritated to find his sleeve damp. The icy water quickly soaked through his linen shirt. He shook his arm to avoid shivering.

"Have you discovered anything new, Captain Ainsley?" Flatman stepped past Nicholas to the walkway, adroitly avoiding the fountain's spray.

"Nothing very new, just confirmation that someone may have attempted to access Lord Taunton's bedchamber. The painters Taunton hired left their ladder in the alleyway last night. I found evidence showing that it may have been used by a thief." He gestured for them to follow and walked through the alley to the rear of the townhouse. Past the edge of the small patch of lawn, he knelt to point to the rectangular depressions abutting the walkway. "There are bits of relatively fresh grass and earth on the feet of the ladder. I also discovered flakes of white paint matching the windowsill."

"How is that proof? They are painting the shutters—there are bound to be marks from the ladder in several places. I would expect just that," one of the men protested, gesturing toward the depressions.

Nicholas nodded. "Indeed. Except you will note that they have not painted any of the shutters or window frames in the rear. That includes Taunton's bedchamber. So while there should be marks in other places, there should not be any in precisely this location." He stood and dusted off his right hand on the side of his jacket. "The painters are here now if you wish to speak with them and examine the ladder."

Flatman nodded, his expression thoughtful. "It does appear to confirm our suspicion that Lord Taunton surprised a thief in his bedchamber and was murdered."

"It certainly accounts for the missing knife." A prickling sensation like ants crawling over his useless left arm made him grip his wrist with his right hand. He gritted his teeth, willing the feeling away. When he caught Flatman studying him, he turned to face the townhouse. "It is odd, though, that nothing appears to be missing."

"The thief was scared away. Perhaps his lordship made some noise when he was murdered." Flatman shrugged. "We will see what the jury makes of it. Although it seems likely that we should ask the constable or a Bow Street Runner to assist us in finding this thief. Unless you wish to pursue that matter."

"I will investigate it. There is no need to involve more men." He rubbed the knotted skin between his brows. "When do you expect to hold the inquest?"

"Tomorrow." Flatman glanced at his men. Several of them shook their heads. "Thursday, then. Day after tomorrow. You will attend, Captain Ainsley?"

"Of course."

Flatman nodded and smiled grimly. "This is one case where I am thankful that the inquest must only determine the cause of death. Some other poor souls will have to decide the innocence or guilt of anyone involved in this tragedy. I doubt it will be easy." He flicked a glance at Nicholas and his smile relaxed. "Unless you have the answers for us already."

"No, not at the moment."

"You appear to be a thoughtful man, and I hope you don't mind a suggestion?"

"I never object to advice."

"The easy answer is often not the right answer."

Nicholas chuckled. "You are a philosopher, sir."

"Not I." Flatman grinned. "But I have seen these matters go awry too many times. I would rather five guilty men go free than one innocent man hang."

"You will get no argument from me. And it certainly appears that there may be complications." He thought of Miss Whitethorn-Litton and Mr. Silsbury. Complications might be too mild of a description. "I hope we can get to the truth of it."

"Well, do not let it become a case of the expeditious answer overruling the strict truth. There will be pressure, you understand, to wrap this up in a neat package. But methinks you are not one to be content to do as he is bid."

Nicholas smiled, recognizing a kindred spirit in Flatman despite the man's taciturn manner. "Some would say I am rarely content with anything."

Laughing, Flatman and his men bid Nicholas good day. The group entered the alley, apparently intent on questioning the painters to confirm what Nicholas had told them. He watched until the last man disappeared around the corner before he mounted the front steps once more.

Entering the townhouse, he looked around, feeling ill at ease despite the comfortable furnishings. The very air seemed thick with suspicion and fear, as if the overwhelming emotions of the inhabitants filled the hallways with a rank odor. A sense of urgency impelled him forward. He stopped at the bottom of the grand staircase and gripped the elegantly carved ball on the top of the newel post. If he wanted to present his findings at the coroner's inquest, he had only today and tomorrow to follow the faint trails he had uncovered.

Not that he had to present anything at that time, but still... He wanted to find the answer. He needed to.

The easy solution would be to accept that a minor theft had turned into murder when Lord Taunton had interrupted the thief. But like Flatman had said, that seemed too expeditious and unsatisfying. Was he making a mystery out of nothing more than the elusive scent of something more intentional than a burglary gone wrong?

The evidence he had uncovered in the bedchamber and alleyway supported the robbery theory. The missing knife, the condition of the ladder, and the marks at the window provided circumstantial evidence to support that notion. On the opposing side stood

Taunton's purse of coins and the fact that nothing appeared to be missing from his bedchamber.

Wouldn't a thief have taken the money? Perhaps he only stole part of the purse's contents to obfuscate the evidence and hide his crime. Nicholas grinned at the notion. He had never known a thief to behave with such circumspection.

And there was Silsbury's story that he had heard Taunton speaking to a woman. Surely, the burglar had not been a female, although it was not beyond the realm of possibility. Silsbury obviously thought he heard Miss Whitethorn-Litton. He believed she was responsible, though whether he thought that because he was jealous or because he honestly suspected her was debatable.

His grip on the newel post tightened. At this point, while he could not discount the possibility that a theft had turned violent, he was unwilling to accept that easy answer. He just hoped his client, Silsbury, would grant him sufficient time to discover the truth and not force him to provide an answer for the coroner's inquest.

Chapter Ten

5:33 PM October 23, 1821

While they didn't have their roast beef and Yorkshire pudding as anticipated, Toddy and Bottom still managed to make an excellent dinner of shepherd's pie, pickles, and some very acceptable beer at the Ten Bells in Spitalfields. Toddy chuckled as he wiped his mouth on his sleeve and gestured to his partner to pay their impatient waitress. Clearly nervous about spending the late earl's gold, Bottom paid for their sumptuous feast with the last few coins he found after digging through all the corners of his capacious pockets.

They did not linger in the comfortably warm but altogether too busy pub. Several other patrons eyed them in a way that Toddy did not like. He brushed a bit of grease from his jacket's fraying lapel and considered which streets would be safest. Nothing too dark or too narrow, certainly. They needed to slip away without any undue unpleasantness.

After an assessing glance at his nervous partner, Toddy fixed an expression of calm optimism on his face to inspire confidence. It wouldn't do for Bottom to panic now. Once Toddy was sure they were not being followed, they could proceed to meet with his old, but highly suspicious, associate who harbored a deep interest in small, highly portable trinkets like the slender dagger.

For once, he would be the one with money, the one who could buy whatever he wanted. Toddy sucked on a bit of gristle caught between his teeth. The coins would be a bit more ticklish than the knife. They had no business with gold coins. The men they regularly dealt with would suspect that the two men were hiding a cache of untold wealth if they saw the guineas. Toddy would certainly come to the same conclusion if one of his friends suddenly pulled a gold coin from his pocket. If they weren't careful, their associates would try to rob Toddy and Bottom, knowing full well that the two men were not in a position to retaliate or report the theft to the authorities.

And Toddy knew of no one who would have sufficient funds to even come close to the value of a guinea, or at least close enough to make the exchange seem like a reasonable trade. He was too wary of stepping up to the wealthier sorts of fences. Too many posh fences were working hand-in-glove with Bow Street. It lent them an air of honesty and provided an excellent cover for their shadier side-dealings. They were simply far too treacherous for Toddy and Bottom to deal with.

As they walked along the busy streets, Toddy dug around in the inner pocket of his once quite elegant coat. A piece of gristle had lodged between his molars, making them ache. He pulled out the dagger and poked at the annoying morsel.

"Put that away, Mr. Toddy!" Bottom knocked his elbow into his side and glanced around. He pulled Toddy away from the pool of light they had strayed under.

No one was staring at them. Of course, that didn't mean some curious passerby hadn't noticed the gold and jewel-encrusted weapon. They might even be inclined to alert the authorities, although Toddy doubted it. No one in this neighborhood wanted anything to do with the watch or the boys at Bow Street.

Unless they needed a favor.

Toddy frowned and then elbowed Bottom back with a laugh. "Leave off! No one is going to notice this little trinket, and I have a stubborn bit o'lamb dug in between me teeth."

"My teeth," Bottom corrected under his breath. His large eyes bounced around, searching the shadows, as if he feared the entire King's guard was about to rush them.

Toddy usually remembered his grammar lessons but at this moment, with his stomach full and warm, it seemed like far too much effort. He grinned at Bottom and picked at the teeth on the other side of his mouth.

"It does not do to flaunt the ridiculous thing, indeed it doesn't. Put it away before someone sees it. Or decides to steal it."

"I am not some pigeon waiting to be plucked, and I'd like to see the man what can put the bite on me for this lovely bauble."

"Please, Mr. Toddy. Have we not moved

beyond this dreadful cant? Put the knife away and make haste for I am anxious to be rid of it and those coins. They belonged to a dead man, and I fear they may bring bad luck with them. I wish I had never found them."

They rounded a corner, and Toddy snorted scornfully in response to Bottom's pleas. Much as Bottom's fear annoyed him, he hated to see his friend so pitifully worried. When he dislodged the final bit of gristle, he finally did as bid and tucked the knife back into an inner pocket.

"We will live like kings for months, perhaps years, on our takings. But only if you can rise above this faintheartedness. I have never known you to be so lily-livered, Mr. Bottom, and cannot think why you should start, now."

Bottom opened his mouth. Then he flapped his lips like a fish pulled out of the water as he walked right into the wide, red waistcoat of a Bow Street runner.

Despite his native *savoir-faire*, Toddy looked at the owner of the waistcoat and felt his stomach clench. The runner was as tall as he was wide with a wickedly cruel face. He blocked the walkway completely.

When the runner caught Toddy's frown, he held out his arms, clutching a knobby cudgel in his right fist. "Here now, where are the two of you fine gents going on this lovely night?"

Toddy stiffened.

If that was the way it was going to be, then so be it. But, he wouldn't go down without a fight.

Before Toddy could move, Bottom staggered with shaking knees between him and the officer, waving his arms.

Toddy could almost read his friend's thoughts in his gray, panicked face. Bottom thought he could distract the runner or get himself arrested while giving Toddy a chance to escape with all the stolen gewgaws.

He couldn't allow that. Bottom would never survive a night in gaol without him. He was too soft.

"We are out for a stroll, if it is any of your business." Toddy leaned forward, clenching his hands into tight fists.

Bottom pushed him back with his shoulder. A sickly grin covered his sweating face. He looked like he was about to be ill. "A fine night for a stroll, sir. I trust you are enjoying the fine weather."

"I am enjoying it immensely. You see, I have unexpectedly come upon the very individuals I hoped to find." The officer tapped his cudgel against his shoulder, his eyes glittering with anticipation.

"Good news, sir, good news indeed." Bottom's words trembled through the chilly air. "Well, sir, we must be on our way. Good night to you."

"Not just yet, my fine friends. I have been

on the lookout for the pair of you—"

It's now or never, old boy. The officer was still talking when Toddy spun on the balls of his feet and sprinted away.

Unfortunately, the walkway behind them was uneven and far too crowded. The loose sole of his right shoe caught on a crack. Toddy tripped. He barreled into an elegant young man out for a stroll. The toff swore at him and raised his lacquered walking stick, face livid with anger.

Toddy raised an arm to protect his head as the brass knob of the stick hit him just above the elbow. He yelped and kicked out, trying to force the young man away. The stranger struck again and again, landing blows that flared with bright pain.

Toddy fell, his head slamming against the brick walkway.

He struggled to regain his feet. Another blow hit him on the back of the head. Bright lights buzzed through his vision before he fell into the cold darkness.

*

Unable to prevent the unfolding disaster, Bottom watched the Bow Street runner push aside a wealthy gentleman and hit Toddy on the back of the head with cruel expertise. His partner's eyes rolled back in his head, and he collapsed with a sickening thud. With a vicious grin on his flushed face, the officer repeatedly kicked Toddy's prone body until he ran out of breath.

Bottom rushed forward and grabbed the officer's arm. "Please, sir! You cannot pummel an unconscious man in this manner. We will go with you willingly if you would only stop this battery. Please, we meant you no insult."

The officer gave Toddy one final kick in the ribs. Bottom winced and glanced away. Before he could do anything, the officer yanked Toddy's jacket back, ripping it at the shoulder as he searched through the pockets.

Faint-headed, Bottom held his breath. A trickle of blood seeped through Toddy's matted hair, staining the icy walkway beneath him. Bottom bent down and carefully pulled out his handkerchief to wrap around his friend's head, all the while watching the officer for fear that any sudden gesture would call down the wrath of the Bow Street runner on him, as well.

"Ah, there it is." The officer discovered the gold dagger and held it up. His dark eyes danced with vicious mirth as he looked from the knife to Bottom. "A pretty little thing, indeed, for a pair of rapscallions like you." Emboldened by his success, he ripped the remaining pockets open and let their contents spill out into the street. A crust of bread, a dingy handkerchief, and two pence rolled into the gutter, along with several small puffs of lint.

A filthy child solemnly watching them scrambled forward and grabbed the pennies. He ran off before anyone could catch him. Bottom watched him go, wishing him better luck than he and Toddy had found.

A minute later, the officer found the guineas Toddy had brought with him. While it wasn't their entire hoard, it was sufficient to make the officer straighten and give Toddy another sharp kick in the stomach. Bottom flinched and gripped his friend's shoulder. He felt as sick as if he had received the blow himself, however he was determined to block any additional violence.

"Pair of thieves, the both of you," the Bow Street runner commented as he tucked the coins in his own pocket. Then he hauled Toddy up and pulled one unresisting arm around his neck. "You take his other arm," he ordered. "And if you try to escape it shall be so much the worse for you."

"Yes, sir," Bottom said dully. He gently picked up Toddy's limp arm and eased it over his shoulder, flinching when Toddy moaned. "Sorry." He barely breathed the apology, shaking with fear. He could not leave his unconscious friend to the officer's less-than-tender mercies, and he knew the runners would find him again even if he did manage to escape.

No, he would stand by Toddy. What else could he do? Toddy's breath gurgled in his throat. A small bubble of blood burst from his left nostril.

Men perished in gaol after a session of savage questioning. With Toddy already injured, how would they survive? Toddy might not even survive this night. The chill of fear clenched Bottom's bowels.

His unusually heavy meal gurgled in his stomach. His body was more used to starving than eating. For a moment, he wondered if he would be able to keep the food down.

Toddy had always been the cagey one, the one who protected both of them as they trod the dark twisted paths through the back alleys of London. Now it would be Bottom's turn to protect Toddy, and he wasn't sure he was up to the task.

Not that he had a choice. His friend would need him after such a brutal beating, at least until the hangman put nooses around their necks.

Bottom struggled to keep his friend upright. He had no illusions about their fate. The officer would probably keep the guineas he had pocketed, but he would hand over the dagger.

That dagger would convict them. The object was cursed.

If only Toddy had listened to him this one time.

Chapter Eleven

10:30 AM October 24, 1821

"How could you tell that inquiry agent that you heard me talking to Taunton last night?" Kathryn asked when Harry finally strolled into the small breakfast room in search of his favorite Sally Lunn bun and cup of coffee.

Harry shrugged and examined the chafing dishes on the sideboard, lifting the ornate silver lids and frowning with disappointment. "I merely told our dear captain the truth, my dovekie. Would you have me lie?"

"I would have you speak honestly. You know it was not my voice you heard. Have I ever visited Taunton's bedchamber?"

"How would I know such a thing? I do not keep an account of your movements. All I know is that I heard a woman's voice." His slim hand hovered over the covered basket of bread and buns, a thoughtful expression replacing the frown.

She had already eaten her share while the buns were so hot that fragrant steam clouded her vision when she broke one open to slather on a dollop of rich butter. She smiled to herself when Harry picked up a bun and frowned at finding the delectable bread barely warm.

He deserved a cold bun and even colder coffee after what he had told Captain Ainsley. Harry had all but accused her of murder. The thought made her full stomach churn uncomfortably.

Sipping her coffee, she considered what she should say to Captain Ainsley and anyone else who asked. Certainly, she could never confess where she had been the night Taunton had died. Any admission that she had visited an abortionist in the company of a pregnant girl would result in nearly the same fate as being found guilty of murder. The truth served no purpose but to make her bleak life worse.

There seemed no way she could avoid a miserable and very short future. She was damned no matter what she said or what course she took. A bitter sense of ill-use filled her as she studied Harry's blithe expression. Apparently, his biggest concern this morning was the temperature of his breakfast.

But then, he had always been the fortunate one.

"Have you considered that you heard another woman? You could not possibly say it was my voice." She rolled a small crumb of bread under one finger.

He sighed and placed several buns on his plate. "My dear little dovekie, I can only express my honest opinions to you, as I expressed them to the oh-so-charming captain." A malicious gleam lit his eyes as he flicked a glance at her. "I have not lied, if that is what you fear. In any event, I am convinced the captain will discover the truth, whatever that may be. I am not worried on that score."

"And I am convinced you will do your best to convince him of my guilt!" She flung her napkin onto the table and stood, shaking with sudden anger.

Harry sat back and studied her, a smile curving his mouth. "Your guilt? Then you are guilty?"

"You know I am not!"

"Your innocence or guilt is no concern of mine." He shrugged. "But you had best take care, my dovekie. Your tempestuous nature may get the best of you some day, if it has not done so already."

"I—" Shaking, she choked back a flood of bitter words and strode out, cold with fear. How could she defend herself? Any display of temper would be dutifully reported to Captain Ainsley.

She had to think clearly. Unfortunately, that was a trait her father and Lord Taunton had never encouraged. The realization increased her panicked sense of helplessness and ill-usage. The men in her life had always described her as a carefree creature and encouraged her to express her emotions freely. They told her that logic was for men and bluestockings, not pretty young women. She realized now that their indulgent attitude had not done her any favors.

Taking a deep breath, she worked to bring order to her chaotic thoughts. She had to rely on sense, not sensibility, and apply logic to help her escape this false accusation.

The twenty-two pounds she had saved

would not support her for long. Perhaps if she sold her dresses... And then what? She could not sell all of her clothing and possessions unless she planned to wear one frock for the foreseeable future. The sum she would realize even if she did such a thing would not afford her with the tiny cottage she dreamt about at night.

She was as well and truly trapped as any fish on a hook. Her exchange of her reputation for a place to live and the chance to uncover the truth about her father's death appeared to be a poor exchange.

She touched one finger to her pale lower lip as she paused in front of a mirror. Her reflection today looked haggard with dark circles under her eyes and pale skin. She was growing old and undesirable.

No one wanted her. She'd never have a family of her own. Or children.

The thought of a baby sleeping in her arms brought to mind Mary's sad experience and the dress Kathryn had balled up and thrown inside her wardrobe. The blood-streaked hem would surely damn her if it were found. When she regained her room, she pulled open the wardrobe doors and searched the shelves. Several shawls were neatly folded on the bottom but there was no sign of the dress.

Panic fluttered through her chest. Had one of the maids found it?

She ran to the corner of her room and yanked the embroidered bell pull. Unable to stand still, she paced from the door to the window. The October sun shone brightly through the glass, the shaft hot against Kathryn's face and hands when she paused to look outside. The view was limited to a small garden and alley, and beyond them, the solid bulk of the townhouses lining the other side of the block. She'd never paid any attention before to the narrow, uninspiring view, but now it made her feel hemmed in, trapped by the brick walls and narrow alleys.

A soft rap sounded on the door before a maid opened it a fraction. Nancy peered through the crack as if afraid to enter.

Kathryn felt her face flush with impatience. Did she fear Kathryn was a murderess, determined to kill everyone in the house?

"Come in, Nancy." Kathryn gestured to her neatly made bed. "Did you clean my room today?"

Nancy's blue eyes widened, and she raised the hem of her apron to cover her mouth. "Yes, Miss. Is it not to your satisfaction?"

"It is fine." Kathryn paced to her chest of drawers and stared at her reflection, forcing herself to take a deep, calming breath. "I was— well—did you happen to find a dress in the bottom of my wardrobe? I, um, began my monthly courses early, and I was afraid the dress would be ruined if I did not soak it. Did you find it? If you did, I hope you thought to wash it. It was one of my favorite gowns. I do not want it stained."

"Why no, Miss. I never touched your wardrobe, not this morning nor yesterday neither."

"Did any of the other maids?" Kathryn's voice rose sharply. She took another deep breath to control her surging emotions and smiled at the maid in an attempt to reassure her.

The maid stared back, appearing even paler and more frightened than before. "No, miss. I w-were the only one working upstairs."

"I am not angry." The smile on her face felt stiff. Her cheek muscles ached with her effort to appear calm. "I simply did not want to lose the dress through my own carelessness. I should have soaked it immediately."

"Should I ask the other maids, Miss? Them as work downstairs?"

"No. I must have been mistaken about where I left it."

"Do you need anything else? May I go?"

"One more question, Nancy. You are responsible for Lord Taunton's bedchamber as well as mine, are you not?"

"Yes, Miss." Nancy stared at the floor and twisted her apron, deepening the wrinkles already covering the faded garment.

"Did Lord Taunton speak to you Monday evening?"

"Wh—what?" Her stammer grew more pronounced.

"Harry—Mr. Silsbury—says he heard a woman speaking to Lord Taunton. I just thought you might have exchanged words with him when you brought him fresh water for washing."

"I never—you can not say I killed him—you can not!"

Kathryn gripped the poor girl's shaking hands, trying to reassure her. "I did not think you hurt him. I just thought you might have spoken to him."

"He—he ..." Nancy stared at her, her eyes reddening and filling with panicked tears.

"Nancy, you are not in trouble. We are all simply seeking the truth. You did speak to him, did you not? When you brought him a fresh ewer of water?"

"I can not say!" The maid pulled her hands away and covered her face with her apron. Her shoulders shook with a sob before she turned and fled.

Staring at the open door, Kathryn felt sure, now, that Harry had heard Nancy's voice in Taunton's room. Perhaps the water had not been warm enough. Kathryn had heard him berate maids for bringing cold water to his room in the past.

For the first time since she'd heard the news of Taunton's death, a small flicker of hope bloomed inside her. If she could convince Nancy to speak to Captain Ainsley, she might be able to prove she had never been in his room. She was not a murderess.

Unfortunately, before she could call Nancy back, Kirby paused in the hallway in front of her open door. The butler coughed discreetly into his gloved hand to catch her attention.

"I beg your pardon, Miss Whitethorn-Litton, but you have a visitor. Miss Mardling is awaiting you in the Chinese Drawing Room." He bowed and gestured with a wide sweep of his right hand toward the staircase.

Distracted, Kathryn glanced around her room before she realized with a sigh that there was nothing else she could do. Her stained dress was not here. Preceding Kirby, she felt a momentary flush of irritation as she caught the skirt of her simple cotton print day dress. While there were flounces decorating the neck and cuffs as well as piped bands around the hem, it was by no means the latest fashion. The skirt was too narrow and the design was cheap, roller-printed blue flowers strewn among wine-colored grasses. She was dressed well enough for reading or writing letters, however her dress was hardly what she would have wished to be wearing to receive the very fashionable and wealthy Rose Mardling.

"How good to see you, Rose! How are you?" Kathryn held out her hands as she entered the drawing room.

Instead of gripping her hands, Rose rushed to her and threw her arms around her, giving her a tight hug. Tears leapt to Kathryn's eyes. She blinked rapidly, holding her friend tightly as she swallowed, grateful for her friendship. She had not realized how alone and frightened she had been until she saw the sympathy in Rose's eyes.

"My dear, the question is, how are you?" Rose's warm gaze searched Kathryn's face. "I was so worried about you when I heard the news about Lord Taunton. What happened? How could he be dead?"

Kathryn shook her head, her throat constricting painfully. It took her another moment before she could speak. "I honestly don't understand it, Rose."

"You were not there, were you?" She caught Kathryn's hands and squeezed them, her brow tightening with worry lines.

"No, I was not here. I was with Mary."

"Another dreadful affair—I am so sorry. You have had such a fearful time the last few days. I don't know how you can appear so calm." She released Kathryn's hands and sat down, straightening her skirts before patting the settee cushion next to her.

As Kathryn expected, her friend exemplified the height of fashion. Rose wore a lovely pale blue walking dress with rich embroidery and piping enhancing the flounces around the hem and neckline. She looked as ethereal as an angel.

"Appearances can be deceiving." Kathryn shook her head ruefully. "I am far from calm."

"No one can blame you." Rose frowned

and touched Kathryn's wrist. "I should have gone with Mary in your stead."

"Why? You could hardly know that Lord Taunton would be—that he would die the same night. I am already ruined. There would have been little sense in allowing you to be ruined, as well."

"You cannot possibly mean that."

"Mean what? That I am ruined?"

"You know you are not. Everyone knows Lord Taunton was your guardian and therefore your presence here is perfectly respectable."

Kathryn laughed and briefly squeezed her friend's wrist. "Thank you for that, but you know as well as I that your father merely said that to make our friendship acceptable."

"My father is a pompous—"

"Rose!"

Rose laughed. "Well, he is, as you well know."

"It matters little. I am simply relieved you were not involved."

"Was he truly murdered?"

Overwhelmed by sudden grief, Kathryn nodded, unable to answer.

The hot sting of tears blinded her. She blinked quickly, staring down at the floor. Oddly, it was her friend's sympathy that destroyed her attempts at self-control and called forth her unbearable grief. She had thought it would be easier to manage her emotions in the company of a friend.

"My parents were horrified when they heard," Rose said.

"Oh yes, I had forgotten about your own situation. What will your family do now? Your father was so set on an alliance with the earl, wasn't he?" She suspected that Mr. Mardling was the one enamored of the earl's social standing, not Rose. Saddened, Kathryn remembered the bitter discussion between Rose and her father at Wexford, and Rose's desperate threat. Based upon that, a stranger might conclude that Rose had finally been pushed too far and had murdered Taunton.

Or, he might decide that Kathryn had murdered Taunton out of a jealousy she had never felt.

Rose turned away slightly and tucked a blond curl under the lacy edge of the cap she wore under her bonnet. "It may seem cruel to you for me to admit this, but I have hopes they will finally entertain Mr. Westbrook's offer. He may not be titled or as rich as Lord Taunton, but he loves me."

Since Frank Westbrook worked for Rose's father in the position of secretary, he had been thrown into Rose's company on a regular basis. The two had developed a warm relationship despite her parents' ambition for their daughter to marry into a noble family.

If anyone could make Rose happy, it was Mr. Westbrook. Rose could never go for long without mentioning his name.

Kathryn could certainly sympathize with her friend. It was far better to marry someone for love. She ached for an end to her own loneliness and could not imagine being forever tied to someone who harbored more affection for her ability to produce children than for her company. Kathryn knew what it was like to live with a man who maintained only a polite interest. She would not wish such empty coldness on anyone.

"I hope they accept Mr. Westbrook's offer, then, for your sake, Rose."

"They should. I know of no other titled gentlemen interested, particularly not any rich enough to suit my father." A grim smile brushed her lips. "It is rather disheartening to witness your father bowing and scraping to men he would normally not speak to in hopes of convincing one of them to make an offer."

"You cannot view it in that light. Your parents want what is best for you, and Lord Taunton was a kind man." Kathryn gripped her friend's hands and leaned forward. "I'm sure that over time, the two of you would have developed warmer feelings for each other. I'm told that often happens. In fact, many harmonious marriages start out in just such a manner."

"You did not develop warmer feelings for him," Rose replied sharply. "Or so you said."

A stab of pain surprised Kathryn. She released Rose's hands. "He...well, we did not suit." She faltered, unable to admit the truth. How could she explain that Taunton preferred the company of men? "I'm sure I must have explained our situation before. My father passed away while we were visiting Lord Taunton. I don't believe Lord Taunton was aware I was even present in his household for the first few weeks after papa's death. Certainly, he was not concerned until he tried to send me home, and I informed him I had no home and no place to go." She glanced away, her gaze coming to rest on the smooth, calming surface of one of the blue-and-white vases. "Lord Taunton was kind enough to allow me to remain."

"What would you have done had he married me?"

Kathryn stared at her, nonplussed. "Done?"

"You could hardly have expected to remain, my dear, despite our friendship. It would have been very uncomfortable for all of us. Surely you see that."

"But we were friends—and I had not considered what might happen in the future."

"Think of how awkward it would have been." She gave an elaborate shiver. "You do see that, do you not? The gossip would have been dreadful, intolerable in fact."

"I suppose I do understand," Kathryn replied slowly. Why hadn't she considered this before, when she heard Mr. Mardling discussing it? And yet, she could not help but wish that her friendship with Rose was stronger than Rose's fear of gossip.

"Then it truly is for the best, after all. I am relieved," Rose said with a satisfied smile.

"No, it is not for the best," Kathryn replied sharply, angered by Rose's callous disregard of Taunton's tragic death.

"Whatever do you mean?"

"They are investigating Taunton's death. I fear it is not going well." At least, it was not going well for her. At least, Rose was fortunate that Harry had not mentioned Rose's rash remarks at Wexford.

"I thought—I heard a rumor that he was murdered by a thief." Rose frowned in confusion.

"That is one theory, certainly." Kathryn sighed. Speculation certainly flew on rapid wings through London. "Some may believe that I killed him."

"You? But you were gone. You were in the company of Mary Dudley, were you not?"

"You know very well I was. However, that has placed me in an awkward position. I could never tell anyone about Mary, or where we were, and neither can you. It would ruin her and only trade one crime for another."

Rose smiled encouragingly and patted Kathryn's hands. "Nonetheless, you were not here. They cannot possibly blame you so you have nothing to worry about."

"You don't understand. Harry hired an

inquiry agent. I believe he suspects me. If he were to discover that Lord Taunton had offered for you, he may believe that I was jealous and murdered him to prevent the marriage."

"Don't be ridiculous." Rose laughed outright and leaned forward to hug Kathryn. "No one could possibly believe such a thing. There is no one kinder or gentler than you. You are borrowing trouble, my dear Kathryn, as you often do. You must have faith that this inquiry agent will discover the truth. A thief murdered Taunton and that is all there is to it."

Studying her friend's face, Kathryn was not so sure.

She had not considered that Rose would have requested her to leave once she married Taunton. If she had known, she would have had a very good motive for trying to stop their marriage. And since Harry could confirm that Kathryn had known that Taunton was considering marriage for three months, she had no way of proving that she was not jealous and had not jumped to the conclusion that she would be told to leave.

If Captain Ainsley spoke to Rose and she admitted this, he was intelligent enough to understand how powerful that motivation would be.

Kathryn would surely be arrested once that happened.

"You must make me a promise, Rose," she said, her heart pounding with urgency.

"Promise that you will not tell Captain Ainsley, that is the inquiry agent, any of this."

"But papa will surely tell him that they were writing the marriage contract."

"I understand, but please don't tell him that you would not have allowed me to remain once you married Taunton. Please. This is important, Rose."

Rose frowned. "I cannot lie, you know that. I am a terrible liar."

"I know. But you could avoid saying anything about it, could you not?"

"I suppose." She smiled suddenly, her blue eyes brightening. "He may not even discover I exist. And even if he does, he will most certainly speak to my father instead of me. I am sure this Captain Ainsley of yours need never discover the awkwardness of our situation. So truly, this is all for the best." Rose leaned forward and tapped Kathryn's wrist with her fingertips. "What will you do now?"

"I beg your pardon?" Kathryn eyed Rose, confused.

"Well, I understand Lord Taunton had a younger brother, a married, younger brother. Surely, he will arrive soon to attend to his brother's business affairs. Where will you go?"

"I—I don't know."

"I wish I could take you home with me, but my parents never truly approved of our friendship, despite my father's public satisfaction with it. In fact, I believe they only allowed us to speak because they hoped it would bring me to Lord Taunton's notice. But what of Mary Dudley?"

"Mary?" Kathryn laughed. "She can hardly acknowledge that she knows me. Her parents only allowed us to associate because of you. Her reputation is already fragile enough without acknowledging a connection to me."

"Well, you shall think of something, I'm sure. After all, you managed to fall on your feet when your father died and left you impoverished and orphaned. You shall manage now."

"I wish I had your confidence."

"Oh, Kathryn, you must believe me. You shall find a new home soon. You will see." Rose stood. "Now I'm afraid I must not tarry. My parents believe I went to Floris to shop for a new perfume, and my maid is waiting in the hallway. Will you be all right?"

"Yes. I am fine."

Rose's blue eyes searched Kathryn's face. "If you find yourself in need, send word to me. I will do whatever I can to help you, you must believe that."

"I do. And I hope you find happiness with your Mr. Westbrook," Kathryn replied out of habit, realizing now that Rose could, and would, do very little to assist her despite her protestations. They lived in a society that would not forgive Kathryn for living in the household of an unrelated, single man. If Rose did not want to face the same stigma, she could not openly associate with her now that the reason for their friendship, Lord Taunton, had passed away.

The two women hugged before Kathryn escorted her to the grand hallway. Rose took her heavy shawl and bonnet from her maid and nodded to Kathryn.

"Please let me know how the inquiry goes. I am anxious to ensure your wellbeing and will assist you however I can."

"Certainly. Goodbye, Miss Mardling, and have a good afternoon." Kathryn watched Rose and her maid depart, feeling dispirited.

Usually Rose managed to bring a whirlwind of optimism and joy with her, but today she had only aroused a new worry. What would Kathryn do when Lord Taunton's younger brother arrived?

Grief filled her, sudden and tumultuous, breaking through the final shreds of her self-control. A deep, gasping sob wracked her. She pressed her hand against her mouth as she fled upstairs. She had not realized how much she would miss Taunton's company, how alone he had left her. He had been distant and oblivious at times, but he had also been warm-hearted and full of joy.

If only she could see him smile at her and laugh one more time, anything to relieve the aching emptiness inside her.

Chapter Twelve

11:30 AM October 24, 1821

Although Nicholas waited to visit Croftson House until he was fairly certain Silsbury would be awake, he did not catch him home after all. When he arrived at Lord Taunton's residence, he was surprised to be advised by the stiff-necked butler that Silsbury had already departed.

"Do you know where he went?" Nicholas asked, glancing past the butler on the off chance that Kirby had been given orders to inform visitors that Silsbury was not at home.

The butler's dark clothing and black cravat reflected a house in deep mourning, as did his haggard face. A hatchment hung above the front door to remind passersby and visitors of the tragedy. The black lozenge-shaped frame held the earl's coat of arms painted over the Latin phrase, *Resurgam*, meaning "I shall rise again."

Nicholas couldn't suppress the cynical thought that if Taunton's murderer happened to see the hatchment and understood what the Latin phrase meant, he might find it a bit unsettling.

"Mr. Silsbury does not confide in me, sir," Kirby said, clasping the edge of the door in one gloved hand in preparation to close it in Nicholas' face.

"I must see him on the matter of Lord

Taunton's death. Do you have any notion of where he might have gone?"

Kirby stared at him for a long moment before he grudgingly admitted, "He had a parcel under his arm." He frowned in thought before continuing, "Generally he leaves posting his packages to me. I believe it may be possible that he took something to Mr. Flatman. I, well, I overheard him asking one of the footmen about the coroner."

"I see." Nicholas turned. At the last moment, he pressed his palm against the door to keep it open. As long as he was here, he might as well make the most of the opportunity. "Would it be possible for me to view Lord Taunton's bedchamber one more time?"

The butler wavered, concern and confusion wrinkling his forehead before his grip on the door relaxed. He stepped back into the hallway. "Yes. It would be best if this matter could be brought to a successful conclusion as quickly as possible. We sent word to Lord Taunton's younger brother after the death of his lordship. We expect his arrival at any moment. I would not wish to add to his grief by informing him that the culprit remains free."

"I will certainly do my utmost to ensure the guilty party is apprehended." Nicholas followed Kirby up the stairs to the master bedroom.

The bedchamber had obviously been cleaned. The air smelled of strong soap and the rug on which Taunton had been lying in front of the hearth was missing.

"We removed Lord Taunton in preparation for his burial. His mortal remains are now resting in the sitting room downstairs. Do you wish to view him and pay your respects?"

"No. That is unnecessary," Nicholas replied. Seeing the clean, redressed body would tell him nothing new.

Kirby nodded. "As you wish."

Walking through the empty room, Nicholas felt a crawling sensation trickle down his spine. He glanced over his shoulder. The butler watched him from the doorway. "There is no need to remain. I'm sure you have other duties to attend to."

The butler studied him. His gaze intensified before he said, "Very good, sir. If you require any assistance, ring the bell."

Nicholas raised his hand in acknowledgement, already working to get a sense of the man who had lived here and what his last moments might have been like. The room had an overabundance of fragile baubles and knickknacks, and none of them had been broken. So there had been no struggle.

Surely if a thief had surprised him, he would have struggled. He should have called out. Why had no one heard him?

He tried to imagine the scene. The murder had played out late at night, lit only by the wavering glow of the fireplace and a few candles. Lord Taunton must have been taken by surprise, though one would think he would have noticed or heard the window open. He should have felt the disturbance in the quiet air of his bedchamber.

Why hadn't he noticed?

Had the thief been too quick for him? After all, he had been stabbed in the back. Perhaps he had never realized there was a stranger in the room.

Nonetheless, the open window troubled Nicholas. How could Taunton not have seen it? And if he were already in the room, why would the thief enter? He must have seen Taunton standing in front of the fireplace where his body had been found, the flames would certainly have illuminated him.

If Taunton stood there in front of the fire, how could he have missed the sound of the window opening? And if he heard it, wouldn't he have investigated and prevented the burglar from entering? Wouldn't there have been signs of a struggle?

The thief could have been in the room before Taunton entered it. And he could have closed the window afterward if he had managed to avoid detection long enough to stab Taunton in the back.

That alternative seemed equally unlikely. No burglar worth his salt would have closed off his best, and perhaps only, avenue of escape. Not to mention that the window made noise when Nicholas had previously examined it. Each time it was opened or shut, the creak would increase the chance of the perpetrator being caught. A thief would have wanted to minimize that risk, so he would not have shut the window unnecessarily.

None of it made any sense, unless... He studied the room again, searching for any details that would provide a logical sequence of events leading up to the tragedy of Taunton's death. The bare floor near the fireplace yielded nothing new. There had been so little blood that none of it had seeped through the missing carpet to stain the oak floorboards. Taunton's final moments had left precious few traces behind in his bedchamber.

Nicholas straightened and slowly walked around the perimeter of the room, stopping once more at the window. The maid had cleaned away the faint smudges of dirt left by the thief's shoes, but there were still fine scratches and missing paint on the sill where the ladder had scraped it down to the wood. At least that small piece of the puzzle was clear.

Turning away, he continued another step or two before he paused. The late morning sunshine streaming through the window at his back cast the wooden bedframe, curtains, and high canopy into bright relief. A tingle flickered through the hairs on the back of his neck. The sharp shadows behind the headboard seemed odd to him, although the anomaly might just have been the angle from which he viewed the inconsistent darkness.

He moved closer, tilting his head from side to side. No. The black shadow nearest to him was thicker than the shadow on the other side of the headboard. The bed was not evenly flush against the wall. The near side was out about two inches.

Eying the bed, he realized the simplest solution to see if the gap meant anything more than simple carelessness would be to pull the thing away from the wall. He wedged his right shoulder between the bedpost and the wall and pushed. The screech of the bed's legs scraping over the floor made him wince, but the noise did not mask the softer thud of an object hitting the floor.

Dropping to his knees, he lifted the bed skirt. A faint ripple of dust tickled his nose. A small, leather book lay on the floor, wedged between the bedpost and the wall. After several attempts, he managed to hook the edge of it with his fingertips and bring it out into the open.

Elegant, green leather with a soft, buttery feel covered the book, but there was no lettering on either the front or the spine. When he flipped it open, he saw that it also lacked a title page, indicating it was not a published or professionally printed work. The first page was entirely blank, but on the second page someone had scrawled "Reginald Croftson, Earl of Taunton" in bold flourishes.

A diary, then. Nicholas flipped through the book. The pages were dated, but only the first third of the book was used. The rest was blank. The last page with writing on it was dated the week before Taunton had died: October 15, 1821.

Feeling uncomfortably as if he were an intruder stealing an object that he had no right to view, he tucked the small book into his pocket. The volume might tell him nothing at all or it might shed some light on the earl's death. Either way, he knew he could not overlook such an obvious source of information.

Although he spent nearly twenty minutes more searching the room, he found nothing else worth noting. Feeling as unenlightened as ever, he left the bedchamber and quietly closed the door.

Downstairs, he discovered the butler ensconced in his small anteroom near the front door, reading a newspaper. He jumped to his feet when he saw Nicholas and smoothed his lapels as he escorted him to the door. A pile of small, white cards on a silver salver sat atop a delicate console table near the door. Several people had visited to show their respect for the deceased earl while Nicholas was upstairs.

"If there is anything else, you may wish to send word first, Captain Ainsley," Kirby said. "Mr. Croftson should arrive soon, and he will be occupied with his late brother's affairs. I'm sure you understand."

Nicholas nodded. He was fortunate to have been allowed as much access as he had had thus far. In truth, if it weren't for his title of captain, he suspected he would not have been allowed through the front door and would have been relegated to the servant's entrance in the rear. Most people considered inquiry agents and thief-takers to be hardly better than the thieves they purportedly investigated.

He was only vaguely surprised that Kirby had not shut the door in his face at the start of the investigation.

Nicholas hesitated, his hand patting the small journal in his pocket. He should read it, but perhaps the book could wait. If Silsbury had a package containing something he felt important enough to carry personally to Flatman, then Nicholas wanted to view that same evidence, as well.

Taking a chance that Silsbury visited the coroner at his personal residence, Nicholas walked through Mayfair to a more modest part of London. Richard Flatman, Esq. lived on the first floor of a narrow townhouse in the middle of a row of similar townhouses. When he knocked at the door, Nicholas was relieved to discover from the flustered maid that Mr. Flatman was at home and still entertaining Mr. Silsbury.

"Good afternoon, Captain Ainsley, to what do I owe this pleasure?" Flatman stood and gazed expectantly at Nicholas when he entered the sitting room.

"I heard there was new evidence in the case." He glanced from Flatman to Silsbury.

Silsbury lounged on a horsehair settee with a cup of tea in one hand and the other arm stretched out along the back. He nodded and smiled before taking another sip of the milky tea.

"Yes." Flatman lifted a wrinkled piece of brown paper from the low table in front of his chair. He held it to display the folded garment that lay within the torn wrappings. "Mr. Silsbury found this dress in Miss Whitethorn-Litton's armoire." He dropped the paper onto the table, picked up the gown, and shook it out. Dark splotches stained the hem, as well as a round area roughly twelve inches above the hem. "You can see the blood. She never even bothered to wash it out."

Before Nicholas could reply, Flatman dropped the dress onto the paper and picked up something else from the table. Gold flashed in his hand as he held out an ornate knife with a ruby set in the handle. The long, thin blade looked dangerously sharp, and there was a dark stain near the guard that appeared to be dried blood.

"Mr. Silsbury has identified this stiletto as belonging to Miss Whitethorn-Litton, as well." Flatman glanced at Silsbury, who again nodded.

"The knife was not present when I

arrived. Where did you find it? Was it in Miss Whitethorn-Litton's room?" Nicholas asked, his mind leaping in several directions simultaneously.

"We obtained it as part of our investigation," Flatman said, his voice deep with satisfaction.

"From the woman?" Nicholas reframed his question, his thoughts flashing over various possibilities. Flatman was hiding something important.

The heaviness in his pocket reminded him that he was hiding something, as well. He shifted feet uneasily, reluctant to offer up the diary until he could read through the contents. He could only hope it would let him gain a better understanding of the circumstances leading up to the earl's death and reveal some modicum of clues.

For some reason, he had the notion that the murder was not the calamitous result of a theft gone awry or an eruption of uncontrollable rage. The circumstances of the earl's death felt contrived, as if the intelligence behind it had planned every last, dreadful moment and then expertly redirected their attention in the direction he wanted it to go.

The whole thing was eerily reminiscent of a magician's trick he had seen as a child. He had disliked the sensation of being deliberately fooled then, and the feeling doubly irritated him now.

"I am confused, Mr. Flatman," Nicholas said. "Do you believe Miss Whitethorn-Litton murdered her lover, or do you still subscribe to the theory that Taunton surprised a thief and was killed by him?"

Flatman shook his head and laughed in a deprecating manner. "It is a puzzle, certainly, and I am relieved my only responsibility is to determine the manner of death. I will leave it to you and the magistrate to determine the guilt of those involved."

"And you, Mr. Silsbury? You are remarkably silent. What is your conclusion from all of this?" Nicholas asked.

Silsbury eyed him thoughtfully as he leaned forward and placed his empty cup and saucer on the low table in front of him. He sat back and once more stretched his arms out along the back of the settee. "It is my opinion that Lord Taunton was murdered by Miss Whitethorn-Litton."

"Why?"

"Three months ago, I overheard a discussion concerning Taunton's plans to marry. A few weeks later, Taunton confided to me that he was indeed considering marriage. He had recently celebrated his thirty-fifth birthday, and he was an earl, after all. He had to produce an heir at some point."

"So you believe he gave Miss Whitethorn-Litton her *congé*?" Nicholas tried to keep the anger out of his voice and maintain his detachment. Why did the thought that she might have murdered the earl bother him? He knew it was a distinct possibility, and he had no reason to defend her.

Silsbury smiled at him as if he knew precisely what Nicholas was thinking. "I suspect it strongly, very strongly, indeed."

"And what of you? Did he ask you to leave, as well?" Nicholas flung at him. The tips of his ears burned with anger.

"Why should he?" Despite Silsbury's careless tone, his eyes narrowed as he locked gazes with Nicholas. "He was my patron. One would presume he would maintain his interest in poetry regardless of his matrimonial state."

"Indeed, one might make that assumption," Nicholas agreed blandly.

In truth, he was beginning to suspect that the relationship between Mr. Silsbury and Lord Taunton might have been much more intimate and interesting than that between Miss Whitethorn-Litton and Lord Taunton: more than just a poor artist and his patron. The weight in his pocket reminded him that he might find some of the answers to these puzzles by sitting down with Taunton's journal and reading what the earl had been thinking before his untimely demise.

"I beg your pardon, gentlemen, but I fear I have an appointment." Mr. Flatman glanced at the brass clock clicking melodiously on the otherwise bare mantle above the fireplace. "In fact, I am late."

Silsbury stood, and Nicholas noted that he looked curiously relieved. Perhaps he wanted to avoid additional questioning.

"May I return tomorrow to take a more thorough look at that gown?" Nicholas asked.

"What could you possibly hope to gain from such an inspection?" Silsbury interrupted abruptly, cutting off Flatman's reply.

"I don't know. That is why I'd like the opportunity to examine it."

Flatman picked up the gown, his forehead wrinkling. "I could allow you to take it with you if you vow upon your honor to return it unharmed tomorrow morning. It is, after all, evidence in this case."

"Of course." Nicholas executed a half-bow and held out his right hand. He had not expected the generous and trusting gesture, and he studied Flatman's face.

The coroner's expression remained bland as he refolded the dress and handed it to him. "I shall not return until late this evening, and I am anxious to hear your opinion, Captain. In truth, although my jury will not concern itself with the identity of the culprit, I would like to gain an understanding of the circumstances surrounding Taunton's death. It is an ugly affair and would be better solved as soon as possible. There are more suspects than I am comfortable with and it needlessly complicates matters."

"I agree wholeheartedly, and thank you

for your faith in me. Would ten o'clock tomorrow morning be too early to return the garment?"

"Not for my day maid." Flatman led the way to the door and opened it. "If I am not available, she certainly will be. I will be sure to give her orders as to the disposition of the gown when you return it."

"Then I bid you both good day." Nicholas tucked the parcel under his arm and exited ahead of Mr. Silsbury.

Silsbury seemed disinclined to continue their conversation outside and bid him a curt adieu on the front steps before he hurried away. Nicholas watched him for a few minutes before he turned to make his way to his own set of apartments.

By the time he arrived at his front door, he felt as if his empty stomach was rubbing against his backbone. He was just about to explore the contents of the narrow pantry in his kitchen when a loud knock stopped him. When he opened the door, he discovered both Jack Jones and Sergeant Dalton standing outside.

"I see you found him," Nicholas commented to the boy, Jack.

"I told you I would and I'm a man of my word." Jack held out his hand, palm up, and eyed him expectantly.

"And did the two of you discover anything about a thief seen near Lord Taunton's townhouse?"

"That we did, Captain," Dalton replied, pushing the child to the right. "'Though it were two of them, not one."

Bracing his feet on the wooden floor outside the door, Jack held his ground. He pushed Dalton back with his elbow. Jack shook his open hand to remind Nicholas of the payment he clearly expected.

Nicholas pressed a sixpence into Jack Jones' grimy palm and eyed Sergeant Dalton. "Are you sure? Two thieves?"

The sergeant leaned forward on his crutch. "Yes. They arrested the two scoundrels yesterday eve. And I heard they still had a knife on them." He shook his head. "A right gaudy bauble from the sound of it."

So Flatman got the knife from the constables who arrested the thieves. At least that much made sense, and Flatman was also correct about one other aspect of the case: there were too many suspects. The thieves had the knife, but Miss Whitethorn-Litton had a bloody dress in her wardrobe.

How could the guilt of either party be established under such circumstances?

Jack glanced from the sergeant to Nicholas with an eager expression, clearly hoping to hear something he could use to earn another easy sixpence.

"Who were they?" Nicholas asked.

"I know!" Jack pushed his way forward slightly, trying to squeeze in front of the sergeant. He nearly toppled the one-legged man. However, before the sergeant fell backward, Jack grabbed his wrist. His good deed didn't obscure the fact that he was now positioned in front of Sergeant Dalton. "And I can tell you—for a price."

"Go on with you! I'll tell the captain what he wants to know, you flea-bitten pup. You've earned your coin so get on with you." Dalton leaned ever more precariously forward to block the boy once more.

"Come in, both of you." Nicholas stood aside and waved the pair through the door. When he took a deep breath and realized how fragrant they were, he breathed through his mouth, regretting his impulsive gesture. "I was about to have a slice of cheese and toasted bread—"

"And beer?" Jack interrupted, his brown eyes gleaming, appearing impossibly large in his thin face.

"I believe I have a few bottles," Nicholas answered dryly.

He turned toward the back reaches of his apartment where his small kitchen was located, trying not to glance around. He rarely had visitors, and he felt vulnerable when others looked around, assessing him and drawing their hasty conclusions from the sparse wooden furniture and stacks of books lining the walls.

The flat consisted of two floors in a building owned by his brother. Nicholas rented the space and before he had been there a month he had realized there was more space than he needed. However, the extra rooms allowed him to separate the area where he might entertain guests from the floor where he slept. Having his bedchamber on the upper floor seemed to provide him with more privacy, and that was something he desperately needed when he returned from Corunna, wounded and trying to learn how to live with his useless left arm.

The two floors gave him another advantage. Strange though it sounded, even the mere fact of having to go up and down the stairs gave him a sense of competence, as if a man who could climb stairs was not entirely disabled. Certainly it was minor, but it felt like a victory nonetheless in a life that had experienced too many defeats.

Reason enough to persuade him to rent from his brother.

"Have you no man to do for you?" The sergeant stared around at the Spartan furnishings, a V cutting into the skin between his brows. He ran his left hand over a small piecrust table and scowled at his fingertips.

Ignoring them, Jack had already taken a seat on a wooden chair near the fireplace. He kicked his heels against the chair legs and chewed hungrily on his lower lip. He clearly didn't care about Nicholas' domestic arrangements as long as there was food in the offing.

"I have not employed domestic staff as yet. A woman comes in twice a week to clean the flat. I make do." Nicholas rotated his head. His collar suddenly seemed too tight.

In truth, Dalton's question made him feel as if he had failed to meet a basic standard for men in his social circle. Gentlemen were not expected to do for themselves. He had always intended to hire a man of all work, but he kept avoiding the task, and he had no excuse he cared to offer.

"You need a batman." Dalton glanced around again and nodded. "Someone to keep things right and proper." Straightening, he moved to stand directly in front of Nicholas. "I could do it."

"You!" Nicholas exclaimed in surprise. The sergeant had only a single leg. Then Nicholas looked at his left arm and frowned. To be honest, the sergeant probably got around just as well as Nicholas. When the sergeant's shoulders sagged and he glanced away, flushing, Nicholas added, "I—well, yes. I have not had time to consider the issue, but I see your point. I could certainly use someone like you. When could you start?"

Dalton and Jack stared at him, round-eyed.

Jack recovered his senses first, at least his sense of speech, for he hopped up from the chair and said, "What about me, then?"

"What about you?" Nicholas struggled

not to laugh. He had the notion that he had suddenly gone from a staff consisting solely of one part-time woman to two full-time employees. Oddly enough, the idea didn't bother him as much as he suspected it should. He was lonely and had been for some time.

"If you're handing out the jobs, what about mine?" Jack asked.

"What can you do?"

"Now, Captain Ainsley," Dalton interrupted. "There's no need to hire a whole staff in an instant. You know nothing about the lad."

"He knows I found you, doesn't he?" Jack flung at him. "I didn't run off with his sixpence like he might a-feared I would." He risked a quick glance at Nicholas, seeking his concurrence. The vulnerability in his young face caught in Nicholas' gut.

"True enough," Nicholas agreed. "However, you must both realize that I..." He paused, unsure how to explain his situation. He wasn't a rich man himself despite his brother's wealth, and he hardly knew if this new career would support him. Certainly, the rent his brother charged for these quarters was negligible, but expanding his household and paying even minimal salaries might strain his wallet past its sad limit. "You may believe I am wealthier than I am."

"Is that all?" Dalton snorted. "I can guess your situation better than most." He plucked at

Nicholas' woolen sleeve. "Why look at your cuffs—threadbare—aren't they? Anyone can see you aren't what anyone would call rich, so you need someone to care for what you do have. I'd say a roof over my head is better than a piss-stinking alley, and I can make do better than most. And I can cook—probably better than you."

"Nonetheless, you'd expect a salary." Somehow, Nicholas managed not to glance down at the sleeves of his jacket. When he had dressed that morning, he thought this was his most presentable garment. It appeared he was mistaken.

"I believe a salary might be negotiable." Dalton smiled at him. "And agreed upon at a later date."

Jack, who had been studying first one man and then the other, objected, "Are you saying you won't be paying us?"

"You'll be lucky enough to get a bite to eat on the odd occasion." Dalton pushed the boy toward the front door. "And if you don't appreciate that, then there's the door, my lad. Go on with you and get out if the terms don't suit you."

A disappointed frown dragged the corners of Jack's mouth down. His grubby fingers disappeared into his pockets, twisting and straining the thin wool. "Was this your last sixpence, then? Do you need it back?"

"No." Nicholas laughed. "And I expect I

can come up with a few other sixpence once in a while, if pressed. You and the sergeant won't be totally without funds should you decide to accept positions here."

"How many sixpence and when?" Jack asked, amply proving he understood the priorities even if Nicholas and Sergeant Dalton didn't.

"None of your concern." Dalton shifted his crutch and nodded toward the hallway leading to the diminutive kitchen. "And we'd best wash up and prepare dinner for Captain Ainsley if you ever want to see another sixpence. Consider yourself lucky to have a coin in your pocket, my lad. It is more than you deserve."

Jack stuck his tongue out in reply, but he followed the sergeant obediently despite his high-pitched complaints about washing and the ill-effects of water on the constitution. He apparently held the belief that removing even a particle of dirt from his skin would lead inevitably to a protracted and painful death.

Left alone momentarily, Nicholas suffered a sudden flash of panic. Had he made a terrible decision? How could he possibly maintain his privacy with not one, but two servants living in his flat? How could he support them?

Well, if it were a mistake, he would find out soon enough. And while he didn't necessarily believe Sergeant Dalton's boast about his prowess as a chef, Nicholas was relatively sure that Dalton could not possibly be as bad a cook as he was. At least they all had a better than average chance at a decent meal.

While he waited to discover if Dalton the chef he claimed to be, Nicholas opened the package and took out the dress he had received from Flatman. He shook it out and draped it over his chair, angling it to catch the sunlight streaming through the window at his back.

The dark stains were clear enough in the harsh light. He picked up the hem to study it. The faint metallic odor of dried blood rose from the material, and he felt his stomach clench. He had seen so much blood and pain ... he could almost hear the screams and smell the sulfurous stench of the battlefield. Gritting his teeth, he shut off his memories, struggling to concentrate on the here-and-now.

Blood had soaked the fabric. As he had noted earlier, another spot in the rough shape of a knee stained the dress about a foot above the hem. The stains were not splatters from a violent attack or even fluid dripping from a wound. The material had wicked up the fresh blood pooled on the floor.

He examined the rest of the dress, holding up the bodice, sleeves, and cuffs to the window. Dust streaked some of the material, but there were no other signs of blood. Holding up the dress against him, he tried to imagine what must have happened, but he could not. The patterns did not make sense if Miss Whitethorn-

Litton had murdered Lord Taunton.

There had been no pool of blood on the rug or floor. The slender knife had caused mortal damage, but that damage was internal. The hilt had prevented most of the blood from escaping, so there was nothing for the hem to brush through or absorb. Even if she had knelt next to his body to determine if he had survived her blow, her knee would have remained mostly clean and dry.

So where had the stains come from?

It would be ironic indeed if she had murdered some other poor fellow while a stranger killed her lover.

He refolded the dress and laid it on top of the stack of books. If he wanted to discover the truth, he would have to question Miss Whitethorn-Litton again. The thought sent a burst of excitement through him. He frowned and gazed out of the window at the townhouse across the narrow alley.

If he was going to become a successful inquiry agent, he had to learn to maintain his objectivity.

When he finally turned away from the window, Nicholas was surprised to see a suspiciously solemn-faced Sergeant Dalton tottering out of the kitchen, closely followed by Jack. The child carried a large, wooden tray covered by a white cloth. The tip of his tongue peeped through his tight lips as he struggled to keep his burden level.

Nicholas quickly cleared off a rickety wooden table by the simple expedient of brushing his right arm over the dusty surface and knocking the books, papers, brass candlestick, and other odds and ends to the floor. As Jack placed the tray on the table in evident relief, Nicholas collected the wooden chair by the fireplace and placed it by the table. Two chairs. He glanced around and noticed a stool by the window. A waistcoat he was trying to repair draped the seat.

"Bring that stool over, Jack," he said. When the boy picked up the waistcoat and glanced around, he added impatiently, "Just put it on the floor."

With elaborate care, the boy folded the garment and placed it on the windowsill before returning with the stool. Since he had retrieved the piece of furniture, he seemed to suffer from the belief it was now his. Jack set it on the other side of the wooden armchair Nicholas stood behind and eased his hip over it. Legs dangling, Jack then leaned over the table and whipped the white cloth away to reveal the plates hidden beneath it.

Stomach rumbling, Nicholas sat in his chair at the head of the table. He studied the food with a critical eye before he waved to the sergeant. "Sit, Sergeant Dalton."

The sergeant gently propped his crutch against the table and sat down opposite Jack. He pressed his wrists against the edge of the table, hands fisted, and watched Nicholas expectantly.

Jack and Dalton had apparently located the pantry and managed to assemble a very acceptable meal from the meagre contents. Nicholas knew that the only bread was half of a stale loaf leftover from yesterday, but Dalton had sliced and toasted it to capture any remaining ghost of flavor. Then he had sliced the heel of a ham thinly and laid it on the bread, following it with some shaved cheddar. Dalton had placed the lot of it in front of the fire to melt and brown the cheese.

The fragrance of warm bread, ham, and melted cheese made Nicholas' stomach grumble anew.

Grinning, Jack took the lid off a bowl and pointed at the contents. "We found a few apples, too. The sergeant heated them with some sugar and crumbs from the bread. I tasted it. It's right good."

The sergeant flushed and grunted before busying himself placing glasses and brown bottles of ale in front of each of them. Task completed, he paused for a moment, his shaggy brows drawn down in concentration. Then he handed around plates and picked up a huge fork to serve each of them several slices of the toasted cheese and ham.

Perhaps it was simply his hunger, but Nicholas' mouth watered. When he bit into the first piece, he thought he had never tasted such delicious food in his life. A twinge of dismay pierced him when he glanced up to see all them eyeing the main platter.

Not even a stale crumb remained.

After a long sigh, the sergeant served up the pudding. The apples and sugar were welcome after the salty ham, and once more Nicholas wished he had spent a little more time filling his larder. Yesterday, shopping had seemed to be a ridiculous expenditure. He couldn't cook, and he was tired of cutting the mold off food to salvage a few bites before going to bed.

Now it appeared he had a cook, and cooks expected to have supplies.

He leaned back in his chair and eyed Dalton and then Jack. "So, gentlemen, back to the business at hand. Who were these two thieves and what do you know of their history?"

"Well, sir." Dalton picked a bit of ham out of his teeth and studied the empty plates in front of him. "It were a Mr. Albert Bottom and Mr. Richard Toddy. The pair of 'em were seen in Mayfair, a few blocks from Lord Taunton's townhouse just a bit after midnight."

"They had no business being there," Jack interrupted. "The watch seen 'em and said they had no business there."

"When they were apprehended, a knife— a knife of gold—was found in Mr. Toddy's pocket," Dalton said.

"Was anything else found on them? Any stolen items?" Nicholas asked.

Jack shook his head. "They said not. Just the knife. It were the one used to murder that earl, weren't it?"

"And what do you know of the two gentlemen?"

Sergeant Dalton shrugged, but Jack straightened, swinging his legs excitedly and kicking his heels against the chair's legs. Each time he bumped the chair, his pale hair puffed up on the breeze. An errant lock fell over his forehead into his brown eyes. "I know 'em."

"You?" Dalton eyed him. "What could you know about 'em?"

"I do know 'em. They was kind, that Mr. Bottom in particular. And he were helping me learn to read, though I didn't get far. He were a teacher, you know."

"A teacher?"

Jack nodded. "He were once, he told me. But he got caught thieving. He couldn't help himself, you understand. It were just small things, a spoon or a saucer or the like. He said he just saw the thing and couldn't help himself. It were like they called to him, and he couldn't rest until he put them in his pocket. So that school, they let him go, and he took up with Mr. Toddy."

"What do you know about Mr. Toddy?" Nicholas prompted him when he paused to take a sip of his ale.

"Oh, he's all right. Leastways he knows his way around London."

"You said the knife was in Mr. Toddy's pocket. Has he ever killed anyone?"

"No, sir," Jack said, his brows drawn down in concentration. "Leastways not that I've heard."

"What about fights?"

"No, sir, not Mr. Toddy. He were a cracksman pure and simple. Oh, he has a temper right enough, but he were more disposed to letting the watch take care of anyone who annoyed him, if you understand my meaning."

"By that I suppose you mean he would place stolen items where the watch would find them and ensure the watch searched in the right places to apprehend the villains," Nicholas murmured in a dry voice.

"There you are." Jack grinned and ran a finger over his plate to pick up any remaining crumbs. "I knew you was a bobbish one."

"Here, none of that cant talk, my fine pup," Dalton said sharply. "Speak proper or be quiet."

Nicholas shifted in his chair. "So would you judge that either of the men were violent?"

"No, sir, not Mr. Bottom." Jack pulled his lower lip. "I wouldn't want to be on the wrong side of Mr. Toddy, but only because I don't want nothing to do with the watch. Now them, well, you want to walk softly around them. Men of the law are like that—vengeful sorts—not soft and quiet like Mr. Bottom."

"So if he was not violent, how is it that

Mr. Toddy had a knife in his pocket?" Nicholas murmured to himself.

"Why he stole it, then, didn't he?" Jack's brows rose to hide under his shaggy hair.

Nicholas nodded. "And if he stole it, he might have seen who committed the murder. Considering your friend's predilection for exposing those who wrong him to the authorities, he might have thought he could use it in the future."

"Or he might have thought to pawn it," Dalton interrupted. "Seeing as how it was gold."

"The puzzle is why these two didn't pick up anything else." The more Nicholas considered it, the more certain he became that he needed to interview Bottom and Toddy.

Dalton shrugged and grabbed his crutch to struggle to his feet. "We don't know they didn't, do we? Come on, pup, and clear these away before they start to stink."

"And while you're washing the dishes, I suggest you both boil some water and take baths. There is a tin bath in the corner of the kitchen, by the fireplace. Use it." Nicholas stood and walked over to the window.

While Jack and Dalton collected the dishes with undue violence in retribution for his suggestion they bathe, he considered the facts. He had known thieves before and most were not murderers. Jack's assessment made sense to him. Given Nicholas' previous difficulties in thinking through a series of events relating to the burglary and the murder scene that made sense, he was fairly certain that Bottom and Toddy were innocent of the earl's death. The only conclusion that made sense given the facts indicated the two had come upon Lord Taunton's body after he had been murdered.

They had taken the knife and fled. Strange that they had taken the weapon, but perhaps the jewels and gold were too much to resist.

The real question was whether they saw the murderer or not.

Chapter Thirteen

3:40 PM October 24, 1821

"Mr. Toddy, wake up. Toddy!" Bottom shook his friend's shoulder, feeling a smoky curl of fear wreath him. The air in their dank cell smelled of blood, human waste, and most of all, sweaty desperation. "For God's sake, Toddy, please. You must wake up."

Toddy moaned and shifted slightly to move his arm off his chest. The limb flopped with a dull thud over the edge of his narrow cot and Bottom winced at the sound. Toddy breathed stentoriously and occasional fine droplets of blood sprayed over his chin.

Broken ribs, if not worse. Bottom swallowed a surge of panic. He'd begged the warden for a doctor, but he didn't have the funds to pay for one so the warden ignored his pleas. There had barely been enough coin in Bottom's pocket to buy a pot of beer, mutton soup, and loaf of bread.

If he didn't eat something, Toddy might never recover from his beating. Bottom glanced around their dim cell. What would he do if Toddy never regained consciousness? Gaol fever was common and even though they had not had their day in court and had not been formally convicted, they were in Newgate. That was bad enough.

He had no illusions. They would be lucky to be convicted of theft and transported. The knife found in Toddy's pocket meant they were more likely to hang for murder.

For the first time since he fell upon hard times, he wondered if transportation to Australia, or even Bermuda, might not be a better alternative than the life the two men led. A dozen years or so of hard labor and then new opportunities might open up for them. Yes, that would definitely be better than remaining here where they could be condemned to serve their time on one of the rotting hulks on the Thames. Neither of them would survive that.

He unwound the none-too-clean linen neckcloth from his neck and gently removed Toddy's worn, woolen jacket, waistcoat, and linen shirt. The livid bruises covering his ribs made Bottom catch his breath, but he pressed his lips together and wrapped the strip of linen around his friend's chest, hoping to bind the broken ribs and allow Toddy to heal.

When he was done, he eased Toddy's shirt down and smoothed his waistcoat and jacket over the wrinkled linen. The cell was chill and damp, and he could hear other prisoners coughing wetly in the cells around them. Bottom shivered and rubbed his arms, hoping the tattered clothing covering Toddy's thin body would provide a bit of warmth to the sick man. Toddy's lips looked bluish in the dim light, and Bottom pushed away the thought that his friend weighed little more than one of the children Bottom had taught before fate had caught and punished him.

"Toddy, please. We've soup and bread here. You must eat to keep up your strength." He gave his friend a few light slaps on his whiskery cheek.

When Toddy's eyes finally fluttered, Bottom helped raise him a bit, frightened at the light, bony feel of his back. He felt as light as a sparrow. Toddy had always been whipcord strong despite his thinness. Now, he felt as if there were no muscles left, just skin covering his brittle bones.

Toddy groaned again and tried to twist out of Bottom's grip, but when he moved, his moan deepened. "Leave off," he whispered.

"No," Bottom replied, the firmness in his voice surprising even him. "You have to eat. You promised to stand by me, and I'm holding you to it, Mr. Toddy. I've good soup here and you can just eat it while it's hot. Never fear, I'll keep you upright."

His hand shook and he slopped a little of the barely warm soup on Toddy's jacket, but he managed to press a beaker of it to the sick man's pallid lips. Despite Toddy's weak protests, Bottom poured a few drops into his mouth and waited for him to swallow.

Slowly and with infinite patience, Bottom eased nourishment down Toddy's thin throat, refusing to give up the hope that they would find a way to survive. They had always managed before. They simply had to manage it now.

Chapter Fourteen

6:00 PM October 24, 1821

The prison keeper unlocked the cell door and stood aside as Nicholas ducked his head and entered. The thick, foul air caught in his throat.

"Ten minutes, Captain Ainsley. No more." He let the door swing shut behind Nicholas.

Nicholas stiffened, but he heard no sound of a key turning in the lock. He let out a long breath and watched as the guard checked the watch he carried in his pocket before he walked away. Inside the cell, Nicholas held up the lantern the guard had provided to him.

One man sat hunched on the floor. He leaned against a poorly made wooden cot where the figure of another man lay under a thin woolen blanket. Next to the bed were several dishes containing the remains of a loaf of bread, some sort of unappetizing soup or stew, and a container of beer. When Nicholas took a step forward, the man on the floor lumbered to his feet, using the edge of the cot to steady himself.

"Which one of you is Mr. Bottom?" Nicholas asked.

The standing man shifted his feet and he blinked rapidly in the light from the lantern. His shaking hands flew to his neck before smoothing the lapels of his jacket. He was missing his neckcloth and even in the dim light, his pale face and red-rimmed eyes bore the marks of fear.

"I'm Albert Bottom, sir."

Nicholas set the lantern down and reached forward to shake his hand. After a moment's hesitation, Bottom returned his handshake with a surprisingly firm grip.

"I take it, then, that this is Mr. Toddy?"

"Yes, sir. Mr. Toddy is indisposed, as you can see."

"What is wrong with him?"

Bottom cast a frowning glance at his friend. He pulled on his lower lip as he returned his attention to Nicholas. "He had an unfortunate mishap when we were apprehended."

The watch had beaten him.

Nicholas felt his jaw tighten. "I see. Well, I am Captain Ainsley. The family of Lord Taunton has asked me to investigate his murder."

Bottom seemed to sway, his hands flapping uselessly at his sides. Nicholas reached out, fearing the man would faint at his feet.

However, Bottom recovered quickly, though his gray face grew even more sickly-colored under the greasy sheen of sweat. "We never hurt a soul, Captain Ainsley. You must believe me. We would never do such a terrible thing."

"Your associate had a knife on him when you were apprehended, a knife that came from Lord Taunton's household. How do you explain that if you did not kill him?"

"He was dead before we arrived! I swear it, sir. And I never wanted to touch the thing, but..." His involuntary glance at Toddy spoke volumes.

"What rooms did you enter?"

"Rooms?" Bottom stared at him, once more pulling on his lower lip. "Rooms?"

"Yes. You entered the earl's house. Illegally, I might add. What rooms did you explore?"

"Just the one. Just his lordship's bedchamber."

If he wanted the truth, he had to allow Bottom to provide the details without providing any information that would reveal how much he already knew. "How did you enter if you only visited that one room?"

"The ladder, sir. There had been painters at the earl's townhouse earlier. They left a ladder behind. We used it to climb up to the master bedchamber on the second floor."

"Why would you risk such a thing? Surely you knew the earl was in residence."

"Yes, but Toddy and I had been watching the house for some time. The earl had habits—particular habits—and we believed his room would be empty for an hour or two."

Nicholas studied Bottom. The man stood hunched with his head forward, wringing his hands as if fearing Nicholas was prepared to get the truth out of him by any physical means necessary.

The thought sickened and angered him. "What were these particular habits you were you relying on?"

"We watched the lights and shadows, sir. Almost every night he would go into his room for twenty minutes or so, and then he would go down the hall to another room. He stayed there for an hour or so, sometimes all night."

Had Lord Taunton been in the habit of visiting Miss Whitethorn-Litton? The thought irritated Nicholas although he should have expected it. She was his mistress after all.

"How did you know this? How could you be sure?"

"The lights, sir. And shadows, as I said. You could see him moving about and the light appearing and then disappearing."

"Surely he drew the curtains at night."

"Not until he retired. Some nights, the curtains in the master bedchamber were never drawn. That's how we knew he spent the night elsewhere on many occasions."

"And how do you know he went to another bedchamber?"

"He never left the townhouse, and we would see the lights brighten in another room, sir.

"What time was this?"

"Near midnight I should imagine. Unless he went out, he always had the same routine."

"I see." Nicholas clasped the wrist of his dead hand, considering what the earl's habits might have been. He had been a man of regular habits, it appeared. Nicholas filed the information away. "So what happened the night you entered his house?"

"Well, sir, as I mentioned, we used the ladder and climbed up to the earl's bedchamber. There was firelight, but someone with a lamp or candle had gone out earlier, so we believed the earl had gone to another room as he usually does. Unfortunately, when we, er, glanced around, we found his lordship on the floor in front of the fireplace. It was a terrible sight, sir, with that knife sticking out of his back."

"Did you notice anything broken or out of place?"

Bottom shook his head, his hands gripping his lapels and pulling on them. Anxiety deepened the lines on his face. "No, sir. That was certainly peculiar, wasn't it? There was no sign of any struggle, but then, he was stabbed in the back, wasn't he? He wouldn't have known what was happening until it was too late."

"And what did you do when you discovered him?"

"I, er, searched for signs of life." He sighed. "His spirit had fled and his flesh was already growing cold. There was nothing we could do."

"Except steal? What did you take?"

"Mr. Toddy thought the knife was—well, there was a ruby and the hilt was gold. I couldn't convince him it would be bad luck. And as

Toddy observed, the earl had passed away and there was nothing we could do for him."

"So Mr. Toddy took the knife and what did you take?"

"Me, sir?"

"Yes. You cannot convince me that you did not take advantage of the situation. You were already there, and the earl was dead. What did you take?"

Bottom flushed and glanced at his friend as if seeking a reason to delay. "I took a few coins. That's all."

"Where are they?"

"Gone." Bottom's mouth thinned as he pressed his lips together. "We don't even have the funds to acquire the services of a physician for Mr. Toddy, or another meal if it comes to it. We may be able to borrow a few pence from some other prisoners to purchase a loaf of bread and bowl of soup, but certainly not much more."

So the watch had beaten Toddy and then to add insult to injury, robbed him. Sadly, the harsh actions of the authorities didn't surprise Nicholas. Times were difficult for everyone and the watch earned little enough. However, Bottom's reticence in blaming them showed a great deal of charity and cunning on his part. He obviously did not want to create enemies unnecessarily.

"Did you see anyone?"

"See anyone?" Bottom's mouth gaped as he stared at him.

Amy Corwin

"Yes. Either before you entered the house or afterward. Did you see anyone enter or leave the premises?"

Bottom thought for a minute, shuffling his feet over the cold floor. Even Nicholas could feel the chill penetrating the soles of his boots. He cast a measuring glance at Toddy. How could an injured man survive this dismal place? It seemed impossible.

"Well, sir, Mr. Toddy might have."

"What do you mean? Did he see anyone or not?"

"He mentioned it, sir, when we were moving the ladder."

"Wake him up, then. I need to question him."

"I'm sorry sir, but he's ill. I doubt he can answer your questions when he could barely eat a few mouthfuls earlier."

"Then what precisely did he say to you?"

"That he saw a woman, or what looked like a woman in a long cloak."

Had they seen Miss Whitethorn-Litton? She said she had gone out, perhaps they had seen her leave.

But then, that meant she had told the truth about being absent from the townhouse that night. And if she had just murdered her lover, could she truly go out for the evening? And why, for heaven's sake, would she come back? Wouldn't she flee, fearing she would be caught and hung for his murder?

How could she return and sleep in a room just down the hall from the master bedchamber where the earl's body remained?

Unless she had gone out to try to create an alibi for herself. Even that notion seemed ridiculous. If she had gone out to create an alibi, she would have ensured that she had witnesses. She would not keep her friends' identities secret.

All of which seemed to support the simple explanation that she had gone out as she said and had not been in the townhouse when Lord Taunton died.

"Did she leave through the front door?" Nicholas asked.

"No, sir. She used the servant's entrance at the back. I remember Mr. Toddy saying she must have been a maid sneaking out for a dalliance."

"Is it possible he saw a man in a cloak?"

"As I did not get a clear look, I can't say, sir. You must ask Mr. Toddy."

"But did he see her clearly enough to know? Did he see her face? Would he recognize her again, or know if he observed a man or a woman?"

"I believe he saw the figure quite clearly, but I don't know." A sly expression crossed his face. "If he had the care of a physician and were to recover, he might be able to answer your questions. It is unfortunate that we do not have the funds to pay for his care."

Even if Toddy recovered and could

identify the mystery woman either as Miss Whitethorn-Litton or a servant, Nicholas had to admit that the two thieves were not trustworthy witnesses. The jury might not consider their testimony credible. Despite knowing this, he needed to know if another woman was involved.

If it was a maid out for a dalliance as Toddy opined, at least he could establish that much.

He nodded. "Is there anything else?"

"No, sir. But Mr. Toddy might have more information if he were in a position to present it."

"I understand." Nicholas smiled as he dug out his rapidly shrinking leather purse. He took out a few coins and held them out to Bottom. "For your meals. I will make arrangements with the prison officials to provide medical care. Send word to me when Mr. Toddy recovers enough to speak."

Bottom's hand shook as he accepted the coins. "Yes, sir, and thank you. I shall send word immediately."

Nicholas opened the door and walked out to find the guard a few feet away. After paying him and providing additional funds for a physician, Nicholas left, glad to get outside of the thick, suffocating walls of Newgate.

Thinking he could use some of the information Bottom had shared, he headed toward the earl's townhouse in Mayfair. The streets were dark between the pools of dim light cast by the streetlamps. He increased his pace, aware of stealthy movements in the Stygian depths of the alleys he passed. Although he carried a knife at his belt and a stout walking stick, with only one useful arm, he would be no match for footpads and others who thought he looked likely to carry a few bob in his pocket.

The dark sky oppressed him despite the twinkling of the distant stars. He hated the sense of being observed as he walked, his boots clicking loudly over the uneven walkway. Eyes glowed at the mouth of the alley on his left. A half-starved dog peered at him, baring its teeth before disappearing into the darkness when Nicholas glanced its way.

It was late, but he could not return to his rooms yet. He had too little to show for his efforts thus far. The earl's younger brother would be arriving soon, and Nicholas had only one more day before the coroner's inquest. If they did not uncover the culprit, there was every likelihood that either the two thieves or Miss Whitethorn-Litton would be indicted for the sake of expediency, just as Mr. Flatman feared.

Nicholas wanted justice, not expedience, but he knew he did not have sufficient evidence to prove the innocence or guilt of anyone with the possible exception of Miss Whitethorn-Litton. The facts were not in her favor. Her dress had blood on it and the knife used to kill her lover was apparently hers as well. Most would consider that sufficient to damn her.

Could she convince the jury that there was insufficient blood pooled at the scene to account for the stains on her dress? They would have to weigh that against her position as Lord Taunton's mistress and his supposedly stated desire to be rid of her in order to marry. While most jurymen would be reluctant to believe any female capable of such a heinous crime, the fact that she lacked a reputation as a decent woman would weigh against her.

He could argue what he believed to be the truth about the blood stains, however that would serve her better if she would confess how her attire became stained. The vital fluid had soaked into the material from the outside, not from the inside, so any tales she might spin about monthly courses would be pure fiction.

And the knife, well, that would be difficult to explain away if what Silsbury said were true. Who else would know she had the knife? Had she noticed it missing and said anything to anyone concerning the loss of the weapon?

He could only hope she was at home and ready to reveal the truth. With a rueful grin, he amended that wish to include the fortitude not to be disappointed if the truth she revealed was that she had, indeed, murdered her lover.

When he paused at a street corner, he realized he was already nearing Taunton's townhouse. He rounded the corner and approached the front door only to stumble to a halt. He stared in surprise.

A cluster of people stood in the open doorway. Even from where Nicholas stood, he could hear the buzzing sounds of their argument. A member of the local watch blocked the walkway and waved his staff around in a futile gesture to restore order. Walking rapidly, Nicholas arrived in time to witness Silsbury maliciously knock Miss Whitethorn-Litton off the middle step with his elbow.

She threw out her arms for balance and tried to catch Silsbury's sleeve. Her hand missed. With a small scream, she fell off the step and landed on her feet near the edge of the fountain. She wavered there for a moment, her arms windmilling. She almost appeared to regain her balance, but then her backward momentum grew too much to overcome.

The marble edge of the fountain caught her in the back of her knees. She went down, splashing into the cold water.

There was a moment of silence. Glancing around, Silsbury caught Nicholas' gaze. With deliberate insouciance, he seated his tall hat on his head, descended the stairs, and strolled away into the shadows in the opposite direction. As he hurried away, Nicholas noted a heavy, leather portmanteau clutched in Silsbury's hand.

Another small valise and a bandbox stood on the top step. As he watched, the front door of the townhouse closed with a snap.

Something was terribly wrong.

"I'm sorry, Miss." A watchman extended his hand to Miss Whitethorn-Litton. "But you'll have to come with me."

She glared at his hand as she struggled to stand up. Her drenched skirts weighed her down, preventing her from escaping the icy water. When she caught sight of Nicholas, she actually leaned back into the fountain. Using her hands as scoops, she poured additional water over herself as if bathing on a hot summer day.

"Come on out of there, Miss," the watchman said in a firmer voice. "You're making a right spectacle of yourself, and that's the truth. Now you just come with me, quiet and lady-like, and make the best of it. We all have to make the best of it, don't we?"

"What's going on here?" Nicholas asked abruptly, putting one booted foot on the bottom step of the front stairs.

"Nothing that concerns you, sir," the watchman said.

"I'm Captain Ainsley and this matter does concern me. So I ask you again, Mr.—what did you say your name was?"

"Lambert, sir."

"Well, Mr. Lambert, will you explain?"

"I can. Mr. Croftson arrived an hour ago and asked these two to vacate the premises."

"And what is your role here?"

"Keeping the peace, sir. I'm to take this young lady to the workhouse, or so says Mr. Croftson."

"Mr. Croftson told you to escort her to the workhouse?" Nicholas asked, appalled. "Did he tell you so himself?"

"Him?" Lambert snorted with derision as he jerked his staff toward the front door. "'Course not. His butler, that starchy old Kirby, gave me my orders. Said she had no place else to go and might as well be delivered where she'd end up anyway. Though how any of this is your business is a mystery to me."

"There is nothing mysterious about it. This lady is—" He caught Miss Whitethorn-Litton's glance and the panic in her gaze made him say the first thing that came to mind, "my sister." When her mouth gaped at his rash claim, he added sardonically, "And I'm embarrassed to say, she is quite mad."

"Your sister!" Lambert looked from Nicholas to Miss Whitethorn-Litton and then back, slapping his staff against his leg. "I'm very sorry, sir. I was unaware that she had a brother to take responsibility for her."

"As was I," he quipped as she frowned at him, unable to resist the unexpected impulse to tease her. "But then, it's understandable, isn't it? One doesn't want to discuss such things."

"No, of course not, sir. Will you be taking charge of her, then?"

She finally managed to stand, although she remained in the fountain, water dripping steadily from her hair and gown. In the fitful light from the townhouse windows and the gas lamp at the corner, she looked for all the world like a naiad who had lost her native stream and was trying to make do with a small fountain.

"I will indeed. I believe there will be no need to escort anyone to the workhouse." He caught her gaze and smiled. "And there will be no more disruption of the peace."

"I believe I can speak for myself," she interrupted.

Lambert ignored her, concentrating instead upon Nicholas. "Will you need assistance getting her out of the fountain, sir?"

"Why don't you ask me if I would like some assistance?" she asked, her voice rising.

"I don't believe so," Nicholas replied to Lambert. "Did I mention that she is as mad as a hatter?"

"You did, sir. Though you hardly needed to tell me, considering."

"Considering?" Her voice rose ominously.

"Yes, I suppose it is fairly obvious. She was never one to shun notoriety." As Nicholas watched, her expression shifted from annoyed to thoughtful. She stared at his mouth. When she glanced up, her eyes twinkled. The change in her expression made him grin in return. He could guess the direction her retaliation might take. "I feel obliged to mention that she believes she is Lord Byron and that I am Lady Caroline Lamb."

"Lord Byron?" Lambert repeated, clearly

confused as he glanced from Nicholas to Miss Whitethorn-Litton. "Didn't you intend to say she thinks she is Lady Caroline Lamb?"

"No. Definitely Lord Byron," Nicholas said. "Did I mention that she's mad?"

"Indeed, sir," his dubious tone indicated he was beginning to suspect Nicholas was jesting. "Shall we assist your sister, then?"

"Yes. It does appear to be a bit cold for a public bath, doesn't it?" Nicholas nodded to him and stepped down to stand at the base of the fountain. "Are you ready to climb out of that fountain or do you need another few minutes?"

She stretched out her arms toward Nicholas, and he obligingly put his right arm around her narrow waist to lift her out. Icy water sloshed over his boots as she grabbed his shoulders and scrambled over the rim. He flinched at the chill dampness as it soaked into his trousers.

When her feet touched the ground, instead of releasing her hold on him, she tightened her grip and pressed against him to ensure that every inch from his shoulders to his toes was properly drenched.

"I should thank you properly, dearest." She eyed Nicholas and then the watch officer. A bland smile stretched her blue-lipped mouth before she laced her hands behind Nicholas' head and kissed him soundly on the lips.

"A-hem. Well yes, there we are, then. That's done, and I ought to be on my way."

Lambert's face flushed visibly despite the poor light. Without waiting for Nicholas' reply, he walked away rapidly, his stout form moving from one pool of light to the other until he disappeared around the corner of the townhouse.

"I can not believe he did not arrest me." She pushed Nicholas away and climbed the stairs to pick up the valise and bandbox.

"Perhaps he believed me when I told him you were mad."

She turned to stare down at him, the bandbox dangling from its ribbon to hit her on the knee. "Yes, I heard. I simply can not understand why he believed you."

"You can not?" He laughed. "He was quite sold that you believe you are Lord Byron."

"I should have thought he would believe you are the one who is quite mad. Why should I be Lord Byron? Why couldn't I be Lady Caroline?"

"Any lady might believe she is Lady Caroline, but only a madwoman would believe she is Lord Byron."

"Well, if I wasn't insane before, I certainly am now." She jerked the bandbox, making it thump more rapidly against her leg. "How could you do such a thing?"

"I must admit that I did so in anticipation of your somewhat tempestuous action when I helped you out of the fountain." He grinned, remembering the taste of her icy lips.

"But for heaven's sake, why Lord Byron and Lady Caroline?"

"Well, I'd previously explained to Mr. Lambert that we were brother and sister. I hoped to forestall any unpleasantness about our exact relationship."

"They were only half-brother and sister," she objected, her eyes glinting in the darkness.

"True, and we are even less closely related. However, we needed some relationship to permit me to keep you out of the workhouse considering that Mr. Lambert seemed determined to escort you there. It also seemed to be one of the better ways to preserve your reputation when I escorted you home."

"I'm not sure I prefer to be thought mad."

"Better mad than bad, trust me. Now if you feel you've exhausted the possibilities of these stairs and fountain, would you like to depart?"

She slowly descended the remaining two steps and then stopped on the walkway next to him. Her silence revealed that she was no longer in a teasing mood. In fact, from what he could see through the shadows surrounding her, she looked wet, cold, and utterly miserable. Water dripped incessantly from the hem of her dress and splashed on the walkway.

Without speaking, he shrugged out of his jacket. He wrapped it around her as she shivered and glanced around, clearly unsure what course she should take.

Amy Corwin

"What happened, Miss Whitethorn-
Litton? Mr. Lambert indicated that Mr. Croftson
had arrived, but I know little beyond that."

Her lips, still tinged blue, curved into a
bleak smile. "Please, call me Kathryn. After all,
we are brother and sister."

"I would be honored to do so." He
executed a small bow. "And I am Nicholas."

"Lovely." She sighed and shifted the
valise from one hand to the other before
Nicholas gently removed it from her grasp. She
pushed the ribbons of the bandbox further up
her arm. "In truth, there is not much more to
add. Mr. Croftson arrived with his wife and
children a few hours ago. He summarily
removed both Harry and myself with the remark
that he believed we would be an unhealthy
influence on his loathsome offspring."

"He said his children were loathsome?"

A fleeting smile curved her mouth. "No. I
added the adjective, and I believe it to be
completely accurate. When I was packing, I
heard one of them screaming as it ran down the
hallway, having a tantrum because there were
insufficient sweets in the nursery. I pity poor
Nancy and the rest of the staff. They are not used
to children."

"No, I don't suppose they are." He
prodded her gently with his bent elbow until he
felt her slip her frozen hand into the crook of his
right arm. Once again, he was aware of his
disablement as he awkwardly maneuvered his

walking stick to avoid hitting her. "Do you have a destination in mind?"

"The workhouse?" Bitterness darkened her voice. "It should be good enough since I doubt I will remain there long. I believe Harry has been diligent in his efforts to implicate me in the earl's murder."

"I would not take advantage of your situation or leave you in the tender mercies of the workhouse," he said slowly as he considered the matter. "Have you no female friend you could visit for a few weeks?"

She shook her head as they walked. "None that would wish to invite me in at this time of night."

"Do not take this amiss, but there is an empty flat that I know of. My brother owns the building, and you might be able to arrange to rent the rooms."

"You mean by becoming his mistress? Am I so repulsive that even you cannot stomach the thought of bedding me and instead must throw me at your brother's head?"

"No, that is not my meaning." He brought her up short, anger smoldering in his gut. *Even you.* The words burned inside him. Apparently, she had not forgotten that his left arm hung useless at his side. She assumed that his injuries meant he could not manage a mistress.

Only his sense of honor kept him from making a rash statement. *I am as competent as the next man.* The thought startled him.

"Then how do you expect me to pay? I have nothing but a few dresses and a small purse."

"Surely Lord Taunton must have provided you with an allowance? Jewels?"

She laughed. "Certainly. But his brother took care to take possession of any baubles his brother mistakenly showered upon me. I have enough for a few nights lodging perhaps, but that is all." She flicked a sideways glance at him, her mouth hidden behind the collar of his jacket. "You understand Mr. Lambert's wisdom, now, in recommending the workhouse. It is either that, or I keep walking until I arrive in Whitechapel. I have enough to live on for a while, and I may be able to earn a few more pence to pay for a place to sleep if other men don't find me too repulsive. Unless you have need of a maid? I'm afraid I don't have any references."

"Don't be ridiculous." He gritted his teeth, angry with himself that he couldn't seem to think of a reasonable arrangement. There had to be a solution, but if there was, he couldn't see it. He could not jeopardize the investigation by supporting her himself, particularly when he suspected the authorities were a hair's breadth away from arresting her.

He was reluctant to force her to take a room alone, draining whatever meager funds she had managed to save. And he could not abandon her on the streets of London.

His thoughts raced, always returning to the same starting point like horses circling around a racetrack.

Did he truly mean to harbor a murderess? It went against his better judgment but at that moment, he could not bring himself to do anything else.

Chapter Fifteen

8:40 PM October 24, 1821

Kathryn glanced sideways at Nicholas, trying not to feel as if he were a knight riding to her rescue. A thoughtful frown creased his forehead, and he hurried her along as if he knew a destination where she would be safe.

Or perhaps he was just cold without his jacket. She shivered as her wet skirts slapped against her ankles. Icy water squelched from her thin shoes. The night air was cold, with a sharp edge that bit through her wet clothing despite Nicholas' heavy woolen jacket. The fabric smelled faintly of smoke and perspiration, and she breathed more deeply. The scent filled her with a sense of security and a longing to lean against him and raise her face to his.

She clutched the garment more tightly around her neck with one hand as she gripped his elbow with the other. His skin felt warm, almost hot, through the thin linen of his shirtsleeves.

"You must be cold," she said, breaking the silence.

"It is of no importance."

"Where are we going?"

He brought them up short at a corner of Compton Street, waiting for a hansom cab to clatter past. "You must have friends. You said you were out with them the evening Lord Taunton passed away. Surely one of them could provide you with a place to sleep for at least one night."

"I already explained: none of them want to see me on their doorstep." She thought of Mary Dudley and Rose Mardling. Frustration with the limitations imposed upon women filled her.

Isolation surrounded her with walls of ice, segregating her from the rest of London, from the warmth of life. Taunton hadn't purposely prevented her from forming friendships, but he might as well have. Her disreputable reputation meant that most respectable women shunned her. Her situation had never seemed so desperately lonely, and her heart contracted hollowly in her chest.

She raised her chin and eyed Nicholas' handsome profile. If decorum held no answers, perhaps boldness did. "Perhaps I should stay with you."

"Me?" He stared at her as if he thought she had suddenly grown as mad as he had claimed earlier to Mr. Lambert.

"Yes." She shrugged. When a gap between the carriages presented itself, she tugged his arm. She gingerly stepped over the damp cobblestones, pulling him with her. "Why not?"

"Surely you are intelligent enough to realize why that would be highly inappropriate." The light clatter of a phaeton barreling around the corner drew his gaze away from her.

He glanced up at the vehicle, jerked his arm out of her grasp, and slipped his arm around her waist. The valise and walking stick he held awkwardly in his hand bumped her hip as he hauled her forward through the small gap in the traffic. The horse's sharp hooves brushed the hem of her skirt as the two of them scrambled breathlessly to the safety of the walkway opposite.

Kathryn glanced over her shoulder. The driver of the phaeton never even looked her way. Whip in hand, he urged his horse to gallop ever faster along Compton Street as if the hounds of Hell were chasing him through the darkness. She might as well have been a discarded newspaper fluttering in the gutter for all the attention she received.

Edging closer to Nicholas, she slipped her hand around his elbow again before she looked up at him. "I don't understand why you believe it would be inappropriate. I have no reputation to consider. What other reason could there be?"

"I'm investigating Lord Taunton's death." His gruff voice warned her that she had ignored the obvious.

"If you believe I murdered him, then why don't you save yourself a great deal of trouble and simply escort me to Newgate? I'm sure they would be delighted to provide me with a room for the night. And many more nights to come."

She felt his arm stiffen before he asked

coolly, "Are you confessing? Did you kill him?"

"No." She sighed. "I had no reason to murder him and every reason not to. His death was a tragedy, not just for his family, but for me, as well. I lost a friend and my sole means of support. If he were alive, I would still be safely ensconced in my comfortable bed in his townhouse."

"Surely not." Despite the darkness obscuring his features, she could hear the smile in his voice. "It is barely nine at night. It's a trifle early to retire, isn't it?"

She tried to laugh and lighten her bleak mood. "Perhaps. But my point is that his death has upset everything. I don't know what I will do now."

"I wouldn't worry overmuch. You are young and attractive. Surely you will marry."

"Surely, indeed. Who would have me?"

"Other women in your position have married."

"With no dowry?"

"There are many men who would overlook a lack of fortune. Think of the Gunning sisters."

"Would you marry such a woman?"

He shook his head. "That question is inappropriate as you well know. There can be no appearance of impropriety if I am to prove you innocent."

"Then you believe I am innocent?" Hope fluttered through her, only to die abruptly in the silence that greeted her remark. The air felt colder than ever as she pulled his jacket more tightly around her shoulders.

"I would like to believe you are innocent," he said at last.

"But you do not."

Silence.

Then he cleared his throat. "May I ask you some questions?"

"Of course." She shrugged. "I can hardly prevent you from doing so, can I?"

"The authorities have located the knife used to kill Taunton. It was a stiletto with a handle chased in gold and embedded with a ruby. Mr. Silsbury identified it as yours. Does it sound like a knife you owned?"

"Yes."

"Can you explain how it came to be used in this crime?"

"No, I cannot." Bitterness tasted sour in her mouth. She nodded, uncaring. "If that stiletto was used, then it was indeed mine. Taunton designed one such as you described and gave it to me. The knife was created to slip into the front of my corset so that the ruby and gold would show at my neckline as if it were a jeweled broach. He thought the device would be amusing and insisted I wear it to protect myself when I went out at night."

"He must have cared a great deal for you to devise such an expensive gift."

"I daresay. It proved how clever and

generous he was, at any rate. That was the point of the gift." The muscles in her jaw clenched.

"I see, and I'm sorry." Nicholas' thoughtful silence tightened her nerves until she wanted to scream.

Suddenly, she didn't want his sympathy or his understanding. She just wanted someone—anyone—to treat her as if she mattered more than a bauble she wore.

Just when she turned her head to say something, he asked, "Was the stiletto missing? Stolen?"

He was obviously searching for some excuse for her.

While she could appreciate the sentiment, it only increased her desperation. Why couldn't he simply believe her?

"No." Her voice rang, hard and bitter with anger. "I was not aware that it was missing. I suppose it is obvious that if it served as the murder weapon, it must have been stolen. I certainly did not use it against Lord Taunton." She frowned. "And it was not among my things when Mr. Croftson supervised my packing and removal."

"When was the last time you saw it?"

"To be truthful, I don't know. I—I did not like it. It was gaudy and frankly, ugly."

"Well think, will you?" The muscles in his arm tightened under her hand.

"I am thinking! I wore it once and then put it away in my wardrobe. I have not looked for it since."

"Who knew you had it?"

"Well, Lord Taunton, of course, and Harry. And Taunton's friends. He had me model it during one of his supper parties at Wrexley Hall." She blushed again, remembering her mortification when Taunton had thrust his fingers into her bodice to draw out the stiletto. He had laughed and elbowed her away to display it to his glittering throng of guests. Since the jeweled hilt had fooled many of them into believing the piece was merely a brooch fastened to her bodice, they were all amused to discover it was a deadly weapon, instead.

"What friends? Who were they?"

"Just *friends*. Why do you pester me so?"

"Your life may depend upon your answers. Try to remember."

A sharp pain throbbed from one temple to the other. She rubbed her stiff, icy fingers against her forehead. "Well, Mr. and Mrs. Mardling were there, along with Rose." She caught Nicholas' glance. "Rose is their daughter." And Rose had been as amused as the rest of them until Kathryn ran back to her room, unable to face Lord Taunton's guests any longer. "Harry was there, of course, and several other young men. Mr. and Mrs. Dudley attended, along with their daughter, Mary." The pounding in her head increased. "There were several others..." Slowly she went through the list of attendees, rattling off the names of people she never wanted to see again.

Except Mary and Rose. She wondered how they were, if the two girls would still speak to her now that she had lost her usefulness in bringing them to Lord Taunton's attention. She'd been so grateful to Rose when she had come up to Kathryn's room later that dreadful evening, dragging Mary along with her, to see if Kathryn were well. Rose had assured her that no one had been laughing at her. The two girls had been quick to agree with Kathryn that the stiletto was a ridiculous conceit that would be better off left in the bottom drawer of her wardrobe, although Mary's lingering glance belied her words.

Even if Kathryn didn't quite believe Rose's comforting words, she was moved by Rose's insistence on making friends with Kathryn, even knowing that Mr. Mardling only encouraged it in hopes that Taunton would notice Rose. Rose even surprised her by seeking her out the very next day while Taunton was out riding with the men and would therefore not notice what the women did. The two girls had subsequently established an almost daily routine that Kathryn looked forward to when most of the older women ignored her.

"Then a number of people knew about the stiletto," Nicholas commented at last. "The question would therefore be: did anyone visit you in your room or otherwise have access to the knife?"

"All the maids and any of Taunton's guests may have done so if I were elsewhere." She shrugged. Although Nicholas was trying to assist her, she was realistic enough to realize how futile his efforts were. In truth, anyone could have removed the knife at any time after that last disastrous night when she had worn the thing. "Is the stiletto the only evidence against me?"

"There was also a dress."

She froze in mid-step, jerking Nicholas to a halt beside her. The stained dress she had worn the night Mary had attempted to obtain an abortion had gone missing. Was that their final proof that she was involved in this murder? She stared ahead at the dark street, still busy with people from all walks of life hurrying home. Her eyes fastened on the lamp lighter ahead. The golden glow from the gas lamp he lit did little to dispel the sooty mist beginning to fill the streets. Her cold feet ached from the icy cobbles pressing against the soles of her thin shoes, but she barely noticed her discomfort in her despair.

She had been so shocked by Taunton's death that she had forgotten about the garment. Now, that dress, stained with Mary's blood, could be Katheryn's undoing, one way or the other.

"Tell me about the gown." Nicholas voice was soft, almost apologetic.

"I can't." She choked. "I promised."

"Whose blood is on it?"

"I can't tell you, I can't explain. I promised I would not."

"Then tell me one thing: is it Lord Taunton's blood?"

"No, of course not! How could it be?" Her hand tightened on his forearm. If she let him go, would he abandon her here, alone in the icy mist?

"I did not think it was, but I had to be sure."

"You're taking my word for it?" She stared at him in wonder.

"Yes. I will take your word for it if you tell me one more thing: is the blood a woman's blood?"

"Yes," she whispered. Forgive me, Mary. I'm so sorry, so sorry about everything.

Leaning forward slightly, Nicholas guided her around the next corner. The lamp lighter had not reached this street. Shadows covered his face, obscuring his expression.

Kathryn felt a sudden pang of fear. "What are you thinking? Do you believe I murdered a woman and got her blood on my skirts?"

"No." He jerked to a halt, a startled expression on his face. "Why would I believe that?"

"The blood. If I did not kill Taunton, you might think I did something else equally as bad."

"Did you?"

That was the question she feared. She

could not lie to him, but she could not answer with complete honesty, either.

"I was with a friend, a woman, as I mentioned." Her hand tightened on his arm as he started forward again. "She—please promise me you will not speak of this to anyone, under any conditions."

"I do not know if I can make such a promise. If your dress is presented in court, some explanation must be given."

"It was an accident. My friend miscarried."

"Who?"

"I can not and will not reveal that. I promised her I would not tell anyone, and I will not break my promise."

"It may come out, nonetheless."

"Not through me."

"While I understand, you must realize you may be ensuring your own destruction through your silence."

"Then so be it."

He did not look at her but stared straight ahead, his brows crinkled in concentration.

The tread of their feet echoed the throbbing pain in her head. She pressed her fingers again to her temple. She had to say something and break the terrible silence wrapping around them like the icy fog, but her fears strangled her.

She took a deep breath. "If you were not investigating this murder, would you have taken me home with you tonight? If I had nowhere else to go?" The words flew out of her mouth without thought.

Spoken, they hung in front of her like a ghost, more humiliating than any admission she might have made.

"Would you have gone, had I asked?" The grim quality in his voice increased her tension unbearably.

She raised her chin. "Yes, I would."

"Because you have nowhere else to go?"

"No—not only that."

"That is the main reason, however. You would not have come otherwise."

"You are mistaken." To her surprise, she realized she meant it. If she ever trusted a man, that man would be Captain Nicholas Ainsley. He was the first decent man to treat her with anything even approaching respect. "I would go even if I had another place to stay."

"Don't patronize me, Miss Whitethorn-Litton."

"Please, it's Kathryn. And I am telling you honestly that if you were to ask me, I would come live with you."

"You can't possibly mean that." The harshness in his voice nearly broke her heart.

"Why? Why do you refuse to believe me when I tell you quite plainly that I would be honored if you were to ask?"

"You know why, and it is cruel of you to play the innocent. You know my left arm is useless. Why would you consent to live with half a man under any circumstances except the most dire?"

His words echoed her own bitterness over her situation so closely that she could not reply for a moment.

True, she had seen his inability to use his left arm, but it seemed an unimportant matter. But the wound apparently ran deeper with him, and she hesitated, fearing that pity would only ignite his fury. She knew what it was like to try to hide a weakness and pray no one would see it. Her inability to rule her own life in any meaningful way was as much of a weakness as his arm, though perhaps less visible.

"You are a man, Nicholas, no more and no less than any other." Her grip on his arm tightened. "And if your arm bothers you, perhaps a specialist could recommend some exercise. You may regain your strength in it one day—"

"Do you think I have not tried?" His furious voice cut through her words. "I've tried the last dozen years and more. It's useless."

"No it's not. You must simply work harder."

"Harder." He laughed bitterly. "And what if I never get the use of my hand back? What would you say then?"

"I would say, you must continue to try." She looked around, not recognizing the street. "Where are we going?"

"Since you seem determined to ignore both the facts and common sense, I suppose we shall go to my apartments. At least for the night."

A flutter of excitement and relief tickled her stomach. "Are you sure?"

"I'll have to find a woman, of course, to stay with you."

"A woman?"

"You can't stay alone with a man, even half a man, without a chaperone." He spoke quickly, sounding impatient. "I wouldn't dishonor you that way."

"How sweet of you," she murmured, although it didn't feel sweet at all. It felt annoying. Very annoying.

Only a remarkably unattractive woman could inspire such a lack of desire in the men around her. And if no one desired her, how would she survive? Neither the workhouse nor prostitution held any hope for a pleasant future.

She shivered and walked faster, her damp skirts slapping her ankles. Perhaps she put too much faith in Captain Ainsley's ability to prove her innocence. If he failed, the courts might decide a rope around her neck was the most suitable solution for her present difficulties.

Cold and utterly miserable, she couldn't decide if that fate was really worse than her situation.

Chapter Sixteen

9:15 PM October 24, 1821

As Nicholas guided Kathryn through the icy streets, he grew increasingly frustrated in his attempts to find a reasonable solution for her. Common sense suggested he take her to a boarding house, pay for a month's rent, and leave her to get along as best as she could. However, he could not convince himself to behave so callously. It felt like he was abandoning her simply because it would save him the difficulty of finding an alternative. He could not do it, knowing that she had no resources with which to pay the rent after the first month.

Most likely she wouldn't need to worry about rent. In less than four weeks, she would probably be in prison. Despite his belief in her protestations, even he had to admit that the circumstantial evidence implicated her. Many men had been sentenced and hung on much less.

And if she were innocent, a month would be enough time for her to find another patron.

A small voice whispered that he could be her protector. He was not such a fool that he didn't recognize the temptation to escort her to his flat. She did not have the resources to refuse any offer he cared to make.

But he wouldn't take advantage of any woman like that. His jaw muscles clenched as he remembered what it felt like to be helpless and wounded, lying in the mud of Corunna. He'd prayed desperately for help and prayed not to die despite the pain. And then like a miracle an unknown soldier had found him and dragged him to a British ship during their retreat.

How could he mistreat anyone when a man who didn't even know him had risked his life to give him another chance?

He had to find a safe place for Kathryn. Once he had done that, he could read Taunton's journal and puzzle out a possible motive for his death.

As he glanced around, he was startled to see he had one foot on the bottom step of the stairs to his front door. Without realizing it, he had returned to his flat. He turned around and caught Kathryn's puzzled gaze. He shook his head and continued walking. Her grip on his arm tightened, and he could feel her stumbling next to him as cold and exhaustion took their toll. The misty night could not conceal her pale face and the dark circles forming around her eyes. Her lips trembled and she bit her lower lip to stop it. She looked terrified, despite the brave front she tried to maintain.

As they continued down the street, his anxiety offered a new solution. "My brother and his wife live a few blocks away. I can find a hansom cab if you are too tired to walk."

"I'm certainly capable of walking a few blocks, but I fail to see why I should do so,"

Kathryn replied.

"You may stay with them until you find a more congenial situation."

"You can't possibly mean to foist me upon your brother!" She stared up at him, her eyes looked huge and black in the golden glow of a nearby gas lamp. Mist bedewed her skin and eyelashes. The moisture glittered on her white cheeks like tears.

"It is only temporary."

"What will you tell him? No man would want me around his family, particularly if he knew you suspect me of murder." She laughed, the sound raw and bitter. "Aren't you afraid I may kill him and his wife?"

"I'm not afraid of what you might do. I trust you will act with propriety." The more he considered it, the more he believed it was the correct and honorable course to pursue. The decision gave him an enormous sense of relief.

She would be safe with his brother. Despite her attempts to appear bold and worldly, she had a lost air about her that made her seem much younger than her age of three-and-twenty. In many ways, Kathryn seemed just as naïve as Helen, his brother's thirteen-year-old daughter.

She jerked back on his arm as if to bring him to a halt. He kept walking, pulling her along with him. "What if I am arrested?"

"Should you be?"

Her fingers dug into his tender inner

elbow. "No." Her voice whispered past him, as soft as the breeze from the Thames.

"Then it is settled."

Nicholas brought her gently to a halt in front of his brother's townhouse. Lamps blazed in several of the ground floor windows, and he could swear he heard laughter and the tinkle of silver despite the solid walls and closed front door. As Nicholas studied the windows, he thought uneasily that the baron, his elder brother, appeared to be entertaining guests.

Maybe that was for the best. His brother would be less likely to ask awkward questions if a party occupied him. Nicholas shifted uneasily from one foot to the other, wishing he could think of some other alternative. Unfortunately, his other brother, Thomas, was a vicar. He was kind and known for his generosity; however, he was also exceedingly proper. He was more likely to suggest Kathryn go to a workhouse than to offer her a temporary haven.

"Is this your brother's house?" Kathryn took a step forward before looking up at Nicholas. She shivered as she stood beside him, reminding him of her disheveled state. Her damp gown clung to her limbs. Her right hand gripped the collar of his jacket to draw it closer at the neck.

"Yes."

"You don't want me to stay here any more than I wish to do so." She gazed up at him with huge, luminous eyes. "Please, let me stay with you. I won't be any trouble. I don't want to live with strangers, and I certainly can't meet them in this state. *Please!*"

"I can't allow you to remain with me," he replied more harshly than he intended. "I'm sorry, but you must see that I can't—not if I intend to finish this investigation and prove your innocence."

A sob broke from her before she pressed fingers against her mouth to stop the heart-wrenching cry. "I can't face him—not like this."

"You must." He dragged her up the short flight of three steps and shook his arm out of her grasp, fearing that her touch would break his resolve to do the right thing for her. Taking a deep breath, he slammed the brass doorknocker against the glossy plate in the center of the door.

He had barely lowered his hand before the door flew open. "Good evening, Soames."

"Captain Ainsley! How good it is to see you, sir. Come in, come in." The butler bowed and opened the door wider, waving Nicholas inside. "I did not realize you would be attending Lord Hampton's supper."

"I'm not." Although Kathryn had stepped back, Nicholas dropped her valise to catch her by the wrist and drag her into the grand hallway next to him.

Soames' plump face registered surprise when he saw her, but he was well trained. A bland expression quickly replaced his astonishment although he could not prevent his brows from rising.

"This is Miss Whitethorn-Litton. She was the unfortunate victim of a carriage accident near here. As I knew her family, I could not leave her stranded in the middle of London. I thought Lady Hampton would not mind providing her with a room temporarily until I can make arrangements to return her safely to her relatives."

"Of course, Captain Ainsley." Soames smiled in relief and bowed again. "I shall inform Lady Hampton immediately."

"Before you do that, I would appreciate it if you could show us to a private sitting room. As you can imagine, Miss Whitethorn-Litton is exhausted. She is in no condition to meet the other guests."

"I should have thought of it sooner, sir. I apologize." Soames flushed and glanced around as if he had never seen the townhouse before.

"The sitting room on the second floor?" Nicholas suggested.

"Of course, of course, sir," Soames repeated as he bowed and waved them toward the elaborate staircase winding up to the first floor. Hesitating, he glanced over his shoulder at the front door. "I beg your pardon, sir."

"Are you expecting more guests?"

"Yes, sir," Soames answered in a distracted tone, flicking anxious glances at the door.

Nicholas suppressed a smile. He had

always liked Mr. Soames. The plump, dapper little man had been with the family for as long as Nicholas could remember and had been happy to join in their games when his duties allowed him to. Soames had few faults except one: he was exceptionally single-minded and could not manage situations involving multiple people. If he was supposed to greet guests for the earl's supper, Soames found it necessary to call a footman to escort other parties to the sitting room or any other room in the townhouse.

"Why don't I escort her to the front sitting room while you inform Lady Hampton that she has a temporary houseguest?" Nicholas suggested, guiding Kathryn toward the staircase.

"Yes, sir, thank you. I shall do just that." Soames bowed again and fled in the direction of the huge, gilded dining room that occupied half of the ground floor.

Nicholas pressed his hand against the small of Kathryn's back, encouraging her to mount the stairs. "Would you kindly pick up that lamp?"

"You lied to him," Kathryn whispered as she grabbed the small lamp sitting on a table to the left of the staircase. She walked ahead of him with jerky movements.

"Just a small, white lie."

"How could you?"

"I thought it was the easiest way to

explain your disarray and lack of a maid."

"What will your sister-in-law think when she discovers the truth?"

"She will find it vastly entertaining," he replied, sure of himself for the first time that evening.

"How could she find anything humorous in this dreadful situation?"

As they reached the landing, he gripped her elbow and nodded to the left. "You are not the only one with a rather, well, *unusual* past."

"What do you mean by that?" She came to a halt in the middle of the hallway, shaking her elbow out of his grasp.

"Let's just say my brother married his wife for love, not her dowry." He tried to push her forward.

She resisted. "Explain or I will leave this instance!"

"Do you really want to do that?" he asked in a gentle voice. "Wouldn't it be better to have a safe place to sleep?"

"Then explain!"

He shook his head. Despite her resistance, he slipped an arm around her waist and nearly carried her to the doorway of the sitting room. He had to release her to open the door, but at least she did not run away. She flicked a glance at him and then entered, raising the lamp to shoulder height to look around.

Pushing past her, he took the lamp out of her hand and walked confidently into the room, using it to light several other small oil lamps. "Come in and sit down," he said when she didn't follow him.

The shadows in the room wavered like spiders crawling over the walls. Kathryn frowned and wrapped her arms around herself, gripping his jacket with white fingers. After a moment, she entered. However, instead of sitting in one of the comfortable armchairs near the fireplace, she remained near the doorway.

"Sit down." Nicholas waved at the chairs before bending down in front of the fireplace. A small pile of sticks, tented over two larger logs, stood ready. He fumbled with the lamp, hoping to light the fire with its flame. He was chilled to the bone after the long walk without his jacket. Kathryn had to be in a similar condition after her dunking in the fountain.

She knelt beside him with a sigh and took the lamp out of his hand. "Let me do this. I may not excel at most tasks, but I am capable of lighting a fire."

"Have at it, then." He braced his hand against the brick edge of the fireplace and rose stiffly, watching her efforts to pack a bit of tinder between the sticks and then light a small stick with the flame from the lantern.

In a few minutes, a fire crackled on the hearth, quickly consuming the tinder and settling down to burn the thick logs beneath them. Kathryn sat back on her heels, smiling as she watched the flames with satisfaction. The light of the fire gilded her skin a rich, golden color and deepened the highlights of her chestnut hair. One of her hands caught the light as she reached up to push a curling tendril of hair away from her forehead. Nicholas felt another deep pang of attraction as he watched her.

As if feeling the weight of his gaze, she looked over her shoulder at him, a warm smile still glowing on her face.

Before either of them could break the silence, the door behind them opened. Nicholas' oldest brother, Henry, walked into the room, followed by his wife, Eleanor.

"Nicholas, I understand you have brought us a guest." Henry gripped Nicholas' right hand and drew him away from the fire before grinning and pounding his shoulder. "Good Lord, man, where is your jacket?"

Since his marriage to Eleanor, Henry always seemed to be in a cheerful mood and Nicholas had never felt more grateful for the change than at this moment. A deep sense of relief warmed him as his brother grinned at him. Nicholas smiled in return as he turned slightly to Kathryn. She remained on her knees in front of the fire, clutching his jacket lapels, almost as if she wished to remain hidden behind the two men.

"Ah, I see, now," Henry said, catching sight of her. "A damsel in distress."

"They are frozen, both of them!" Eleanor

held her husband's arm and peered around his shoulder at Kathryn and Nicholas. She glanced back at the butler who remained in the hallway, just outside the door. "Soames, fetch two blankets—"

"And a bottle of brandy!" Henry interrupted. "You are both wretched-looking specimens. Soames indicated there had been a carriage accident?"

Nicholas took Kathryn's cold hand and tried to draw her to her feet. She leaned away and tried to pull her fingers out of his grasp until he tightened his hold and pulled her up. The force of his grip made her stumble, and he put his arm around her to steady her. When he glanced up, he caught Eleanor's warm, brown eyes watching him.

"Lord Hampton, may I present Miss Whitethorn-Litton?" Nicholas guided her forward, ignoring her stiffness and the desperate look she flashed at him. He knew she feared his brother would humiliate and slight her, but for all Henry's impatience and mercurial moods, he was too kind to ignore a person in need. "Miss Whitethorn-Litton, Lord Hampton."

Henry bowed to his guest and clasped his wife's arm, drawing her to his side. "And may I present my wife, Lady Hampton?"

Staring at the carpet, Kathryn murmured a greeting in such a low voice that Nicholas was sure no one could possibly hear what she had said.

"I beg your pardon," Soames said as he entered the room carrying two, thick blankets draped over his arms. "Here are the blankets you requested, your ladyship." He handed them to her and bowed. "Is there anything else you require?"

"The brandy," Henry reminded him.

"Of course, milord." He turned slightly and waved in the direction of the door. A footman hurried through carrying a large silver tray. A crystal decanter of brandy sat on it, surrounded by four small snifters. Soames took the tray away from the footman and glanced around before placing it on a table near the fire. "Is there anything else you require, Lord Hampton?"

"Yes," Eleanor said. "Have the rose bedchamber prepared and ensure the fire is properly lit. We will have a guest for a few days. Warn Alice that her services will be required, as well. I see you managed to rescue a few of your belongings, Miss Whitethorn-Litton." She picked up the valise and bandbox before Kathryn could answer and handed them to the butler. "Take these to her room, Soames."

He accepted them with another bow and glanced at Lord Hampton. He nodded and Soames bowed again before leaving, shutting the door softly behind him.

As Henry handed a blanket to each of them, Eleanor stepped behind Kathryn to help her by accepting Nicholas' jacket. "Oh, your skin is like ice!" She brushed a handful of damp curls off Kathryn's neck to pull the blanket up more closely around her shoulders. "I do hope you don't both fall ill. Come closer to the fire. Where are your things, or are they just as damp?" Without waiting for an answer, she glanced at her husband as she rubbed one of Kathryn's hands. "Push the chairs nearer, Henry, and pour them some brandy."

"I appreciate your concern, Lady Hampton, but I assure you there is no need. I feel quite restored already." When Kathryn caught Nicholas' gaze, she rolled her eyes. She clearly was unused to having anyone fuss over her.

However, she did not know Eleanor. His sister-in-law liked nothing better than to hover over anyone on whom she could lay her hands, making her a fine compliment to her warm-hearted husband. No wonder he had wrested her away from her previous lover. He had married her within four months of their meeting when she spent the first month of their acquaintance fussing over him.

Despite Kathryn's claim that she required nothing, Henry poured two fingers of brandy into each snifter. He handed one to Nicholas and a second one to Kathryn before offering his wife a glass with a smile. Eleanor winked at Nicholas and downed her portion in one gulp so she could set her glass back onto the table and return her attention to Kathryn.

"Please, my dear, sit here." She maneuvered Kathryn into the chair closest to the fire and wrapped the blanket more tightly over her lap. When Kathryn did not sip her brandy, Eleanor slipped her fingers under the base of the snifter and forced her to raise the glass to her lips. She had to take a drink or risk dribbling the golden liquid over her chin.

Kathryn choked and coughed over the first sip, but the second swallow went more smoothly. A soft, rose color filled her cheeks.

"There." Eleanor took a step back and smiled at Kathryn. "Now, isn't that much better?"

"Yes, Lady Hampton. Thank you." Kathryn's lips had finally lost some of their blue color. She shyly returned Eleanor's smile, although her gaze flickered to Nicholas as if seeking reassurance.

He nodded at her and drank his brandy, grateful for the warmth of the alcohol and the fire at his side.

"So, Nicholas." Henry slapped him on the shoulder and then draped his heavy arm around his neck to draw him slightly away from the women. "Though I'm glad to see you looking so well, I must admit I'm surprised."

"Yes, well, I didn't know—"

"What else to do." He nodded. "Certainly. That much was clear from the start." When Nicholas glanced at him, Henry laughed. He took a sip from the brandy snifter he held in his left hand, although his right arm remained on Nicholas' shoulder. "Eleanor shall take care of her. You need have no fears on that score."

"She has had a difficult time, and there are complications."

"There always are, but I am pleased to see your interest in this woman. Or any woman, for that matter. You are already looking better for it." His brother squeezed his shoulder with a grin. "It has been a long road back for you, hasn't it? Too long and hard a road."

"Perhaps." Nicholas shrugged his arm off and tossed back the rest of his brandy. When Henry offered to refill his glass, he held it out in silence, trying to think of a way to explain the situation. It was damned awkward.

What would Henry think if Kathryn were arrested for the murder of Lord Taunton? If it were Nicholas, he'd be furious that his brother had placed a suspected killer in his house, endangering both him and his wife.

How could he face his brother if that happened? How could he explain that he had saddled them with a murderess?

Except he was sure she wasn't the one who had stabbed Taunton in the back. He had to read Taunton's diary. Then he had to perform due diligence and search Kathryn's jewelry to discover if a stone was missing from any of the pieces. Despite his confidence that he was not mistaken about her innocence, he had to prove it if he wanted to avoid his brother's anger and Kathryn's untimely end at Newgate.

So he could not remain in the comfort of his brother's sitting room. He had to read the diary, go to Taunton's townhouse, examine Kathryn's jewelry, and then find a way to discover who the true murderer was.

"I have to be honest with you, Henry, and I need your help," Nicholas ground out, his voice vibrating harshly in his throat.

"Anything. You know that."

"Miss Whitethorn-Litton may be accused of murder. She didn't do it, you must believe me—but someone is attempting to make it look like she killed her protector." He stared at his brother, daring him to comment about Kathryn.

Henry nodded, although the skin around his gray eyes tightened.

"I need your assistance to prove her innocence."

"I will do what I can, you know that. However, if you are looking for a political favor—"

"No!" Nicholas interrupted him so forcefully that both women glanced over at him. He forced a smile and nodded at Eleanor. In a quieter voice he said, "You misunderstand me. I must flush out the person who did this thing. Whoever it was, he stole a stiletto that Taunton—"

"This is about Lord Taunton's murder, then?" Henry asked in a low voice, his brows lowering to shadow his eyes.

"Yes. Does it matter?"

"I suppose not, though I may regret getting pulled into that viper's nest."

"Why? What do you know of him?"

Henry shook his head. "He was likeable enough. And I had heard lately that he was intending to marry, so perhaps the other was just a rumor and an ugly one at that."

"What rumor? What are you talking about?" Even as Nicholas asked the question, an image of Silsbury's haughty face rose in his mind. He shifted uneasily and glanced again over his shoulder at the women chatting near the warm fire. They looked so peaceful, so unconcerned.

"There were rather unsavory rumors about his private life, the types of house parties he hosted. Particularly the ones at his country estate in Somerset." Henry shrugged uncomfortably and sipped his brandy. Surprise crossed his face when he realized the glass he held was empty. He chuckled and shook his head. Relief eased the tightness around his eyes. He turned to the small table behind them and busied himself refilling his glass.

"What kind of parties?"

"They are just rumors, Nicholas."

"I have his journal, Henry. I suppose I shall find out soon enough, but it would still be useful to me if you could tell me what you've heard."

"Ah, I see." Henry stared thoughtfully at the snifter. "If you have his journal then you should be able to sift through any fiction to find the truth." He caught Nicholas' gaze. "There were, uh, too many men at his parties. Never any women, in fact."

"So?" Nicholas rubbed the back of his neck impatiently. "So he liked to hunt or shoot and had far too many male friends. There are a number of reasons—"

"Indeed, there are. And as you said, he had a great many male friends." His brother shrugged. "As I said, they are just rumors."

"I wish you would stop fencing and speak plainly."

To his surprise, his brother flushed and looked away. "I'm sure you will come to the appropriate conclusion if you consider it."

He searched for a polite way to phrase his next question, but finally blurted out, "You mean he was attracted to men?"

Henry nodded. "A confirmed Miss Molly, by all accounts. However, as I said, I had heard he intended to marry so I can't say that I paid any particular attention to the rumors. And even if it were true, what Lord Taunton did in private was none of my concern."

Studying Kathryn, Nicholas frowned. Had he found the reason behind Silsbury's insistence that Kathryn was responsible for Taunton's murder? Had Silsbury been jealous because Taunton intended to do the right thing and marry his mistress?

Surely Kathryn would have mentioned it if it were true.

"Whom had he planned to marry?" Nicholas asked.

"I regret that I can't say."

He sighed and stared over his brother's shoulder as he considered matters. "Perhaps his journal will shed some light on these matters. Do I have your blessing, then, to leave her with you?"

"Yes, I suppose if you are sure about her innocence?"

"I'm sure." Nicholas straightened his shoulders. "And I have another favor to ask of you. Would you be willing to host a supper?"

"A s-supper? When?" Henry stuttered, surprised.

"As soon as possible. Tomorrow night would be best—no, make that the day after. The twenty-sixth would be best." Nicholas smiled, knowing his request was next to impossible. However, that would give him almost two days to complete his investigations and prepare to identify the killer before the coroner's inquest concluded.

"The twenty-sixth? The day after tomorrow? My wife will be hysterical. I don't think it is possible."

"Then when?"

"May I ask why?"

"The stiletto used to murder Taunton

belonged to Miss Whitethorn-Litton. He had her show it off at a supper he hosted. So only a few knew of its existence."

"They most certainly gossiped about it."

"It doesn't matter if they did. I believe the sight of that knife sparked the notion in the killer. Someone in that group killed Lord Taunton."

"And you want us to host a supper for a murderer, then?"

"Yes. I will ensure your safety. Trust me, I will not allow anything to happen to you or your family." Even as he said the words, he felt self-conscious. With only one arm, he was even less capable of protecting anyone than his mild-mannered brother.

"A supper party?" Eleanor slipped her hand around her husband's elbow and gazed up at him, interrupting the two men. A few feet behind her, Kathryn stood swathed in her blanket, studying them.

"This rascal wants us to host one the day after tomorrow." Henry placed his hand over his wife's and grinned down at her.

"That soon?" She laughed and shook her head. "There shall surely be violence if we do so."

"Violence?" Nicholas frowned, on edge.

"Yes. However, I shall soon be able to solve the new mystery that shall arise from this ill-fated supper. Your brother and I shall be the victims and our cook shall most definitely

Amy Corwin

murder both of us if we ask him to prepare a large supper on such short notice."

Watching the two of them laugh as they leaned into each other, Nicholas felt an ache in his chest, wanting to feel that closeness, that easy companionship. When he glanced at Kathryn, she held his gaze. For a moment, he thought he saw the same hunger in her eyes. Then she looked away and stared down at the floor, shutting him out.

A deep sense of isolation seeped through him. He stood in the center of the room, separated from both Kathryn and the married couple by a few feet of carpet and an invisible wall he felt helpless to break.

When his brother finally glanced at him, Nicholas forced a smile. "Tell your cook that you can find another chef to assist him if he cannot manage on such short notice. I'm sure he'll find a way to accommodate you."

"That's positively cruel." Eleanor pressed her fingers against her mouth as she giggled. "I cannot play on his pride in such an unforgiveable fashion."

"However, it would most definitely reduce his complaints to manageable proportions." Henry rested his chin briefly on his wife's lacy cap as he looked at Kathryn with a faint crease in his brows. "How many will be attending this supper party?"

"Fourteen, excluding the four of us," Nicholas said.

"Then eighteen," Eleanor amended. "A not unreasonable number." She gave her husband's lapel a light tug. "I shall leave it to you to notify Cook, then. And you should do so tonight so he will be able to send his lads to the market as early as possible tomorrow morning."

"And so he will be able to spend the next two nights sleepless with worry over the arrangements." Henry chuckled. "Very well, though it is uncommonly cruel of you, my dear. And what about the guest list?"

"I shall take care of the invitations if you will provide me with a supply of your writing paper." At least he could put Jack Jones to work tomorrow delivering invitations.

If he could identify the addresses of the potential guests. Unfortunately, since Mr. Croftson had taken possession of Taunton's townhouse and booted Silsbury out, Nicholas had no idea where to find him. Silsbury was one guest he particularly wanted to attend. The man had been far too assiduous in trying to fix the blame on Kathryn and it raised Nicholas' suspicions.

"What if your guests have previous engagements?" Henry asked.

Nicholas smiled grimly. "The invitations shall be irresistible, I assure you."

"I did not realize my wife and I were so popular." Henry's dry tone elicited a giggle from his wife.

"You *will* be on the twenty-sixth."

259

Nicholas studied Kathryn's pale face and shadowed eyes before he added, "Miss Whitethorn-Litton has had an exhausting day. She should retire, and I should be on my way. I'll provide you with the list of guests on my way out."

"Very well, dear brother. And I shall rely on your assurances that everything will go as planned."

Chapter Seventeen

1:00 AM October 25, 1821

After several hours of reading Taunton's diary, Nicholas rubbed his tired eyes. They burned as if dust had been substituted for tears. His muscles ached and he felt bone-weary.

The rumors about Taunton's personal life had apparently been true. He had invited men to his house parties because, quite simply, he preferred men. And sadly, he barely acknowledged Kathryn's presence in his household, often questioning why he allowed her to stay after her beloved father passed away during a weekend visit. Initially, Taunton had felt sorry for her and in some way responsible for her well-being. As she matured, however, he found her to be nothing but an encumbrance, at least until an entry dated a month ago.

... After my comment last month about Kathryn, I am embarrassed to admit she proved to be of some value to me last night. Lord Dewhurst and his cronies have been spreading rumors about my dearest Harry, but when I arrived at his pathetic little supper with Kathryn in tow, well, what could he say? The look on his face was beyond price. It was all I could do not to laugh at him. I wish Harry could have witnessed it for it might have improved his mood upon my return. He grows as tetchy as an old woman these days.

Nonetheless, despite last night's

triumph, I grow weary of her presence for in her face I see her beloved father. Her eyes and the color of her hair only serve to remind me of how much I miss him. I had thought she might ease my grief when I allowed her to remain after her father's untimely death, but she has only increased the ache in my heart. He cared, truly cared, about me and had no interest in the extent of my wealth or title. Some days I can scarce look at her without feeling the pain of his loss again and longing for the touch of his warm hand. For all his efforts, Harry is no replacement for Charles. I suspect he realizes it, however nothing he does can hide the shallowness of his feelings. And I have seen how he treats Kathryn—she is an easy target for his ill-temper since her father is no longer here to block his barbs.

In fact, I grow weary of them both. Their incessant arguments and demands prey upon me and leave me not one whit of peace. This afternoon, I am ashamed to say, I stooped to purchasing an emerald ring for Harry simply to put an end to his peevish complaints. The more he insists I send Kathryn away, the more I give in to my cruel impulses and flaunt her in front of him. If Harry gets a ring, then Kathryn receives an ornamental stiletto, and I will laugh and exhibit the silly knife to our friends when he protests. He will learn to curb his jealousy, or he will suffer the consequences of his irrationality.

When I reflect upon what I have written, I realize that perhaps my brother is correct, after all, though he will undoubtedly be unhappy at my agreement with him. It is time for me to perform my duty and marry. The change will certainly bring a breath of fresh air through the over-heated atmosphere in this house. Sadly, Harry will have to learn to fend for himself. But what of Kathryn?

What will become of her? I feel some duty there and shame for having failed her father. Surely, he did not want her to become a member of the demi-monde, regardless of his lack of foresight or provisions for her future. But she was too useful in fending off the worst of the rumors about me and my men over the last few years for me to consider giving her up so easily.

Perhaps some shopkeeper or widower will find her pleasing enough to overlook her lack of fortune. She is still young and not unattractive. In fact, it is a pity I cannot bring myself to forgo a dowry and marry her. However, if I am to do my duty then I must insist on an ample settlement to repay the sacrifice this entails. If I must give up my pleasures then I demand some compensation in return.

So marry I shall, and both Kathryn and Harry must go whither they will.

Nicholas skimmed the remaining pages, finding a few more tantalizing hints that shed a bit of light on the situation in Taunton's household.

I have come to an agreement with Mr. Christian Mardling to take his daughter off his hands. According to her mother, the chit has fallen in love with some obscure man with no title and little fortune to offer. I am more than happy to accept the fat purse Mr. Mardling has offered as her dowry, despite the efforts of his women to oppose this contract. Miss Mardling and her mother have visited me several times with the obvious intent of persuading me to find another. Oddly enough, the more they beg, the more inclined I am to proceed. Miss Mardling is presentable and her spritely manners please me. In the end, I suspect Mardling is relieved by my determination for he applauds my steadfastness.

In any event, the news of our betrothal should discourage the fortune hunter Mardling fears, and Miss Mardling will soon grow used to the idea.

In the end, I shall have things my way. As always.

Nicholas closed the journal and stretched, his stiff muscles crackling with each movement. His left arm ached, reminding him of its awkward presence. He massaged the cold, useless hand. In the distance, he heard a clock's melodious chime. It was two in the morning, but as he gazed through his window at the dark, misty streets, he wondered if Kathryn were asleep or awake. Was she worried about her fate?

Her loneliness and confusion were understandable after reading Taunton's journal. Society believed she was Taunton's mistress and a member of the demi-monde. Nothing could have been further from the truth. At best, Taunton behaved like a disinterested father to her and tolerated her presence out of love for her deceased father. At worst, she was a social convenience he used to stop rumors about his sexual preferences. Unfortunately, Taunton also planned to get rid of her. That decision gave her a motive to murder him if he had informed her of it.

And Silsbury was in as precarious a position as she was.

Nicholas sighed and rubbed his dry eyes. He had a great deal of work to do tomorrow and the next day to prepare for the supper party. For now, though, he needed at least an hour or two of sleep. He stared at his bed, loathing the lumpy thing. Exhaustion pulled at him but he hated the thought of sleep. When he slept, he could not control the nightmares. They pulled him back into the blood and desperate screams of battle. He felt helpless, surrounded by explosions and unable to save the men who died trying to follow his orders. The acrid odor of gunpowder lingered in his throat despite the intervening years.

The ache in his dead arm increased, and

he rubbed it absently. When had it become a test of courage to simply climb into bed? Was he really so cowardly? Pushing away a gut-churning feeling of foreboding, he eased under the blanket and kneaded away a few of the larger lumps in the mattress. He forced himself to close his eyes.

Then, in an effort to avoid sinking into a nightmare, he brought Kathryn's face to mind. Not blue-lipped and frightened as he had last seen her, but smiling and filled with warmth. Perhaps for once the pleasant image would suffice.

*

9:00 AM October 25, 1821
"Five pounds ought to be enough, Sergeant," Nicholas said as Dalton stood in front of him, his calloused hand held out. "You're not feeding an entire battalion after all."

"So you say and be that as it may, there's not a crumb to be had in your cupboards. Even the rats are starving. And I had to borrow—"

"Steal!" Jack yelled, interrupting him.

Dalton scowled at him. "I *borrowed* a shilling from yon heathen to buy our breakfast, meager though it was."

"The beer is all gone, too." Jack's face twisted as if he were about to cry.

"A terrible misfortune to be sure." Nicholas eyed him, suppressing a smile. "However, five pounds is all you'll get. And I have more pressing matters for the two of you than the state of your bellies."

Jack straightened immediately, his intelligent eyes flashing with anticipation. "Yes, sir!"

Grinning, Nicholas ruffled the boy's ragged hair. If only he could live in the careless moment the way the boy did. When Jack twisted away and snorted in disgust, Nicholas laughed. He picked up the pile of invitations he had written earlier that morning when sleep deserted him. "Can you read, Jack?"

Dalton snickered as the boy's face fell. However, to give him credit, when the sergeant saw dismay stain Jack's eyes, he immediately sobered.

"Never mind." Dalton gripped the boy's thin shoulder and gave him a shake. "I can read well enough. I'll read whatever it is."

"That won't do." Nicholas frowned.

"I tried to learn, but it is hard going." Jack shook off Dalton's hand.

"I can teach the lad, Captain."

Too bad Bottom had not been released from gaol. Given sufficient time, he might have been able to continue his lessons with Jack and finally taught him his letters.

"Not in the next hour, I'm afraid. And I need the sergeant for another errand." Nicholas paused in thought. "Can you remember a list of seven names?"

"Yes—I can do that. I know I can."

"Then here is your task." Nicholas handed Jack the pile of invitations. "You will take these to the homes of seven families. When you arrive, you must tell them that they must take the invitation with their name on it. These invitations are for a supper party at Baron Hampton's townhouse. The party is at nine tomorrow night. Can you remember what I've told you thus far?"

Jack nodded. "I'm to take these notes to folks who are to go to Baron Hampton's supper tomorrow at nine. Will I be going, too?" He licked his lips in anticipation.

"I'm afraid not." When he saw the disappointment in Jack's eyes, Nicholas added, "And you wouldn't want to. It will be very tedious and boring."

"But the food—"

"Will be equally bad. Trust me, you'll be happier here. Now are you ready for the list?"

"Yes, sir." Jack leaned forward, the pink tip of his tongue protruding from between his teeth as he concentrated.

"Mr. and Mrs. Croftson, Mr. and Mrs. Hugo Dudley and daughter, Mr. and Mrs. Christian Mardling and daughter, Mr. and Mrs. Daniel Reeve and daughter, Mr. Bartholomew Palmer, Mr. Harry Silsbury, and Mr. George Inglewood. Now repeat those names back to me."

"That's only four families. Three of 'em be bachelors."

"Be that as it may, repeat the names."

Hands behind his back, Jack scowled in concentration as he tried to repeat the list.

Nicholas shook his head. "You forgot Mr. Inglewood and it was the Reeve family, not the Palmer family. In fact, I believe Bartholomew Palmer is one of your bachelors. Now repeat the names again."

It took several more tries before Jack could recite the list verbatim, but Nicholas finally declared him ready. "One last thing, Jack. I do not know where Mr. Harry Silsbury lives. You may try asking at Croftson House when you give the Croftsons their invitation. However, be prepared for a bit of tracking because they may not know. Finding Silsbury will be one of the most important aspects of this task."

"I'll find him, never fear, Captain!" Jack executed a smart salute and spun on his heel before racing out of the apartment.

In his excitement, Jack forgot to shut the door. Dalton tottered over and pushed it closed with his crutch. "Now that he's off, I suppose you have some task for me?"

"Filling our larder for one thing. And visiting an employment agency."

"An employment agency?" Dalton stared at him. "What the devil do you want with an employment agency?"

Nicholas chuckled. "You don't fancy a real job?"

"I've got one, Captain. I'm not looking for

another unless you're trying to tell me you're done up and I should find a new situation."

"Not at all. I'd like you to find a female able to act as both a lady's maid and housekeeper."

"You want me to interview a *woman*?" Dalton's eyes bulged at the daunting prospect.

"Yes. An acquaintance of mine has need of a personal maid."

Dalton leaned back and leered at him. "Oh, I see."

"I don't think you do. She is a decent young woman and has suffered quite enough hardship already. This is a temporary measure. You will show her respect, or you can apply for employment in another household. Is that all perfectly clear?"

"Yes, sir. Though what I know about female servants wouldn't fill a thimble."

"Do the best you can. Find a no-nonsense woman, and one who is not too young. If she's knocked around a bit, she shouldn't be too flighty. Now, I have several errands to run, myself." Nicholas donned his hat and picked up his walking stick on his way out, pretending not to hear Dalton's dire muttering about single females and their ability to destroy a well-run household.

After all, no one could claim that the Ainsley household was in any way well-run despite its recent increase in members.

*

The weather was cool but fine with just a few tendrils of early morning mist clinging to the shadows in the darker alleys. Nicholas walked quickly to Mayfair, heading for Taunton's townhouse. The inquest was due to start today if Flatman had his way, and Nicholas had a bit more investigation in mind. Then he had to prepare for the party tomorrow evening.

His shoulders tightened as he walked. When the townhouse came into view, his stomach clenched the way it always did when preparing for battle. So much depended upon the next few hours. This case would prove he was not a useless shell of a man.

But he could not depend solely upon the silly parlor trick he planned for the dinner. He needed to interview a few more of the earl's acquaintances to make up his mind. Information and preparation would ensure he knew well enough in advance to properly target his quarry.

Then, if the supper at his brother's residence went well, he might be able to publically identify the murderer. If it did not, well, he felt it very likely that Silsbury would succeed in casting the blame on Kathryn despite Nicholas' confidence in her innocence.

Too bad Silsbury's emerald ring hadn't been missing a stone. It would have been satisfying to throw a little suspicion and discomfort his way. And a small sliver of doubt remained about his innocence. He certainly had both opportunity and motive.

There was the distinct possibility that he possessed another ring. And Toddy might recognize the beautiful face of the woman who had crept out of the townhouse at midnight as that of an innocent housemaid.

Therefore, Nicholas couldn't discount the possibility that Silsbury had murdered his lover. Taunton had written that Silsbury was jealous. Jealousy often indicated a passionate nature. If the earl had informed Silsbury that he was to vacate Croftson House, Silsbury might have flown into a rage and murdered him. He might then have decided to hide his crime by incriminating Kathryn.

However, something in that chain of events did not feel right to him. And in the back of his mind, Nicholas worried about Bottom and Toddy. If Toddy had gotten worse, then his efforts to arrange the supper would become riskier and less certain. He had guesses, but very little proof unless he could trick the murderer into displaying the ring with the missing stone. If the killer learned that he had the diamond, the ring would vanish forever.

Worse, he could not necessarily connect the person Toddy saw to the murder without the ring. The ring might be the strongest link in the chain, but he also needed the other links including the identification of the person slipping out of the house at the time of Taunton's death. He was relying on Toddy to identify her—or him.

He knew that circumstance was important. It would be too much of a coincidence for that figure to be a maid slipping out for a dalliance with some man. And since there would be no reason for a member of the household to leave if he or she committed the murder, that meant that the murderer had to be someone who did not live there.

Of course, he could be mistaken and it could have been a love-struck maid.

The events at the supper would forge the strongest links and decide the issue. There were far too many questions and too many motives, otherwise, to present a clear case.

He rapped on the front door at Croftson House and turned slightly to watch the traffic as he waited. A rag man was working his way down the street, pulling his narrow, two-wheeled wagon. He disappeared down the narrow alley across the road to ask for tattered clothes and scraps at the servants' door. Before he reappeared, the door behind Nicholas opened.

"May I help you, Captain Ainsley?" the butler asked.

"Is Mr. Croftson available?" Nicholas stepped forward and placed his booted foot on the doorjamb in case the butler decided to shut the door in his face. "It is in reference to the earl's death."

The servant's eyes shifted, and he stiffened before executing a slight bow. "Please come inside. I shall endeavor to determine if Mr. Croftson is at home, sir."

Catching the butler's arm, Nicholas detained him. "Do you remember any visitors the night Lord Taunton died?"

"I believe I already answered that question, sir." The servant's brows creased as the corners of his mouth turned down.

"I'm not simply referring to guests—I'm wondering if Mr. Croftson may have arrived in London a few days early."

The butler's eyes flickered. He glanced over his shoulder at the grand staircase. "I'm afraid I couldn't say."

"Could not or will not?"

"I'm sorry, Captain." He stared over Nicholas' shoulder, the muscles in his jaw working.

"I understand." Nicholas changed directions, hoping a more oblique question would encourage the servant to answer. "Before you see if Mr. Croftson is available, can you at least tell me if the message about Taunton's death was sent to a London address or to Croftson's country estate?"

"It was a London address. A club, sir."

"Is Croftson a member of that club?"

"Both Lord Taunton and Mr. Croftson were members."

Croftson had been in London when his brother died. No wonder he had arrived so expeditiously.

"Is that all, Captain?"

"Yes." Relieved to pass the first barrier, Nicholas waited in the entryway, marshaling his thoughts. Taunton's diary had answered many of his questions, but his brother might provide additional insight into the events that precipitated Taunton's death.

Of course, given what the butler said, Croftson might also have been responsible for his brother's death. Nicholas could not discount him, now, knowing that he had been in London at the time. It would also explain the supposed "maid" that Bottom and Toddy had seen. Croftson could have used a cloak to disguise his identity, and he would have had to return to the club if he hoped to use that as an alibi should anyone discover he was in London.

"Please follow me, Captain Ainsley. Mr. Croftson can spare you five minutes."

The servant led the way past the wide staircase to the ground floor library occupying most of the rear of the townhouse. When Nicholas entered the room, the butler announced him, bowed, and shut the double-doors.

Sitting behind a large, mahogany desk, Mr. Croftson did not rise when Nicholas strode toward him. As he neared, Croftson waved at a single, wooden chair placed directly in front of the desk.

Nicholas removed his hat and sat down.

For some reason, Croftson's appearance

startled Nicholas. His rosy-cheeked, round face and blue eyes leant him a cherubic appearance that his frown belied, and the deep lines bracketing his mouth suggested that his displeased expression was habitual. He appeared to be young—certainly still in his twenties—and he had the same blond curls as his brother. However, his chest and shoulders were thicker, almost stocky, and he was far less fashionable. He wore a sedate, dark blue jacket that did not fit very well, a black waistcoat, and a black neckcloth wrapped around his throat.

"As I'm sure Kirby informed you, I am very busy. I don't have a great deal of time to spare. He indicated you have some questions?" He laced his fingers together on top of the desk and leaned forward slightly, his blue eyes focused on Nicholas' face.

"Yes, I'm investigating the earl's death—"

Croftson let out a sigh and sat back. "If you wish to be paid then you must present your bill to Mr. Silsbury. I have no interest in your inquiry."

"Surely, you want justice for your brother?"

"Of course. However, from my observation, inquiries of this sort merely serve to expose the families involved to sordid gossip. It is my understanding the authorities have two men in custody. I am happy to let matters remain as they stand. My late brother's affairs are private and therefore no one's concern."

"I understand you were in London at the time of your brother's death."

Croftson stilled. His hard eyes gave nothing away as he stared at Nicholas. "Where did you hear that?"

"I can't remember who mentioned it. I'm puzzled though: why would you stay at a club instead of here?"

"Though this is none of your concern, I will tell you that I felt it would be more convenient. I had business to attend to."

"Surely it would have been just as convenient to reside here."

"My associates were also members. They stayed there, as well." He folded his hands in front of him in a gesture that conveyed finality. "I do not see the point in discussing this any further. My affairs are no concern of yours."

"Did you visit your brother while you were here?"

"No." His stare grew colder. "We did not socialize. We moved in different circles, and he had peculiar taste in friends."

"Nonetheless, he was your brother," Nicholas commented softly. "Surely you would have come here at some point to pay your respects."

"Certainly. Before I left London. Unfortunately, I did not have the opportunity."

"Were you familiar with his household, then? Would you know if anything were missing?"

"That would depend, I suppose." Croftson rubbed his thin upper lip. "Do you believe something was stolen?"

Instead of answering directly, he lifted his hand in a gesture of uncertainty. "Did you ever see a knife—a stiletto—in your brother's possession? One with a gold grip set with a ruby?"

"Is that what was used to kill him?"

"It is possible. Had you ever seen it here?"

Croftson shrugged. "I cannot say. It is possible he owned something like that. I have never taken any particular interest in his belongings."

Unlikely.

Nicholas suspected that jealousy ate at Croftson and he knew precisely what his older brother had owned. He would have watched his brother enjoy the privileges of his position while ignoring the duty to marry and produce heirs. Envy seethed inside him, and Nicholas could almost smell it like the odor of milk gone sour. Croftson had probably known every yard of silk, every piece of silver in the house, bitterly resenting the obvious differences between his brother's residence and his own, more modest, situation.

Did Croftson realize that Taunton had finally realized he had a responsibility to marry, and marry well enough to enhance his title and estate? Had that brought him to the breaking point?

"Now, if there is nothing else?" Croftson half rose, ready to dismiss him.

Nicholas leaned back, relaxing in his chair, amused to see a V of annoyance settle between Croftson's brows. "I'm sorry, I forgot my main purpose in coming here. Do you know where I may find Mr. Silsbury?"

Croftson's mouth thinned. "I do not. He and that strumpet left at my request. That is the last I saw of them. I have no interest in their whereabouts."

"Why did you insist they leave so precipitously?"

"I have a wife and children, sir." An ugly, crimson color stained his cheekbones. "Those two were an unhealthy influence on my brother and his household. I could not allow them to exert a similar influence on my family. It was beyond all reason. I'm sorry, but I cannot assist you any further."

"Did Miss Whitethorn-Litton leave any jewelry behind?"

"Yes. She had no right to any items acquired by Taunton."

Nicholas bit off a remark that as Taunton had given the items to her as gifts, they belonged to her. Angering Croftson would not get him what he wanted. "May I see the jewelry?"

"Why?"

"They may assist me in this case."

"You fail to understand me: I don't wish

any further inquiries into this affair."

"You were very clear on that score. However, the two men in prison are not guilty. That fact will certainly come to light during their trial and then inquiries will resume." Nicholas studied him, sensing an imminent dismissal despite his argument. "If I promise that I will only share information with the coroner, will you allow me to examine her jewelry? I do not wish to intrude or cause any further gossip, but the rumors will only increase if I can't discover the truth."

"Wait here." Croftson stood and went to the door. He whispered to someone who remained hidden behind the door, and then waited.

As he stood with his hand on the doorknob, the sun glinted off an elaborate ring on his right hand. The light caught Nicholas' eye.

He blinked and then frowned. "That is an interesting ring, sir. May I see it?"

Croftson thrust his hands into his pockets and turned partially away. "It is a trifle, an inheritance from my mother. Nothing more."

A few minutes later a servant knocked on the door, opened it, and handed an object to Croftson. When he turned, Nicholas saw a wooden box about the size of two large books stacked one atop the other. He placed the box in front of Nicholas and then circled around the desk to his chair.

"Open it."

"Is it all here?" Nicholas lifted the lid. The flimsiness of the wood surprised him. It felt cheap and brittle, not at all what he expected. Surely Taunton could have given Kathryn a more appropriate jewelry box?

The implication angered him. He knew from Taunton's journal that he didn't care two pins about Kathryn, but at least he could have provided her with decent belongings.

"Yes, it is," Croftson replied, pursing his lips in distaste. "I have not had time to dispose of the items she left behind. I expect the servants may appreciate the gaudy trinkets. There is nothing there I would wish to give to my wife or children."

Several necklaces and thin, gold bracelets were jumbled together on the bare wood inside the box. His heart hammered as he shifted the box in his hands. He could be wrong about Kathryn. If he found a ring missing a diamond, he would have to have her arrested. Some of his confidence returned when he lifted one of the necklaces and studied it in the light streaming through the window behind Croftson's back. The gems were paste. Cheap trinkets, indeed. Even if Kathryn had kept the jewels and tried to sell them, she would not obtain more than a few pence.

Three rings rested in one corner, but as he lifted them one at a time, they proved to be no more valuable than the necklaces. Even the bracelets were worthless brass.

Kathryn was innocent.

"Is there anything else?" Croftson asked when Nicholas dropped the last ring into the box.

Yes. You could show me your ring.

"Yes." Nicholas rose. "I would like to speak to the servants."

Croftson leaned forward and grabbed the box, unwilling to let even a few pence out of his grasp. "Very well. Kirby can assist you. Then you may go. And I trust we will not be bothered again. If Silsbury hired you, then you must take your instructions from him."

While Kirby was remarkably efficient in organizing interviews with all the staff, Nicholas did not discover anything new. The maids were all in bed well before midnight, as confirmed by the housekeeper. The housekeeper and Kirby had spent a few hours going over household matters in the butler's office and confirmed that neither of them had left the house at any time that evening. The servants seemed to all be accounted for.

As he left, Nicholas hoped Jack would have been lucky in finding Silsbury. There seemed to be little hope of discovering any additional clues at Croftson House, at least if Edward Croftson had anything to do with it.

Chapter Eighteen

10:00 AM October 25, 1821

Bottom listened to Toddy's snores, trying to sleep. There was little enough to do during the day and sleeping passed the time well enough.

"One, two, three..." He counted the seconds between Toddy's snorts, "...seven, eight..." He sat up in a panic and shook Toddy's shoulder.

He seemed to have stopped breathing.

"Wake up!" Bottom rolled him over and held his hand in front of his nose.

A burst of faint, warm air puffed from Toddy's mouth, fluttering his lips. "Wh—what is it?" He groaned as he raised a hand to his face, rasping his palm over his whiskers.

"You weren't breathing."

Toddy yawned, his jaws cracking. "'Course I was breathing. Why can't you leave a body in peace? My ribs ache something awful." He gripped his middle and let out a rasping moan as he struggled to roll over into a more comfortable position.

The doctor the captain had sent had examined Toddy and wrapped his ribs properly, throwing Bottom's now-unnecessary neckcloth into his lap. Before he left, the physician bled Toddy until he closed his eyes, slipping into unconsciousness. His lined face grew so pale he seemed to glow in the darkness. Bottom had watched the doctor carefully and soon concluded that the supposedly learned man was nearly useless. He did no more than Bottom had already done and hadn't even offered Toddy a draught to alleviate his pain.

What had the captain paid him for, then? A few strips of linen and not much else.

Bottom leaned over Toddy, studying his gray, gaunt features and feeling chilled with fear. "Don't die. You can't leave me here alone," he whispered. "How am I to survive?"

The sharp slap of leather soles drew near and then passed their door. In the distance, Bottom heard the clang of a door shut. For once, Newgate seemed relatively quiet, but the silence only deepened his terror.

The living were a noisy lot, swearing and fighting. Only the dead were silent.

He picked up one of Toddy's cold hands and rubbed it. "Please don't die, Toddy. You can't die, yet. I'm depending upon you and so is the captain. You can't leave us—you can't be such a coward as to die." His words grew increasingly incoherent as fear ate away his confidence. "Please, Toddy. Don't leave me here. I'm frightened."

Rocking, Bottom closed his eyes and continued talking nonsense to Toddy, trying to ignore the icy cold drafts seeping into his aching bones. "We're going to get out, Toddy, you'll see. We'll be out soon. You just have to hang on a bit longer."

*

11:00 AM October 25, 1821

Nicholas paused on the steps and decided his next interview would be the Mardlings. He needed to get an understanding of the people who danced attendance upon Lord Taunton and had been present when he flaunted the dagger that had ultimately killed him.

The Mardling residence was situated near the east edge of Mayfair, on Conduit Street. The butler seemed to be expecting him because he barely heard his name before he escorted him into a small but exquisitely furnished sitting room on the first floor. The butler announced him and then stepped back to shut the door behind Nicholas.

Two women sat near a window, the older one sewing while the other flipped through the pages of a magazine with a bored look on her pretty, young face. As he neared, the older lady glanced up at him. She placed her sewing in her lap and gently folded her hands on top of it, her cool gaze on him all the while. He guessed she was Mrs. Mardling and the younger woman her daughter, Rose.

A few grayish-blond curls peeped out from under the lacy edge of Mrs. Mardling's cap, but her clear skin was unlined except for a few wrinkles around her eyes. She had been a beauty once and remained handsome. A sense of calm assurance flowed around her, lending her a regal presence that her daughter would be wise to emulate.

Unfortunately, while Miss Mardling was as fair as her mother, with pale blond curls framing her face and wide-set blue eyes, she lacked the older woman's poise. She retained an air of innocent childishness that many men might find attractive. He did not, and the droop of her mouth betrayed a petulance that did nothing to change his assessment.

Spoiled. He wondered why Taunton had decided to marry this particular girl. Had her dowry truly made her irresistible? Ill-temper was already developing in her young face and showed signs that she would grow into a truculent, shrewish woman. Surely, she was no bargain.

"I am sorry to intrude, Mrs. Mardling," Nicholas said, bowing in her direction.

"Indeed, Captain Ainsley. To what do we owe this honor?"

"I had hoped to speak to Mr. Mardling as well as you and your daughter."

Mrs. Mardling raised one hand and flicked her fingers at the empty room behind him. "As you can see, my husband is not here. You will have to make do with me or return at another time."

"When do you expect Mr. Mardling to return?"

"My husband does not share his schedule with me." Although her face remained beautifully composed, a bitter tone lurked in her voice. She resented her husband's freedom or felt abandoned by him. Either way, she was not happy with the state of their relationship.

No reply he could make would change her mood, but perhaps he could redirect her thoughts to something less disturbing. "May I offer my condolences to you and your daughter? This must be a difficult time for you. I understand Miss Mardling was to marry Lord Taunton."

Miss Mardling glanced at him, her eyes wide with surprise before a laugh escaped her. When her mother looked at her sharply, she covered her mouth and cast her gaze down at the magazine in her lap.

"My daughter is hysterical," Mrs. Mardling stated firmly. She studied her daughter for any sign of inappropriate behavior but Miss Mardling kept her eyes demurely downcast.

"Quite understandable. She must have been very much in love with him. I understand Lord Taunton was a very handsome man."

Miss Mardling shifted, her fingers playing with the edges of the magazine. She did not look up at him, but the corners of her mouth turned down. A frown pressed a deep V between her fair brows, clearly indicating that she did not agree with his words.

"It was a business arrangement, Captain Ainsley. This family is not one to indulge girlish flights of fancy." Despite her words, her hands picked at her sewing, showing the same nervous mannerisms as her daughter. "Of course, we are saddened by his death as we would be by the death of any acquaintance. It was a dreadful thing. Mr. Mardling took it all very badly."

Not surprising. Mr. Mardling would now have to find another gentleman to marry his daughter. Or allow her to marry the man of her choosing.

He sensed the latter alternative would not meet with his approval. Mr. Mardling obviously controlled the women in his family and expected them to do his bidding. Perhaps that explained Miss Mardling's peevish temper. It could not be easy to be treated like a common household item that Mr. Mardling could dispose of as he saw fit.

"You may have heard that I have been tasked with investigating Lord Taunton's death, Mrs. Mardling. As your husband was contracting an alliance with Taunton, I hoped you might know, or have heard, something that may shed some light on this matter. Do you know of any reason for someone to murder Lord Taunton?"

Mrs. Mardling's hands stilled. She stared down at her sewing as if she had never seen it before. "My husband had more dealings with him than I. Or my daughter. We could not have enjoyed his company more than half a dozen times, is that not correct, Rose?"

"Yes, Mama," Miss Mardling replied obediently without glancing up at Nicholas.

"I understand that Miss Mardling had struck up a friendship with Miss Whitethorn-Litton."

"Mr. Mardling knew Mr. Whitethorn-Litton. They were friends a long time ago. He felt sorry for the girl when she was left under the guardianship of Lord Taunton after her father died. He hoped Rose and Miss Whitethorn-Litton's friendship would make it easier during Lord Taunton's courtship of Rose."

"Did you agree?"

She glanced up at him. The flash in her eyes startled him, but she controlled her expression too quickly for him to know what to make of it. "My husband makes the decisions for us. It is usually for the best."

"No doubt. Was it for the best in this instance, Miss Mardling?"

Mrs. Mardling's gaze jerked to her daughter and she lifted a hand as if to grip Miss Mardling's hand, but her daughter ignored her. She looked at Nicholas with blue eyes as empty of emotion as the sky. "Of course. I enjoyed Miss Whitethorn-Litton's company."

"Didn't your friendship mean you met Lord Taunton a few more times than a mere half-dozen?" he asked gently.

"Perhaps." She waved her hand airily. "I do not keep track of such things."

"Were you pleased with your betrothal?"

Miss Mardling glanced at her mother and then stared down at her magazine again. "I am always pleased to obey my father's wishes."

"Forgive me, but I had heard that you were in love with another man. I would have expected you to be disappointed with your father's choice if you had already given your affections to another man."

"A girlish infatuation, nothing more." Anger hardened her words into stones that she flung at him.

"My daughter's feelings would have matured into affection and perhaps even love after her marriage to Lord Taunton." Mrs. Mardling touched her daughter's wrist. The gesture looked like a warning to Nicholas. "If that is all, I'm afraid you will have to excuse us. We have another appointment, and I do not believe there is anything more we can tell you."

"I beg your indulgence for one more question. Do you remember where you were the evening of October twenty-second? It was a Monday."

Mrs. Mardling's eyes turned glacial. "Are we considered suspects?"

"I'm hoping that someone may have seen or heard something. That is all. Perhaps it seemed inconsequential at the time."

"It was my understanding two men had already been apprehended."

"There are two men in custody, but I am not convinced they are responsible. They are petty thieves, nothing more."

"Thieves may become murderers."

"No doubt. Nonetheless, I'm hoping either to find enough evidence to convict them or discover the true culprit. Were you at home Monday evening?"

"We attended a dinner, at Mr. Thurston's home," Mrs. Mardling said in a firm voice.

"Where is his home?"

"On Grosvenor—"

His interest quickened. "Lord Taunton's townhouse is on Grosvenor Street."

"Yes. Mr. Thurston lives nearby."

"When did you leave?"

"I haven't the faintest notion. Rose, do you remember?"

"No, Mama." Miss Mardling had begun flipping through her magazine again, clearly uninterested.

"Do you think you left before midnight?" he asked. Had the Mardlings seen Toddy and Bottom? Not that he needed their statement to prove where the two men had been. They had already admitted to breaking into Lord Taunton's house. However, when he was putting a puzzle together, it was important to have all the pieces.

"It is possible, I suppose."

"Did you see anyone unusual on the street when you passed Lord Taunton's townhouse?"

"We were in a carriage and had the curtains drawn. I'm sorry, but I really don't know what else we can tell you."

"Wait, Mama. I do know when we got home. Do you remember the clock in the hallway? It started to chime and then failed. You said we needed to get it repaired, although it still keeps time well enough. It was eleven-thirty." Miss Mardling straightened, her gaze fixed on a point beyond Nicholas' shoulder as she frowned in her effort to remember. She smiled at Nicholas. "Papa hates to stay out late, you see. He claims it ruins the digestion to be wandering around in the damp night air."

"Can you think of anything else that may be relevant?"

"No, I cannot. And I really think we must get ready for our appointment." Mrs. Mardling clasped her hands and stared at him, clearly expecting him to accept his dismissal this time.

Nicholas rose and bowed to both ladies. "Thank you for your time, Mrs. Mardling, Miss Mardling. I am grateful for the information. If you think of anything else, please send word to me." He handed Mrs. Mardling his card.

She accepted it with alacrity, as if she thought taking the small, white square would hasten his departure. "I will inform Mr. Mardling of your visit. He may think of something that will assist you in your inquiries. I am sure he will send word if he does."

"I would appreciate it." He bowed again as Mrs. Mardling stood to ring for the butler.

Nicholas paused on the front stoop to adjust his hat. The interview with the Mardlings went about as he expected, given what he knew of the situation from Taunton's journal. After meeting Rose Mardling, however, he was surprised that Taunton had found her so pleasing. Perhaps he meant her dowry pleased him. Or her father may have controlled her enough to ensure she remained on her best behavior.

Well, like "The Taming of the Shrew," if Taunton had married her, he may have found her to resemble Bianca and in the end, the demure little mouse might prove to be a shrew. Considering her mother, however, it was possible that she could acquire such calm poise in time. Taunton may have assumed the daughter would mature into a woman similar to Mrs. Mardling. It was a reasonable assumption.

He paused at the next busy corner to consider his best course.

Time to report to Gaunt at Second Sons and ask for his assistance. After that, he hoped to visit Newgate and renew his acquaintanceship with Toddy and Bottom.

Chapter Nineteen

1:00 PM October 25, 1821

"This case sounds more complicated than I anticipated," Gaunt commented when Nicholas finished a brief summary of his inquiry.

"Yes, but I believe I am making headway. I do have a ticklish situation, however, that may require assistance."

Gaunt nodded and folded his hands in front of him on his desk.

"Two men, Albert Bottom and Richard Toddy, have been arrested in conjunction with the case. They were known thieves and were caught with the weapon used to murder Lord Taunton in their possession."

"That should make your case easier, I would assume."

"It might appear that way, but I don't believe they murdered Lord Taunton. And one of them, Toddy, received a severe beating when he was apprehended. I am afraid he will not survive for long in prison, and I need him alive. He witnessed someone leaving Croftson House shortly before they found Taunton dead in his bedchamber."

"And you would like them released into your custody."

Nicholas smiled in surprise at Gaunt's rapid understanding of the situation. "I need Toddy alive."

"However, they are thieves, even if you could prove they did not commit murder."

"Yes, but no one seems inclined to prosecute them."

"What about Mr. Croftson?"

"While he was happy to let them rot in Newgate, he did not seem to want his brother's affairs aired in public. I doubt he will want to take any legal action against them."

"I see." Gaunt steepled his fingers and tapped his fingertips against his mouth. Then he smiled. "I am friends with a magistrate who might be convinced to release the fellows in your custody if you agree to ensure their presence in the courtroom should that be required. He owes me a favor."

"Could you see him this afternoon? I would like to have Bottom and Toddy released as soon as possible."

"Why the urgency?"

"Toddy's health is poor, as I mentioned, but also because I've invited the suspects to a supper at my brother's house. Toddy can identify the individual he saw leaving Taunton's townhouse, but I need him as healthy as possible to do so."

"Surely you are not relying solely on that? It would make a very weak case."

"No. That is but one piece of the puzzle." Nicholas explained the rest of his plan as succinctly as possible.

He was relieved when Gaunt finally

nodded and agreed to visit the magistrate. "By the time you get to Newgate, you should be able to extract your two miscreants without too much difficulty."

"Thank you, Mr. Gaunt."

"Just make sure they don't steal anything else or slip away before your case is concluded. I would hate to try to explain that to the magistrate."

Nicholas laughed. "Never fear. Toddy is in no shape to be climbing through windows, and I doubt Bottom will go anywhere without him."

*

2:30 PM October 25, 1821

"I will be responsible for them." Nicholas studied the warden's impassive face. "No one is willing to pay for their prosecution, and in fact, they appear to have been arrested in error. I understand the magistrate was going to send word to you concerning this."

The warden, Mr. Griffiths, frowned thoughtfully and rested his fingertips on a folded piece of paper. He pushed the note a few inches. "I did receive instructions, as you indicated. However, by rights we should wait for the assizes. If no one is willing to prosecute, then the two may be released at that time. Though if you want my opinion, we'd all be better off if they were transported."

Nicholas shook his head. "You're overcrowded as it is. And as I told your assistant, this has all been a dreadful mistake. The magistrate agrees."

In fact, there wasn't as much proof of the two men's misdoings as the officers of the law might hope. The watch officer who had taken Toddy and Bottom into custody certainly would not admit that he had found any of the stolen guineas on them, and that left just the stiletto.

Well, that was easy enough to take care of. Nicholas had learned to lie well in the battlefield. He had been ashamed the first time he had given his men false assurances to build their courage in the face of a grim and hopeless battle. The odds were against them—most of the men under his command would perish and knew it. But he had done it, his heart hollow in his chest. Now, under these innocuous circumstances, he felt more tired than uncomfortable.

"I understood they had a knife in their possession," the warden said. "A knife used to murder a man."

"Yes. The two of them discovered the stiletto and were bringing it to Bow Street. Unfortunately, their reputations are not of the best so when they ran afoul of the watch, they were arrested for possession of the weapon. The officer was simply a trifle overzealous. And I can certainly understand how he might have believed Mr. Bottom and Mr. Toddy had stolen the knife, given their somewhat shady past. As I mentioned, it was a misunderstanding and no one could fault the watch. In fact, I intend to reward the officer if possible. His actions brought the weapon to our attention, and I'm grateful to him for that. If he had not arrested Bottom and Toddy and had not delivered the stiletto to Bow Street, the weapon might still be collecting dust on someone's desk."

"The magistrate indicated you are to pay for these two gentlemen to be released." Mr. Griffiths had a peculiar habit of sitting bolt upright without moving. Nicholas found it unsettling. Perhaps Griffiths had developed the technique to intimidate the inmates and encourage them to blurt out the truth in order to escape his office as quickly as possible.

"Yes. I understand the costs involved in running this institution. I would be happy to settle any debts they have incurred. I also intend to add a small sum to defray your costs."

Griffiths' pale, blue eyes watched him carefully. Nicholas resisted the impulse to shift in his seat and look away. Would the warden accept his offer of a few pounds to release Toddy and Bottom? Or did he prefer to hold them despite the note from Gaunt's friend, the magistrate?

"Very well." He stood and held out his hand. Nicholas hurriedly scrambled to his feet and shook Griffiths' cold, stiff hand. "See my secretary on your way out. I will have your two inmates meet you at the door. Good day to you, sir."

"Good day and thank you." By the time Nicholas turned to leave the office, Griffiths had already reseated himself and picked up a paper from the short stack in the center of his desk.

Nicholas waited over twenty minutes at the door before Bottom and Toddy shambled into view, escorted by an officer who cheerfully prodded them forward with a thick stick. Bottom held one of Toddy's arms looped around his neck. He lurched awkwardly as he struggled to keep his companion on his feet and moving. When Nicholas opened the door, he got a closer look. The men's skin looked gray and unhealthy, and Bottom blinked continuously as if his eyes could not adjust to the pale, afternoon sunshine streaming over Nicholas' shoulder. Bottom's skin hung over his bones and his jowls sagged, his cheerful plumpness worn away by privation.

Nicholas' stomach clenched at the sight of them. He had seen that same hopeful look before on men who had suffered mortal wounds, but didn't realize they were dying. Hopelessness, frustration, and rage churned in his gut. Bottom and Toddy were little more than walking corpses, waiting at the edge of their graves for a slight push to topple them into the muddy darkness.

"There you are, gentlemen." The officer nodded at Nicholas. "I hope you enjoyed your visit and do come again soon." He snorted with laughter at his wit. "We're always glad to see the likes o' you."

"Thank you." Nicholas grasped Toddy's free arm and draped it around his neck. He glanced at Bottom. "Are you ready?"

"Yes, sir. And may I say—"

"Save your breath. You're going to need it."

Stumbling through the busy streets, Nicholas guided them for several blocks before he stopped to catch his breath. Bottom gasped harshly. Sweat rolled over his hollow cheeks, and exertion flushed his skin with unnatural color. A harsh, white circle ringed his mouth.

They would never make it to Nicholas' flat like this.

He released his grip on Toddy's wrist. "Hold him up, Mr. Bottom."

Bottom struggled to support his friend's weight, breathing noisily and weaving with exhaustion, unable to speak.

"Have you got him?"

Bottom nodded and wiped his sleeve over his brow.

Frowning, Nicholas stepped into the street and glanced around. Two blocks away, a hansom cab had stopped to disgorge three fashionably dressed women. When the driver folded up the steps and shut the door, Nicholas waved his arm.

At first, he feared the driver would ignore him. However, when the man looked around and saw no other likely prospects, he touched the brim of his tall hat to acknowledge Nicholas.

He climbed into his seat and flicked his whip over the heads of his horses.

"A cab is coming."

"Thank you, sir," Bottom said as Toddy's head lolled on his shoulder. "I don't know how much further Mr. Toddy could walk."

Since Toddy had failed to walk the last four blocks, Nicholas shrugged impatiently, keeping his gaze fixed on the slowly moving cab. When it finally halted in front of them, he jerked open the door and pulled down the steps before the driver could descend.

"Get inside, Bottom," he ordered. "I'll hand Toddy in to you."

"If I may ask, where are we going, sir?" Bottom gasped and struggled to ease his friend into the seat next to him.

Toddy fell, headfirst, onto the floor of the conveyance before Bottom heaved him up onto the seat. Nicholas gave directions to the driver and then clambered inside. He jerked and fell into the rear-facing seat when the carriage lurched forward.

"We're going to my flat." Studying Toddy, Nicholas' chest tightened. Had he left them in Newgate too long? Toddy appeared to be dying. He might not regain consciousness long enough to help anyone, much less provide the final tidbits Nicholas needed to make his case against Taunton's murderer.

He had to live.

Closing his eyes and leaning back,

Nicholas tried not to think about the condition of the two men. He ought to be callous enough after all he had witnessed, all he had been through himself. Nonetheless, worry slipped cold fingers under his collar and slid down his back. He knew only too well how helpless and frightened Bottom must feel as his friend grew steadily worse.

He'd wrestled with that desperation, edging to panic, in the past. He remembered a man's hot blood soaking through his coat sleeve while the man—little more than a lad—died in his arms. There were no words to ease the pain, no draughts strong enough to wash the images from his mind.

Despite the chill in the October air, Nicholas rolled up the leather curtain. He stared out of the window, trying not to think.

"I should not wish to appear ungrateful, sir, but may I ask the reason for your generosity?" Bottom blinked at Nicholas as he held Toddy steady.

Toddy nodded in the corner, mumbling and jerking as the carriage rattled over the uneven cobblestones.

"I need your assistance."

"My assistance?" His brown eyes glanced from Nicholas to the window then down at the dusty floor. His blinking grew more rapid. "While I'm more than happy to provide anyone assistance, I fail to see what I—that is—I should say, I'm afraid I don't understand."

"I need Mr. Toddy and you to help me identify a murderer."

Placing a hand protectively on Toddy's shoulder, Bottom studied his friend and then transferred his worried gaze to Nicholas. "While I would be happy to do so, I don't know how we can perform such a miracle."

"You said Mr. Toddy saw the face of the person who left Croftson House, did you not?"

Bottom nodded.

"And he might be able to recognize that person?"

"Yes, sir. But Toddy is ill. Very ill, sir."

"I can see that," Nicholas answered sharply. He rubbed a hand over his face and behind his neck. His muscles felt sore and tight. "I'm sorry, but I do realize that Mr. Toddy is very ill. If he rests this afternoon in a comfortable bed and is given decent food, do you believe he could be roused tomorrow? He only needs to identify the person he witnessed leaving that house."

"Perhaps. Mind you, I should not like to make any promises, but he might recover enough. And if he does, what then?"

"I'll be honest with you and admit I have not thought beyond that point."

"If the matter comes to trial, you do realize that Mr. Toddy may not make the best witness, do you not?" His precise tone reminded Nicholas that Bottom had once been a teacher.

A smile touched his mouth briefly. He couldn't help but like the man. Bottom had shown remarkable loyalty to his friend and the type of courage one often saw in men whose surface timidity hid a deep heart. Why couldn't he have remained safely ensconced in his schoolroom where he obviously belonged?

Even a mouse will bite if pushed hard enough.

"I am hoping that neither of you will be called upon to testify. There may be other proof—I simply hope to make sure."

"Do you suspect someone, then?"

"I strongly suspect several people." His mouth twisted. Now was not the time to reveal his pet theory. If asked, he could supply a short list that included Silsbury, although he was inclined to believe that Taunton's lover was not to blame.

Not that Silsbury didn't have plenty of other sins to apologize for, including his attempt to make Kathryn appear guilty of murder.

Finally, the carriage slowed and came to a halt. The vehicle swayed and jolted as the driver descended. The horse's hooves clattered sharply against the cobblestones as the animal shifted.

To Nicholas' surprise, Toddy roused enough to glance around in evident confusion. "What is this, then? Where are we?"

"We've been released, my lad." Bottom stumbled down the two steps, nearly falling against Nicholas before he regained his balance on the walkway. "The captain, here, has obtained our release." He reached into the cab and tapped Toddy's bony knee. "Come on, then. We'll have a bit of dinner when we get inside. You must be as famished as I, I should think. So come and give me your hand, Mr. Toddy."

Muscles shaking, Toddy stuck his grizzled head out and glanced around before gripping Bottom's hand. The steps defeated him, however. He nearly fell before Nicholas and Bottom caught him under the arm and lowered him to the walkway.

Toddy sucked in a sharp breath as they steadied him. His face paled at the sight of the four steps in front of him. "What manner of pub is this, then?"

"It's my apartment," Nicholas said.

"And why should we go with you, then?"

"This is Captain Ainsley, Mr. Toddy." Bottom leaned over his friend's shoulder to whisper into his ear. "He has obtained our release."

"And why should he do such a thing?" He studied Nicholas with a scowl and distrustful look in his red-rimmed eyes.

"There is no reason to discuss this on the street." Nicholas gripped Toddy's shoulder and guided him up the steps. "There's another flight of stairs and then you can rest and get a bite to eat. I'll explain the situation inside. Make up your mind to cooperate or it's back to Newgate."

Grumbling and wheezing, Toddy placed one hand on Bottom's shoulder and another on

Nicholas' arm and managed to enter the building. He blanched at the sight of the steep staircase leading up into the dimness above them. After casting a dark glance at Nicholas, he struggled up those stairs, as well, though he was wheezing badly when they reached the small landing in front of Nicholas' door.

When he opened the door, he discovered Dalton and Jack arguing boisterously. They had apparently completed their tasks and returned to the apartment, convinced that the other party should have had the foresight to prepare some nourishing fare before the other had arrived.

"Be it on your head, then, if I perish of hunger before he returns!" Jack waved his arms in an extravagant gesture that barely missed the end of Nicholas' nose.

"You don't appear to be dead, yet." Nicholas chuckled when Jack jerked around at the sound of his voice.

"No thanks to him!" The boy pointed an accusing finger at Dalton. "He's the most miserly old—"

"That's enough, Jack. Sergeant Dalton, we have two guests for dinner. I hope your shopping this morning was successful." Nicholas propped up his walking stick in the corner behind the door.

When he glanced around, a flush washed over his face. He had never realized how his apartment might look to others with its paucity of furnishings and lack of comforts. No rugs graced the scarred floor planks and the hems of the drapes covering the windows were partially undone. He wasn't even sure if he could find enough chairs to seat them all at the table in his sitting-cum-dining room.

It had never mattered before. He had few, if any, visitors and preferred to entertain those he did have at the military men's club. He'd never expected to have so many people in his flat at one time.

He waved Bottom and Toddy to the molting horsehair settee in front of the fireplace, relieved to see that Dalton had a warming fire blazing on the grate. As Bottom settled Toddy on the settee, Nicholas pulled Dalton toward the door.

"Do we have anything suitable for a convalescent?" He glanced over his shoulder. Toddy was stretched out on the settee with his legs hanging over one arm.

Bottom sat awkwardly on the floor next to him and called loudly enough for them all to hear him, "Broth or something similar?"

Dalton scowled. He scratched his chin. "Broth takes time, sir, and a bone. I bought a bit of ham and few other bits and pieces. A few potatoes. Cheese, onions, and the like." His frown deepened. "There's a bone in the ham, but it would take a while."

"You said there is cheese? Toasted cheese might suit him well enough." Nicholas ran a hand through his hair. His scalp felt tight, as if the skin had shrunk and a slight burst of pain throbbed in his temple. "Can you assemble some sort of lunch for now? When we're done, put the pot on to boil for soup and set Jack to stirring it."

"I can make a pot of soup well enough without that scamp." Dalton eyed him, ready to guard his position against any competitors, including Jack.

"I'm sure you can. However, I have another task for you after we sup. Mr. Bottom and Mr. Toddy need more presentable raiment. There's a fellow who sells second hand clothes a few blocks up the street. I'm relying on you to acquire what we need."

"They look fine to me." Dalton scowled at Bottom.

"No, they don't. At least not respectable enough to visit my brother, the Baron Hampton."

"What business do they have visiting a baron?"

"That is none of your concern, sergeant. You presume too much." Nicholas eyed him, tired of arguing. "They will be accompanying me to my brother's tomorrow evening to assist me in identifying a murderer. I need them dressed in presentable clothing. Nothing too flash, no bright colors."

"Ah." Dalton nodded. "You want them in the background, like. Black, then, something dark and discreet."

"Precisely. Do you think you can accomplish it?"

"Of course, sir. Now that I have an understanding, I can certainly find what you require. I know a man who has a little collection of what you might call second hand togs. All somber and very tasteful, sir. And it won't cost you as dear, neither."

"At least tell me they're not stolen—no, never mind." He had visions of one of the guests leaping to his feet, pointing a shaking finger at them, and exclaiming that Bottom was wearing his favorite jacket.

The way Dalton grinned did nothing to reassure Nicholas. "Very good, Captain." He winked and nodded. "Now I'll be off to the kitchen. I'll have your lunch ready and that scamp, Jack, can get it on the table in two ticks, see if I don't."

*

After eating, Nicholas sat back, forearm resting on the edge of the table. He examined his guests. Toddy had displayed a healthy appetite despite his gaunt appearance, and after eating, he showed a great deal of improvement. A bit of color had returned to his sallow cheeks, and he seemed more alert, although he couldn't hide the fact that his ribs pained him when he moved. He tried to keep his mouth pressed shut, but small gasps escaped when he lifted his arms or twisted his torso.

Brows creased, Bottom watched him incessantly and worried over him like a mother cat anxiously nosing a newborn kitten.

"Leave off, Bottom. You're mauling me something fierce," Toddy complained. A sharp gasp clipped his words when his friend tried to wrest the mug out of his hand. "I can hold me own beer, can't I? See?" He lifted the mug only to jerk and spill a foamy wave over his knuckles. He sucked in a harsh breath as he paled from the pain. When Bottom raised his hand, Toddy scowled. "Get away with you. For God's sake, give me a bit of peace, will you?"

After exchanging glances, Dalton and Jack left the table as soon as they finished the remaining crust of melted cheese. Nicholas could hear them clattering around in the kitchen and the mumble of Dalton's voice as he instructed Jack on the intricacies of soup making. Once Dalton arranged matters to his satisfaction, he disappeared on his errand.

Nicholas finally turned to Bottom. "How would you like to accompany me on a small reconnaissance and resupply mission?"

"I beg your pardon, sir? Reconnaissance?" Bottom turned away from Toddy.

The injured man closed his eyes and let out a sigh of relief.

Nicholas stood and waited while Bottom scrambled to his feet. "Come on, leave him be. We're only going to the attic."

Over the years, tenants had come and gone, abandoning household items they no longer wanted. Sometimes, they were forcibly removed due to insolvency and their belongings remained. So the attic was filled to overflowing with all manner of goods. Nicholas had raided the large, cobwebbed space once before to obtain the settee and the wide table they had used for their meals. He had a vague recollection of other useful items.

The attic was little more than a series of rooms that opened from one to the next. The room closest to the narrow staircase held the most items, and they were stacked up in dusty piles against the walls. Fortunately, a narrow window draped in soft, gray cobwebs provided sufficient light in each room to identify the haphazard stacks as furniture.

Bottom stared around, his mouth slightly open, as if he viewed the treasures from Aladdin's cave. Unfortunately, most of the furniture was broken and better off used as fuel in the fireplace. Only a few pieces were sturdy enough to be rescued for his rapidly growing household.

"I need your assistance, Mr. Bottom." Nicholas yanked a brittle chair missing one leg off of a stack in the furthest corner. When it came free, he threw it toward the opposite wall, watching it clatter and raise a small cloud of dust from the gritty floor. Motes of dirt sparkled in the light slanting in through the small, gray panes. Nicholas sneezed as the dry smell of old wood tickled his nose. "There are two chairs here that might serve us well in my dining room."

"Yes, sir." Bottom edged past him and gently removed the two items. "There's a third one here with all four legs." He looked at Nicholas with raised brows and a hopeful sparkle in his eyes.

"Go ahead. Take anything that isn't broken." He pushed through a few more stacks, disgusted as seemingly good furniture broke apart when he pulled it free. "I believe there are a few beds here, as well. If we can locate them, you can move them into one of the bedrooms. I saw mattresses in the back room, as well." He dusted off his hand and flinched when he felt a sliver plunge deeper into his palm from the gesture. He tried to remove it with his teeth and once more felt the burn of frustration. Even the removal of a sliver defeated him. What use was he with only one arm?

Sweat made his shirt stick to his back. He shrugged angrily and blinked when a cobweb caught on his eyelashes.

"Allow me, sir." Bottom gently took Nicholas' hand, turned it over. He worked gently with his fingernails until the sliver slipped free.

Nicholas pulled his hand away and brushed it off again. To cover his frustration and ill-temper, he forced a chuckle. "You should be a physician, Mr. Bottom. You always seem preoccupied with curing the ills of others."

"The boys often got into scrapes." He shrugged, staring down at his own grimy palms. "You see, I used to be a teacher, sir. One had to deal with illnesses and such mishaps."

"You miss it, don't you?"

"Well, they could hardly keep me on, sir. Not when I persisted in picking up trinkets here and there. But that's all over, now, isn't it?" He rubbed his hands together and glanced around, clearly trying to avoid the topic of his past. "What else do you require? There is a lovely little piecrust table in the corner. I'm sure it would polish up quite nicely."

"Take it. Take anything you think will be useful. There are four bedrooms on the second floor, including mine. Furnish them as you wish. Toddy will regain his health more quickly if he has a decent bed."

"That is very generous of you, sir." His brows pinched together, and he flashed a quick glance at Nicholas. "Begging your pardon, sir, but what is to happen to us? I should say, after tomorrow night, that is?"

Nicholas turned away and stared at the glistening dust motes. The pale light created the illusion that powdered diamonds filled the air when it was nothing but dirt. Life was very adept at such illusions, and the notion depressed him.

Just like his left arm. Its presence created the illusion that he was whole, that he had two strong hands. The reality was bitterly different.

He wished that reality matched the lovely illusion.

"I'm considering the matter, Mr. Bottom." He sighed. He could not keep collecting people like so many snuffboxes, and yet the thought of walking away was intolerable. They had no place to sleep, no resources to buy food. And they would freeze as the October mists drifting through London's dark streets turned to sleet when winter settled around them.

Sick, hungry, and frightened, they would have no choice but to rob another house.

Their faces haunted him like the desperate men he'd tried to save in Corunna. He would never forget their pleading eyes following him, begging to live despite their suffering, to go home even if it was to die.

Part of him whispered that his concern for the two men was simply a way to forget his own situation, his own sense of incompleteness and failure. Whatever the reason, he could not escape his sense of responsibility for this odd band of men.

He rubbed the back of his neck again. Well, he would think of something after this affair ended. Tomorrow night. For now, he needed their assistance to catch a killer, although he still had only the vaguest idea about how he could prove what he knew was true. Unless the guilty party could be convinced by his parlor trick to confess.

The Illusion of Desire

It all depended upon a sense of guilt.

Chapter Twenty

10:00 AM October 26, 1821

Another night filled with nightmares of blood, gun smoke, and muffled screams. Nicholas awoke in a tangle of sweat-soaked sheets and got up only to wobble over and sit down at the shaky table near the window. Desperate for a distraction, he wrote another list of the people who had attended Taunton's dinner. Who else had witnessed Taunton's smiling humiliation of Kathryn as he showed off the jeweled stiletto he had commissioned for her?

Nicholas was inclined to exclude Croftson, however he could not do so in good conscience. Croftson had never admitted whether he knew of Kathryn's stiletto, but he had been in London. Nicholas never saw his ring clearly enough to know if any of the stones were missing.

Before the supper tomorrow night, he needed to interview the rest of the guests from Taunton's dinner. He had something in mind, not precisely a trick but something that might seem like one to some of them. In order to carry it out, he needed to familiarize himself with those who would attend.

He crossed the Mardlings and Silsbury off the list.

The Dudley name caught his eye. They would be next.

After returning Kathryn's bloodied dress to Mr. Flatman, Nicholas walked briskly to the narrow townhouse the Dudley family rented in Mayfair and knocked. With a sense of chagrin, he realized he could have delivered the dinner invitations as easily as Jack. However, sending Jack saved Nicholas from getting caught up in a discussion or questions about the dinner. He wanted to focus on gleaning any tidbits of information he could about the night Taunton died, not what his brother's cook intended to serve.

A whip-thin butler opened the door, and a short time later, he ushered Nicholas into a drawing room. He was fortunate to find the entire family, Mr. and Mrs. Dudley and their daughter, Mary, seated by the fire. Mr. Dudley was reading a book while his wife knitted. Mary Dudley leaned toward the crackling flames with a heavy shawl drawn tightly around her shoulders. She glanced up at him as the butler introduced him.

Her pallor, bloodless lips, and deep circles around her red-rimmed eyes shocked him. The girl was ill, but whether it was a physical illness or something else was beyond Nicholas' skills to determine. Mrs. Dudley's lips moved as she counted stitches, the needles clicking between her fingers. Her attention seemed completely absorbed in her task. Her husband, however, closed his book and studied him without offering his hand or suggesting he sit down.

"What can we do for you, Captain Ainsley?" Mr. Dudley asked. His clipped voice made it clear he was not a man to suffer fools, or delays, with good humor.

A smile played over his wife's mouth, dimpling her rosy, round cheek. She shook her head as she shifted her knitting to start a new row, clearly used to his abrupt manners and finding them amusing. Nicholas bit the inside of his mouth to keep from ginning, himself. At least Mrs. Dudley did not seem either resentful of her husband or downtrodden.

"As you are no doubt aware, I am inquiring into the matter of Lord Taunton's death. I was hoping you could assist me—"

"I don't see how."

"Hugo..." Mrs. Dudley placed a hand briefly on her husband's arm as if to remind him that politeness cost nothing. She smiled at Nicholas. "As my husband said, it is difficult to see how we can assist you."

"Were you anywhere near the Taunton townhouse the night of October 22? Could you have seen anything or anyone entering or leaving the premises?"

"No," Mr. Dudley said in a firm voice. "We were at home."

"We don't go out much," Mrs. Dudley clarified. "Except to visit a few close friends, of course."

"I see. Well, I am also trying to build a

picture of the man, to understand how this
tragedy could have happened. What were your
impressions of Lord Taunton?"

A furious crimson tide washed up Mr.
Dudley's neck. The vein above his left brow
throbbed as he frowned. "If it is rumors you
want, you can go elsewhere, young man."

"No, not rumors," Nicholas responded
hastily. "I am interested in your own thoughts
and opinions. Your judgment concerning his
character would be valuable to me. If there is
anything you can tell me that would assist the
inquiry, I would be grateful."

Mrs. Dudley tightened her grip on her
husband's wrist and brightened her smile. Her
brown eyes gleamed in the firelight. "We
admired Lord Taunton greatly. He was a very
kind and generous man. I'm sure we can't
imagine why anyone would want to do away
with him, can we, dearest?"

"The man was an earl and acted as befits
one."

"Perhaps." Mrs. Dudley sniffed and her
smile faded. "I must say, though, that his
behavior toward that girl was not what one
would hope."

"That girl?" Nicholas studied her
troubled face.

"Miss Whitethorn-Litton. First, her
father passed away under peculiar
circumstances while visiting the earl, and then
we all though Lord Taunton would do the right

thing and marry her. But of course..." She sighed and made a small, exasperated gesture with her hand. "Is it any wonder that she murdered him?"

"She couldn't have! She was—" Miss Dudley straightened. She stared at her mother, blinking.

How could Miss Dudley be so sure unless she was the friend Kathryn was protecting? This young woman must be the person she had been out with, not a member of the demi-monde.

"She was...?" Nicholas prompted her.

Miss Dudley flushed and then grew paler than ever. "She was too sweet to do such a thing."

Sweet? Kathryn was *sweet*? He could think of many ways to describe her, including intelligent and headstrong, but insipidly sweet did not leap to mind.

"You don't know, Mary, dearest." Her mother patted her on the shoulder.

Miss Dudley hunched forward, moving out of reach of her mother. "I do know. She could never do such a thing." Her voice quavered, but beneath the thin notes was a firm sense of the truth. She knew beyond a doubt that Kathryn was innocent, although Nicholas suspected she would never explain why in the presence of her parents.

"What made you assume Miss Whitethorn-Litton was responsible, Mrs. Dudley?" Nicholas asked, diverting attention away from the vulnerable Miss Dudley.

"Rumors." Mr. Dudley's mouth thinned. "Mr. Silsbury was here earlier and mentioned it. I should have known better than to believe him."

"Harold Silsbury visited you? Was he in the habit of calling on you?" Nicholas shifted from one foot to the other, tired of standing still for so long.

"No." The word burst from him before he snapped his mouth shut. After a minute, he continued in a harsh voice as if he regretted the necessity of explaining but could not bring himself to remain silent. "He had never been here before except in Taunton's company. He apparently felt pressed enough to do so today, however."

"Why?"

"He wanted a loan. I sent him on his way with a flea in his ear. Why should I provide him with funds, I ask you? His affairs are none of my concern."

"Completely understandable," Nicholas said. "And he is the one who indicated that Miss Whitethorn-Litton was to blame for Taunton's death?"

"Yes. He said it was her knife. Apparently, Silsbury was convinced Taunton was about to cast the girl off and she killed him in a fit of pique."

"I'm afraid Mr. Silsbury mislead you."

"I am not surprised." The anger slowly leaked out of Dudley's face, relaxing his heavy features.

"Mrs. Dudley mentioned her father... What happened?"

"I thought that tragedy might have been at the root of it," Mrs. Dudley said. "I must have misunderstood."

"We don't indulge in gossip." Mr. Dudley caught his wife's gaze and gave a slight shake of his head.

"I dislike gossip as well. However, you never know what bit of information may be important. What was this tragedy?" Nicholas asked.

"Mr. Whitethorn-Litton..." Mrs. Dudley watched her husband but he did not stop her. "Well, he was visiting Lord Taunton at his country estate when he passed away. It was, um, quite sudden and it left his daughter quite alone in a houseful of men. The entire affair was disgraceful."

"Was Mr. Whitethorn-Litton's death suspicious?"

She frowned and then raised her brows at her husband. Mr. Dudley answered, "I believe it was the unexpectedness that caused the rumors. Nothing ever came of it. He apparently died in his sleep."

"What is your opinion?" Nicholas asked.

"I lack sufficient information to have an opinion, as does my wife."

Ancient history. But after his cursory view of Taunton's journal, Nicholas realized there might be more to the tragedy than he had thought. He would have to go back and read the older entries. The Dudley's view of the tale was interesting, however Nicholas couldn't allow that mystery to distract him. He suspected that Taunton's killer had a more immediate reason to commit murder. He nodded and tightened his clasp on his left wrist.

"Is there anything else, Captain Ainsley?" Mr. Dudley rose and strode over to a bell pull.

"No, and thank you for your assistance." Nicholas accepted Dudley's dismissal with good grace. He had learned more than he expected and now had to sift through everything he knew to ensure he did not overlook any critical factors.

When he arrived at the Reeve household, the butler informed him in no uncertain terms that the Reeves were not at home. He did not elucidate whether they were truly out or simply not at home to Nicholas. He suspected they were not home specifically to him since it was too early in the day for them to be out for the evening.

The bachelors, Mr. Inglewood and Mr. Palmer, were both in, but they laughingly supplied Nicholas with a solid alibi: they had spent the evening of October 22 at their club. They had not returned to their apartments until well after two in the morning.

"If you're looking for a reason to kill him, I would investigate his ridiculous notion to marry," Mr. Palmer said.

Mr. Inglewood smothered a laugh. "Marriage makes even the wisest man ridiculous." He sprawled over a sofa with one arm and a leg hooked over the back. His foot swung lazily as he stared at the gilded ceiling. "We advised him it was ill-considered, but he was never one to listen to others. He wanted what he wanted. No one could dissuade him once he made up his mind."

"He always claimed that decisiveness was one of his better qualities," Mr. Palmer added.

"Ah, is that what it is called?" Inglewood smiled at Nicholas. "And here I have been describing it as sheer stubbornness. How dreadful to be so terribly wrong."

"Can you think of anything else that might help us? Anything Taunton might have mentioned?"

"Not that I recall," Palmer said. "Dear Harry said it was that girl—Whitethorn-Litton. Perhaps you should ask her."

Silsbury had been a busy lad spreading his version of the events to all and sundry.

"Rest assured she has been questioned. Do either of you have an opinion concerning Lord Taunton's death?"

Palmer shrugged and glanced at Inglewood who simply smiled benignly at Nicholas and remained silent.

He could play that game as well as the two indolent young men in front of him. He waited.

Palmer shifted and even Inglewood began to look uncomfortable. The foot he had hooked over the sofa back swung faster and faster. The two men exchanged glances.

"Well," Palmer said.

"Yes. Well. Right." Inglewood swung around to sit properly. His hands gripped his knees. "Right. Well."

"So." Palmer took a step forward and then back.

"Well. I suppose that's all, then," Inglewood said.

"Oh, yes. Well." Palmer thrust his hand out to Nicholas. "Er, thank you for dropping by."

"If you think of anything, send me word." Nicholas shook Palmer's damp hand.

"Of course, of course." Palmer pumped his hand enthusiastically. "Happy to do so, aren't we, Inglewood?"

"Indeed, yes. Happy to do so."

Not much the wiser, Nicholas left, much to the evident relief of Palmer and Inglewood.

Chapter Twenty-One

4:00 PM October 26, 1821

Kathryn studied Lady Hampton, wondering if she knew. She suspected she might. Lady Hampton seemed very ... worldly, far worldlier than Kathryn, herself. However, she was also a married woman and that might account for it.

"Where were you going, my dear?" Lady Hampton's needle flashed in and out of the soft lawn, adding an embroidered design of delicate white flowers to the hem of a baby's christening gown.

"I beg your pardon?"

"Nicholas, my brother-in-law, indicated you were in a carriage accident." She glanced at Kathryn, her brown eyes flashing with amusement. She had such a quaint, doe-like appearance that Kathryn could not help but like her, despite her awkward questions.

She sighed. "I am not adept at fairytales."

"I rather thought that might be the case." Lady Hampton placed her sewing on the table next to her and leaned forward to place her hand over Kathryn's. "Nicholas is a difficult man. I understand completely if you do not wish to talk about your adventures with him, though I may be able to help if you are in a difficult position."

"No, no, it is not that. Nicholas—Captain Ainsley—is very kind." Kathryn's hands balled into fists. "He has treated me with nothing but respect."

Lady Hampton sat back, smiling, and picked up her sewing again. "I would expect nothing less of him. However, despite your defense of him, he *is* difficult. He persists in believing himself less of a man simply because his left arm is damaged. We have never been able to convince him otherwise."

"Well, if he does, it is understandable. He must have gone through a terrible ordeal." She defended him, a spurt of anger making her words more forceful than she intended. How could they be so obtuse and fail to understand him? He went through a terrible ordeal in Corunna, and everyone seems to treat it as no more tragic than falling off a horse during a hunt.

"Then you feel sorry for him? Pity?"

"No—that is not what I meant. I, oh, what is the use?" She raised her hands, frustrated. She could scarcely explain her feelings to herself. How could she possibly explain them to anyone else?

"I suspect there is a great deal of use in understanding how you feel about him, my dear. And you do have deeper feelings for him, do you not?"

"I—I suppose I do, though it's hardly surprising." Bitterness twisted her mouth as if she had eaten a teaspoon of alum. "He's the first man I've met who has bothered to listen to me or ask my opinion in a long time."

Lady Hampton nodded and continued sewing. "Yes. He was always good at that. It is one of Nicholas' better qualities." She bit off the thread and picked up a spool to rethread the needle. "How did you happen to meet?"

"He was pursuing an inquiry." She sighed. "You might as well know, I am a suspect in a murder."

"Really? How delightful. I must say you seem to lead a very exciting life, much more exciting than mine. Whom did you murder?"

"Lord Taunton. That is, I didn't murder anyone, but he, well, I was living in his townhouse when he died. Naturally everyone assumes I, um, well, you must guess already..."

"At the very least, I would imagine everyone believes you are a light-skirt. But you are not, are you?"

"No." Kathryn shook her head. Oddly enough, it was more embarrassing to admit she was not Taunton's mistress than that she was. The admission meant that Taunton had not loved her and did not even find her desirable.

"It is not surprising, after all." Lady Hampton's offhand comment surprised her. "You must have realized quite some time ago that Taunton had no interest in that direction."

"I beg your pardon? He was engaged to be married to Miss Mardling."

"A rather recent development, however."

"Yes, but—"

"That wouldn't change his proclivities.

After all, it was his duty to marry and produce heirs. One needn't like, or enjoy, one's duty. One simply needs to perform it."

Kathryn's temper flared. For all his faults, Taunton had been good to her. At least, he had given her a home when her father died, and that alone showed his compassion. How dare Lady Hampton criticize his private life? It was no business of anyone except Taunton.

She let out a long breath. Perhaps Lady Hampton had only tried to point out the truth and not condemn Lord Taunton.

"And what of my brother-in-law, Nicholas?"

"Nicholas?" Kathryn repeated his name and glanced down at her clasped hands, feeling her face flush. "What do you mean?"

"Have you discussed your situation?"

"I have no notion what he knows or does not know." She couldn't stop a bitter note creeping into her voice. She knew he thought she was "damaged goods." The only thing that surprised her was that he had not attempted anything improper. Unless he also found her unattractive. She couldn't help but think that despite his "proclivities," Taunton might have been interested in her if she were as beautiful as the woman sitting across from her.

"Have you told him the truth? About the murder and your situation with Taunton?"

"He is the inquiry agent. He should have discovered it already."

"And how would he do so if you refused to tell him the truth? Come, I know it is difficult and your pride may get in the way, but you must tell him you were not Taunton's lover and you did not kill him."

"I told him I was not even in the house at the time Taunton died." She hesitated to say more. She had promised Mary and could not betray her trust even if she sensed that Eleanor would be more sympathetic than a man. The fact remained that seeking an abortion was illegal and their actions would damn them both. "There is truly nothing more to be said about it. He either believes me or does not."

"Who do you think killed Taunton?"

"I don't know." Kathryn pressed her lips together, feeling stubborn and angry. If she had not been able to discover the truth about her father's death in seven years, how could anyone expect her to know who murdered Taunton?

"You must have some notion. Come, I will not tell anyone if you don't wish it."

"Why do you persist in asking me?"

"Why do you wish to pretend ignorance?"

"But I am ignorant." She brushed a curl off her forehead with the back of her hand in an annoyed gesture. "I'm sorry, but it is so painful, I'd almost rather not know."

"That is often the case. However, you cannot continue in this manner. Eventually the truth will come out, and it might prove better to face it sooner rather than later."

"There are many who might have done such a thing." She smiled, though not in amusement. "My first thought was Harry. That is, Harry Silsbury. He has a terrible temper, and Taunton often went to his room when he thought I had retired for the evening." Her grim smile changed to a frown. "However, if it were Harry, I would have expected the body to be found in his room. He rarely went into Taunton's room. In truth, I have never known him to go in there. Taunton liked his privacy too well."

"And his control, no doubt." Lady Hampton nodded.

"And truth be told, Harry and I were both too beholden to Taunton. We had no place to go and lived there on Taunton's sufferance. There would be little point in killing him."

"Unless he told you that you must leave."

"There is that. Even so, with him alive, we could expect something from him, a settlement or funds to assist us in moving elsewhere." She shrugged. "I know it sounds terrible, but we—both of us—had more reason to keep him alive despite any desire on his part to be rid of the two of us. If he wished to be rid of us, that is. Nicholas mentioned it, so I suppose it must be true. But Taunton never said anything to me." Only Rose had been so adamant that Kathryn would have to leave.

"So if we eliminate love, because you don't believe Mr. Silsbury was responsible, who was?"

"His brother?"

"Mr. Croftson? Surely, not." Lady Hampton's brows rose.

"He inherited, didn't he? And if Taunton married and produced an heir, it would have cut him out." She sighed and rubbed her forehead, hating the thought that Taunton's own family might have betrayed him.

"Was he in London?" Lady Hampton asked.

"I believe he might have been. I heard Taunton mention him earlier that day."

"And he was in the townhouse, then. Yes, I see."

"No—no, Mr. Croftson never stayed at the townhouse. He preferred his club. I don't think he and his brother were close, at least that is the impression I had." She straightened, refusing to speculate, not wanting to remember an argument she had overheard when Taunton first decided to allow her to stay.

His brother had been livid at the impropriety of her presence in the household. Taunton had laughed at him, asking in a cutting voice if it weren't better to have her live with him than the men he preferred.

Cheeks flaming, Kathryn had run away feeling too ashamed to listen to them. When Taunton used that voice, it always made her feel ill. It felt as if he were about to say something that would cut her heart out and lay it bare in front of him where he could dispassionately watch the life bleed out of her.

"So Croftson wasn't there that day?"

"No. At least, not that I was aware. Perhaps it was a business associate? If the motive was not love, it must have been money." Despite her words, Kathryn could not dismiss a niggling doubt that they might not be able to dismiss love quite so easily.

"Ah, a nameless business associate. How comfortably convenient." Lady Hampton tucked her sewing into a wicker basket and smoothed her skirts, making the silvery-blue silk glow in the soft light from the windows. "I hope you will excuse me. Since Nicholas persuaded us to host that ridiculous supper this evening, I must ensure Cook hasn't deserted us in a fit of ill-temper. You may wish to get some rest while you can. It promises to be a long evening."

Kathryn squeezed her eyes shut for a moment. Cowardly though it was, she almost wished they could all just forget Lord Taunton and the need for justice for a few days.

Amy Corwin

Chapter Twenty-Two

6:00 PM October 26, 1821

"How is he?" Nicholas whispered when Bottom opened the door to the tiny back bedroom the two occupied.

"Sleeping, sir. His color is better, and I think he'll do."

He handed Bottom an armful of clothing Dalton had acquired the previous afternoon. "He can rest another half-hour or so, but then you must dress. Dalton will bring you wash water."

"Very good, sir. We will be ready." Bottom nodded and shifted the burden of dark-colored coats and trousers from one arm to the other.

Nicholas shut the door gently and returned to his sitting room, pacing from the window to the door and back. He had re-read Taunton's journal that afternoon, focusing on the earlier sections. Mr. Dudley was right to question Mr. Whitethorn-Litton's sad death. Nicholas closed his eyes, the words in the journal returning like the faint echo of cannons.

...I found him in the garden, his trousers pooled around his ankles and clothing in disarray. A silken cord dangled from his neck. My poor Charles—what happened to you? Why? How could you meet someone else when you knew so well how I felt about him? Someone who would do such a thing to you...

334

Despite his betrayal, I could not leave him there, not like that. And I have no interest in so-called justice. I will not expose my dear Charles or my own private life to vulgar, sordid gossip. So I made up my mind to grant him some dignity in death and did what I had to do.

Thankfully, it was late and dark in the garden so no one saw me. I could not contain my tears, however. Weeping with despair, I carried him to his room and dressed him in his nightclothes. My tears washed away the dirt from his face and hands.

In a last farewell, I kissed him on his cold lips and pulled the coverlet up to his chest. I shut the door.

I could do no more for him.

My grief would not let me sleep. An hour before dawn I promised myself I would remain alert and uncover the culprit, if possible. The thought filled me with bitter despair. I do not know who could possibly have done such a thing.

Finally, the maid knocked on my door, carrying a tray with my usual chocolate. A short time later, I heard a scream and like all the others, I ran into the hallway and pretended surprise when the maid found him. Dead in his sleep. My physician was happy to concur with my assessment.

Rest in peace, my love...

Later entries indicated that unmasking the murderer continued to elude Lord Taunton.

As the years passed, he put it out of his mind.

Unfortunately, the tragedy of that death reverberated to this day, causing pain for all concerned.

And at last Nicholas had pieced together what had happened, and how the sad threads have been woven together into a dark tapestry. The tale was tragic, and unhappily, not as uncommon as one might hope.

He only hoped he could prove his theory this evening.

*

Nicholas arrived with Bottom and Toddy at his brother's house an hour before he was expected. The surprised butler informed him that Lord and Lady Hampton were in their rooms dressing for dinner and could not be disturbed. Uncertainty wrinkled Soames' brows as he eyed Bottom and Toddy.

"Show us to a sitting room, then," Nicholas said. "Tell Lord Hampton we're waiting for him."

Soames nodded and led the way, grandly ignoring the two men who followed Nicholas like a pair of diffident dogs with their tails tucked firmly between their legs. The butler left them with a promise to send in a tray of some excellent elderberry wine that he was sure they would appreciate, clearly deciding not to waste his lordship's fine sherry on such disreputable specimens.

Toddy coughed wetly and pulled out a large, blue handkerchief with yellow spots to wipe his mouth. He frowned and glanced around as Bottom stood nearby, his dented and tattered hat clutched in his hands.

"What're we here for, then?" Toddy asked, his tone belligerent.

"As I explained, I'm hoping you can see if any of the guests look like the person you saw leaving Croftson House the night Lord Taunton died."

"Hmmm." Toddy hummed, but it sounded more like a dirge than a cheerful tune.

Bottom's knuckles whitened as he crushed the brim of his hat. "Pardon, sir, but how do you plan on carrying out your plan?" He flushed, his eyes widening as if he heard his words echoing back to him. "Not that it isn't a grand plan, sir. But it seems a trifle awkward— no disrespect, sir. We can hardly stand in the hallway eyeing the visitors as they arrive. And we are not dressed for serving the guests." He clasped Toddy's shoulder as if to reassure him.

While he had recovered enough to join them this evening, Toddy was not in any condition to act as a servant, even supposing Henry wanted the two to pretend to be members of his staff.

"Sit down before you fall." Nicholas shrugged. "And help yourselves to the wine. My sister-in-law makes it, and it is quite good." He poured himself a glass before handing the bottle to Bottom.

Truth be told, he actually *had* hoped to pass the two of them off as servants when he asked his brother to host this supper. However, he recognized that Toddy's condition made that impossible, and he reluctantly gave up on the notion. It was unfortunate that Bottom hadn't seen the face of the Taunton's visitor more clearly. With his clear diction and courtly manner, he could easily have passed as a footman or even a butler in Soames' stead.

Toddy grunted and gingerly seated himself on the damask-covered chair nearest the small table where Soames had placed the wine. His friend watched him, his brows beetling over his eyes in concern, before he poured two glasses.

"Mr. Toddy." Bottom bowed as he handed Toddy a glass.

"Thank you, Mr. Bottom." Toddy's eyes glinted with anticipation. He took a sip and licked his lips before emptying his glass in a long gulp. "A pleasure, Mr. Bottom. A rare pleasure." He held out his glass.

Bottom bowed and instantly refilled it.

"I believe that's enough," Nicholas said, eyeing the pair. "At least for now."

"Nicky!" Henry blew through the sitting room's grand double doors like a cheerful south wind. He pounded him on the shoulder blade and then stopped, rubbing his hands together as he eyed Bottom and Toddy. "So, are we ready? I must say this is damned exciting. I shan't complain again about your choice of careers, Nicky my boy. But I insist you include me whenever you plan on unmasking a murderer. It makes it worth getting up in the morning, doesn't it?"

"I suppose it does." He couldn't help chuckling. At least his brother didn't view his desire to be an inquiry agent as somehow beneath him. Of course, if Nicholas went from chasing murderers to the somewhat less exciting work of locating missing maidservants, his older brother might change his opinion.

"Now, what is our plan of attack?" Henry asked.

"I had thought Mr. Bottom and Mr. Toddy could assume positions on your staff, however Mr. Toddy is in no condition to do so. He has been ill."

"And which is Mr. Toddy? You failed to introduce us—where are your manners, Nick?"

As Toddy scrambled to his feet, Nicholas performed the introductions. Henry shook their hands solemnly as if they were hitherto unknown peers of the realm.

"And I take it Mr. Toddy, here, is the one who can identify the foul miscreant who did away with Taunton?"

"Possibly. His observations will certainly assist me."

Henry pulled his lower lip. Then his eyes brightened. He snapped his fingers. "I have it!

Mr. Toddy will sit in the dining room next to the bell pull. I often have Soames waiting in that corner, ready to summon the next course. The bell is much more efficient than running back and forth between the kitchen and the dining room."

Nicholas grinned, knowing that the truth was that Soames was getting old and rather than getting rid of him, Henry devised a scheme to allow Soames to rest between courses while keeping an eye on things. As each course came to a conclusion, Soames would ring the bell to bring forth a long line of footmen carrying delicacies on silver trays. Soames could then take over serving, assisted by one of the footmen, before resuming his seat.

"Mr. Bottom can help Soames at the door, then. He was once a tutor and can round off his vowels almost as expertly as Soames."

"Very good. Excellent." Henry picked up the remaining glass and held it out to Bottom who filled it with alacrity. "My wife's elderberry wine, I presume?"

"Yes, it is very good."

"Excellent. Much more refreshing than sherry, don't you agree, Mr. Toddy?"

"Yes, your lordship, sir." Toddy, just having taken a sip, sputtered. His handkerchief flashing as he wiped droplets of wine off his chin and lapels.

"Have another glass and a seat, Mr. Toddy." Henry motioned to Bottom to refill his glass. "And tell me how you came to witness Taunton's murderer."

Toddy flicked an agonized glance at Bottom before gulping down the entire contents of his glass. "I, er... Mr. Bottom, another glass if you please? I'm right parched."

Paling, Bottom flicked a glance at Lord Hampton and took a deep breath. "We, well, we happened to be in the small yard behind Croftson House when we noticed the person in question."

"Very exciting, eh?"

"Yes, your lordship." Bottom refilled his glass and Toddy's, thereby finishing off the bottle of deep purple wine. He touched his sleeve to his damp forehead, delicately blotting a few beads of sweat.

Henry pulled out an elegant, gold pocket watch and thumbed it open. "Our guests should be arriving shortly." He smiled. "If you are to play the parts of servants, you must assume your posts, men. Let the play commence!"

Chapter Twenty-Three

9:00 PM October 26, 1821

The next two hours left Nicholas regretting his idea of a supper. He was forced to be polite and find topics of conversation that did not involve Lord Taunton. It was not as easy as he hoped, but he thought he managed to avoid putting anyone on his or her guard.

Of course, the guests had quite the opposite objective and talked about Taunton whenever they sensed an opening. Avid whispers filled what might have been awkward silences as everyone shared the latest gossip about the murder.

Kathryn avoided most of the questions and appeared pale, almost ill. She pushed her food from one edge of her plate to the other, and her hands shook so badly that very few forkfuls made it to her mouth. Those that did spilled half their contents.

After trying to wring the details of the case from Nicholas and finding the conversation ruthlessly turned to the damp weather, most of the guests turned their shoulders to him. A few of the men questioned him about Corunna and the hectic British retreat. However, his terse answers finally discouraged them from pursuing the topic.

The Dudley and Mardling families appeared to know each other well. Mrs. Dudley and Mrs. Mardling sought each other out and sat together in the drawing room, both before dinner and after. The plump, self-satisfied ladies were so much alike they looked like sisters, down to their gray-streaked hair, although Mrs. Dudley was dark while Mrs. Mardling was fair.

Their daughters, Mary and Rose, linked arms after the meal and bent their heads together. The girls whispered behind their hands as they flashed coy glances at the three bachelors. The young ladies had smilingly included Kathryn when she sat down in a chair near them, although Nicholas noticed that Rose glanced uneasily at her mother for approval before speaking to her.

As for the men, the older gentlemen formed a loose circle a few feet away from their wives. They seemed off-hand and almost disinterested in the event, while the women's eyes glowed with barely repressed excitement. The women clearly anticipated some interesting news, if and when Nicholas finally decided to share it with them.

The three bachelors seemed to prefer each other's company and stayed in a tight cluster. The young men were dressed in bright colors that seemed a bit strident against the more subdued jackets and waistcoats of the older men. The dark haired, black-eyed Bartholomew Palmer, in particular, glowed like the sun in a golden yellow jacket over a black waistcoat elaborately embroidered with rich crimson and gold threads in a Chinese design. His friend, the brown-haired, brown-eyed George Inglewood, was hardly more subdued in a bright blue jacket over a green brocade waistcoat.

Silsbury, at least, wore a subdued, dark blue jacket with a black cravat encircling his neck. His waistcoat was black with silver embroidery, and of the three men, he seemed the most nervous. He kept flicking glances at Nicholas and Mr. Croftson as if he expected one or both of them to grab him bodily and throw him out the door.

The trio drank too much and spent a great deal of time poking each other in the ribs with their elbows and laughing uproariously at some shared joke. Despite Rose and Mary's scowls and exasperated glances, none of the young men paid the women the least attention. In fact, they scarcely looked their way.

Croftson, however, seemed determined to maintain a pretense that the three bachelors did not exist. He stood in the semi-circle with the other married men and managed to look both bored and angry at the same time. His brows jutted out over his eyes and every time he caught Nicholas' glance, the frown lines around his mouth tightened. He spoke only when specifically addressed. His fingers kept playing with his pocket watch, although he managed to restrain himself from pulling it out and flicking it open more than two or three times an hour.

"Are you ready, Nicky?" Henry whispered before he winked at Eleanor.

Eyes gleaming with laughter, she bit her lower lip and shook her head. She bent over a silver tray of bone china tea cups that were so fragile Nicholas could see through the sides and watch the tea sloshing around inside. Kathryn assisted her in handing cups to the other ladies, smiling politely but noticeably quiet. Nicholas felt a stab of concern that they would snub her. His tension eased slightly when Mary returned her smile and made a harmless remark clearly aimed at including her in their conversation.

"Nick?" his brother prompted.

Feeling his shoulders tighten, Nicholas nodded. "Yes. We might as well begin."

"What do you have in mind?"

"Do you have a bowl of some sort?"

"Would a silver presentation bowl suit you?" Henry waved in the direction of a console table set near a group of silk-covered chairs.

"Yes." He cleared his throat. His stomach felt hollow despite their excellent dinner. Henry's cook had outdone himself with a succulent beef roast, potato soufflé, and a rich fish chowder that was a meal in and of itself.

The food sat heavily in his stomach, making it hard to breathe.

Would this really work? Now that he was on the point of executing his plan, the entire thing seemed absurd, a childish attempt to expose a murderer who would probably be far too clever for his simple ruse.

But they needed that confession, in combination with the missing stone in the killer's ring, to prove what had happened that night. He had no illusions that his theory would be hailed as the final, brilliant solution without something more concrete.

He strode over to pick up the bowl. His hand felt icy as he flicked his fingernail against the side to elicit a low, melodious ting. Eleanor and Henry glanced at him, but the rest of the guests continued to chat, oblivious to the sound of anything except their own voices.

"May I have your attention, please?" Nicholas asked.

The conversations stopped abruptly. Everyone stared at him. The sudden, expectant hush made Nicholas' nerves tighten.

"What is this all about, Captain Ainsley?" Croftson took a step forward.

"About? Why just a pleasant supper, Mr. Croftson. Nothing more than that." Nicholas smiled. "And since things seem a trifle flat, I thought it might be amusing to show off a skill I picked up in Spain. From a gypsy, I might add."

"Oh, a gypsy!" Eleanor's slim fingers touched the base of her throat. Her eyes burned with excitement. "How exciting! Can you tell us our fortunes?"

"No." He chuckled and handed the bowl to his brother. "I'm not that talented. The trick consists in reading a person's character from his or her rings."

"Our rings!" Croftson frowned and looked around at the other guests, clearly irritated and searching for a kindred soul. "It won't be much of a stretch for you. You know most of us and have seen our jewelry during the meal."

"Trust me, I have a poor memory. And even if I did not, I cannot say that I noticed anyone's jewelry in particular. To make this fair, I'll ask my brother and his wife to collect your rings and place them in the bowl." Nicholas sat in one of the uncushioned chairs facing the wide bow windows. "Therefore, I will not see the jewelry again before Lady Hampton brings the bowl to me."

"A bit ridiculous, don't you think?" Mr. Dudley's diffident voice floated over Nicholas' shoulder.

Before Nicholas could answer, he heard Eleanor's sweet laughter. "Come, Mr. Dudley. It sounds like such a novel game and very amusing. Surely you can't be so cruel as to disappoint the rest of us." Her voice trilled over the less enthusiastic comments, cajoling and convincing even the most reluctant participants to add to the collection clinking against the bottom of the bowl.

Finally, Eleanor handed him the bowl. He placed it on a nearby table, his excitement mounting. While there was no guarantee that the ring with the missing stone would be part of the glittering pile of jewelry, somehow he knew it would be. When he prodded through the collection, he noticed his brother's onyx ring. He picked it out with a smile and hooked his arm over the back of his chair so that the others in the room could see the ring he held in his fingers.

"Ah, yes. This is an interesting ring to start us off. It belongs to a singularly humorless individual—onyx is well known to induce quarreling and nightmares."

"That certainly explains a great deal, my dear." Eleanor laughed. "And as long as you wear that ring, you shall no longer be allowed to claim that I instigate any argument. Clearly your lack of humor and irritable nature are responsible for any disagreements."

Henry laid a hand flamboyantly over his heart and widened his eyes with feigned, wounded innocence. "Alas! I have been unjustly accused. You are all witnesses to this foul insinuation. I am the least quarrelsome man alive, and in fact, am known for my excellent sense of humor."

"Not to mention your modest and retiring nature," Nicholas said in a dry voice as he threw the ring to his brother.

Henry caught it in one hand and slipped it on his finger. "There, at last a true assessment of my fine character. Though I must say, Nick, you have not impressed me in the least."

"Then I shall have to do better with the

next one." As he hoped, a marked lessoning of the tension in the room followed his initial "reading."

Most of the guests had finally taken seats and leaned back in relaxed attitudes, smiling and laughing with their neighbors. Even the tension creasing Mr. Croftson's face had eased. A small smile played over his mouth, and he no longer gave the impression of a man about to leave.

Nicholas sifted through the contents of the bowl. Rings of all sizes and colors trickled through his fingers. A large, square diamond with emeralds on either side caught his eye. The setting was thick, heavy gold suitable for a man's ring. He held it up, letting the candlelight glint off the jewels.

"Another interesting ring—a man's ring if I am not mistaken." Someone stifled a chuckle before he continued. "The owner is a bold, flamboyant man given to extremely fashionable dress." A slightly louder laugh cut him off. He frowned and pretended to examine the ring more closely. "But he is also a true and dependable friend, generous and open-handed. His acquaintances can count themselves as fortunate."

"What else do you see?" Bartholomew Palmer leaned forward in his seat, his hands on his knees.

"Only the common wisdom that diamonds promote fortitude and good fortune

while the emeralds will make the wearer clever."
He held it up. "Now, if I have not made a hash of
the reading, would the owner care to claim his
possession?"

Palmer jumped up as Nicholas expected.
He took the ring with a smile, clearly pleased.
"Excellent. Of course, anyone may have guessed
such things, but in truth, I found the reading
quite accurate. And to think, you recognized all
of that simply from my ring."

"I'm relieved you are pleased. Now for
the next one." He fumbled over the bowl until he
found a delicate woman's ring comprised of a
small opal surrounded by four tiny emeralds
and four diamonds. A closer look revealed that
all the stones were present. "This is certainly a
lady's ring—a delicate thing for a young lady
whose heart is easily given and sadly, just as
easily crushed. She was born in October and has
only recently made her curtsey to Society." He
wasn't sure which of the young ladies owned the
ring, but his guesses were general enough to fit
either Miss Mardling or Miss Dudley. "Her
friends are fortunate to know her. She is loyal
and will not forget to return favors ten-fold."

The silence in the room gave him no
notion if he had blundered or not. Regardless,
he did not glance away from the center jewel. It
might be a game, but it had a more serious
purpose than amusing the guests. He only
hoped to sweep them along with his nonsense
until he discovered if any of the rings in the

collection lacked a small diamond.

"Opals can bring bad luck, but the emeralds and diamonds surrounding it will offset that and bring good fortune. Of course, a ring set with an opal will improve the wearer's eyesight, as well as help fair-haired ladies keep their hair color longer." He held it up as he had the previous one. "Would anyone care to claim it?"

"Yes." Mary rose, her left hand protecting her neck as if she felt vulnerable. She sounded breathless. "Thank you very much."

Over the next fifteen minutes, the pile dwindled. He could sense his audience growing restless. Nicholas felt just as irritable. None of the jewelry thus far had been damaged. Try as he might, he could not remember which of the rings had been worn by the person he believed had murdered Taunton. There were only three pieces left in the silver bowl when he plucked out a delicate pearl ring.

The remaining two were heavier rings belonging to men, and none of them sparkled in the wavering lamplight. Disappointment made him barely glance at the pearl. The murderer could have noticed the missing stone and disposed of the ring. He turned the pearl ring over in his hand. He could not remember who had worn it.

Was it whom he suspected, or would his theory unravel? His second reading of Taunton's diary had given him what he felt were the critical clues that explained what had happened. But obtaining proof would be next to impossible. He had to find the owner of the piece of jewelry missing the diamond and have Toddy confirm that he had seen the person leaving the townhouse at the time of the murder.

He had to prove the person had been there.

Tension cramped his shoulders. He just wanted the charade to be over. If he could not find the ring, then he could only hope that his explanation, in conjunction with Toddy's identification of a familiar face from those who attended the dinner, would suffice.

Even now, Toddy waited in the corner of the sitting room, installed in a simple wooden chair next to the bell pull. Nicholas had not intended to involve him until he had the first piece of evidence confirmed, but now he might not have a choice.

"A lady's ring." He turned the ring over and slipped it onto the tip of his index finger to hold it up to the light. "A ring for a modest, unwed lady, certainly, for it is unlucky for brides or those engaged." In the golden gleam of the lamp next to him, he saw the glint of a very small diamond. The brilliant was set next to the pearl.

The pearl was indeed unlucky, then, for those engaged. In fact, it had ended in murder.

The hush in the room held a breathless quality. He risked a small glance. Several faces were so tense they seemed bloodless.

"I see blood—the pearl has been unlucky indeed for the wearer of this particular ring."

"That is enough, sir!" Mr. Mardling stood shakily, his face gray. He gripped the back of his chair to support himself. "How can you be so callous? You must be aware of our loss— Taunton's death—this is nothing short of a disgrace. You play on our grief—it is a disgrace."

Nicholas stood to face him. "I agree with you, Mr. Mardling. However, I'm afraid worse awaits us. You recognize this ring, do you not?"

"Of course I do." He glanced at his wife but his gaze drifted and finally rested upon his daughter. Both of the women kept their gazes fixed on the floor, their faces pale but demure, the pictures of good, obedient ladies caught in a difficult position they are obliged to weather.

"May I ask to which lady the ring belongs?"

Miss Mardling half-rose before her mother caught her wrist. The older woman shook her head. Her daughter looked at Nicholas and then her mother before subsiding in her seat, her eyes huge with fear. When Mrs. Mardling rose, she pressed her hand on her daughter's shoulder, firmly pushing her back into her seat.

"No, mother. Please," Miss Mardling said in an agonized voice. She caught her mother's wrist.

"Mr. Mardling, can you tell us the owner of this ring?" Nicholas repeated, holding the piece of jewelry out between two fingers.

By this time, the rest of the guests had realized that this was not simply an idle game. Whispers filled the corners of the room. The three bachelors straightened and stared at Nicholas. Silsbury rose and strode to the door. For a moment, Nicholas feared he was going to leave, but Silsbury stopped. He turned with his back to the door as if he expected someone to attempt to flee, and he intended to stop him. Or her. His eyes glittered with the hungry, vengeful light.

His expression reminded Nicholas that he had loved Taunton. Silsbury had lost everything when Taunton died.

Nonetheless, Nicholas moved closer to the exit. And Silsbury. If his self-possession deserted him and he decided to exact revenge, Nicholas wanted to be in a position to prevent any further violence. They did not need another murder committed in the name of love.

Mrs. Mardling shook off her daughter's restraining hand and took a step closer to Nicholas. Her round, worn face bore an almost beatific expression as if she were convinced she was about to do the unarguably right thing.

"It is my ring," she declared, holding out her hand. When Nicholas made no move to drop it into her palm, she jerked her hand slightly in a peremptory gesture. "I insist you return it to me. Immediately."

Nicholas glanced at Mr. Mardling for

confirmation. "Is this your wife's ring?"

"No! It is mine." Miss Mardling pushed between her mother and Nicholas. She grabbed the ring out of his hand and tried to thrust it on the third finger of her left hand. The ring's band proved too small. It would not slip over her knuckle.

Her mother held up her right hand briefly. A narrow line of paler flesh encircled the base of her middle finger.

"Don't be foolish, Rose. Your hands were always larger than mine—your father's gift to you. The women in his family always had ridiculously large hands. Give it to me."

"No—it is a trick. It is mine, I tell you." Rose Mardling put her hands behind her back, hiding the ring in her fist. "I—I borrowed it from you, don't you remember?"

Her mother laughed and shook her head. "No. And you shouldn't lie, my darling."

"But there is something wrong—some trick. Can't you tell? He is planning something—something wicked." Frowning, Rose flung a hostile glance at Nicholas, her eyes hard with suspicion.

"You are hysterical, Rose, and I insist you stop this ridiculous behavior." Her father looked from Rose to her mother. Then he held out his hand to his daughter. "Give me the ring, or hand it to your mother and sit down. I trust this ridiculous game is over, Captain Ainsley?"

"Yes, it is." Instead of elation at his

success, a sense of intense weariness filled Nicholas. In truth, he realized he hoped he had been wrong. If only the murderer had been a stranger, after all, an unknown person who had murdered Taunton and then fled into the night, never to be seen again. "And I must confirm: the pearl ring does indeed belong to Mrs. Mardling, does it not?"

"Of course it does," Mr. Mardling replied. "Rose, return it to your mother."

"If you don't mind, I'm afraid I require it for a while longer." Before she could move, Nicholas reached behind Rose and twisted the piece of jewelry out of her grasp.

"Give it back!" Rose clawed at his hand, trying to pry his fingers open.

Her father grabbed her by the arm and pulled her away. "Get control of yourself, Rose." He raised a hand as if to slap her.

Nicholas stiffened, but held back, ready to step in if necessary.

As he expected, Mrs. Mardling stepped between her husband and daughter. "Christian!"

The sound of his name made Mr. Mardling lower his arm. He stared with cold eyes at Rose. "Sit down and cease embarrassing us, daughter. Your behavior is disgraceful." He turned to Nicholas. "I insist you return my wife's ring immediately, sir. And we will leave as soon as you do so. We have had quite enough for one evening."

"Just a few minutes more." Nicholas waved to Toddy.

The thin man rose awkwardly. He grimaced as if his bones ached, and he placed a hand against the wall as he took a deep breath and straightened. "Yes, Captain?"

"Do you recognize anyone?"

Toddy nodded.

"The lady you observed leaving Croftson House around midnight was Mrs. Mardling, was it not?"

Toddy nodded again before coughing wetly into his hand.

"Sit down, Mr. Toddy." He studied the guests in front of him. Suspicion and confusion wrinkled many faces while others studied him with half-smiles as if thinking he was about to announce that the entire, mysterious discussion had been a joke. Mrs. Mardling knew better. She had assumed a content expression as if she knew what was coming and was happy, almost relieved, about it.

Nicholas faced her. "Mrs. Mardling, I'm afraid I must take you into custody for the murder of Lord Taunton on the twenty-third of October."

Clasping her hands in front of her, she nodded. A small smile flickered over her mouth.

"This is ridiculous!" Mr. Mardling exploded, striding toward Nicholas with his hands clenched into fists. His face flushed a deep purple as the veins in his bullish neck throbbed.

Before Nicholas could do more than throw up his forearm to protect his face, Mardling struck him. The blow glanced off his arm and landed on his neck, just below his ear.

Nicholas stumbled back and instinctively lashed out. He hit Mardling in his soft, unprotected belly. Mardling grunted and tripped over the chair next to him. Caught by the momentum, Mardling flailed his arms and stumbled before he righted. He glared at Nicholas from under lowered brows and hunched over, preparing for another attack.

Instead of plunging forward to press his advantage, Nicholas straightened. "Get hold of yourself, man!" he commanded in the voice he used to quell the fear and confusion on the battlefield.

Mardling blinked. His frown deepened and he took a step forward. Then he paused, letting out a deep breath as Nicholas' order finally penetrated the haze of his anger. Mardling covered his eyes with one hand and rubbed them. He sat down abruptly, sucking air in sharply as he struggled to contain his emotions.

"You can't be serious, Nick," Henry said at last. "Surely you can't believe Mrs. Mardling was responsible for that tragedy."

"I'm sorry, but it's true. And I think Miss Mardling suspected her mother, as well. Didn't you, Miss Mardling?"

"How could you know? How could you possibly believe such a thing?" Rose's voice rose, quavering with fear. "She had no reason to murder Lord Taunton. If you must suspect anyone, then you must suspect me!"

"I'm afraid not. Your mother was seen leaving Taunton's townhouse by Mr. Toddy. He saw her face clearly, and he will testify that she was there. And your mother's ring proves it." He held the ring up so everyone in the room could see it. "There should be twin diamonds on either side of the pearl. The one on the left is present, but the one on the right is missing. You can see the prong—the stone must have been loose."

"What does that prove?" Miss Mardling asked, her face flushed and voice strident.

"I found the missing diamond caught in Lord Taunton's jacket."

Miss Mardling sniffed. She rubbed the side of her nose with her handkerchief, pressing so hard that she left a long, red streak in the pale flesh. "That ring could have been damaged at any time. Taunton and my father were working out a marriage contract, as you must know. We were frequent guests. She could have lost that diamond at any time. My mother had no reason to do such a thing."

"No, Miss Mardling, you're wrong," he replied gently. "The diamond was held fast by the drying blood. Your mother lost the brilliant when she dealt Taunton the fatal blow." He held up a hand to stop her protests. "Your mother attended the dinner where Taunton insisted on showing off the stiletto he had given to Miss Whitethorn-Litton. Your mother knew about the knife and where it could be found. And she knew that you were desperately unhappy with the engagement. Both of you had gone to Taunton several times to ask him to break the engagement, but he had refused."

"This is ridiculous. My wife would never do such a thing. She knew Rose would do what she was told," Mr. Mardling said.

"Yes, she would. And that was the problem. At any rate, I believe that seeing how Taunton treated Miss Whitethorn-Litton at that supper disgusted Mrs. Mardling and gave her the solution to her daughter's unhappy situation. She hoped to murder Taunton with the stiletto and leave Miss Whitethorn-Litton to take the blame. Miss Mardling would then be free to marry the man she loved." He studied Miss Mardling's pinched face with pity. "You must know that your mother loved you too much to allow you to marry Lord Taunton."

"All I wanted was your happiness," Mrs. Mardling murmured. "All I ever wanted was your happiness. How could you find contentment with a man such as Lord Taunton?" She glanced at her husband, her mouth pressed into a straight line of contempt. "Your father may have denied the rumors, but I knew what that man was, peer or not. You would have been miserable married to one such as he.

I could not bear the thought of you with him, with his foul men and *that* woman. No. No matter what happens, I do not regret what I did."

"Oh, *mother—*" Miss Mardling's words broke off with a sob. When she reached out to hug her mother, her father stopped her.

"Stop this foolishness immediately. I will not have you making a spectacle of yourself in this manner." Mr. Mardling put an arm around his daughter and pulled her away from her mother. He never glanced at his wife. It was as if she had ceased to exist for him. "We're leaving. Good night to you, Lord Hampton. We will await our carriage in the hallway."

Nicholas watched father and daughter leave, filled with sorrow for the pair. Mr. Mardling was not the sort of man to face scandal well and his daughter would surely suffer. He could only hope that the man Miss Mardling loved would not desert her in the face of the unpleasantness that was bound to come and that Mr. Mardling would show the good sense to allow her to marry him. If not, they both faced a grim future. It was unlikely any other man, and certainly no peer, would ever offer for Miss Mardling after this tragedy.

"I am sorry." Nicholas turned back to the remaining guests, heaviness compressing his chest. He gave the remaining rings to their owners and then held up his hand. "Unfortunately, Lord Taunton's death is not the only matter we must discuss."

Silence greeted his remark. Once again, he was the focus of attention.

"What else is there?" Mr. Dudley shifted impatiently and glanced around as if hoping the others would protest the delay to their departure.

"There was another incident, years ago." Nicholas fixed his gaze on the group of young men standing near the door. "Another death."

"I'm sure there have been many deaths over the years," Mr. Dudley said.

"No doubt." Nicholas smiled grimly. "However, this involves another murder that appeared to be a natural death—the death of Mr. Whitethorn-Litton."

Kathryn paled and let out a small, surprised gasp. "That can't be true!"

Eleanor put an arm around her shoulders and drew her closer.

"I apologize for the shock, Miss Whitethorn-Litton, however, it is true," Nicholas said. "When I began the investigation into Lord Taunton's death, someone made the remark that your father had been strangled in the garden. I nearly forgot it until I found Taunton's journal. In it, Taunton said he had found Mr. Whitethorn-Litton's body and moved it. He did not want to cause a scandal or let anyone see Mr. Whitethorn-Litton in such an embarrassing state. So he placed the body in bed and let the servants discover it the next morning.

"According to the journal, the doctor was called the next morning and judged Whitethorn-Litton to have died in his sleep. I'm sure Lord Taunton encouraged him to come to that conclusion. There must have been marks if the physician looked closely enough."

"I don't see why this matter should concern us." Mr. Dudley frowned and glanced around the other guests, clearly searching for support in his desire to leave well enough alone. "It is over and done with."

"Perhaps so. Except for that comment," Nicholas said.

"That comment could only have been made by the murderer." Henry moved in a casual manner to stand in front of the door.

"Precisely. Even Miss Whitethorn-Litton did not realize that her father's death had been anything but natural." He studied her. "Did you know?"

Pressing her fingers to her mouth, Kathryn shook her head. Tears gleamed on her pale cheeks. Eleanor hugged her more tightly and pressed a handkerchief into her hand. After wiping away her tears, Kathryn cleared her throat and said, "Who? Who told you he had been strangled."

"Mr. Silsbury."

Silsbury took a step forward, his hands fisted at his sides. "I never said anything like that—you are lying!"

"No, I'm not. You told me Lord Taunton had allowed Miss Whitethorn-Litton to stay at his home because her father had been strangled in his garden. And Taunton's journal confirmed that. But only Taunton and the murderer knew."

"Taunton could have killed him—"

"No. Taunton was—too fond of him. He was devastated by his death and did everything he could to make it easier for Miss Whitethorn-Litton. He would never have murdered her father."

"And why would I do such a thing? What possible reason could I have?"

"You know better than I, but I can guess. You were jealous of their friendship. That was the root of it." Nicholas watched Silsbury uneasily.

The man was volatile and capable of deadly violence.

Silsbury's eyes flashed with rage as he glanced around the room, clearly judging the possibility of escape. "I am innocent and admit nothing. You have clearly taken a dislike to me and hope to build your reputation at my expense. Well, you won't find it so easy, my good man."

"I have nothing to gain professionally or personally. You were my client in the matter of Taunton's death." A lopsided, self-deprecating grin grew on Nicholas' face. "In fact, this makes it highly unlikely that I will be paid for my troubles."

"At least you are intelligent enough to realize that much," Silsbury said.

"It hardly matters if you wish to deny it," Henry said. "My brother's information is sufficient for me to pursue pressing charges on behalf of Miss Whitethorn-Litton. And we have the evidence of Lord Taunton's journal and your own remarks. I assure you, it will be enough."

"I think we have all had enough surprises for one evening." Mr. Dudley placed a heavy hand on his wife's back to encourage her to move toward the door. "We bid you good night, Lord Hampton."

"Good night and I hope you will forgive us for this rather sad ending to the evening," Henry said.

Mr. Dudley nodded, but the frown creasing his face did not lighten.

As the other guests followed the Dudleys, Henry bid them a quiet adieu. Finally, only a few remained. A pair of constables arrived a short time later to take charge of Harry Silsbury and Mrs. Mardling to gaol.

Only Mrs. Mardling appeared unconcerned, even relieved, as the two were escorted outside. Despite her conviction that she had done the correct thing, she must have been under intolerable strain, praying for news that her ruse had worked and that Kathryn had been arrested.

As he watched them leave, Nicholas wondered how long Mrs. Mardling would have been able to live with the guilt. Would she truly have allowed another woman to hang for her crime? Or would her conscience have made her confess before that terrible miscarriage of justice? Nicholas was relieved it had not come to that.

And as for Silsbury—he could only hope the killer would finally face justice after so many years.

Chapter Twenty-Four

1:00 PM October 27, 1821

While Nicholas had resolved two tragedies, he soon found he had another difficulty facing him. He had remained awake late into the night, considering what to do. He felt drained and his mind sluggish. What would happen to Toddy, Bottom, and Kathryn? Before he had accepted a position at Second Sons, he had chosen to live like a horse with blinders on, blind to the activities around him. Even though the war had ended over a decade before, he had seen so much suffering at Corunna that he preferred to remain oblivious.

To his surprise, he had discovered that sometime during the last few days, his courage and a small measure of his confidence had returned. A strange, newfound sense of freedom lifted his spirits.

Where there is life, there is hope. He thought of Corporeal Myles and his wife, Violet, and smiled. Hope and perhaps a chance for happiness.

He waited until Dalton and Jack were clearing away the dishes before he turned to Toddy and Bottom. "I am going to visit my brother, and if you don't have anything planned, I would like you to accompany me."

"What for?" Toddy's brows jutted out with suspicion. "It's not your brother you're planning to visit, is it? Taking us back to

Newgate, I reckon?"

"Not at all. I simply wish for your company for an hour or two. Now will you come?"

"Of course, Captain, sir, of course," Bottom interjected hastily, glancing from Toddy to Nicholas. His plump fingers played with the buttons of the jacket he still wore from last night.

When they stepped outside onto the walkway, a chilly mist dampened Nicholas' face and hands. He drew his cloak around his shoulders and set a brisk pace as he strode toward his brother's townhouse. The two men padded after him in silence, not wasting their breath on complaints, and leaving Nicholas to consider their future.

Nothing would be accomplished by inaction. As he walked, the seed of the idea he'd had the previous night germinated. The roots dug firmly into his restless mind and his shoulders straightened.

At least Henry's butler seemed pleased to see him. His cheerful features had never truly attained the appropriate, gravely impassive expression befitting his position, and Nicholas was heartily glad of it. He'd had enough of disapproving butlers to last a lifetime.

"Lord Hampton is in, Captain Ainsley. If you will step into the library, I shall inform him of your arrival." He stopped in confusion when he saw Toddy and Bottom, but he quickly recovered and stepped aside to let them enter, as well.

"Come on, you two." Nicholas nodded and strode down the hallway. He barely entered the room before he heard the slap of his brother's leather shoes on the steps of the grand staircase which debouched just outside the library door.

"Nicholas!" Henry gripped his hand and shook it briskly, slapping him on the shoulder with his left hand. "You're looking well. I suppose you've come to visit your damsel in distress and crow about your success?"

He shifted uneasily and motioned to the two men standing behind him. "Yes, but not right away. We have a small matter to discuss."

"So you have something more serious on your mind, then?" His brother's sharp gaze flashed over Nicholas, leaving him feeling as if all of his inner thoughts and uncertainties were written on his face.

"Yes." He paused, staring at the window in the front of the room and conscious of the two men staring at him, their faces tense with anxiety. How to begin?

"Shall we sit?" Henry motioned to a pair of chairs in front of the fireplace and then strode to the door. He murmured something to the footman lingering outside and then turned back, rubbing his hands. "Bit of a chill, but it's early yet for brandy." He grimaced. "It's a bit of a woman's trick, but I've ordered tea. Go on, sit and tell me what this delicate proposition is that has you so twisted with concern."

"It's Mr. Toddy and Mr. Bottom, here." Nicholas waited until his brother took the chair closest to the fire before he motioned the two men to sit in the wooden chairs nearby. Then he sat down.

"Ah, yes. The witnesses. What about them?"

"It seems they are rather destitute."

Bottom cleared his throat and then pulled out a handkerchief. He held it to his nose, his cheeks flushing with embarrassment as Toddy stared at Nicholas with a hard gleam in his eyes.

"Have they no profession?" Henry asked.

"Thievery." Nicholas chuckled. "If you wish to call that a profession."

"Sir, I protest!" Bottom said. When Henry glanced at him, Bottom's face turned almost purple with mortification. "I beg your pardon, your lordship."

"I see." Henry stretched out his legs and pulled on his lower lip. "And how is this any concern of yours. Or mine for that matter?"

"Mr. Bottom was once a teacher. It is my understanding that he lost his position due to an unfortunate predilection for pocketing the belongings of others." Nicholas paused when the footman returned with a large, wooden tray. He set it on the table near Henry, bowed, and waited until Henry dismissed him. "You once told me you were interested in starting a charity school for the indigent."

Henry nodded as he filled a cup with tea and handed it to Nicholas. "And you think Mr. Bottom would make an adequate teacher, despite his light-fingers?" He grinned. "Perhaps you believe destitute children would have nothing to tempt him?"

"In part." Nicholas laughed as Bottom sputtered incoherently. "In fact, what I propose is to hire Mr. Bottom as a teacher with Mr. Toddy as his assistant."

"Now see here, Captain—" Toddy started to rise, a frown creasing his angular face.

"Remain seated, Mr. Toddy. If you please." Nicholas studied his brother. The years, and perhaps his experiences with politics, had given Henry a certain measure of self-control that now made it difficult for Nicholas to know exactly what he was thinking. "I gather that Mr. Toddy has a certain expertise that might prove invaluable to us. If Mr. Bottom should forget himself, Mr. Toddy can replace any accidentally borrowed object before its loss is discovered. Is that not so, Mr. Toddy?"

Toddy grunted and glared at the floor, although a slight smile played around his mouth.

"An interesting proposition, indeed." Henry leaned back, resting his half-empty teacup on his thigh. "And what would be the terms of his employment?"

"They could certainly share an apartment in the building housing the school. And they would only require a small stipend."

Bottom stood and placed a hand on Toddy's shoulder. "Now see here, sir. While we appreciate the offer—"

"How much of a stipend?" Toddy shrugged off his friend's grip and got to his feet.

"One hundred pounds per annum." Henry gazed at the two men, his expression unreadable.

"Each?" Toddy asked.

"For the pair of you. More than fair, I should think."

"Of course, my lord," Bottom said in a breathless voice. He bent his head close to Toddy's. The two men whispered to each other for a few seconds. Toddy gestured at Nicholas and his brother several times, frowning and scratching his gray whiskers as he did so. In the end, he shrugged. Bottom smiled and bowed at Henry. "We accept your generous offer and are most pleased to begin at your earliest convenience."

"I'm sure you are." The dry note in Henry's voice made Nicholas smile. "I will leave the matter in my dear brother's hands to organize." When Nicholas straightened and glanced at him, startled, Henry shrugged complacently. "Though I am fairly certain he will be happy to delegate it further to you, Mr. Bottom. And of course, Mr. Toddy. Now that we have settled that, there remains the question of the lady who is, at this very moment, out shopping with my wife." He grimaced. "I can only hope she shows a trifle more restraint than Lady Hampton."

Nicholas couldn't control his uneasy glance at the door, half hoping and half dreading that Kathryn would walk through it. His restlessness last night had convinced him that he knew only too well what he wanted to do about her, but one troublesome question remained: what did she want?

"As you must realize, Miss Whitethorn-Litton has no personal attendant, and I consider that of primary importance," Nicholas said, skirting the main difficulty of how to settle Kathryn's future to her satisfaction. "My man, Sergeant Dalton, is hiring one. He has orders to send applicants here for her approval, if that is acceptable to you."

Henry nodded and made a slight gesture for him to continue.

"Once Miss Whitethorn-Litton accepts a suitable companion, then we can proceed. Is that agreeable?"

The gleam in Henry's eyes revealed that he was only too aware that Nicholas was employing a delaying tactic. At least he did not challenge him. They chatted a few minutes longer on inconsequential matters until his brother finally rose. "I'm afraid I must bid you good afternoon, my dearest brother. I have

business, and you have other matters to attend
to, not the least of which is organizing the affairs
of Mr. Bottom and Mr. Toddy."

"Of course." Nicholas stood with alacrity
and gestured to the two men to follow him. A
sense of disappointment made him pause at the
front door, listening for Kathryn's step. The
hallway behind him echoed with silence.

His gaze searched the crowded walkway
outside, resting briefly on each shadowed face
half-hidden by the bonnets of the ladies walking
by. He caught no glimpse of Kathryn before he
shook his brother's hand and walked away.

Chapter Twenty-Five

2:00 PM November 27, 1821

"Good afternoon, Lady Hampton." Holding her sewing in her hand, Kathryn opened her bedroom door and stepped aside. She glanced over her shoulder at the wooden clock occupying the center of the mantle. Just a few minutes after two. Almost time. She bit her upper lip to prevent a silly smile at the bubbling sense of joy that filled her.

Nicholas had adopted a habit of visiting at two each afternoon, and she could not help looking forward to his visit.

"Captain Ainsley is awaiting you in the little drawing room. Will you join us, or shall I tell him you are otherwise occupied." Lady Hampton briefly touched the dress draped over Kathryn's arm, though the twinkle in her eyes indicated she knew perfectly well that Kathryn would not choose to remain in her room repairing the seam of her dress.

She handed her sewing to her new companion, Mrs. Langley, who hovered behind her. Patting her hair, Kathryn stepped into the hallway. "I can finish that dress at any time." She linked her arm with Lady Hampton. "Is he well?"

"As well as he was yesterday. And the day before, and the day before that."

Kathryn giggled and covered her mouth, trying to suppress her giddiness. "He has been very attentive, has he not?"

"Indeed he has. I do wish you'd tell him how you feel, however."

"I can not. Not yet. He has not revealed his true feelings to me." Her happiness froze in her chest. Despite his visits, Nicholas might not reciprocate her love. What would she do, then?

She knew she was only a temporary guest of Lady Hampton, and she could not remain here forever. The thought of leaving filled her with panic. Lady Hampton had been so kind to her, and she felt so at home with her. She feared losing their tenuous bond. She had no family remaining and no other friends except Rose and Mary.

Since Mrs. Mardling's arrest, Rose had refused to see her, although Kathryn suspected Mr. Mardling had decided she was not acceptable company for his daughter. She had visited Mary twice, but after their experiences, Mary seemed silent and unhappy. Perhaps Kathryn reminded her too much of the unpleasant past, and although she was polite, she did not seem enthusiastic about Kathryn's presence. In fact, Mary seemed relieved when Kathryn stood in preparation to leave.

The future seemed bleak and uncertain.

Each time she considered it, her anxiety increased until it seemed to press the very air out of her lungs. In the meantime, she clung to Lord Hampton's offhand comment that no decision would be made until she selected a companion from the dozens of women Nicholas kept sending over for her approval. If she told Nicholas, would she lose him, too?

So only Lady Hampton knew that Kathryn had already selected Mrs. Langley, the very first woman who applied for the position.

"Captain Ainsley! How are you this afternoon?" Kathryn asked as she entered the drawing room, self-consciously aware of Lady Hampton's presence a step behind her.

Nicholas stood, his right hand grabbing his left wrist in a characteristic gesture to prevent his injured arm from dropping uncontrollably to his side. She caught her breath at the dear sight, loving him for this small reminder of his vulnerability.

"I am well." He bowed to her and again to Lady Hampton. "How are you?"

Kathryn giggled at his formality. "I am very well and pleased to see you. It has been so long since your last visit." She glanced at Lady Hampton for permission to sit.

Lady Hampton strolled over to a pair of chairs by the window and sat down, picking up a basket of embroidery. "Do be seated." She waved toward the opposite side of the room. "Over there, if you please. I am attempting a terribly difficult pattern and don't want to be distracted by your conversation." Kathryn glanced at her, surprised.

Lady Hampton winked.

Obedient to his sister-in-law's command,

Nicholas stood behind one of the silk-covered chairs opposite the door. He waited for Kathryn to sit before he took a seat himself, facing her.

"Have you interviewed Miss Abercrombie?" He leaned forward, his eyes holding hers with an intense gaze that made her feel breathless.

"Yes, she visited this morning. I spoke to her at length, and I'm afraid she will not do. We simply did not suit each other." She shook her head and dropped her gaze to her lap. Her nervous fingers smoothed the folds of her dress.

She could feel Lady Hampton's presence behind them and the heaviness of her small charade. It was true that she had not liked Miss Abercrombie. The thin woman seemed to disapprove of everything she saw around her in the townhouse. Her lips pressed together and grew thinner and thinner during their interview, making their conversation increasingly awkward.

Kathryn could not tell Nicholas, however, that she had selected the first woman she'd met. She felt terrible as she continued interviewing hapless women, knowing they were wasting their time. Mrs. Langley had been installed for nearly two weeks.

Her neck burned as if Lady Hampton were staring at her.

Nicholas accepted her statement, however, and nodded. A smile curved his mouth as if he were relieved by her rejection of Miss

Abercrombie. "I shall request that Sergeant Dalton do better. I confess I was not enamored of Miss Abercrombie and hoped you would not select her."

Lady Hampton cleared her throat.

A flush tingled Kathryn's cheeks. She leaned forward and lightly touched Nicholas' sleeve, her heart pounding. He would be furious. But she could not continue misleading him, most of all because of the poor women he kept sending. The women arrived with such pitiful hope in their eyes, and she felt dreadful when she informed them that she did not think they would suit each other.

"I have a confession." She pulled her hand back and clasped her cold fingers together. "I—I already have a companion. I chose the first lady you sent. Mrs. Langley has been with me for over two weeks now."

"You hired her?" His brows met over his nose as he studied her.

Her hands shook, and she clamped them more tightly together to hide her anxiety. "Sergeant Dalton sent her," she said. Perhaps he had not heard her and thought she had ignored his efforts on her behalf. Panic fluttered in her chest.

"Why didn't you tell me sooner?"

Her eyes searched his face, but she could not tell what he was thinking. "I feared what would happen." She clutched his right sleeve. "Lord Hampton indicated that as soon as you had found a companion for me, I would have to make other arrangements for a place to live. I thought I would never see you again."

He shook her hand off his arm, but just long enough to allow him to pick up her icy hand in his warm one. "You had nothing to fear, Kathryn. I would not have abandoned you." He smiled, his eyes twinkling with amusement. "And I must assume that Lady Hampton knew about Mrs. Langley. As you see, she did not demand your departure."

"Yes, she knew." Kathryn sighed with relief and placed her free hand over his to keep his reassuring clasp. "You're not angry?"

"No, not at all. I confess I've been relieved that you seemed unable to find a woman who would suit you."

She laughed. "We are both horribly dishonest, then."

"Not dishonest, simply delaying the inevitable." He shook his head and withdrew his hand. "Unfortunately, we must eventually make a decision about your future."

"Oh, no, please. I'm not ready."

"I had hoped..." His eyes searched her face. "If you had a father or brother—"

"If I had a father, or brother, I would not be in this position," she interrupted, her voice harsh.

He was going to tell her she had to leave, that he wanted nothing more to do with her.

"No, you misunderstand me. I only

meant to say that your situation is more difficult as you have no parent to speak for you."

"I am perfectly capable of speaking for myself."

He chuckled. "So you are. I am not phrasing this well."

"Then just use plain words, Captain."

"I hoped that over time, you might grow fond of me, at least enough to view me in a more favorable light."

Warm joy blossomed within her, easing the nearly intolerable tension. "I have always viewed you in a favorable light, Nicholas. More or less."

"More or less." He laughed again, making Lady Hampton drop her embroidery. She glanced at them as she bent to pick it up. "Well then, would you consider marriage as a possibility?"

"Of course I would consider marriage." She arched a brow, trying to appear calm. Surely, he had not had time to find a potential suitor, a prosperous cit, no doubt, happy to take her off Nicholas' hands. "To whom?"

"Well, to me, if that meets with your approval."

"You?" She could hardly speak as a rush of joy and relief shook her.

He glanced away as if embarrassed. "Does the notion displease you?"

"No. I was simply surprised." She leaned forward to touch his arm in reassurance and pleased to see him smile in return.

"If it pleases you, my brother can act *in parentus loci* under the circumstances."

"Then you have it all worked out very nicely, don't you?" She grinned back at him, lightheaded with giddiness.

He eased out of his chair and knelt next to her, slipping his arm around her. "There is only one small matter left, something you must know." He gazed at her, his eyes dark with emotion. "I love you—you make me feel hope. I'm phrasing it badly, and I know it may not be so for you. You have no family, no one to turn to, and my damnable arm—"

"Pray don't be absurd." She bent forward and kissed him.

His grip tightened hungrily.

She pulled back after a moment and then placed her palm against his cheek, feeling as light as a feather. "I am forward enough to admit I love you, too, and my lack of a family has nothing to do with it. I would be honored if your brother would act on my behalf."

"Then my sweet, I rely on you to cajole Lady Hampton into remaining as your hostess until I can obtain the necessary license."

She kissed him on the corner of his mouth, laughingly pushing him away when he tried to take advantage of her nearness. "Very well. Then we have only one further matter to agree upon. When will I see you again?"

"At two, my love. I shall return tomorrow,

precisely at two."

THE END

Amy Corwin

Other Titles by Amy Corwin
The Archer Family Series

The **Archer Family series** are traditional Regency romances spiced with a mystery, and *The Earl's Masquerade* is the latest in the series. The books all offer at least a glimpse of John Archer, the instigator of many a fateful adventure. He can't seem to keep from dragging his nieces, nephews, and other unfortunate relatives, with him on escapades that invariably uncover a murder or two. Thankfully, Mr. Knighton Gaunt, of the Second Sons Inquiry Agency is often on hand to help the Archers out of the worst of their troubles, when he's allowed to do so.

While these books do not need to be read in order, the list below presents them in chronological order. Reading them in the listed order may be best to gain a true understanding of the mischief John Archer can create amongst his young, unattached family members.

The Necklace ~ A young woman, a scoundrel, and a family heirloom that might possibly be cursed. **Book 1**

The Necklace introduces John Archer and his exasperated niece, Oriana Archer, who is fed up trying to keep her uncle out of trouble. When Uncle John drags home yet another disreputable, wounded associate for her to nurse, she's at her wit's end. But there's no rest for the weary, and Oriana soon discovers another of her uncle's acquaintances, murdered in a way that points suspicion directly at her!

The Unwanted Heiress ~ An American heiress nobody wants; a duke every woman desires; and a murder no one expects. **Book 2**

In *I Bid One American,* Nathaniel Archer, Oriana's brother, no sooner inherits a dukedom than he's accused of murder. And his Uncle John's schemes don't help. Uncle John is the guardian to an American heiress he's anxious to unload on the first, unwary, English peer, and Nathaniel looks as good as any, despite the shadow of a noose hanging above his head.

But Nathaniel is made of sterner stuff, or so he thinks, and he's got more to worry about than romancing a singularly unromantic heiress when a dead debutante is found in his carriage.

The Bricklayer's Helper ~ A masquerade turns deadly when a murderer discovers one of his victims survived. **Book 3**

The Bricklayer's Helper features Sarah Sanderson, an orphaned girl disguised as a man and working as a bricklayer. She's the sole surviving member of her family, murdered thirteen years ago in a terrible fire. She may, or may not, be the niece of John Archer, and John is determined to bring her back into the family by hiring one of the newest agents at the **Second** Sons Inquiry Agency. Unfortunately, when the killer realizes Sarah escaped, her life is threatened despite the efforts of the attractive inquiry agent and her matchmaking uncle.

The Earl's Masquerade ~ A sabotaged boat forces an earl to investigate murder and discover that love may ultimately be what he's searching for. **Book 4**

Everyone believes Hugh drowned with his brother after their boat is sabotaged, and Hugh fosters that belief trick the elusive killer into revealing himself. But he doesn't count on running into two others also desperate to escape notice behind the comforting anonymity of false identities. Helen Archer lost the fabled Peckham necklace

Amy Corwin

at a ball given at Hugh's home and is desperate to get it back. Young Edward Brown only wants to run away to sea like his hero, Admiral Nelson. When the three meet, Helen and Hugh hatch the perfect plan. By masquerading as servants, they can accomplish their goals in secret. However, Edward objects for purely practical reasons. He wants to go to sea, and he definitely doesn't want to spend his days polishing boots as a pretend servant. But the young boy is overruled and their adventure begins.

Second Sons Inquiry Agency Series

The **Second Sons Inquiry Agency series** are traditional historical mysteries spiced with a romance. The books all feature Second Sons, but do not necessarily focus on the found of the agency, Mr. Knighton Gaunt. Many of the stories feature other inquiry agents, or investigators, as the agency grows and flourishes. Mr. Gaunt is often called to the aid of the Archers, who seem to be inordinately fond of trouble.

While these books do not need to be read in order, the list below presents them in chronological order.

The Vital Principle ~ Gaunt is called to a séance to uncover a fraud, only to stumble upon a murder. **Book 1**

The Vital Principle is the first in the **Second Sons Inquiry Agency** historical mystery series and features coolly intellectual Mr. Knighton Gaunt, the agency's founder. Once accused of murder, himself, Knighton is driven to uncover the truth behind the complex, often mysterious murders that cross his path.

In *The Vital Principle,* Knighton Gaunt meets Prudence Barnard, a spiritualist accused of murder. While those involved are happy to accuse her as the stranger in their midst, Knighton is not so sure and sets out once again to discover the truth.

The two meet again in *The Dead Man's View.*

A Rose Before Dying ~ An earl is enmeshed in a deadly game to prove his uncle didn't murder his mistress. **Book 2**

In *A Rose Before Dying*, Charles Vance impulsively

Amy Corwin

decides to pluck the role of inquiry agent out of Knighton's hands and discover the real killer. Charles is determined to exonerate his irascible uncle, Sir Edward, the only real father he has ever known. Unfortunately, Sir Edward doesn't make it easy for his nephew, and the only clues Charles has are sprays of roses left at the scene.

As **Second Sons Inquiry Agency** grows, you'll encounter other agents who run into odd mysteries and formidable murderers during the vibrant first half of the 19th century.

"Witty historical whodunits in the tradition of Bruce Alexander's *Blind Justice* and Victoria Holt's *The Mistress of Mellyn,* that will keep you guessing until the unexpected end." –A Reader

The Dead Man's View ~ Pru requests Knighton Gaunt's aid to help her prove the death of her cousin was not suicide, but murder. **Book 3**

The Dead Man's View is the second mystery featuring Prudence Barnard and Knighton Gaunt, and the third in the **Second Sons Inquiry Agency** historical mystery series.

When Eric Knibbs invites Pru, his second cousin, to a house party, she's pleased to discover that she has a family, even if it is a distant one. Unfortunately, their reunion is cut short when Eric is found dead, hanging from a noose outside his bedroom window.

The authorities believe Eric hung himself, but Pru begs to differ. Eric was afraid of heights and could never have committed suicide in such a manner. After a quick examination of his room, Pru finds too many anomalies and can't help questioning the circumstance of Eric's supposed suicide.

So Pru does the only thing she can, she asks Knighton to help her prove that her cousin's death was murder.

The Illusion of Desire ~ A new inquiry agent, Captain Nicholas Ainsley, is enmeshed in a murder investigation where even the victim seems determined to obscure the truth behind a series of illusions. **Book 4**

The Illusion of Desire features a new inquiry agent, Captain Nicholas Ainsley and is the fourth mystery in the **Second Sons Inquiry Agency** historical mystery series.

When Nicholas accepts employment as an inquiry agent, he is soon drawn into a complex murder investigation. Lord Taunton has been killed just a few weeks before he plans to marry a young debutante. The dead earl's closest friend claims Taunton's mistress, Kathryn, killed him in a jealous rage over his plans to marry another woman. Despite the evidence pointing to Kathryn, Nicholas believes she may be innocent. Others have equally strong motives and matters are complicated by the complex series of illusions Taunton cultivated to hide the details of his private life. Nicholas is sure that one of the carefully constructed veils may be hiding the face of the killer.

As he digs deeper, Nicholas discovers an older mystery left unresolved. Is the earl's death related to the seven-year-old tragedy, or was his murder committed for entirely different reasons? Nicholas is determined to rip away the illusions and reveal the face of the vicious killer, regardless of personal cost.

As **Second Sons Inquiry Agency** grows, you'll encounter other agents who run into odd mysteries and formidable murderers during the vibrant first half of the 19th century.

Amy Corwin

A Second Chance Paranormal Romances ~ The Redemption Series

The **Redemption series** are paranormal romances spiced with mystery, danger and an "Urban Fantasy" feel that will keep readers enthralled. They do not have to be read in any particular order as each book stands alone.

Vampire Protector ~ *Vampires, a haunted house, and a lost relic, and Gwen's evening is just beginning.* **Book 1**

An anonymous note sends Gwen on a mission to uncover a dark family secret that may be hidden in her long abandoned childhood home. When she asks her handsome neighbor, John, to accompany her, she's not expecting much. Unfortunately, that's her first mistake. John is a vampire and her house is not exactly empty. Secrets—and the dead—won't always stay buried, and John's extraordinary strength and determination may be all that can withstand what awaits them in the shadows.

A Fall of Silver ~ *A woman bent on the destruction of all vampires discovers redemption in the arms of an ex-priest determined to save the undead.* **Book 2**

Their secrets are about to catch up with them.

The only good vampire is a dead vampire: that's Quicksilver's philosophy and she sees no reason to change it. In fact, she's about to kill one of the undead when Kethan Hilliard confronts her, promising redemption for both vampires and humans in exchange for an end to the slaughter.

390

But Quicksilver knows that's not going to happen.

Someone is killing humans and vampires, and sweet words aren't going to end the nightmare.

The events awaken terrible secrets from Quicksilver's past, and she's not about to repeat her previous mistakes by trusting the undead. This time, she's going to end the madness and silence the horror, forever.

Cozy Contemporary Mysteries

A new series of contemporary, cozy mysteries is underway, set in fictitious towns near the Outer Banks of North Carolina.

Whacked! ~ *Cassie's hopes for a quiet vacation go up in flames when she discovers her uncle sharing a smoke with a dead body.*

Love can make anyone crazy, but Cassie, a stressed-out computer expert, has always chosen logic over that uncomfortable emotion. This is, until in a weak moment, she agrees to housesit for her aunt and uncle. Within minutes of her arrival, she finds a murdered man. And her uncle is inexplicably determined to implicate himself. Cold logic suggests he's hiding something and Cassie isn't going to let him get arrested without a fight. Unfortunately, her past history with the sheriff makes him all too happy to accept her uncle's guilt.

But love is supposed to overcome all obstacles, not create them, and Cassie refuses to let a ridiculous emotion stand in the way of logic.

Too bad Cassie is about to discover just how far people will go for love.

Amy Corwin

About the Author

Amy Corwin is a charter member of the Romance Writers of America and recently joined Mystery Writers of America. She writes historical and cozy mysteries with a touch of romance, as well as paranormal romances. To be truthful, most of her books include a bit of murder and mayhem since she discovered that killing off at least one character is a highly effective way to make the remaining ones toe the plot line.

Join her and discover that every good mystery has a touch of romance.

Connect with Me Online

Website: http://www.amycorwin.com

Twitter: http://twitter.com/amycorwin

Facebook: http://www.facebook.com/AmyCorwinAuthor

Blog: http://amycorwin.blogspot.com